WF

Brazilian Contemporaries Series

Tarcisio Lage

WEAVES OF POWER
Politics and Witchcraft in the Same Cauldron

Translated by Américo Lucena Lage

Brás Cubas Press

BRÁS CUBAS PRESS

An imprint of Para Inglês Ler Tradução e Ensino

Copyright © 2024 Tarcisio Lage

Originally published in Portuguese as "As Tranças do Poder" by Editora Batel, Rio de Janeiro

Translated by Américo Lucena Lage

Cover design by Armando Pereira

Proofread by Louise Stahl

ISBN 978-65-982932-0-8

Table of Contents

First Part

-

THE PREVIOUS LIFE

1

"Inmate 3,029!"

The loudspeaker blared out an authoritative, metallic voice, echoing through the scorching prison. Eighty-five degrees in the shade.

Tarquínio Esperidião barely looked up, lost in thought. At the beginning of our story, his world had shrunk to the courtyard where detainees sunbathe while guards watch over them with loaded rifles. His greatest priority was to stay away from the other inmates. He went from here to there in the prison's ironclad routine, alongside the worst criminals, some of them celebrities created by the press. Tarquínio's sharpened senses detected everything around him, especially the creaking iron of the opening and closing bars, the look of revolt and dissatisfaction in the newcomers, the numbness and apathy of those already accustomed to captivity. He belonged to this latter group, of course, made worse by the isolation he imposed on himself. He was almost always unshaven, trimmed once a week at the behest of prison management. Behest is an understatement. Forced would be more accurate. When he had made a face for his first haircut, that had been enough. Two thugs had immediately appeared, batons in hand. A striking duo: one, a European descendant from the country's south, over six-feet, five-inches tall, the other, an equally imposing Afro-descendant. The blond one hinted that the baton was meant to be stuffed somewhere and the black one smiled in anticipation. Also, still fresh in Tarquínio's memory were the two equally brawny nurses who had pushed the barbiturates he refused to swallow down his throat when he was first admitted to the Jacarepaguá Nursing Home. And batons aren't meant to be swallowed, quite the opposite.

"Inmate 3,029! Repeating: visit for 3,029!"

The loudspeaker crackled again, announcing the visit with a tone of impatience.

Tarquínio didn't move, even though he knew it was his number.

The voice called out again, this time using the alphabet instead of numbers. The prisoner, hearing his name called out in full, awoke from his daily, recurring nightmare of the past fifteen years:

"Last call: visit for inmate Tarquínio Esperidião."

After being handcuffed, he walked slowly to the visiting room. He sat in the uncomfortable chair set aside for inmates as he watched a young woman in her twenties approach. Her hair was styled in braids, framing her familiar, piercing, and mesmerizing gray gaze. Otherwise, he would have gotten up and run back to his cell. The girl sat down next to him and immediately asked:

"How are you, Dad?"

"Dad?!"

"It's me, Maria Amélia. I've grown up, sure, but am I that unrecognizable? Don't worry, I forgive you. Crazy people do crazy things, don't they?"

Once again, Tarquínio found that he was no match for the witch who had walked all over him for so many years, leading him to commit crimes that had elevated him to the category of monster in the screeching headlines of the sensationalist media. There she was, sitting in front of him, the one responsible for everything bad that had happened in his life, the murders he had committed, everything. And she looked at him with the determination of someone about to make a request and who won't take no for an answer. He even saw Marlon Brando's face in Coppola's *Godfather*, promising his godson, who some say was Frank Sinatra himself:

"We'll make him an offer he can't refuse."

The girl then confirmed his fears with what sounded more like an order than a request:

"Dad, I'm really, really going to need your help to get me where I want to go. Not just yet, but it won't be long, and you have learned to wait, haven't you? Reward? Of course, you'll be rewarded. Maybe I can pull some strings to free you. You won't believe the crowd I'm involved with."

"Free me?! How? I am past sixty and have more than 100 to serve. Leave me alone, forget about me. Do what you want with your life. I'm out! Out, you hear. You should never have come back here, whoever you are. Guard! This visit is over, take me back to my cell."

"Don't make a scene. You are responsible for me, and you will help. When Mom was still alive, she always said: 'Maria Amélia, we are not alone, your father will take care of us. And it is you, my little *Fiinha*, who will get him out of prison.' She always called me Fiinha. She was such a sweetheart. Even her death was pretty. Remember the bloody rose that flowered on her back when you fired that crazy shot? Well, I'm here to ask for your help and I'm already counting on the support of Dr. Maria da Anunciação."

As the guard approached to ask what had happened, Tarquínio's eyes widened. With a wave from his hand, the prisoner hinted that everything was fine. Curiosity had overcome the indignation, the repulsion, the hatred he felt for that slender figure. Maria Amélia was showing off two very long braids that reminded him of the fashion of the beginning of the last century. But they had nothing *démodé* or vulgar about them in Maria Amélia. Tarquínio asked:

"Dr. Anunciação?! How did you get mixed up with that manipulator?"

Before giving the answer, Maria Amélia's gray eyes radiated mockery:

"Dad, you are perfectly aware of the answer. It was you who put her on my path. She is such a lovely person. She's being priceless in the work I am developing in college about beings born with the natural ability to influence other beings."

"Influence?! Why not outright say dominate, control, manipulate? Or, who knows, trample? And what the hell are you studying?"

"For now, psychiatry. But I won't stop there, and you will help me get where I want to go. That's what dads are for, right?"

Was it real? Was it a nightmare? For the remainder of the visit, Tarquínio was paralyzed, his wide eyes transfixed on Maria Amélia's, a stand-off to see who would blink first. If it had happened in a public arena, people would have said it was staged. Finally, faced with the oppressive determination of the braided girl's unyielding gaze, Tarquínio lowered his head and barely heard the guard approaching to say that the visit was over. She left, announcing that she would return for another visit, his stupor giving way to a hint of curiosity. He wanted to know what the little witch's plan was and what she could do to save him from four consecutive life sentences.

A brief overview of the events leading up to Tarquínio's arrest for three cold-blooded murders.

It all started when he was still a young journalist in Rio de Janeiro and Tarquínio Esperidião decided to research the life of an aunt who had been murdered at the start of the second decade of the last century. She was shot in the chest with a 16-gauge shotgun, the shell ejecting intact like a cannonball. As it exited through the back, it made a huge bloody rose. The shooter—the brother of the victim's stepfather—had been in love with and spurned by the girl. He had filled the cartridge not with lead, but with gold and silver pellets. His aunt's name was Maria Amélia, but everyone knew her by the nickname Fiinha, given to her at birth by her mother. Indeed, it's not just a coincidence that the braided girl claiming to be Tarquínio's daughter has the same name and the same nickname. Let's take it one step at a time. Maria Amélia the First, or Fiinha the First, (let's call her that to distinguish her from the second Maria Amélia, the focus of our tale) was, so to speak, the queen of Capim Alto, a prosperous farm in the interior of the state of Minas Gerais, near the city known as Santo Antônio das Tabocas. The stepfather, the servants on the farm, the regulars of the house, the brothers, and above all, the sisters, nurtured a mixture of admiration, respect, and fear for Fiinha the First. She commanded those around her with a gaze from her gray eyes, except perhaps her mother, Dona Adelaide, with whom she seemed to have sealed a pact during her pregnancy. This birth is worth a separate summary. Here is how it went down:

Adelaide's first husband, Aristides, was a burly man with a dense beard and thick mustache, an authentic people breeder, very much in the mold

14

of late-nineteenth-century landowners. The marriage, celebrated in 1888, had in fact been another pact, aimed at the merger of two large estates: Capim Alto, owned by Adelaide's parents, and Ribeirão Fundo, owned by Aristides' parents.

There was a problem, however. Adelaide, then fourteen, was not your typical maiden awaiting marriage, ready to spread her legs only when her husband told her so and with the primary intention of bearing his heirs. She was a rebel. She rode horses astride, like a Calamity Jane of the Cerrado Mineiro,[1] not caring about the warnings that this could rupture her hymen. If she followed any commandments at all, none dictated "thou shalt always and in all things obey thy husband." She had embodied the spirit of the suffragettes a few decades in advance. The spirit that would do so much damage to the sacred right of domination of husbands, fathers, and brothers.

Already on her wedding night, Adelaide's disdain for her arrogant groom morphed into hatred at the sight of his disgusted expression when she mentioned a potential hindrance to carnal consummation. She was menstruating. In the teenager's mind, there should be no problem if he wanted to proceed. If blood was to be spilled, it was already there, warm and perhaps even serving as a lubricant. But for Aristides, Adelaide was unclean and untouchable, as the Holy Bible decreed. The situation worsened the next morning when Adelaide's prying mother-in-law rummaged through bedroom drawers and cabinets looking for a whip that Adelaide had owned since she was a girl. She liked to mingle with the farm hands, especially when it was time to separate the cows from the calves. Adelaide asked what she was looking for and only got an answer when her mother-in-law finished her search and found it. Then, emphasizing each word, she declared:

"In this house, only men go to the corral and use a whip. Women stay indoors, as they have plenty to do."

Adelaide began softly muttering "Son of a bitch!"—she loved swearing—until it erupted loudly and clearly. The mother-in-law, Maria Aparecida

---

[1] A type of savanna found in the State of Minas Gerais.

15

Ferreira de Andrade, half-deaf, only heard the last part, like an explosion: "bitch!" She paused, surprised for a few seconds. Then she let go a high-pitched crackling scream capable of waking the entire farm. And that wasn't it. She walked over and slapped her daughter-in-law in the face. The fury whirling around the teenager's head indicated immediate retribution, but instead, she jumped up and ran off in her wedding nightgown. Her husband dragged her back by her hair through the cow shit. That night, she dreamt of her husband's death. Many years later, now married for the second time, Adelaide would never tire in answering her companion in the card game *Truco*, Francisquinho, when he asked about her honeymoon:

"What honeymoon? I had a shitmoon!"

This explanatory note on the pact between Adelaide and Fiinha the First might be getting too lengthy, but the episode of the first night is essential for the reader to have an idea of what life was like for the couple and how this influenced the existence of this story's central character. Aristides and Adelaide had four children: Aristides Filho, Orlando Andrade, Sebastião Andrade, and the youngest, Maria Amélia Andrade.

The last pregnancy, Fiinha the First's gestation, was unlike any other—extraordinary in every way. For starters, Adelaide noticed a mysterious quality in her belly, something more rounded, almost luminous. Rather than kicking, the fetus seemed to gently caress her uterus, as if affirming Adelaide's belief that she was carrying a girl. The pregnant woman adopted an unusual practice for the dawn of the twentieth century: she would lock herself in her room, get completely naked, and spend hours massaging her belly with almond oil. And so it happened that, one day when she had forgotten to lock the door, her husband burst in and saw her fully naked and caressing her belly for the first time, something he had not imagined seeing even in a brothel. His reaction was to strike with his whip, leaving a purplish bruise encircling Adelaide's belly. This was also the first time she felt a sudden movement and a sense that the fetus had felt the pain of the whip and was crying out for vengeance, a call for vengeance mirrored in her tears of pain and hatred.

16

What happened next, on the afternoon of the same day as the flogging, could well be more than mere coincidence and not align entirely with the laws of probability. The foreman recounted the story, his eyes wide with disbelief. Everything coincided, to the smallest detail, with the dream Adelaide had had the day after the wedding, after being dragged like a rag doll through the corral's manure.

Aristides' horse had stumbled in an armadillo hole, throwing him off about fifteen feet. He landed on his head, broke his neck, and died in the arms of the foreman who tried to rescue him. Extra detail: during the fall, Aristides flung his right arm upward, causing the whip to lash out. It returned like a boomerang, coiling around his muscular belly, leaving a purple bruise that would only disappear with the corpse's decomposition.

In his autobiographical book, Tarquínio goes into the fine details of the research on the life of Fiinha the First and recreates an image that was revealed to him by the witch herself:

> Adelaide listened quietly and impassively to the report of the foreman, who was still visibly frightened. When women flocked to console her, she begged her pardon, saying that she would like to be alone, went into her room, undressed, oiled up her hands, and began massaging her belly. The soon-to-be-born girl adjusted her head to better feel the caresses, seemingly eager to share in the contentment visible in her mother's eyes.

Up until her murder at age twenty-one, and even posthumously as Tarquínio's research uncovered, Fiinha the First shared a bond with her mother that went a little beyond the affection of mothers and daughters. Severe and ruthless to the rest of her offspring, Adelaide never even scolded Maria Amélia the First, who did everything she pleased, dominating everyone with her gaze, two beacons that issued orders that could not be disregarded. Celma and Sena, two of Fiinha the First's sisters, struggled to conceal their envy toward her, a sentiment that cost them dearly. Tarquínio details all the strange events surrounding the young witch until Juca Trindade, brother of Fiinha the First's stepfather Amadeu, driven mad by unrequited love, shot her in the chest and killed her.

17

In his research, Tarquínio clashed with Rosa, Juca Trindade's niece, who was examining her uncle's life for a thesis at the University of São Paulo. Impelled by the witch—then dead for almost eighty years—Tarquínio ended up murdering Juca's niece, in addition to destroying everything she had written about him. For Fiinha the First, Rosa was rehabilitating the memory of her killer, and this was inadmissible. Tarquínio transformed from a researcher into Fiinha the First's puppet, murdering Rosa and then eliminating the victim's maid and the building's doorman to cover his tracks. The case became known as the *Jardim Paulista Massacre* or the *Carnage on Marechal Castelo Branco Street.* Tarquínio's mind lost all links with sanity and, before being sentenced, he was hospitalized in the Jacarepaguá nursing home, where he came into contact with Dr. Anunciação and Sister Patrícia, one of the nurses at the clinic. When he was leaving the Jacarepaguá nursing home, and before a nosy reporter discovered that he was the monster of the Jardim Paulista Massacre, Tarquínio enjoyed a night of passion with Patrícia, leading to the birth of the new Maria Amélia, or the new Fiinha. In his autobiography, Tarquínio states unabashedly that he wasn't the one who had sexual relations with Patrícia. It was Fiinha the First herself who had taken possession of his body with the confessed purpose of being reborn.

In his autobiography's epilogue, Tarquínio describes the first prison visit from Sister Patrícia and their seven-year-old daughter. She told that the name Maria Amélia came to her in a dream, suggested by a beautiful woman with braided hair and gray eyes, much like their daughter's. Tarquínio lost all control when Sister Patrícia finally asked him:

"Don't you think our Fiinha is beautiful?"

He pounced on the guard like a cat, wrested the rifle from his hands, and fired at the girl. Sister Patrícia flew like only a mother can, making her chest into a shield as she thrust the girl into the accompanying guard's arms. As it exited through the back, the bullet formed a bloody rose, identical to the one on the back of Fiinha the First, eighty years earlier. Tarquínio was hauled out of the visiting room, nearly unconscious from the beating he endured. His autobiography ends like this:

"Yet, despite my dizziness, I couldn't escape the scornful look the girl gave me as she was carried away in a policewoman's arms."

Second Part

-

CHILDHOOD

2

Let's pick up the thread when Fiinha left the crime scene in the policewoman's arms. The girl appeared far less shaken than the uniformed woman, who trembled as she awkwardly placed the girl on the sofa in the warden's office waiting room. Fiinha's gaze shifted from one of debauchery to shock, an orphan lost in the world after seeing her mother get shot in the chest by her convict father. And this is how—with bulging eyes—she fixed her gaze on the warden, who was walking in her direction accompanied by an entourage of aides. In their midst was a beautiful red-haired woman (the warden's secretary?). She seemed the most shaken of them all. The woman pulled a handkerchief from her bag, and Fiinha realized it was meant to comfort her, to wipe away non-existent tears—for now. The girl pressed an invisible button on her crying machine and water trickled from her gray eyes, her lips puckering like a creature alone and abandoned in the vast world. Even before the warden bent down to console the victim of the "visual rape"—as he had classified the incident—the woman from his entourage cut him off and sat on the couch next to Fiinha, hugging her, kissing her forehead, and wiping away her tears. Maria Amélia played the part. She rested her head on the woman's shoulder, sobbing softly in a way that could melt even the most calloused hearts. Camera flashes popped from photographers stationed at the penitentiary. It crossed the warden's mind—one of those calloused hearts—to kick the swarm out, but reason prevailed. In an instant, he realized the front-page photos would be worth more than any advertising money spent to mask the common and ordinary rot of his institution. And that's what happened the next day. A tabloid featured a close-up of the tearful consolation, dominating its front page. The photo of Sister Patrícia sprawled on the floor with a bloody rose on her back was published only in the inner pages.

The entourage's redhead was neither maid nor secretary. She was the warden's wife. Her name was Anita Xavier Nogueira, less than half the age of her husband in his sixties, who was sterile, and she was desperate for a child, preferably a daughter.

Had Maria Amélia secured her own adoption? Let's slow down, because even a warden with so many strings to pull can't sidestep the bureaucracy involved in such matters. Certainly, on Sister Patrícia's side, the path had been essentially cleared. The grandmother was diabetic and a heart patient who had just turned eighty-five. She was also a pensioner on a minimum-wage, surviving out of sheer stubbornness in a room in the Copacabana apartment of her now only living child, Adamastor. He might pose a minor obstacle to the adoption plans of the warden's wife. Whenever Fiinha had visited her grandmother with her mother, Sister Patrícia always tried to avoid contact with her brother as much as she could. However, this wasn't entirely feasible, as the uncle and niece shared a certain rapport, a kind of understanding in their glances that went beyond mere family ties.

"Go, Uncle, everything will be fine today. Lots of fish will take the bait."

"Thank you, Niece. I really need some luck; it's been tough going."

"And what are you guys talking about? Do you even know what your uncle does? If he does anything at all!"

Sister Patrícia was vaguely aware of her brother's involvement in illicit activities. She hoped it was gambling, but feared it was drugs. She couldn't think of any other explanation for the funds required to rent a four-bedroom apartment with an extra maid's room in Copacabana, in addition to the new Volkswagen in the garage he had bought with cash. Adamastor carried a peculiar business card bearing only his first name, the title 'Exchange Agent,' and a mobile phone, prepaid, just in case. Sister Patrícia's suspicion, the worst one, was correct. Her brother managed a stash house in Leme, and at the time, his main commodities of trade were cocaine and marijuana. He felt almost compelled to deal in crack as well, however. Market stuff. After her brother left on business during her last visit to their mother, Patricia remarked:

"I think he's mixed up in bad stuff. Has he ever told you what he does, where he gets so much money?"

"He didn't say and I don't care, my child. At my age, what I want, what I need, is comfort, to be well. What he does is not of the slightest importance. He is a great son; he practically knows my every wish."

"Mother!?"

Before Dona Genoveva could respond to her daughter's outrage, Fiinha, a seven-year-old brat hardly fit for such conversations, interjected:

"Uncle Adamastor does what he has to, and he does it very well. Why are you always snooping?"

"Fiinha!"

However, the scolding ended there. The urge to reprimand was immediately quelled by a pair of gray eyes conveying a message: "You pretentious little nurse, let your brother handle his affairs in peace." And though her daughter's lips stayed shut, she could almost hear:

"People only use if they choose to!"

This was one of the few times Patrícia had scolded her daughter, albeit timidly. Usually, she indulged all her whims and desires, particularly as Maria Amélia exhibited from a young age a rationality and determination rare in many adults.

So, Adamastor might indeed become an obstacle to the warden's wife's aspirations, who hugged Fiinha for over ten minutes in a moment of profound maternal bliss, a veritable mother's orgasm.

"What's your name, my dear?"

"Maria Amélia," she answered amidst sobs.

"Oh, what a beautiful name!"

"Mommy called me Fiinha."

"Oh, my dear. Fiinha! How wonderful, oh, oh ... my poor, lovely little Fiinha!"

The fish was on the hook. Hidden behind Anita Xavier Nogueira's shoulders, Maria Amélia's eyes would have betrayed immense satisfaction. Her mother's corpse with the bloody rose on her back was long gone, buried forever, even though it was still in the prison's visiting room, surrounded by homicide detectives and forensic technicians.

23

But beyond Adamastor and his mother, another obstacle loomed, who knew the biggest of them all. After all, Fiinha had a father. How would Tarquínio react if the warden's vivacious wife arranged a meeting to solemnly ask if she could adopt his daughter?

While we await the outcome of the adoption proceedings, let's go to the burial of Sister Patrícia, scheduled for ten o'clock the next day in the Caju cemetery. With the exception of Tarquínio, who remained behind bars, all those involved were present, including the warden and his wife, the latter wearing a discreet brimmed hat adorned with a black orchid and tucked into a black dress made the day before by her personal couturier. She appeared every bit the grieving family member, far more exuberant than the victim's mother, who was also dressed in black but in a modest outfit from C&A. The brother Adamastor, careful not to draw attention, had put on an elegant blue suit, covering the small tattoo on the inner side of his wrist. A leaf design, which would certainly not amuse Dr. Joaquim Paranhos Nogueira, a man to whom nature had granted no sense of humor whatsoever. Oh, and the most important detail of the funeral: Fiinha's dress was a precise replica of Dona Anita Xavier Nogueira's funeral attire, crafted by the same couturier, naturally.

Fiinha decided to put on a teary face to please the crowd, a feat she executed masterfully as the coffin was lowered into the grave.

And then a fading scream ...

"Mommy, Mommy, Mommy ..."

Afterward, she gave a quick kiss to her grandmother, a vulnerable look to her uncle and a long, and a drawn-out hug to her new mother project, dressed in her ostentatious black. However, law and tradition mandated that the orphan be promptly entrusted to the nearest kin, so Fiinha went to live in the Copacabana apartment with her sick grandmother and drug-dealing uncle. Anita returned home in a cloud of misery. She wept like a woman facing doom as she bid farewell to Maria Amélia, whispering a promise to make her her daughter. For it had been written for tens of thousands of years ... No, those are the words of Nelson Rodrigues, an author this socialite would never deign to read ... It was written in the stars, which don't need numbers. Pulling away from the long embrace, Anita whispered in Fiinha's ear:

"God's will shall be done!"

This particular God's will was expressed to her husband at night, when they were getting ready for bed. Adorned in lingerie, she insinuated a night of passion ahead and declared with conviction:

"I'm adopting her, no matter what it takes!"

3

Fiinha had to be transferred from her school in Jacarepaguá to the Copacabana Municipal Education Center. Maria Amélia had always excelled, ever since kindergarten at the public school in Jacarepaguá, conveniently located near the nursing home where Sister Patrícia worked. She refused to come in second, in either play or study. She adored all kinds of puzzles, assembling and disassembling maps, building and demolishing castles, and frustrating Dona Neide, who couldn't win a single game of checkers against this little girl with braids, who was already reading at four and speaking with a grammatical finesse that could embarrass a college freshman.

"This girl will go far!"

The teacher was even more impressed when Fiinha started attending primary school. She feared that she would not stay at the school long and be attracted to a more prestigious establishment, perhaps an institution for extraordinarily gifted children. Fiinha was also aware of this possibility, but something told her that it was best avoided. A school for the gifted meant isolation, she reasoned, a world apart filled with geniuses inside their bubbles, unprepared to navigate the web of emotions and frictions of ordinary mortals. It's the stupidity of others that fuels the thirst for knowledge, perhaps even more than competing with the privileged winners of the evolutionary lottery. It was astonishing how this person-in-the-making, not even four-feet tall, could harbor such complex thoughts, concluding that the other gifted were not suitable as companions. They were just competitors to beat, preferably in a public arena, with a large audience of mere mortals.

When a Department of Education official visited the school to identify gifted students, Dona Neide nominated only Maria Amélia, convinced that the girl would be selected. She was mistaken. Fiinha purposely failed a few questions so that the employee had nothing else to communicate to school management, except:

"She's a totally normal girl. Maybe a little more dedicated and studious than the others. Nothing more."

As she left, the talent scout for the highly intelligent passed Fiinha and was pierced by the mocking gaze. She realized then that she had been mistaken. The girl was much more exceptional than a simple test for putting together figures could ever reveal.

Maria Amélia's transfer to the Municipal Education Center of Copacabana occurred without a hitch. In a letter to the principal of the new school, Dona Neide expressed her deep admiration for the girl, describing her as exceptionally intelligent for her age, despite not passing the Department of Education's test for the gifted. The new principal, Dona Esmeralda, quickly skimmed her colleague's lengthy report, which spent more than half its content lamenting the girl's failure on the exceptionality test. The principal was only interested in the name of the student and the grade in which she should be enrolled. She asked her secretary:

"Do we still have openings in second grade?"

"Yes, we have, Dona Esmeralda."

The principal stamped 'Enrolled' on the petition and passed it to the secretary:

"Report it to those responsible."

Aware that her time at the Copacabana school would be short, Maria Amélia resolved to breeze through it. From the first day, she was unexpectedly discreet: she chose a place right in the middle of class so that she could hardly be seen by the teacher, and effortlessly kept up with the classes, which offered her nothing beyond what she already knew by heart. She didn't want to make friends. Something told her that this was not the right place to fulfill her destiny. In her uncle's apartment, the seven-year-old girl became the mistress of the house and subjected her grandmother to her whims and commands. With an innate arrogance that required no shouting to impose her will, she dictated the maid's routine: "Alzira, do not leave without cleaning the bathroom. Alzira, put less salt in grandma's soup. The sink faucet is dripping, call someone to fix it." And so, it was done. Maria Amélia distributed her orders while the apartment turned spotlessly clean and organized. Nothing out of place. Alzira occupied the apartment's maid's room from Monday to Friday. On weekends, she returned to her shack up the hill in the Chapéu Mangueira favela, home to her four children—two boys and two girls, aged between seventeen and eleven. The boys—Gilberto and Agenor—were the oldest and already properly employed. Their employer was the same as their mother's—they worked as drug runners for the stash house overseen by Adamastor.

Maria Amélia's request was, as always, an order:

"I want to spend the weekend with you, at your place."

With trembling lips, Alzira replied:

"Oh, dear god! Amelinha, it's very dangerous up there. Would Mr. Adamastor allow it?"

The two familiar gray eyes pinned her down:

"You know very well that Uncle does what I ask. And secondly, don't call me Amelinha. Maria Amélia, please! I'll pack my bag. We'll leave after the nurse has arrived to take care of Grandma."

Alzira called Adamastor in secret, unaware that the girl was listening in on an extension that she had pulled to her room:

"She wants to spend the weekend with me in the favela, Mr. Adamastor. What do I do?"

"This girl! Once she sets her mind on something, there's no stopping her. Just act normal and don't let her suspect anything. It's probably better if Gilberto and Agenor don't stay in the shack while she's there. This girl, I'm telling ya!"

27

Adamastor then called Maria Amélia in a last attempt to convince her to stay:

"My dearest niece, what is this story about you spending the weekend in the favela?"

"Oh, you mean Alzira snitched? An ugly and dangerous thing, wouldn't you say, Uncle? Yes, I want to!"

"It's dangerous, Fiinha."

"Not dangerous at all, Uncle! You need to read more newspapers and watch those police shows on TV. The favela has its pacifying police force now, haven't you heard?"

If it hadn't been over the phone, the uncle would have seen her mischievous look. How could he not have known when he had already spent three sleepless nights because of the UPP,[2] which was being praised in song and verse by the newspapers of the status quo. But he was also aware that there was no denying the request, with or without peacekeeping police.

Before Fiinha heads up to the favela, however, let's turn our attention to Anita Xavier Nogueira. Her first measure, a week after Sister Patrícia's burial, was to get rid of what she thought was the largest stone. She went to see Tarquínio, and this prison visit was decidedly different from the others. There was no call through the loudspeakers shouting the inmate's number instead of his name. Two guards escorted him, his arms and legs cuffed, directly to the warden's office. Dona Anita was sitting to the side in a comfortable armchair. Despite the empty sofa in front of her, they brought in a hard, armless chair for Tarquínio. He didn't exactly sit down. The two guards sat him down. Dr. Paranhos Nogueira spoke:

"Inmate Tarquínio, it is my wife who has something to tell you."

Dr. Nogueira nodded, but frowned immediately when his wife began addressing the prisoner as 'sir.' He became even more annoyed by the begging tone coming from his wife's lips:

---

[2] Pacifying Police Unit.

"Sir ... It's a request, a favor I ask of you. I'll get right to it. I want to adopt Maria Amélia as my own daughter. I already have the papers with me declaring that you renounce the condition of father and won't stand in the way of the adoption process."

"Where do I sign?"

"Don't you want to read it first? It is a total and definitive renunciation. Maria Amélia will never visit you again. It's forever."

"Excellent, that's exactly what I want. I just can't sign with my hands tied."

Joaquim Paranhos Nogueira shot Tarquínio his commanding look and ordered the guards to remove the handcuffs. Hopping—his feet remained shackled—the prisoner was practically dragged by the guards to the table. He signed the document, and with a smile of pure satisfaction, addressed Anita without further ceremony:

"You will regret this. The little witch is no good. I'm here because of her. You were captivated by the girl, weren't you? The interests charged for gullibility are steep and paid for a lifetime. My warning is free. You'll regret this."

Tarquínio's speech was interrupted by Dr. Nogueira's outburst:

"Take inmate 3,029 back to his cell immediately."

Tarquínio met the warden's fury with loud laughter, the laughter from someone with nothing left to lose, but when his eyes crossed those of Dona Anita, which expressed a mixture of gratitude and compassion, he felt disgust. Even the baton of the blonde one would be preferable to that look, he thought.

Two large stones were still in the way: the grandmother and the uncle.

At that moment, the uncle was concerned with Maria Amélia's ascent to the favela. He made a point of going up first to ensure the stash house remained operational and discreet. The first order of business was finding a temporary way to send Gilberto and Agenor away.

"You two need to stay away from the favela this weekend. There's a place for you to sleep in Pavãozinho. I'll tell your mother."

Freed from the pair of runners and with the rest of the arrangements made, Adamastor decided to take Maria Amélia and Alzira in his car to the vicinity of the shack, not far from the tip under the "S" formed by the sloping Ary Barroso. On the way up, even though he knew that the car could hardly deviate from the slope's zigzag, he asked Alzira:

"Show me how to get there."

He caught Fiinha's sly look in the rearview mirror that seemed to say, 'You're a terrible actor, Uncle.' Then she spoke out loud:

"I want Gilberto and Agenor to show me the favela. I want to go up there, beyond the road. They say the sprawling wealth of Avenida Atlântica is quite a sight from the peak of poverty."

Adamastor and Alzira spoke at almost the same time:

"What kind of ideas are they, Fiinha? Did your teacher tell you that?"

"Oh, Holy Lady of Perpetual Help!"

"No, Uncle, it just came out of my head now! Why are you so afflicted, Alzira?"

"It's just that my children are not at home. They went to visit relatives there in Minas Gerais."

"And that's why you're terrified? Does the boogeyman live in Minas Gerais? Uncle, put up some Luiz Gonzaga! I suddenly feel like listening to 'Oh what a lie, what a pretty yarn.'"

Without a word, Adamastor continued up the hill, eager to fulfill Maria Amélia's wish. Then he stopped the car and declared solemnly:

"There is Avenida Atlântica, at your feet, my dearest niece."

Up there, a gentle breeze was blowing. Below, the first lights were being turned on, but not even the twilight had managed to expel the simmering heat of a scorching day. Maria Amélia got out of the car, spread her arms, and turned her head to take in the landscape from all angles. Her eyes gleamed with satisfaction, less from the view and more from knowing she had complete control over the two in the car.

4

Adamastor knew she knew, but he pretended she didn't. It wasn't easy to admit that such a little brat could have mastered the tangled web of drug trafficking, offering him wise advice in her indirect manner of speaking.

After spending a weekend in the favela, frequently accompanied by Alzira's daughters, Genivalda and Arlete, Maria Amélia couldn't help but remember the respect she received on the hill. It was as if everyone made way wherever she passed without her having to ask with words or eyes:

"Why don't you charge me for the ice cream?"

"It's covered, it's covered. For the girl, everything is covered."

"In that case I want some for my friends too."

"No problem, no problem. Whatever the girl wants."

Meanwhile, Dona Genoveva's health wasn't good at all. Her cough had worsened, and at night, the old woman's wheezing was audible from Maria Amélia's adjoining room. They were having dinner—Alzira assisting Dona Genoveva with the challenging task of guiding the spoon to her mouth—when Maria Amélia almost whispered in Adamastor's ear:

"Uncle, there's a guy from the Pacifying Police Unit everywhere we go in the favela."

And she had a few other comments to make.

"Strolling through the hill's alleys and backstreets has become safer than jogging along Avenida Atlântica's boardwalk; Nighttime traders must adapt to these new circumstances."

Adamastor frowned:

"I have no idea what you're talking about, Niece."

He was shot down by the girl's glare, who then kissed him on the cheek and whispered in his ear:

"Take care, Uncle, take care ... I think this peacemaking police is temporary, for now. And also, trade is for the benefit of all, isn't that right, Uncle?"

Adamastor, instead of responding, nearly choked and had to ask Alzira for help, who was assisting his mother sip her soup, completely oblivious to what was happening around her:

"Water ... a glass of water ... hurry, Alzira!"

Maria Amélia wasn't done speaking, however. She motioned to Dona Genoveva and said, in the same whispering tone:

"Poor thing! After she is gone, it would be best if you accepted Dona Anita's offer to adopt me. We would all win: Dona Anita, a daughter; me, a mother; and my dearest uncle, a niece in the right places to help him in his every need.

Dona Genoveva's pneumonia was reaching the point of no return. On top of that she was a heart patient, diabetic, and old. The doctor recommended immediate hospitalization. While waiting for the ambulance, Maria Amélia entered the room and told the nurse that she wanted to be alone with her grandmother. She gazed into the old woman's eyes with the cold, unfeeling intensity of a shark, as if she were death herself, poised to strike. With no trace of compassion or pity, she commanded in a firm tone:

"Grandma, it's time to go. There's no point in waiting for the ambulance. It's better for you and for everyone."

Dona Genoveva stammered and died with her terrified eyes fixed on her granddaughter. Fiinha switched from the cold stare of death's messenger to the expression of an eight-year-old child witnessing her grandmother's agony. She screamed at the top of her lungs:

"Maria (the nurse's name), Uncle Adamastor, quick, Grandma is dead! Oh, how awful! Grandma's dead!"

And she cried the tears of the falsest crocodile to ever crawl the face of the earth.

5

Maria Amélia didn't want to go to an institution for the gifted, but neither did she plan to suffer through the entirety of third grade at the terrible Copacabana school. It also wasn't the ideal environment to make the kind of friends who would align with her goals. To encounter poverty, the rabble, the marginalized, and especially the masses ripe for manipulation, she needed only to step into the streets or visit the favela where her uncle called the shots. Those pulling the strings, held up in their well-guarded condominiums, typically demanded a pass for entry through their electrified fences. Beyond these barriers you'd only find servants or the anointed by fortune, even if they had to face sordid and fetid labyrinths to get there. In addition, the braided girl reasoned that she needed to find a suitable school, one that would enable her to advance directly from junior year to university, seamlessly and without drawing undue attention. Maria Amélia made a point of picking up the phone herself to tell Anita Xavier Nogueira about her grandmother's death and invite her to the burial.

Dr. Joaquim Paranhos Nogueira did not go. When his wife insisted, he claimed to have appointments that couldn't wait. The Caju cemetery was the scene of a great show. Anita arrived with two bodyguards in black suits, very well dressed for the occasion.

"It is the funeral of Maria Amélia's grandmother. She is our daughter! I can't think of her any other way. Our daughter!"

Dr. Joaquim was stubborn, but not enough to quell his wife's growing obsession with adopting this child—an idea he secretly hoped to thwart. The thought that inmate 3,029 could be right thundered through his mind: a killer's daughter couldn't be any good, she was a bad egg! Yet, he kept his reservations private, not voicing his concerns to shield the beautiful, naïve woman who had opened so many doors for him. Doors that were often closed to prison wardens.

Maria Amélia's dress was black, but different from the one she wore at her mother's funeral. She was growing up and there was already a hint of adolescence in the girl who was yet to turn nine. After Sister Patrícia's burial, she gave the dress to Alzira's youngest daughter, who had erupted in thank-yous while her mother raised her hands to ask providence to shower the sweet, braided creature with blessings. Maria Amélia, her eyes fixed on the gift's receiver, had replied:

"Oh, you're welcome. Maybe one day you'll pay me back with a favor."

Anita was also wearing another black dress. She was not the kind of woman to go to two wakes in the same outfit.

As soon as the coffin was lowered into the grave and the priest had finished the tedious process of shipping off a soul, Maria Amélia, holding Adamastor's hand, led him to her future mother:

"Uncle, I think Dona Anita needs to talk to you."

The adoption was arranged between the graves of the Caju cemetery, even before Dona Genoveva's bony corpse had attracted the first worm.

Adamastor and Anita went ahead, followed by the two bodyguards. Between them, like a bouncing wedge, was the object of the conversation up front. Maria Amélia smiled, glancing from one man to the other. She then held the brutes' hands and asked:

"Which one of you will drive me to school? Or are you exclusively Mom's? Dona Anita is straightening things out with Uncle Adamastor, ever heard of him? She's ironing out the last details for my adoption."

The bodyguards held firm. Not a word, certainly not a smile. Maria Amélia let both their hands go, but continued between them, imitating the seriousness of their faces. As if just to herself, she said:

"Fools!"

The men exchanged glances, as if to share the fear that afflicted them, conveying in the typical silence of those who care for the security of others: "This little thing is going to give us more trouble than the adults."

Adamastor put up some obstacles at first, even though his niece had already convinced him to give in. After all, it said 'Exchange Agent' on his card, so he could hardly deliver the goods without bargaining. He was the one who started talking:

"I know you adore my niece and would do everything for her that my sister would do had she been alive. But I must say, it's not easy on an uncle's heart to part with such a wonderful creature. (His eyes widened.) Not easy. If it hadn't been for her, I think my mother would have died long ago. But I'm single, busy all day. I know I can't take care of Maria Amélia as I should ..."

He was cut off by Anita:

"Fiinha—that's what I want to call her—told me you sell cleaning products in the favelas of Zona Sul, is this true?"

Adamastor was startled, but he didn't lose his composure or train of thought:

"Yes, it is. As you know, poor people aren't dirty by choice, it's the lack of money to get clean ... Pardon the joke. But yes, it's true, I do what I can. Life is not easy in trade. It is hard enough already to part with my dearest niece. That's what I call her. Did you know?"

Anita had an impulse to take Adamastor's hands. She held back. She was content sharing the most sentimental look witnessed at the Caju cemetery that day.

"I understand. I understand you perfectly. I can only promise you that our Fiinha will want for nothing, absolutely nothing. She's the daughter I always wanted."

"I don't want to lose her for good. I don't want to be deprived of her occasional company. I know you made her father ... that creep ... promise he would never see our lovely Fiinha again. You can't ask that of me. How could something so terrible produce the most beautiful and wonderful child I've ever seen in my life?"

This time emotion triumphed over all modesty. Anita, however, quickly, clasped Adamastor's hands and said to him, locking her glistening eyes onto his:

"You will always be welcome in our home. I know I also speak for Joaquim."

Then she turned, stooped down and shouted to Maria Amélia:

"Come, give me a very big hug, my Fiinha!"

The girl's eyes were triumphant, and while she hugged Anita with her left hand, she pulled Adamastor in with her right. Uncle and adoptive mother almost touched faces in their eagerness to indulge the girl.

6

Anita hired the Sonho Dourado Buffet, considered by her friends as Rio de Janeiro's finest. Only the best, the most sophisticated, was good enough to present her daughter to Rio's society. Six hundred invitations went out. The husband raised a feeble objection:

"Don't you think that's a little too much?"

"It's not too much. Maria Amélia deserves so much more. My wish is to invite the entire world, to put up a poster in Cinelândia, to announce over a megaphone: 'I have a daughter, the most beautiful, most adorable, most intelligent daughter in the world!'"

Dr. Joaquim answered with a smile, but he lacked Fiinha's finesse in the art of pretense. If someone were to transcribe the wrinkles of the ill-represented smile on his face, they would read: 'imbecilic creature, exposing me to ridicule, throwing parties for a convict's daughter. If she gave me trouble before, imagine now with that little brat looking at me sideways, challenging me. Insolent!'

The mistress of the house felt their Lagoa mansion was unsuitable for the grand party she intended to host. They rented another mansion, fully equipped for major events, nestled in the Atlantic Forest. Joaquim Paranhos liked this, because the idea of exposing his own house to so many people displeased him.

Maria Amélia made sure that Alzira's sons and daughters were among the guests. Above all, she demanded the presence of Gilberto and Agenor, even though Gilberto preferred the favela's funk parties. But he too had already learned that an invitation from the braided girl was not to be refused. It wasn't an invitation; it was a summons.

"Alzira, I want your four children at my party."

36

"But, my angel, they don't have the right clothes. How are they going to look among so many fancy people?"

"Why, as favelados among high society. Don't rich people go up the hill? There is nothing keeping the favelados from coming down. Gilberto and Agenor have a knack for navigating such problems."

Knowing with certainty that the girl was aware of far more than she ought to be sent shivers down the maid's spine. With a final pleading glance, Alzira asked for Adamastor's help. This occurred during the final dinner before Fiinha departed the Copacabana apartment for the Lagoa mansion, where she would have a bedroom, a study room equipped with computer and television, and a large gym with all the necessary equipment just for herself. Adamastor answered the maid's cry for help with a look of utter helplessness. And although expressing the plain truth, he said in jest:

"May my dearest niece's will be done."

Apart from Alzira's children, Maria Amélia had almost no interest in inviting other kids. She only called one classmate from her school. The only one, incidentally, who occasionally matched and rivaled her in the staring game, when two people stare at each other until the first blinks. Her name was Maria das Dores, though she went by the nickname Das Dores. The other invitees were children of Anita's friends, all anointed as the *crème de la crème*, with rights to mansions in the Lagoa, penthouses in the Zona Sul, and bank accounts in Switzerland or some other tax haven.

Maria Amélia did not insist when Adamastor said he would not attend the party. She figured her uncle was right. The time was not ripe yet. She knew that a *tête-à-tête* between the uncle and the warden could not be avoided, but she wanted to lay the groundwork first.

More than thirty waiters were responsible for letting the champagne flow freely. If a napkin fell, one of the several servants was there to pick it up. Gilberto and Agenor walked among the members of high society with their fingers itching to pick their big pockets. They resisted because they knew Adamastor's wrath would be unrelenting. They had been warned:

37

"Watch what you do at my niece's party, you brats! I've spent a lot of money on these suits you're wearing. I want both of you to blend in like two little spoiled preppies. And make sure your sisters don't make a spectacle of themselves as well."

Adamastor did not anticipate the two might cross paths with some customer. They did. One of them, Adalberto, had just married one of Anita's youngest friends and had a feeling of foreboding, almost dread, when he saw the two runners circling among the guests. He went over to another member of the *blow* gang, who was standing on the other side of the room:

"Did you see that?"

"The two runners? Stop shaking, man. I've figured it all out. They are the sons of the maid of the guest of honor's uncle. And you're going to flip out when I tell you who the uncle is. Care to guess?"

"I have no idea."

"It's Adamastor of Chapéu Mangueira."

Adalberto grew even more unnerved upon realizing he was under the intense gaze of the guest of honor's gray eyes, less than sixteen feet away. Had she overheard the conversation? The confusion didn't last.

Maria Amélia came over and asked:

"Did I hear you say my uncle's name? Do you know him? Are you friends or customers?"

Adalberto's friend, his defenses down after his tenth glass of champagne, bent over and spoke in Maria Amélia's ear:

"Customer of what, miss?"

"Cleaning products. That's what my uncle sells. Or do you prefer pharmaceuticals for nasal use?"

As Maria Amélia walked away, blowing kisses to the audience waiving at her, Adalberto left his drunk friend, walked resolutely to his wife, and said in a low but decided tone in her ear:

"Let's go!"

Security measures were extreme, unprecedented for a party to introduce a nine-year-old girl to society. Half the prison guards had been dispatched to secure and patrol the vicinity of the Mansão da Colina. The guests had to go through a metal detector. Some objected, but Anita would swiftly intervene, smoothing things over with the sunny disposition befitting someone born with a silver spoon in her mouth:

"Come on guys, just pretend you're boarding a plane."

Dr. Joaquim didn't find anything about it funny. He was nevertheless quite happy, a joy that superseded the fact that he was having to accept the daughter of a maximum-security inmate as his own. His happiness owed to an important absence. As for the exceptional security measures, Dr. Joaquim had plenty of reasons. He had kept the newspaper clippings reporting the death of a colleague, who had been shot sixty times in his white Mercedes on Avenida Brasil. He had been an ally of Rio's Secretary of Penitentiary Administration. However, he criticized the victim for his lax security and for not using a bulletproof car. He never let his guard down when it came to those matters. When they told him there was no money for an armored vehicle, Dr. Joaquim had looked down from his perch as blue-blooded heir to a Minas Gerais farm from the "*Café com Leite*" days[3] and answered:

"I'm paying out of my own pocket!"

He didn't go anywhere without his armored car and three bodyguards, one in the front seat and two in the back, armed with revolvers, two machine guns, and a 12-gauge shotgun. Anita's car was also armored, and she was followed by two scowling security guards.

The party's missing person was precisely the Secretary of Penitentiary Administration, Dr. Anacleto Batista de Mello, even though he had been one of the first to be invited. His wife, Maria Piedade, was also absent. She was Anita's friend and confidante, a companion in the philanthropic works involving the vast field of the prison population. A field ripe for charity, which Tarquínio often fiercely and bitterly criticized as the inseparable companion of injustice. Anyway, they were not there, and instead of displeasure, Dr. Joaquim felt satisfaction.

---

[3] In the early decades of the twentieth century, Brazilian politics were dominated by the states of São Paulo and Minas Gerais, major producers of coffee and milk.

Less than a week prior, the couple Anacleto and Maria Piedade had visited Dr. Joaquim and Anita. Maria Amélia would be introduced to them first. The friend had whispered her concerns into Anita's ears, not mincing her words. She expressed doubts about the wisdom of adopting a killer's daughter. She had read his file and her husband fully agreed with her.

"These things run in the blood, Anita! I hope you won't regret it."

The rebuke was blunt and loud enough for the entire room to hear:

"Stay out of it, Maria Piedade! Don't talk about my daughter like that!"

It happened when Maria Amélia was entering the room to be introduced. With a smile, she approached the visibly shaken women, extended her hand to the visitor, and said with her mocking gray gaze:

"Nice to meet you, Maria Amélia. Mommy, what happened? Dona Maria Piedade looks like she's seen a ghost."

The visit lasted the ten additional minutes required by etiquette, masking the end of a friendship.

However, the incident from the previous week wasn't the primary reason for the secretary and his wife's absence. The cause was revealed in a phone call that Dr. Joaquim Paranhos Nogueira had received on the morning of the party. It came from the governor's office, summoning him to an audience at the Guanabara Palace.

"May I know what this is about?"

"Yes, but please don't mention to the governor that I'm already offering congratulations to the new head of Rio de Janeiro's entire prison system. That is, if you accept."

He was being asked to take the place of his former friend, who in turn was asked to resign after his name appeared in a tabloid headline:

"Anacleto Behind the Massacre at Bangu 1 Penitentiary"

Unlike his wife, Joaquim Paranhos Nogueira liked to savor his successes alone, a private moment for him and his vanity, mingled with indulgence. Thus, he was savoring his whiskey on the rocks and smoking a Cuban cigar, its aroma filling the entire studio. It was already the day after Maria

Amélia's presentation party. His appointment as Secretary of the Penitentiary System of the state of Rio de Janeiro was but a step in his plans. He wanted to go much further. He lamented expending so much energy and countless nights poring over books to complete his PhD thesis, which had led him practically on one single path. "Repression and Authority in the Maintenance of Penitentiary Order" had even been published as a book. Paid for by the author, sure, but even so, it had already been adopted in some of the law schools sprouting like mushrooms in the cities of the countryside. Joaquim Paranhos Nogueira had dreamed big since his time as mere police officer and freshly graduated lawyer. He aspired to rank among the true puppet masters. His talent for using force to quell rebellion, and his knack for balancing repression with speeches that stirred the prejudices ingrained in the inmates' cultural psyche, led him on the path of prisons. A guardian of the marginalized masses, Brazil's chief jailer. Or Rio de Janeiro's, for now.

He smacked his lips after sipping his whiskey and inadvertently thought out loud:

"No, I want more. Much more than that!"

It was then that he saw he was not alone. Maria Amélia sat on the studio's sofa, less than ten feet away. She had her hands on her chin as if she had been watching for some time. She smiled.

"Daddy. I can call you Daddy now, right? What is it you want so badly?"

Joaquim Paranhos choked on his whiskey and only regained composure after downing the entire glass, ice cubes included. This was their first moment alone because of Anita's near omnipresence. And it was also the first time he was challenged, for an instant that seemed like an eternity, by the inquisitive eyes of his adopted daughter.

"Just nonsense. Work-related issues, adult concerns. You wouldn't understand."

"Thoughts that spill over into words are never nonsense."

This she said with an unusual gravitas for a nine-year-old, but she soon proceeded in a mischievous and playful tone:

41

"Adults sure fuss over lots of silly things, don't they? Silly things that somehow make life interesting, right? Once Daddy gains more confidence in his daughter, she'll be a great help in tackling all those silly things that make life worthwhile."

When leaving the studio, skipping, Maria Amélia blew a kiss (the first) to Joaquim Paranhos, who was unable to say a single word. But he did make a decision: he was going to have another talk with detainee 3,029.

From the studio of her adoptive father, Maria Amélia skipped to the living room and saw three girls about her age standing next to two of Anita's friends. No doubt the mothers. Among them were curly-haired blonde twins, Frederica and Camélia. They moved in impressive alignment, which is how they cast their critical looks on Maria Amélia. A good interpreter would have translated them like this: "does the braided nitwit think she is in a circus ring!"

Undeterred, the princess of the house (one of the many nicknames given to her by her adoptive mother) waved to the group:

"Hey guys!"

"Come, my dear, I want to introduce you to your new schoolmates and friends."

She skipped over and made a long bow for the twins. When she raised her head again, she shot both girls down with sparks of defiance from her grey eyes. She then turned disarmingly to her third future classmate, Esmeralda, sending her a kiss.

"I see that you will get along very well."

"Anita, your daughter is so charming."

The twins looked at each other, kissed her with ill-concealed contempt, and were taken aback when Maria Amélia stepped between them, grabbing their hands and leading them away from their mothers' view.

"Let's go!"

"We don't want to go!" both said in unison.

Letting go of the twins' hands, Maria Amélia burst out laughing and then commented, her words dripping with sarcasm:

"We're going to get along great. Dona Cleide is spot on."

Esmeralda, the third girl, approached the others with hesitation. But she stepped back when she saw that they were coming back, immediately understanding that a conflict was on between the schoolmates, and at the same time feeling that she was no match in the game that was about to start. Frederica and Camelia were famous in school. Inseparable, like peas in a pod, each always watching out for the other. In fights, they were unbeatable: if one scratched, the other would kick, bite, or throw elbows. And when they saw themselves at a disadvantage, they would—without fail—scream for help like two innocent victims. They were also invincible in word games, in the art of maneuvering friends, of imposing play, anointed— as it were—with the so-praised grace of natural-born leaders, movers of ordinary people, those seen only as flock. The mothers didn't notice any of it. Neither the look of aversion stamped on the twins' rosy faces, nor the challenge sparkling in the gray eyes of the braided girl.

7

Tarquínio was not called over the loudspeakers. Two guards escorted him from his cell, forgoing the handcuffs. The prisoner shot them a questioning look, but they responded only by firmly gripping his arms, guiding him forward with their hard-way-or-easy-way demeanor. When they entered the office, Dr. Joaquim was standing, gesturing toward a chair for Tarquínio. He signaled the two guards to leave, and upon noticing their slight hesitation, the warden simply pointed authoritatively to the door, meaning "Get Out Now!" At the same time, he made a show of the .38 caliber Taurus revolver secured at his waist. Tarquínio remained calm the entire time, almost oblivious to everything. Dr. Joaquim prepared to clear his throat to get his attention, but decided to make his authority explicit:

"Wake up, prisoner 3,029! What we need to talk about is very important."

Tarquínio responded with a look that clearly said, "I couldn't care less."

"I want to know more about your daughter. Does the detainee know that she is already in my house and loved by my wife, more than anything in this world? Is the detainee listening to me?"

Tarquínio shrugged.

"You really don't care about your own daughter, do you, scumbag?"

"My dear warden ..."

"Don't address me like that! I demand respect and will not accept mockery."

"As you wish, my most esteemed prison warden! I see that your honor has become acquainted with her, but I'm afraid this is just the beginning. Maybe you should find my book in a discount bookstore—it covers every detail about her. Read it!"

"I'm not interested in your pulp literature. I want to know, here and now, if the girl had any disorders, any problems at delivery. Anything that may have influenced her behavior."

"And how am I supposed to know? I've been stuck in this fucking prison and only had contact with ... the other one, to put it that way. But none of that matters. The girl's a witch. She's going to drain you and your dear wife completely. Brace yourselves!"

Dr. Joaquim approached Tarquínio, his arm raised to slap him. Tarquínio didn't flinch.

"Come now, your honor, a warden doesn't slap, he orders the slapping. Wouldn't it be more fitting to summon your two henchmen? Besides, I've nothing more to say."

"You little shit! Scumbag! Murderer! Guards!"

As he was being dragged out of the office, Tarquínio shouted:

"Oh, so the little witch has shown her face! This is just the start. Tell her I'm dead. Perhaps the dead can escape the little wretch!"

The conversation with Tarquínio was Dr. Joaquim Paranhos Nogueira's last act as prison warden. The next day, he took office as Secretary of Penitentiary Administration of the state of Rio de Janeiro in a ceremony at Guanabara Palace.

Dressed meticulously, as though in uniform, Anita and Maria Amélia both moved to hug him as soon as he'd received the governor's handshake. Tears of happiness filled Anita's eyes; in Maria Amélia's grey ones, there was only the cold satisfaction of completing a minor stage. Yet, she didn't miss the honoree's discomfort, a palpable revulsion, an urge to free himself from her embrace. Anita, as usual, noticed nothing. The curse of naivety appears to be incurable.

Maria Amélia's confrontation with the twins escalated on the first day of school. She chose to sit next to Esmeralda, who was the very embodiment of a doormat. Esmeralda would prove useful in Maria Amélia's battle against the twins, who sat front and center and were always raising their hands to answer the teacher's questions. Whether in history, geography, mathematics, or Portuguese, it didn't matter—if one twin didn't know the answer, the other did. They were the class know-it-alls. The duo's fame extended far beyond the school's boundaries. Anita was among their admirers and didn't hide her joy at having them as Maria Amélia's classmates:

"I'm so glad you girls got along well!"

History was the last class of the day. The teacher was discussing a chapter called "Economic Miracle, Kidnappings and Repression." During the previous subjects, mathematics and Portuguese, the twins had raised their hands at least ten times, not giving anyone else a chance. Maria Amélia leaned into Esmeralda's ear and whispered:

"Get ready, you're going to raise your hand for the next question."

"Me?"

"Yes, you. I'll write the answer here, right in front of you. All you must do is read."

The teacher's eyes welled up with tears as she described the March of the One Hundred Thousand. She had been a student at the time, she had participated in the protest walk, she remembered Vladimir Palmeira climbing a wall and tearing into the military dictatorship with his words. She spoke of the front of intellectuals: Paulo Autran and Tônia Carreiro

45

in the greatest civic role of their careers. Dona Eulália loved catchphrases. At one point, she turned to the class and asked:

"Who remembers the name of the General-President when Institutional Act Number 5 was enacted?"

As quickly as Maria Amélia had demanded, Esmeralda raised her hand and read the answer in front of her.

"Costa e Silva."

The twins turned and were struck even more when they saw that the challenging voice had come from insipid Esmeralda, the dullest of them all, despite her name. And they were perplexed again when Dona Eulália immediately shot off another question:

"By the way, who was the civilian behind the so-called economic miracle?"

"D. Neto ..."

Maria Amélia only had time to write "D "instead of "Delfim" to prevent the twins from answering first. It was they who protested in unison:

"She doesn't know. 'D' what? Maria Amélia is letting her copy. That's not fair!"

"Calm down, girls," the teacher intervened, almost as the bell rang for recess.

In the courtyard, a circle formed around the twins, seething over the plot orchestrated by the little witch.

Maria Amélia, dragging a terrified Esmeralda by her left arm, stepped into the circle, right hand on her hip, and issued a challenge:

"So, sweethearts, are we settling this with fists or words? If it comes to blows, you might stand a chance. After all, brute force is the only way for troglodytes to prevail. But rest assured, in the end, you'll lose without a shadow of a doubt. My braids forbid me any defeat."

In a rage, the twins lunged at their opponents. Frederica slapped Esmeralda's face. Camélia, however, stumbled during the attack, missed Maria Amélia, and slammed into the ground. Blood gushed from her nose. The commotion drew the attention of the monitor, who arrived just in time to witness the twins' aggression and Maria Amélia's innocent 'I-

46

did-nothing' expression. The twins were taken to the principal's office, defended themselves, talked about the history class plot and got decisive support from Dona Eulália. The teacher said she suspected Maria Amélia had in fact passed information to Esmeralda, who was shy and had never, ever, participated in the classes' Q&As. She concluded her accusation by claiming that evidence could be found in the crumpled papers she had seen Maria Amélia toss into the trash can beside the blackboard. With a nod from the headmistress, the monitor went to check the trash can and found three small, crinkled papers from the braided girl's notebook. They had gibberish written on them, but in the same red ink as the pen that was visible in Frederica's pencil case. The actual notes had been flushed down the toilet at the end of the hallway. The principal looked at Dona Eulália and, with all the weight of the authority invested in her, said:

"It's very clear who the culprits are. Frederica and Camélia will be suspended from recess for two days."

Dona Eulália clammed up in her classes, which were once lively and full of participation from everyone. She adopted the classical routine, ordering students to open the book at Lesson 14 and read everything there was about the pharaonic works of the military government, without a single comment, without the long-awaited Q&As by the twins with answers on the tips of their tongues. Yet, even so, the teacher couldn't escape the braided girl's piercing gaze. Even when she looked down, she could still feel a strange vibration, the restlessness of those who are being watched.

Frederica was the first twin who realized that Maria Amélia could not be faced head-on, every day. They had never encountered such a powerful opponent with such diverse tactics. They were losing, they were becoming demoralized, hopelessly subjected to the thousand and one tricks of the adversary. She proposed to her sister:

"Let's make peace with Maria Amélia."

"Are you crazy? Over my dead body!"

But Camélia didn't die. She was run over when she hurried to catch the school bus. The last thing she saw before being hit by a car speeding at forty miles per hour was Maria Amélia's face peeking through the bus window. A sly, and at the same time cold and determined face, that lingered while her world slipped into immense darkness. A blacked-out television screen that only came back on when she finally awoke from a week-long coma, strapped to a hospital bed with three broken ribs and a cracked skull.

And so it was, slipping between sleep and consciousness, that Camélia saw Maria Amélia holding hands with her sister next to her mother and Anita. She was comforting Frederica as if they were best friends. Camélia wanted to close her eyes again, slip back into her coma, and freeze the little braided witch for eternity. She couldn't. She was woken up again by rushing doctors and nurses. One opened her eyes, another her mouth, another had a thermometer in her hands to stick it in the most appropriate place. She watched as the visitors were ushered out of the room, with Maria Amélia arm in arm with Frederica, whispering in her ear, yet loud enough for all to hear:

"I saw it all. And I mustered all my strength to prevent the worst from happening."

"You're an angel!"—the mothers said at the same time in the euphoria of the moment.

Disgusted, Camélia vomited what little she could.

8

Camélia never fully recovered. She developed a limp. The surgery had made her left leg slightly shorter than the right. Even with orthopedic shoes, her formerly elegant gait couldn't conceal the subtle imbalance. But that wasn't the worst of it. Her keen memory and ferocious sense of humor had also been affected. Her performance in school dwindled, the answers no longer on the tip of her tongue, no longer able to accompany her sister in her studies. She simply sat by, enduring the complicity between Frederica and Fiinha, who coordinated their responses to all of Dona Eulália's questions. Indeed, the teacher had resumed her Q&A sessions, by someone's specific request. You can guess whose. It had come little more than a month after Camélia's accident. At the end of class, when everyone had already left, Maria Amélia stayed behind and told the teacher:

"Why don't you do Q&As anymore? It was so nice. We want it back!"

It was an order, not a request.

Camélia harbored such intense hatred that she felt nauseous every time her gaze met Maria Amélia's. Worse yet, her limp grew more pronounced, and she lost her composure. Her sister, former ally in all things, distanced herself more and more while at the same time forming an inseparable pair with Maria Amélia. She chose to befriend Esmeralda, another girl seething with jealousy and feeling utterly sidelined.

The first day Camélia spoke to Esmeralda was in the yard, when Frederica and Maria Amélia were having a lively conversation. Earlier, Esmeralda had attempted to join the new inseparable pair but was rebuffed by a steely gray gaze, silently conveying that this conversation wasn't meant for fools. Dejected, she sat alone in the shade, on a wooden bench under a pine tree. And with her head down she heard someone say:

"Hey! Can I sit next to you?"

She was surprised to find her former adversary standing beside her. She nodded yes. They remained silent for a couple of minutes, alternating looks between each other and Frederica and Maria Amélia on the other side of the yard, who seemed to be laughing about everything and everyone.

"Do you forgive me?"

"I forgive you," Esmeralda replied.

They held hands and said nothing else that day. And like this, waiting for the next class to begin, the other pair approached, hand in hand, their faces alight with what could either be the glow of wickedness or the sheen of mockery. And while Maria Amélia focused her now commanding gaze on Esmeralda, Frederica addressed her sister:

"You'll grow dumber by the minute keeping company with this idiot. But if that is what you want, you can sit next to her during class. Maria Amélia, you don't mind sitting next to me in class?"

Maria Amélia moved closer, her right braid lightly brushing against Esmeralda's face as she answered:

"Naturally, we will be the invincible duo."

Esmeralda bowed her head and cried softly until the bell rang. Camélia mustered the strength to confront her sister for a few seconds, but then she could feel her eyes being closed in a staring contest of concentrated hatred with the braided witch. She dashed back to the classroom, the sound of Maria Amélia's laughter echoing behind her as she playfully tugged her sister's arm, leaping with joy.

Third Part

-

MAGIC FINGERS

9

After a 300-page report demanding urgent measures to stop Rio's prison rebellions was released, Joaquim Paranhos Nogueira found himself grappling with the most challenging issue of his new role. The report was the result of a study by a commission of experts established by his predecessor. Next to the title, the governor's handwriting read: "Most urgent! Report of the highest political importance."

The governor was right. Every time a rebellion broke out, the press had a field day, sparing no ink, interviewing human rights activists, and trying to paint convicted criminals as saints. The director of Rio's penitentiary system also fretted over the troublesome, blog-infested Internet that disrupted his dignified and necessary work. How did that cheeky woman dare write in her blog—which was even praised by the press—that the governor had appointed a death-squad-sympathizing sheriff to run Rio de Janeiro's prisons? And she had written more: that he was an uncompromising supporter of the death penalty—which he was. Muggers would think twice before making a move. And they would not have time to think thrice. For they would be fried in an electric chair or drool their last saliva after a lethal injection. Personally, he preferred the gallows, which were faster and made more of an impression, relaxing the muscles of any scum to let the shit run down their pants. Cheaper too. A good rope was enough. A wooden scaffold could even be built in every prison yard. This was the simple answer he wanted to give the governor, the most effective remedy for so many rebellions. Human rights, sure, for the working and orderly majority. For the hoodlums, the robbers and even those outraged with authority, the right to prison and the gallows remained. Everything would be simpler; Rio de Janeiro would not have so many muggings. Peace.

During his spiritual exercise before reading the report, Joaquim Paranhos Nogueira had even visualized an extensive cemetery. The graves had no crosses or any other marks, only a single inscription: "harmful element extirpated for the good of society." He thought, almost out loud: "I'm going to clean up Rio de Janeiro." And that's how, almost in a trance, he was called back to reality by Maria Amélia's voice, pointing to the report.

"Daddy, have you read everything?"

He despised being addressed as "Daddy" by the daughter of the criminal whom he wished to see hanged from gallows in Cinelândia. But he struggled to contain his brewing hatred, not solely to appease his wife, but also because the braided girl intimidated him with her domineering gray eyes. He feared Tarquínio was right about her being a witch, despite her being the most beautiful thirteen-year-old girl he had ever seen. He swallowed his pride and answered:

"What might interest you in a prison report, dearest?"

Despite all his efforts, "dearest" came out strained, laden with other implications. Maria Amélia counterattacked with the same term:

"My dearest daddy, I am interested in everything. I read it."

"You read it? Read what?"

"I read it. And if you want, we can discuss it. I have interesting suggestions that will be to the governor's liking."

Joaquim Paranhos stared for a few moments at that cheeky creature, at a loss for words. He was, in fact, torn. Reason told him to end the conversation right there, but something urged him to continue, a hint of opportunism telling him that he might have something to gain, that the girl could be a steppingstone in his career. He was even more startled when Maria Amélia broke the silence following her proposal and added:

"You think people like my biological father should be hanged, don't you?"

And as Joaquim Paranhos pondered whether this little devil was reading his thoughts, she continued:

"Unfortunately, that is no longer possible. If you propose the death penalty or any drastic measure to contain the rebellions by force, it will be the end of your political dreams. You want to run for congress, don't you?"

54

He did indeed. Joaquim Paranhos had already discussed the matter with his wife, but he did not remember Maria Amélia being nearby and having heard. A shiver ran down his spine, he could hardly believe what was coming out of the brat's mouth:

"You must look soft to be hard."

"How?" he asked, automatically.

Maria Amélia laughed and ran over to hug Joaquim Paranhos. She gave him a kiss on the forehead and spoke in his ear.

"We must talk a lot. Read the tome, then we'll talk."

Anita entered the room and marveled at the scene. She had been pained by her husband's inability to hide his rejection of their adopted daughter and had even prayed for their relationship to improve. And there it was, the scene of her dreams. With folded hands and a radiant smile, she said:

"How wonderful! May I know what my Fiinha is talking about with Daddy?"

"We were discussing my birthday party, but Daddy said it will be a surprise."

For the first time, Joaquim Paranhos shared that sly smile of pure mockery with his adopted daughter, while Anita opened her arms to hug the braided girl.

The birthday party should in fact have been a surprise. Every afternoon for the last two weeks, Anita had been discussing the preparations with her friend Cleide, the twins' mother. The party would be held at the newly purchased house near Paraty beach. A huge bungalow featuring seven suites, a 1,000-square-foot lounge, a barbecue area, swimming pool, sauna, and a real fitness center complete with an instructor. Joaquim Paranhos and Anita were sure Maria Amélia did not know about the purchase. But she did. Maria Amélia and Frederica had gone to Cleide's maid and forced everything she had heard about the party's preparations out of her. And not only that. They also learned about Cleide's significant worries, evident from her wearing sunglasses even on rainy days to conceal her tear-swollen eyes. Worries that had led to several meetings with the psychiatrist Maria da Anunciação.

The appointment with the shrink had been arranged at Anita's suggestion, and their acquaintance was not merely coincidental. Dr. Anunciação was the one who had taken the initiative and called her shortly after the adoption.

"You don't know me. I'm Dr. Maria da Anunciação, director of the Jacarepaguá nursing home and I have a practice in Lagoa. I would love to talk to you about your daughter."

Anita was alarmed.

"Is something wrong with Maria Amélia? Oh, my God!"

"No. Nothing is wrong. I'm sorry if I scared you. Her biological mother, Sister Patricia, was one of my best nurses in the ward where Mr. Tarquínio was hospitalized. He was my patient, as you may already have heard. But don't worry, Mr. Tarquínio won't be part of this story any longer, at least not if I have a say in it. Maria Amélia interests me because I know that she is endowed with exceptional intelligence. I know this. The few minutes talking to her when Sister Patrícia introduced me to her daughter in the ward were enough for me. She must have been about four or five years old. I felt that I was in the presence of a privileged mind. Perhaps you aren't aware, but in psychiatry, we encounter so many individuals grappling with various disturbances and fears. We need contact with enlightened ones from time to time."

Hearing the silence on the other side, the psychiatrist smiled and added:

"I know you must be confused. People usually call *me* asking for advice. It is not common for a psychiatrist to call requesting to schedule an appointment. You say when and where. We can meet at your home, mine or the Jacarepagua clinic."

"My place, then. Saturday, three o'clock. But please, doctor, pretend we know each other, that it's just another visit. I don't want Maria Amélia to have the slightest suspicion."

"Don't worry! Dealing with people is my specialty. Until Saturday, then."

The doorbell rang at three p.m. sharp. The butler led the visitor into the mansion's large salon, where a visibly agitated Anita was waiting for her. Dr. Anunciação picked up on the awkwardness, and to break the ice and give credence to the farce that they were old acquaintances, she embraced the wife of the head of the prison system and spoke, effusively:

"My dear. How long has it been!"

It was at this very moment that Maria Amélia entered the salon. She feigned surprise and said:

"I know you too. Aren't you the doctor at the clinic where my biological mother worked?"

"Yes, honey. How do you remember? You were so young!"

Maria Amélia's smile was mockery made flesh.

"I do remember. My working memory has a bit more capacity than the 16 gigs on my dad's computer!"

"What are you talking about, honey?"

"It's nothing, Mommy. Computer nonsense, isn't that right, Doctor? Anunciação, right?"

In her mind, Maria da Anunciação tore up her psychiatrist's diploma. She was stunned, overcome by that little braided thing calling the shots, manipulating them both as if she were a seasoned politician on the hunt for votes. And she almost let her authoritative and confident countenance be overcome by shock. She shuddered when she remembered Tarquínio telling her his aunt's story. She had her chest blown off by the blast of a 16-gauge shotgun, and eighty years after her death, she had borrowed his body to be reborn as Sister Patrícia's daughter. Could he be right? Could his body really have been taken over? "Get a grip, Dr. Anunciação," she thought to herself. "Do you want to lose face in front of your peers." Yet there she stood, with her pigtails and gray eyes, exactly like the other Fiinha of the beginning of the last century, who Tarquínio had described thousands of times when he was her patient. Could he be right? The report she had written on the case had been published in several specialized journals. She presented two rational reasons to explain the patient's insanity but left a crack in the door for Tarquínio's version. Her paper "Patient X: a Case of Obsession" read:

There is a third line of interpretation, of course, but that one falls outside the scope of psychiatry: his aunt really was a witch and came back to dominate him. My background does not allow me to give this hypothesis any credence, but when discussing the case of Patient X with a serious researcher like Dr. Fábio da Mata, an expert in the study of paranormal phenomena, he stated that this possibility could not be ruled out.

This third line of interpretation terrified her. However, what scared her even more was the certainty that, at that very moment, she could no longer free herself from the domineering gray eyes of the braided girl, that their destinies were linked, and that the other held all the cards. She was left with a forced smile, one of concession, almost surrender. She said to her:

"What an extraordinary young lady you are. I'm delighted. My friend Anita is very fortunate."

But this wasn't what she truly wanted to express. She wanted to say Anita was lost, like herself, dominated by the little witch in pigtails. At this point, she had barely any more words left, her vast reserves of arguments locked behind the sly smile of her braided opponent. Dr. Anunciação made some small talk for a few more minutes and said her goodbyes.

In the café of the Leblon Shopping Center where the two met, Anita's talkative enthusiasm about Maria Amélia's birthday party preparations contrasted with Cleide's dreary face. Cleide took off her glasses, no longer caring to hide her tears. And it was crying—to the point of attracting curious glances—that Cleide spoke:

"I don't know what to do with my daughter anymore. Camélia is someone else, she doesn't even look like her sister anymore, always happy, always smiling. Before, her limp was so slight, hardly anyone noticed. Now, it seems like she's exaggerating it on purpose. Oh, my god ..."

"Don't cry, don't cry. The trauma was very severe and thank God your daughter is still alive."

"Oh, you only say that because you don't see your daughter languishing by the day. Sorry, I am being selfish, talking about my problems, spoiling the joy of the mother of such an adorable creature like Maria Amélia. I am so glad she's friends with Frederica and so ashamed of Camélia's jealousy. She doesn't want to go to the birthday party. Oh, how sad! She doesn't want to study. She wants to change schools."

Anita said nothing. She just held her friend's hands. They say that offering consolation is the best balm for the human spirit, not so much for the one receiving it, but for the one providing it, who can get drunk on their own altruism. Anita was so enveloped in her own kindness, bathing in its aura, that she almost forgot the essential point of that moment, which was recommending Dr. Anunciação. But with her eyes closed, holding her friend's hands, she said:

"I know someone who might be able to help you. Maria da Anunciação, a very reputable psychiatrist with a clinic in Lagoa. She's my friend. If you want, we can make an appointment right now."

"I'm not sure, I'm not sure. Astor is trying to enroll her in a nuns' school. Ugh! May God forgive me, but I don't like it. I think nun schools are a thing of the past, and they won't be missed."

"I totally agree. Dr. Anunciação will certainly strengthen your arguments against this option. I'll call her now. I'll set up a date just between the two of you. The meeting with Camélia can happen later. How about it?"

Still sobbing, Cleide consented with a nod.

The appointment was set for the Friday of the following week. Dr. Anunciação wanted at least a week to prepare for the conversation. She knew the broad strokes of the twins' story, but it was Maria Amélia's involvement that really worried her. And because of that, she wanted Cleide to come alone. Or, to put it more succinctly, she did not wish Anita to be present. She was very clear on the phone.

"The first appointment with your friend is scheduled for next Friday at eleven a.m. It's important that she comes alone, as even your presence, being a mutual friend, could impact the necessary professional dynamic. By the way, precisely because of this—because you're a friend—you cannot be present."

If Dr. Anunciação's office had been equipped with an anxiety meter, it would be reading waves coming from both sides. The psychiatrist was far from the secure professional of other consultations. The latent nervousness was expressed in an excessive blinking of the eyes, in a hand-rubbing as if to get rid of something sticky, and above all, in a voice that hesitated during enunciation. On the opposite end, Cleide was confusion personified, not sure where to start. She threw her friend into it.

"Anita must have told you what this is about. I come for my daughter."

"Yes, very briefly. But I want you to tell me everything again."

While she listened, the psychiatrist only paid attention when the name Maria Amélia came up. She was sure of one thing: she was the cause. But she didn't know what to do exactly. How could she inform Cleide without letting Anita find out? But that was not her greatest fear. What she really did not want was that Maria Amélia took notice of the matter. Finally, she said:

"I still want to talk to your daughter, but I am almost sure she needs a change in environment. She can no longer be kept in the same school as her sister. Unfortunately, everything indicates that the bond, the collusion existing between the two has broken with the appearance of a third person. Let's keep all this between us. The feeling of inferiority is perhaps the human mind's greatest pain. It leads to depression, in most cases, and to revolt, in others. From what I've heard from you, Camélia varies between both extremes. I know it is difficult for a mother to admit that one daughter feels resentment toward the other, especially in the case of twin sisters, but that's exactly what's happening. Frederica and Camélia formed a team and one was excluded. We have the resentment of one against the contempt of the other. Maybe I shouldn't tell you what I'm saying so bluntly. But it's not a psychiatrist's job to console the patient. It is to find out the causes of what disturbs them. Come in with Camélia as soon as possible. Next week, maybe. But I repeat, I am almost sure that she must be separated from Frederica and the other one."

Separated from the other one. Dr. Anunciação was ashamed of herself. She didn't even dare say Maria Amélia's name, so simple, so easy, and she could see glimpses of the braided girl's face erupting in victorious laughter.

Camélia was practically dragged to the psychiatrist's office. She didn't want to go. She felt humiliated, branded as insane, or at the very least retarded because of the accident.

"I have nothing to say to this doctor."

"Sweetie, it's for your own good."

"Frederica is your sweetie now. I don't want to go!"

"You're going!"

The father, initially just overhearing the conversation without intending to interfere, lost his temper and forcibly led the girl by the arm into the backseat of her mother's car. During the drive over, almost an hour in heavy traffic, Camélia sulked and didn't say a single word. She grimaced and stuck out her tongue when her mother stopped at a traffic light and told her emphatically:

"It's for your own good!"

Dr. Anunciação seemed more relaxed when she received them. Addressing Cleide, she said:

"Wait for us at the reception if you don't mind. Camélia and I need to talk alone."

The psychiatrist told the girl to sit down and make herself comfortable. Dr. Anunciação sat upright in her chair behind the desk, her eyes slightly lowered, encouraging the patient's imagination: what should I do? Do I speak or do I wait for her to speak first? The psychiatrist cleared her throat, raised her head slightly, and finally spoke:

"Are you okay? Are you comfortable?"

"I'm fine," Camélia replied dryly.

"So, then. Tell me."

"Tell you what?"

"You have nothing to tell me?"

"No!"

"How is your relationship going with Frederica and her friend?"

61

"Cut!"

"Cut? Simply cut? And school?"

"What about school?"

"Are you doing well in your studies?"

"Yes, I am."

"But, before, with your sister, you were among the top of your class. Not anymore. Does that make you think something's wrong?"

"No."

"All right. Would you like to change schools? Who knows? A boarding school?"

"You mean taking me far away from those two?"

"See, you are smarter than average. You catch on very quickly while others keep fumbling around. But it seems you're not in the mood to talk today. However, talking is exactly what we'll need to do in our sessions; a lot of talking. We'll keep that for next time."

While she spoke, Dr. Anunciação pressed a button requesting the assistant's presence, and then instructed her to call Camélia's mother. Cleide entered the office looking anxiously from the psychiatrist to her own daughter.

"Is the consultation over already? So fast! Is everything okay?"

"We'll still have a lot to talk about. Today was just for a brief introduction. Camélia now knows I'm no bogeyman."

Camélia responded to Dr. Anunciação's slight smile with a sideways look of contempt. She then told her mother:

"Let's go."

"Next week I want to see her again. Make an appointment with my secretary."

Joaquim Paranhos finally finished reading the report, making almost a hundred notes about dubious or controversial points. He looked at the document full of scratches and notes, but he didn't know how to begin writing his opinion. He felt stifled by the Penal Enforcement Act, which coerced—this was the word whirling in his head—wardens into treating prisoners as normal individuals. They were not. They broke the law and had to pay. They could not enjoy the privileges of the individual living in society. But the law, passed in 1983 when the dictatorship was starving to death and renewed in 2007, was the Justice Minister's little darling and firmly underpinned by the current Constitution. Rio de Janeiro could not be an exception. The law had to be obeyed. Indeed, indeed. But it was just a piece of paper. It was to be obeyed in theory, in speeches, and in the pathetic refrain of those human rights scum. If it were to be applied, in practice, there could be no discipline. It would be like treating the chaff as the wheat, giving the prisoner the status of citizen, a status he renounced when he committed a crime. Individualized treatment?! What nonsense! Imagine the poor prison guard risking his life every day in the midst of that mob, having to address the worst criminals as *Sir*. Absurd! Sure, he might have to swallow his pride and write the damn report, bowing to liberal discourse, but for himself, in his heart, he would make no compromise. He would not admit that a murderer of Tarquínio's caliber could enjoy so many privileges. Absorbed in such thoughts, Joaquim Paranhos did not realize he was being watched. Maria Amélia, sitting at the other desk in the office, held her chin in both hands with a look of extreme concentration. When the Secretary of Penitentiary Administration of the state of Rio de Janeiro saw her like this, he automatically frowned. But inside, he wanted to know the girl's opinion.

"What are you doing here?"

"Watching the smoke from the gears in Daddy's head. I can see the Penal Enforcement Act is stuck in your throat. But it's no use, Daddy. We must acknowledge the things that are here to stay. They're here and should be part of our discourse, and therefore, of the opinion you are going to write. Praise it, praise it thoroughly, especially those points you don't have the slightest intention of following. We know that if the law were to be applied to Bangu 1, it would be closed the next day, don't we?"

But what the hell does this girl know about Bangu 1 Penitentiary, he thought, unable to hide his shock.

While absorbed in writing the report, Joaquim Paranhos left a working draft prominently on his desk, almost as if inviting his adopted daughter to read it. And he did more: he printed a copy of its pages as he wrote. The next day he could then read Maria Amélia's notes and criticisms. When the document was finally ready, Joaquim Paranhos was a little embarrassed with the help, but he knew that the opinion had everything to please the governor and shut up the Human Rights Secretary.

He slid the 145 pages in a gray folder and wrote "Concluded" on it. The next day, he noticed "Concluded" had been crossed out, with a note:

Minor corrections on pages 8, 18, 23, and 45. But above all, start the introduction with this:
Applying the Law of Penal Executions is the sine qua non for the functioning of Brazil's prisons, respecting the rights of prisoners, and above all, not imposing extra punishment beyond the deprivation of liberty defined in the convicting sentence."

The litany of practical restrictions on the application of the law would only follow after: how to give a prisoner individual treatment with overcrowded penitentiaries? Capacity was enough for a quarter of detainees and many prison wardens—reluctantly, stressed the secretary—found themselves in the dilemma of keeping convicted prisoners and those still awaiting trial in the same cell.

"Against the law, unfortunately, but only because the law does not provide the conditions required for its application."

One of the little witch's contributions. She also cut an entire paragraph about disciplinary measures. Joaquim Paranhos had written:

Respect for the prisoner's individuality and the rule of not imposing extra punishment on him cannot be obstacles to the maintenance of discipline in the prison environment. There is a range of rules covering everyone, such as the time an inmate may remain in the courtyard sunbathing. In our view, prohibiting this practice to a detainee because he violated one of the disciplinary norms imposed on all, does not infringe the Penal Enforcement Act. This is not extra punishment, but the application of a disciplinary rule, without which chaos would be established in the prison environment.

Instead, Maria Amélia wrote:

One way to maintain discipline in the prison environment is the introduction of an award policy. The well-behaved, for example, could receive more time during visits and leisure hours in the courtyard.

Next, in parentheses, she wrote in red letters: "(You should avoid the words *punishment* and *prohibition* as much as possible.)"

The governor liked the opinion so much that he leaked it to the press before official publication. It made front-page headlines in the newspaper that despised Joaquim Paranhos and that had given him the nickname Chief Sheriff.

"Chief Sheriff Bows to the Law"

But apart from the already expected sarcasm in the headline, the piece was all praise. The report was very well bound. On the outside a luxurious cover and on the inside just the right measure of ambiguity to cover up the text's authoritarianism. Joaquim Paranhos had a huge problem ahead of him, however: how to hide the help he had received from his adopted daughter? Luckily Maria Amélia also wanted to keep matters discrete. This was the time for planting, the harvest would come later. Anita, as always, didn't pick up on anything, floating in a madam's holy peace, craving nothing more than the ephemeral sparkle of frivolities. Seeing her husband read the newspapers so excitedly, she commented to her adopted daughter:

"Look how happy Daddy is. Looks like he hit the jackpot!"

"He did, Mommy"—and whispering in her ear—"magic fingers touched his keyboard."

10

It goes without saying that Maria Amélia's thirteenth birthday party was every socialite's dream. The subject of menstruation hung in the air because some of Maria Amélia's classmates and younger guests had not yet had their first experience. Next to Frederica, and after making sure no adults were nearby, the birthday girl spoke as if giving a lecture to the group of girls.

"There's nothing to be ashamed of. Blood is our body's self-purification. A woman's life cycle, a privilege, not this shame advertised by male chauvinist society. The Bible—the tome that sexist bunch loves so much—says it's a punishment and has been hammering that bullshit into people's heads for thousands of years. Look at those swollen-headed boys, as if that thing hanging between their legs gave them the right to boss everyone around. I don't think many of you read the Bible, if any of you read it at all. You've only heard the drivel coming out of Catechism class. I've read it. It's horrible!"

One of the girls who hadn't menstruated yet interrupted.

"What are you talking about?"

"Don't you know? It's understandable that you haven't menstruated yet. But your mother and father never telling you anything about it is just disgusting."

Anita, always wanting to know about her daughter, approached the girls and said:

"What a lively group! What are you girls talking about? Wouldn't it be nice if we called some boys over for the conversation."

"No, Mom, this is no talk for boys, much less for adults. We are going to pull a little prank. It's a secret."

Anita withdrew, looking suspicious—even the gullible harbor doubts at times. Maria Amélia did not lose her train of thought and continued:

"Oh, yes, people. A prank and it will be played on that one."

She pointed her finger to the one some would call *most full of himself*. Bangs slicked back by imported gel, standing at five-feet, nine-inches, just at the start of his last growth spurt, broad shoulders, a judge as father with money coming out of the nose, a socialite mother: Berenice Andrade, Anita's former classmate in high school. The teenage girls swooned as he passed, and at our story's current party, he also incited enthusiastic comments from the forty-something mothers. His name was Leopoldo. For the infatuated girls, the hot stud. Anita, moving her eyes from Leo to Maria Amélia, hinted:

"Berenice, your son is the biggest catch in Rio de Janeiro. And just look, I've got the ideal bride for him right here."

She was sorely mistaken!

No attraction existed between the two. Rather a natural repulsion, a congenital antipathy that went to the bones. Leopoldo could not stand Maria Amélia's stare, especially her sidelong glances, which felt like the words "asshole" or "idiot" yelled directly into his ears. And that was how she rated him, even though she knew that Frederica was smitten, like most of her classmates. Which is why the prank proposed by Maria Amélia displeased her entire audience. Especially Frederica, who was called upon to be the plot's linchpin. But let's close this chapter for now, because developments in the next one could totally change the course of the story. And just so no one says this is an artificial cliffhanger, the reader may very well skip ahead to Chapter 12. There, they will learn in full detail the prank the little braided witch concocted for the hot stud. Then, they can simply return to the following chapter.

11

So far, we've only seen the little witch's thirteenth birthday party from the bratty girl perspective. Adults only entered as supporting characters. But it's time to report on events of paramount importance, both in the circles of women and men. Looks, comments (some might say malicious), innuendos, and above all, poorly filtered thoughts. Let's get to the facts.

Anita was undoubtedly the most exuberant at the party, carrying the typical happy smile of a satisfied woman, but also of mother's pride in seeing Maria Amélia's resourcefulness compared to the other girls. She acted as a famous lecturer. But the adopted daughter did not absorb all her attention. Occasionally, with apparent nonchalance, her gaze would drift toward a small group of men, distinctly not including her husband.

There you have it! All that suspense only to land on the well-trodden path of marital infidelity. But what to do? Maybe monogamy was invented just for that. Cleide, her faithful companion and the mother of the twins, was the first to notice the spark in Anita's eyes and subtly hinted:

"Who's that hunk of a handsome man?"

Anita, feigning distraction:

"Who?"

Cleide's smile was mischievous, and without so much as moving her eyes or finger to the men, she said, more leisurely than necessary:

"That one!"

"Oh, maybe you're referring to Adamastor. Didn't you know? He is Maria Amélia's biological uncle."

"Oh, no, I didn't. You never told me about him."

"Look at our daughters. They are the smartest of them all. Aren't they?"

"Yes, they are. But that's not what we're talking about. What does he do?"

"Who?"

"Come on, who? Him!"

"Oh, him. Right. He sells cleaning products in the favelas. Isn't that a great idea? Maria Amélia said it made him rich. No one had thought of that before. There are poor people who also like hygiene, right?"

"Hang on. Cleaning products in the favelas? You think that story adds up?"

"And why should I doubt it? Maria Amélia has already been with him up the hill. He even said that she gave him very interesting advice."

"Oh, so you guys talked already."

"Of course, we talked! He is my daughter's uncle. A brother."

"Ah, a brother! Careful, girl, handsome brothers like that can get you in trouble."

"Why, Cleide! Do you ever think about anything else? I am a faithful wife. And besides, look how many people are paying attention to our conversation!"

"Okay, girlfriend. We'll get together tomorrow. How about that café in the Ipanema bookstore? Four in the afternoon?"

"Okay. Hi, Suely, join us."

A quick flashback. Shortly after Anita's conversation with Adamastor to handle Maria Amélia's adoption, she had called him:

"To what do I owe the honor of this phone call?"

"I wanted to thank you and assure you that your niece will always be in good hands. More than that. She has and always will have the mother she lost."

"I know. I know. Dona Anita, you don't even have to say that. Anita, you ... can I call you Anita?"

Anita cut him off:

"You can and you should. You're now part of the family. You don't have to worry about my husband's serious face and his reputation as a tough guy. Deep, deep down, he is meek as a puppy."

"Well, I'm very happy to call you Anita. My sister must be very happy in heaven."

"Oh, I'm so delighted!"

"I think we should meet. We have a lot to talk about. Write down my cell phone."

"Yes. I'll call. See you soon."

A mind a little more hung up on sex—like Cleide's—would have heard the smack of a kiss as they hung up.

At the party, Adamastor and Joaquim Paranhos Nogueira barely greeted each other. A weak handshake and furtive looks exchanged by those feeling uncomfortable around each other. Anita received Maria Amélia's uncle with the discretion required by the circumstances, with two kisses, one on each cheek, as Rio etiquette dictates. In São Paulo, it's just one. To save on affection, according to one cynical interpretation. But no affection was lacking here. Even though discreet, the hostess's kisses were quite wet, with a slight tip of the tongue briefly touching the drug dealer's face. Enough to bring back the Sunday afternoon in Adamastor's studio apartment in Tijuca. What did you think? Drug dealers know on which side their bread is buttered. No way was Adamastor going to take the wife of Rio de Janeiro's Secretary of Penitentiary Administration back to some motel in Duque de Caxias or an apartment in Copacabana. Better go to a discreet street in Tijuca, far away from all the buzz in the Zona Sul. The suggestion had been made by Maria Amélia when she visited him one afternoon. The girl opened the window to reveal Nossa Senhora de Copacabana Street, sensed her surroundings as if sniffing something out, and said:

"My goodness, Uncle, what an exposed dwelling you've chosen. Don't you think it's better to get something more discreet, if only for the weekends? So, you can rest instead of having only cleaning supply sales on your mind?"

The apartment in Tijuca was rented the same week for a relatively cheap price, half of which Adamastor paid to the doorman so he would keep his mouth shut about the people visiting him. And after the bribe, he clearly warned the doorman that any indiscretion would have the dire consequences associated with crossing a favelas' cleaning products trader.

The apartment in Tijuca was good for more than just meeting Anita. Adamastor also set up a small office with a telephone number few knew and a computer. Since his drug running days in Pavãozinho, he had always been aware of a drug dealer's ephemeral career in the front lines, in the hill's day-to-day. Fame and prestige in the favela can disappear overnight, competition is brutal and there's a very big chance of waking up in a ditch with a mouth full of ants. And this is also what his niece told him on one of her visits to the Copacabana apartment.

70

"Uncle, it's way past time to stop peddling cleaning products. There is no future in that. I mean, there is, but it's a future that's gone as soon as it arrives. You need to operate behind the scenes, start calling yourself 'doctor,' and join the ranks of those who control the peddlers."

"But what are you talking about, girl?"

"You know very well what I'm talking about. My father ... I mean, Dr. Paranhos ... is dumber than you are. But he was lucky enough to be born in the right environment to enter the true rulers' circle. If you miss out on this initial luck, the golden cradle, you need to force your way to the top. And I'm not talking about the top of the Chapéu Mangueira favela or even the Rocinha and other more profitable markets. At this point, you must know there are a lot of bullets out there with the names of cleaning product peddlers on them."

"My dearest niece, I don't understand a word you're saying."

"Yes, you do. And I am the door to the new world."

"You, the door?"

"Yes, sir. Or the window if you want to jump in. But there is no need to jump, there is no rush. My house is your gateway to the world of true rulers. What's more, my mother Anita feels great affection for you and my father Joaquim has a very big heart."

Adamastor, still a little flushed:

"Oh, I didn't know Dr. Paranhos was such a good person."

"I didn't say he's a good guy. I said he has a very big heart."

"Exactly. Big heart, right."

And the little witch, with her mocking smile:

"No, Uncle, I'm talking about the test he took in the hospital. His heart is very large, swollen. Dilated congestive cardiomyopathy. Ever heard of it?"

"Ah!"

Maria Amélia left and threw her uncle a kiss from the door.

12

This chapter focuses on the prank of Maria Amélia's thirteenth birthday party. The hot stud's circle was engaged in a heated discussion about the wonders of the last video game. In it, the player must run the gauntlet, avoid being beaten up by two rows of opponents and kill them all with a Gatling gun. Headshots scored higher points, and combos that drenched the virtual landscape in blood and gore earned extra bonuses. The absolute champion was the player who reached the end of the corridor without taking a single blow. Hot stud liked to boast that no one in the class could match his skill level, whether he was controlling the members of the corridor or the mad shooter.

"I've already run through the corridor thirty times straight without getting hit. I would like to see any of you do that."

One of the boys asked:

"Would you dare play against her?"

If you haven't already guessed, "her" was Maria Amélia, who at the moment was pulling Frederica by the arm toward the bathroom. Leopoldo glanced over to the two girls and then to the questioner, his brow furrowed.

"We're talking about a man's game, damn it! They're probably still playing with dolls, or who knows, beating the fiddle in the bathroom."

"What's that?"

"How can you be so stupid. Why don't you go ask pigtails."

"I want to see you have the courage to say that to her face."

"Shut the fuck up, dipshit, or I'll smash your little face in right here! Go back to drinking your juice box from mommy. This here is man talk, you fuck!"

The offended party, who shall remain nameless since he won't appear again in this story, did indeed choose to leave the clique, taking refuge in a corner, wishing hot stud's head to be crushed the next time he ran the gauntlet. Had his people skills been more attuned, he would have realized that hot stud's anger stemmed from the fear of being beaten by Maria

Amélia in the gauntlet in front of all his schoolmates. That is why he preferred changing the subject, talking about his latest conquests, at least three of which were present in the group on the other side of the room. At the moment, he was preparing to make a move on Frederica, though deep down, he had to admit he was afraid of the other one protecting her.

In the bathroom, Maria Amélia didn't mince words:

"Pull down your panties, take it out, and hand it to me."

"Take out what?"

"The tampon."

"Jeez, that's gross!"

"Gross? You'll see who finds it disgusting soon enough. Give it here."

Maria Amélia didn't hesitate. Holding the blood-soaked tampon in her hand, she walked over to the group of young men, stopped unceremoniously in front of Leopoldo, and asked him:

"Are you drinking Coke or Cuba-Libre? Did you sneak in a little bottle of rum?"

Leopoldo gestured in a way that clearly meant 'obviously it's a Cuba-Libre.' With the speed of a magician, Maria Amélia deftly slipped the tampon into hot stud's glass and elegantly walked back to the group of girls, her braids swaying. Meanwhile she said:

"Enjoy your Cuba-Libre."

Leopoldo only noticed something in his glass on the third sip. He ran to the bathroom, and on realizing what it was, all he could do was lock the door before puking his guts out in the toilet, where he also threw the tampon with the rest of his Cuba-Libre. Before leaving, he flushed at least three times and returned to his group, yellow green like the Brazilian flag. His parents took notice. Júlio Andrade, a judge on the verge of being promoted to a federal court of appeals, was already mentally drafting the verdict without even considering the pleas from the defense, the boy's mother, who feared her son had been stricken by some virus.

"Drunk again?! Straight home and grounded for the weekend!"

If hot stud had a tail, it would have been tucked between his legs as he left the party, displaying a level of humility that not even the meekest of dogs could mimic. That weekend he stayed home. A punishment he even welcomed. He didn't want to deal with the class or the explanations. But the problem was only being delayed, of course. The following Monday, he would have to go back to school and face not only his friends, but the gang of girls. And Frederica? How would Frederica react, the next in line of his conquests? It didn't bear thinking about. On Monday, he came prepared to slap anyone who had the gall to make fun of him. But oddly enough, he felt no desire for revenge against the mastermind of the prank. He couldn't even think about it, perhaps as a self-defense mechanism. A vague, formless voice in his head whispered something like, "forget about her, try not to cross her path."

When he got to the school, he was surprised. Milton, one of his most eager bootlickers, slapped him on the back and said:

"Wow, you were wasted at the party, bro."

Not far away, some girls who had been at the birthday party joked and talked without even noticing his arrival. Among them were Frederica and Maria Amélia, who told her friend:

"Wait here, I'll be right back."

Leopoldo felt a chill as he saw the little braided witch walking toward him. He felt even worse when she stopped in front of him, looked him in the eye, and said, with hardly any sound coming from her lips:

"Stay away from Frederica!"

It was clear that only the two of them had knowledge of the incident. That is how Maria Amélia wanted it. After slipping the tampon into Leopoldo's Cuba-Libre, she had returned to the group of girls, all eagerly awaiting the prank. But Maria Amélia quickly dampened their excitement:

"Oh, I gave up! Let's keep talking. That's so much nicer."

And when alone with Frederica:

"I was going to pull a dirty trick on that stupid brat with your tampon, but I didn't. Better they stay over there, and we stay here. And don't tell me you've fallen for that halfwit. We're still learning, and that learning should be among ourselves. After, only after, will we give them the right to feel us up. Otherwise, those idiots, who know nothing except how to use their lances, will remain master's only because of the stick between their

74

legs. Sex is good, it's nice. But we don't have to be dominated, on the bottom in every sense. It's all about power, Frederica. The learning should happen among us. And you already know I'm a great teacher."

Frederica felt a sinking feeling in her gut, a flash that her sister was right. But mesmerized by the two gray eyes locked onto hers, demanding nothing less than pure obedience, she relented. All her instincts told her it would be great to learn sex secrets with hot stud, but her forces, once so vigorous when she was part of the duo with her sister, seemed to have been sucked out by her braided friend. Indeed, it was a question of power. And the other one had it. Frederica also understood that Maria Amélia had not given up on the prank, or whatever other name the fate of her tampon could be given. Leopoldo wouldn't have left the party, head down after stumbling out of the bathroom, green and yellow in the face like the Brazilian flag, under the watchful eye of his father with the look of a judge who just handed out his sentence. Frederica wanted to ask, she wanted to be sure, but she couldn't. The coldness of her friend's eyes didn't permit any contestation. She came home with her head down, not daring to face her sister's looks of contempt, as always. She felt worse than a scolded bitch.

Fourth Part

-

BIG HEART

13

The biker was zigzagging as usual, weaving between the cars and packed buses along Copacabana. Just after the short bend past República do Peru Street, the Copacabana-Jacaré bus driver swerved to the left, hitting the biker's head, which was then crushed under the tires of three cars. The rest of his body fared even worse when it fell under the wheels of another bus that caught it between the legs, tearing everything apart, turning it into paste, just like the head.

Not a single organ was left intact, and Dr. Paranhos had been at the top of the donor list for over a year, waiting for the heart of a healthy young man killed in traffic or meeting another violent end.

Luckily for the chief jailer, the first blow knocked off the biker's helmet, sending it hurtling like a cannonball against the wall of a corner building and releasing a shard that pierced the head of a twenty-year-old walking peacefully along the Copacabana sidewalk. He was rushed to the health unit on Siqueira Campos Street, still alive, with his heart stubbornly beating even though his punctured brain was long since dead.

As an undertaker, Zé Onofre could barely feed his family of seven. So, he took up side jobs, like police informant, which that day earned him much more—ten thousand reais in the pocket—when he placed a phone call informing the Penitentiary Administration of the State of Rio de Janeiro about a half-dead young man with an excellent heart, waiting for the secretary.

A year earlier, after a batch of exams, Dr. Paranhos' clinical picture had been defined. The doctor, a childhood friend, bent over backward to break the news to him while raising as little alarm as possible. He tried a forced smile and appealed to humor, with a tremor in his voice betraying the performance.

"Indeed, Mr. Paranhos, we're going to have to change your pump."

"What are you talking about?"

"A transplant, my friend. There is no other solution. But there's no reason to panic. I won't tell you that it is a simple operation, nor that it is easy to find a donor. You'll have to get on the Health Department's list. Fortunately, you have some time—about a year, maybe a year and a half. We'll figure it out. With increasingly advanced techniques, the procedure itself isn't a major challenge. Besides, given all the dealings and violence in the favelas, Rio de Janeiro is a prolific source of donors. You know that more than anyone."

"I don't know if I can handle the uncertainty of waiting."

"Dr. Paranhos, perhaps I shouldn't say this, and I do so confidentiality, of course. But given your position, your office, it wouldn't be difficult to get your name to the top of the waiting list. Or maybe, so as not to give too much away, to the top three."

"But is there no other way? Medication? Diet? Moderation at work? I'm even willing to resign my post, retire. Ban my whiskeys and my Cubans, even on special occasions."

"No, there isn't any other way. I'll be frank. You need to take a leave. Go on vacation, avoid unnecessary stress."

"Vacation? Sitting idle for over a year? I haven't been able to have sex for two months. Your meds seem to suppress everything, not just my heartbeat."

"Not sitting idle, no. The first step is to employ scouts across hospitals in Rio de Janeiro and São Paulo. Ideally, we need someone brain-dead but with an intact heart. If it is still beating after brain death, even better. Many potential donors get lost in the doldrums of the hospitals. Organs such as the heart need to be removed as soon as possible. In principle, a heart should not stop beating for more than four hours."

The heart of the shrapnel's victim beat all night. His father, a bank clerk, even thanked God upon seeing his son still breathing. The expressions of the doctors and nurses pierced his optimism. It was eight in the morning. In the next room, Dr. Paranhos' lawyer waited with a folder full of documents, each marked for signature. One of the doctors on duty took the bank clerk by the arm, led him to a private room, and told him in a slow, firm voice:

"Mr. Damasceno. Your son is still breathing, but he is dead. His brain no longer responds to any stimuli. It's necrotized, for the most part. His heart only responds to a vegetative stimulus. But your child could still help someone. There's a long list of people facing death because they lack a healthy heart, liver, or kidney. Your son could save many lives."

Anguish and despair took hold of the father's insides. He sobbed until he gathered himself, resolute. He had made a decision. No! His son was breathing; his heart was beating; he was alive. Thus convinced, he left the room, leaving the doctor, death's messenger, with nothing to do.

But Mr. Damasceno's resolve lasted barely a minute, deflating like a punctured balloon as he caught sight of a girl with gray eyes whispering into the ear of someone resembling a coroner. Maria Amélia didn't say a word, she merely pinned the victim's father down with the order emanating from her eyes: "Your son is dead. And I want his heart!"

Mr. Damasceno signed all the papers like an automaton, authorizing the plugs to be pulled from the devices and the immediate harvesting of all transplantable organs, including the heart, which was so insistent on beating.

In Maria Amélia's plans, it was not yet time for her adoptive father to die.

14

Under the three o'clock sun, a group of inmates played football on a makeshift pitch on the prison's concrete courtyard. Tarquínio preferred the shade of one of the pillars, meditating with his eyes closed on the best way to send Maria Amélia from this world to the next. In fact, he had repeated the same ritual for more than fifteen years of incarceration. If his thoughts could be projected on a screen, the scenes would be so gruesomely bloody that they'd unsettle even fans of cinematic gore. Tarquínio approaching his daughter, still a girl, and bursting her chest open with a short-barreled shotgun from less than two feet away. Blood, oozing in slow motion, covers her face, while the girl falls on her belly, revealing the void left by the bullet. Sam Peckinpah and his disciples, so adept in technologically sophisticated evisceration, would be envious. And even the most understanding of souls would cry out "monster!" upon hearing the father's satisfied sigh at the sight of his daughter in a pool of blood.

The prison siren put an end to the virtual revenge in inmate 3,029's head. He took a notebook from his coat pocket and started writing. This was the tenth notebook in a series, all titled with the same haunting question:

"Can a witch be exterminated?"

In the first nine notebooks, Tarquínio reviewed traditional methods of killing witches, making a point of accentuating the gender, *witches*. For some reason or other, he was convinced that no man would ever have the necessary strength for witchcraft. Prejudice? He had asked himself the question hundreds of times, but the conviction was ingrained somewhere in the brain where social norms and pressures don't exert great influence. Witchcraft was a woman's thing, they're the ones born with the gift, or whatever the hell it is. Tarquínio's notebook reads:

It is true that the western historical record has many more great wizards than witches. According to various interpretations, this is due to the rise of the patriarchy, which at one point supplanted matriarchy, the great cradle of witchcraft. The Hammer of Witches, the infamous Malleus Maleficarum, was the source that inspired Pope Innocent VIII to promulgate the bull of 1486, the spark for the largest witch hunt in history that lasted almost three centuries. The Malleus Maleficarum, written by German Dominicans H. Kramer and Jacob Sprenger, clearly states that witchcraft is predominantly a woman's domain, although it does not exclude the possibility of warlocks. In the minds of the Dominicans, witchcraft is nothing more than a pact with the devil. And the greatest attraction this creature symbolizing evil has is everything related to lust and women, with their curves and insinuating shapes.

They are Satan's best instrument. In the first part of the Malleus Maleficarum, it is written "All witchcraft comes from carnal lust, which is in women insatiable."

Inspired by this assertion, Tarquínio continued in his notebook:

In the eyes of the authors of the Malleus Maleficarum, the devil was or is the greatest sexual pervert imaginable, but not very inclined to homosexuality, as far as we know. It is with women, the future witches, that Satan performs his devilish feasts, giving his satanic licks and thrusting his pole, sealing the indelible mark of the pact with the victim. There is no record of the devil going crazy for a pair of male butts or a penis like Soriano's dick, so masterfully praised in Guerra Junqueiro's verses. Nor should anyone have to be reminded that the Bible begins with the story of Adam and Eve, in which she is attracted by the serpent (the devil in disguise), leading Adam to eat the fruit of good and evil, or science, desiring the same knowledge as God. Symptomatic. Even in the form of a serpent, Satan did not want any intimacy with Adam. His business was with Eve.

It is possible that Tarquínio's head is filled more with sex than reason or a scholar's temperament. But it is also possible that the sexual question, more specifically lust, really has a relationship with witchcraft that one could call sacred. In this case, patriarchy would be simply the replacement of lust—pleasure itself—with power. Premature ejaculation, assault, penetration of the victim would be the quintessence of male chauvinism. Domination by force. Pleasure, the Faustian bargain of carnal intercourse itself, was condemned in all textbooks of the West, at least until the second half of the twentieth century. A very fashionable book intended for parents and educators in 1940s Brazil, states in no uncertain terms:

Man is the king of the universe. It is incumbent upon him to conquer the world, to subdue the earth, to gain the means of subsistence for the family, with the heavy labor of his hands or brain, in all branches of human activity. Because of this, and to this end, he is stronger in body and intellect than the woman ...

According to this book, *The Sexual Problem and its Solution* by Father Lacroix, written in the mean times of Pope Pius XII, this is what a woman is reduced to if she doesn't sign a pact with the devil and turns into a witch:

> Bodily, she comes down to the ovaries, for procreation. And sex, as such, or libido, is the bitter gall Christian couples must take for the sole and exclusive purpose of procreation.

In his scornful rage, Tarquínio wrote:

> I was suckled with this book. Tormented by little witches who would not let me sleep on guilt-loaded nights of pollution and wanking. Father Lacroix talked about ovaries, but I didn't even know what the hell they were. I saw other things, or imagined them, because not even smut magazines existed. In O Cruzeiro, you could see Rita Hayworth in a one-piece swimsuit, at most. Pussy only in the imagination. But I discovered, like many, that a woman's strength stems precisely from her apparent weakness.

Tarquínio is no exception. Nearly everyone in his era was tormented by such prejudices. And one must conclude that women were the most affected, compelled to suppress their desires to avoid giving the devil an opportunity. Even the most impassioned, who could not contain their lust for sex, ended up paying the price that patriarchal and misogynistic society always exacted.

These things seethed in Tarquínio's head. In his youth, he had been sympathetic to the feminism that shook the sixties of the last century. But now he was revisiting his old positions, coming to believe that gender equality was unachievable on any level. He developed a kind of reversed prejudice, elevating women as superior in the realm of knowledge beyond the so-called scientific boundaries. It confirmed his conviction that witches preferred to remain in the background, purposefully and slyly, allowing men to dominate the roster of renowned sorcerers.

Many books cite the German doctor and lawyer Agripa, born at the height of the Inquisition in the end of the fifteenth century, as the greatest of them all. Heinrich Cornelius Agripa was, in fact, the model for Faust, that other man of science who became a German legend as an example of a pact with the devil, and whose life story became Goethe's masterpiece. The soul in exchange for knowledge. Adam and Eve's story rewritten, without Eve and without the serpent. All of it enacted in some notary office between heaven and hell. A civilized thing with no orgies, no uncontrollable libido, just a clause with the exchange of the immortal soul for passing knowledge on Earth. In Tarquínio's view, a witch would never agree to terms so favorable to Satan, and in a fuck with Mephistopheles she would have asked pleasure for all eternity instead of fleeting knowledge in a life that vanishes in the blink of an eye. Tarquínio was so convinced of female superiority in matters of witchcraft that, at the opening of his first notebook, he wrote:

The Inquisition may not have been entirely wrong in eliminating over 100,000 women accused of witchcraft in France alone, at the peak of the most extensive witch hunt on record. While it's possible some innocents were burnt, such excesses could be justified by the goal of eradicating such malevolent and deceitful beings from the earth. A witch roasted at the stake is worth a thousand innocent lives with the same fate. The existence of witches is intertwined with the history of mankind. They are described in all civilizations, albeit in different ways. It is no mere chance that Exodus 22:18 reads: Thou shalt not suffer a witch to live. The Bible has never been, nor do I think it ever will be, my choice of bedside reading. But on that point, I fully agree.

15

Maria Amélia felt it was time to make a third and possibly last visit to her father. The time had come to make a request he couldn't refuse. She dressed with the elegance of a seductress, donning a black skirt and a bright red blouse that left her shoulders bare, meticulously styled her braids, and proceeded to the prison, carrying herself with the arrogance befitting the daughter of Rio's head of prisons. It was five in the afternoon when she arrived, and she immediately said she wanted to see prisoner

Tarquínio Esperidião. She did not present any documents, her face was familiar to all the guards, having been featured in the press as the daughter of the *Great Jailer*, one of the nicknames Dr. Joaquim had received from the opposition newspapers. Once again, Tarquínio was not called over the speakers. One of the guards personally went to fetch him, saying:

"The girl's here. Come!"

Tarquínio simply stood up, allowed the guard to handcuff him, and followed without a word. He sat in the chair for the inmates, trying not to show any emotion, his gaze fixed on a distant point. Maria Amélia entered, settled in the comfortable armchair facing the prisoner and threw him a mocking smile. It was Tarquínio who spoke first:

"What do you want?"

"Good morning, Dad. How are you doing?"

He answered with complete silence. Not even the slightest deviation in Tarquínio's gaze could be noticed. Maria Amélia continued:

"Well, here I am to make the previously announced request. Do you remember last time I was here? It wasn't that long ago. It's very simple and I promise I will do everything in my power to help you. Getting you out of here is hard, it's complicated. But everything has a cure, and what can't be cured must be endured. Anyway, what I'm about to ask of you is very simple. I want you to deny that you are my biological father. Say you've never had sex with my mother, say whatever you want, but make it clear we don't have any blood ties."

"It's clear we really don't."

"And wasn't it your sperm that fertilized my mother's egg?"

"Don't be cynical; your cynicism is enough to make me puke. It would be my greatest pleasure to sign such a paper. But it's not that simple. There is a record in the registry office. DNA evidence may be required. Witnesses heard. Even your stuck-up friend, Maria da Anunciação, would attest to your mother's lifelong fidelity in everything she did. Either way, I couldn't care less. Give me whatever you want, and I'll sign it."

"Great, then. Leave the bureaucracy to me. I've got it all in writing. Just sign here."

"And how am I supposed to sign with my hands cuffed?"

Maria Amélia motioned to the guard again. When he approached, she spoke to him in her commanding tone:

"Release the handcuffs!"

"But miss ..."

He didn't finish his sentence, simply obeying when met with her piercing gray eyes. Tarquínio took the paper, scanned it, and reached for a pen handed to him by the braided girl. He signed and asked:

"Can I go back to my cell now?"

"You don't want to know the reason for the request?"

"No. I feel as if a weight has been lifted from my soul already."

Maria Amélia motioned to the guard again. And as Tarquínio was led back to his cell, now properly handcuffed, she called out loudly enough for everyone to hear:

"Thanks, Daddy. I mean, thank you, Tarquínio Esperidião."

The plan to renounce paternity had been meticulously devised by Maria Amélia, her adoptive mother, and her uncle, now duly elevated to the status of Anita's lover. Dr. Joaquim, absent from these secret meetings due to his work leave and impending heart transplant, was nevertheless a crucial part of the scheme. He would be Maria Amélia's real father. He was convinced to back the story that he had been involved in a week-long affair with Sister Patrícia, coinciding with the time she became pregnant. If Tarquínio didn't contest and Maria Amélia accepted this version, the case could be closed without needing a DNA test, and all other bureaucratic tangles would be easily unraveled. They were in a position where signatures were easily obtained, with no real obstacles. Dr. Joaquin had tried to object during a dinner.

"But what you are asking of me is outrageous! A falsehood! It is illegal and goes against every principle that guided my professional life."

"Come on, Joaquim. It is our daughter's future at stake. It is better to be the daughter of a worthy man, respected in Rio's ... no, in Brazil's society, than of a convict, a criminal of the worst kind. That would close so many doors for her."

"I'm not convinced, Anita. You're asking too much of me ..."

Maria Amélia didn't say a word. After dinner, both Anita and Joaquim went into the living room in a bad mood, not looking at each other. They each took a side of the wide sofa and did not turn on the television, breaking their usual evening routine. Maria Amélia walked over to the bookshelf and retrieved a well-bound report, "Fundamental Changes Required in Rio de Janeiro's Penitentiary System." Joaquim Paranhos' response to the study published right after he took over the general management of Rio's prisons. Years had passed, yet Maria Amélia's expression remained much as it had been at thirteen, when she had provided all the insights for the report's drafting.

"Really, Daddy, this is a great legal piece. Where did you find so much inspiration to write it?"

Joaquim Paranhos' foundations shook. And his huge heart almost succumbed to the tachycardia that came over him. The little witch was demanding her dues for the help she had provided. He replied with a dry smile, claimed to be tired and retired to his office, a place of refuge when he fell out with Anita. Maria Amélia smiled at her adoptive mother and told her:

"Don't make that face as if you ate something you don't like. Let's watch that soap opera you like so much. Don't torment yourself. Tomorrow, he'll wake up a changed man and sign whatever we ask of him."

And she was right. At breakfast, after signaling the maid with a firm nod to leave, Joaquim Paranhos burst out:

"Alright. I accept the proposal. You'll smooth things over with the prisoner. If he doesn't cause a problem, I'll do my part."

Adamastor signed a statement confirming he had witnessed several meetings between his sister and Joaquim Paranhos, and things progressed quickly from there. All parties to the agreement were in alignment. The fake father assuming, the real father rejecting, and the daughter moving all the pieces on the board. The DNA test that had been haunting Anita's nights was no longer a concern. More than once Maria Amélia said:

"Don't worry, Mom, everything will work out. It's a sure thing."

Judge Patrícia do Amaral of the Third Family Court of Rio de Janeiro, and of Anita's same social circle, merely scanned the paperwork. Her decision was very straightforward, almost defying the legal tradition of complicating clear matters.

PATERNITY REINSTATEMENT CASE

Applicant: Dr. Joaquim de Albuquerque Paranhos

Given that Mr. Tarquínio Esperidião, until this act considered as the biological father of Maria Amélia Feitosa Paranhos, hereinafter referred to as M.A., renounced, as stated in the attached document, the paternity of the aforementioned, and, given that Dr. Joaquim de Albuquerque Paranhos assumed, in an attached statement, to be the true biological father of M.A., there is no reason to delay the matter. It is also reported that M.A.'s maternal uncle, Adamastor Leite Feitosa, witnessed several meetings between Dr. Joaquim de Albuquerque Paranhos and M.A.'s biological mother, Patrícia Leite Feitosa, who died in 1998. Therefore, the paternity claim filed by Dr. Paranhos, with the broad consent of M.A., is granted.

Dr. Patrícia do Amaral
Judge of the 3rd Family Court of Rio de Janeiro

Following the decision, a simple visit to the Civil Registry Office in Lagoa sufficed to finalize the matter. Anita was overjoyed, even though she had to explain her husband's supposed infidelity to her friends. By mutual agreement among the three—the new father, the adoptive mother, and Maria Amélia—they decided against hosting a commemorative party.

"This whole affair calls for discretion, wouldn't you say, Daddy?"

In response to Maria Amélia's derisive smile, Anita uttered a lamentation that seemed to emanate from deep within her:

"Such a shame!"

16

Adamastor was in high spirits, laughing casually as he opened his apartment door, bowing playfully as his niece entered.

"So cheerful! May I know why?"

"You wouldn't believe it, my dearest Niece. I've just closed on my election. It's a sure thing now with the quiet wad of cash at my disposal."

"Oh really? Explain further, Uncle."

"My dear, I've just had a meeting with the heads of the hills. I'll be their voice in the State Assembly. For this, I'll receive no less than ten million reais. Ten million is enough money to elect at least ten representatives!"

"Interesting, Uncle. Very interesting. But you'll refuse."

"What are you saying, Niece?"

"Exactly what you heard. You'll refuse."

"I don't get it ..."

"My dearest Uncle, this is not the path you take to enter politics, the trail of power. Sure, you'll get elected easily, no doubt. But you'll always be seen as a representative of the drug mafia, and therefore heckled by the media. Think of the headlines: 'Drug Dealers get their Representative into the Assembly.' This label will stick for the rest of your political career, should it even last beyond one term. No, you'll refuse."

"But elections cost a lot of money. I've read studies saying it takes at least a million to secure a state representative seat. I could presumably scrape it together, but I don't want to end up financially drained, treading on thin ice."

"Uncle, penny-pinching is a politician's worst sin. Politics is the journey along the intricate path to power. Power is the only word that matters in the political vocabulary. The ability to influence, maneuver, and dictate the laws to be obeyed is the only valid ambition in this game. Corruption in the pursuit of an easy fortune, small or large, will end up becoming an obstacle sooner or later. Have you forgotten?"

"So, I must draw from my own funds?"

"Stop being petty, Uncle! I have a far better proposal than your former associates. Former associates, right, Uncle!?"

"No need to get mad, Niece. A proposal?"

"Yes, a proposal. You're going to write a book. A book confessing that you were a drug dealer and telling all the petty things you did. A book renouncing your past as a cleaning products vendor, all on your own accord. A book oozing sincerity on every page, paragraph, sentence, and word. Like a telenovela. The crowd likes that, it loves that. And most importantly, it forgives and supports."

"I'm sorry, Niece, but if I do anything like that, I'll be in prison by tomorrow, unless a hired thug from Rocinha gets to me first. Plus, I don't know how to write a book."

"Don't worry. I'll help and the necessary care will be taken to not implicate your former associates directly. They won't risk murdering someone who's only remorseful, but who hasn't broken the code of silence. The book will be told in the first person, without naming names. I, the drug dealer asking for passage into another worthy profession. I, begging forgiveness ... no, not forgiveness ... seeking understanding and support to start anew."

"I'll be locked up the next day. And in court, they'll demand names, dates, acquaintances. You know this very well."

"It's a calculated risk. A very small risk, I assure you. Maybe you won't even get elected in the next election. But your name will be in vogue. The repentant drug dealer who had the courage to confess. Public opinion loves that kind of thing. And Justice is not blind, nor deaf. And it is literate, it knows how to read and interpret what newspapers say, what polls say, what the blogs say. Even the strictest judges would hesitate to give you more than a nominal punishment, like community service. You'll be a hero. An example of those who are reborn purified."

"I'm afraid, Niece!"

"Don't be. Politics requires more determination than a game of hide-and-seek with the cops. It will be the decisive play of your life. The leap from marginality to public life. What you need to fear and guard against is the envy of your future peers. The trail of power is a knife fight, but in the end, when you get there, it pays off. The candy of power is the greatest delicacy a human being can taste."

"I don't know where to begin or what to say. You've put me in an untenable position."

"And what's your dearest niece here for? You just tell me, and I'll write it. By this weekend, I'll have the prologue and epilogue done and will bring them for you to read. As for the preface, I'm sure I'll get a prestigious name to sign it."

With a forced smile, Adamastor asked:

"Is there any chance I can avoid doing what my dear niece asks?"

"No, there isn't."

And she let out a triumphant laugh.

Fifth Part

-

NEW LIFE

17

Maria Amélia toyed with the title "A Repenting Drug Dealer" but soon dismissed it, sensing it was a bit tacky, and more fundamentally, feeling a bias against the word "repent." No, the title wouldn't do. "I Was a Drug Dealer" was too obvious, and it still conveyed the feeling of guilt. Discarded. A more positive angle was required, something that signified "water under the bridge," a clean slate with no regrets about the past. But the word "dealer" or "drugs" had to be in the title, the best way for the author to show he is not trying to hide the glaringly obvious and vaccinate himself against future criticism.

The spark came during a ride between Copacabana and the penthouse she had bought in Leblon to make her own, away from her adoptive mother's presence. Just after the Barata Ribeiro tunnel, while waiting at a red light, it struck her: "Social Lessons from the Drug World's Gutter."

When elected state representative and faced with the barrage of criticism from his opponents, who would hold the sin of drug dealer against him, Adamastor could always wave the book in their faces, or, rather, point them to the title, which was the best answer. No regrets, simply the story of a man who descended into hell, learned the devil's ways, and returned to the surface better equipped to serve his community. Adamastor, the reformed dealer dedicating himself to the service of the favela and the people he once exploited. It wasn't very original, of course. Characters walking the path of evil and finding redemption along the way are a dime a dozen. But he would join this group that never lacks for praise.

Now, the introduction had to be tackled and then the uncle interviewed, scrutinizing his life as drug dealer to write a first-person account. Adamastor, the man who renounced drug trafficking, his power over the favelados, to become a citizen full of good intentions. Maria

Amélia wasted no time. She returned home, took a quick shower, fired up her laptop, and started drafting the introduction with her hair still damp and her braids undone:

To those unfamiliar with the drug-dealing underworld of Rio de Janeiro's hills, I introduce myself candidly, without any mask or disguise. My name is Adamastor Leite Feitosa. But every dealer or user in town knows me as Adamastor of Chapéu Mangueira. Simply because, for years, I was in charge of the cocaine and marijuana dealing in all the slums facing Leme beach. This illegal, yet profitable and extremely dangerous trade, taught me about the needs of the favelas' inhabitants. The lack of perspective of its youth, the arrogance of the police breaking into houses and shacks without a court order, the relationship of respect and fear between us, the big drug bosses, many of us using public roles as cover and living in mansions in the city's high-end neighborhoods. These are all elements of an apprenticeship. One that took a long time. I gradually became aware of my part in an oppressive system that has no respect for the people involved. A web of domination formed by us, the police, a cadre of politicians and high officials. Dealers, like I was, are only intermediaries in this vast chain the mainstream media sometimes calls organized crime and others just trafficking. A shared trait among those involved is their radical opposition to legalizing the drug trade. This may seem strange, but that is how it is. Even if the risks are enormous, an average dealer has the chance to accumulate more wealth than anything he could have amassed in such a short time in a legal trade, paying taxes and labor costs. The police also have no interest in legalizing the sale of drugs, even if in a controlled manner. The most corrupt see clearly that the illegal trade represents a source of extra income, but even many honest cops would lose their jobs if the drug dens were replaced by legal commercial establishments. The war the newspapers insist is taking place in the hills would probably cease to exist. A successful example in the controlled trade of certain drugs are the famous coffee shops in the Netherlands, where marijuana and hashish can be freely purchased for consumption. Statistics indicate that in other European countries, with stricter enforcement against soft drug users, there's a higher rate of drug-related crime and increased consumption of hard drugs, such as heroin. This is not to condone the use of drugs, whether hard or soft, a group that should include tobacco and alcohol. However, as we're well aware, dealers of these latter products are readily accepted in social circles without any qualms, even welcomed in clubs like Rotary and Lions. It should also be stressed that cocaine was once a perfectly legal substance, sold in pharmacies at the beginning of the last century, consumed mainly by old women to fight migraines. Not to mention that according to records, sixty-nine brands of beverages used cocaine in their composition around 1909, including that famous soda everyone knows, which years later replaced cocaine with caffeine. There is no news of the youth of the time being addicted to the substance, although there are records of notorious adepts of cocaine from that time, like Arthur Conan Doyle, creator of the character Sherlock Homes. Cocaine has probably been used for more than five thousand years and its great boom in the so-called Western world occurred after the turn of the nineteenth century, when Sigmund Freud wrote a treatise on its pharmaceutical use. Today, cocaine is mainly used by the executives of large companies as an instrument to keep them awake, so to speak, during long work meetings. Since cocaine is expensive, the poorest strata have to use its contaminated by-products as alternatives, such as crack cocaine.

The point that needs emphasizing is the following: the criminalization of drugs does not achieve its main objective, which is to curb their use, especially regarding the youth, rebellious by nature and always attracted by what is forbidden. To the contrary, the prohibition of the drug trade has created a chain of interests generating billions of dollars, involving not only cartels and intermediate dealers, as I was, but also the entire repressive system. To give you an idea, the American narcotics police DEA has at its disposal an annual budget of more than USD 2.5 billion and more than ten thousand employees—half of which are agents. A strong political component is involved here, but I would have to deviate from the scope of this book with references to the so-called Plan Colombia, for example. I just want to emphasize that the DEA's budget has skyrocketed since the 1990s, when the FARC issue in Colombia took over the mainstream news as far as Latin America was concerned. In 1972, the DEA could only count on USD 65 million and fewer than 1,500 agents. Given the constant influx of drugs into the U.S., especially cocaine, it is fair to suspect that all that money and manpower is being wasted. Or that there is a lot of corruption along the way. Brazil is no different in terms of corruption and waste, although on a much smaller scale. The Federal Police's budget hovers around BRL 350 million and dealers in the country have never complained about a shortage of merchandise. That is, drug trafficking seems to increase as the means and money to fight it also increase.

My lessons as a drug dealer for more than fifteen years may seem obvious, but they deserve to be made explicit. People live in the favela because they are poor and can't afford to buy or rent a house or apartment in the urbanized areas. And whatever any given favelado may do, he has already been brandished by the rest of society with the mark of marginality. It is fair to ask whether all the money funneled into repression would not be better spent building more popular housing, and above all, new public schools with decent teachers. My maid spends the day with her belly pressed to the stove for a measly minimum wage, but two of her children were my runners, the term used for those who deliver drugs to the consumer. Neither finished their lousy primary school, and as such, both only had two options: sacrifice themselves in a menial job, to be manés—or chumps in favela slang—or join the marginality, in their case dealing drugs. I doubt they would have become drug runners in a more supportive environment with decent housing and schools. At least, it's fair to say that they would have other worthy alternatives.

In short, it's cases like this that led me to the decision to give up trafficking, but without foregoing the position of leadership I earned on the hill. I can and want to take advantage of it on another front, in social engagement, perhaps in politics. With this book, I step into a new world with an open heart and a cleansed soul, sharing my experiences as a dealer, yet without revealing names or denouncing anyone. I don't believe in repression in the fight against drugs. The educational path seems to me more effective and less costly, especially regarding the preservation of human life.

Perhaps the introduction could have been shorter but let's not dwell on it. It's unwise to edit a witch's copy. She wrote it and that's how it's going to read.

Adamastor couldn't sleep all weekend, even before reading the introduction. He couldn't shake off the images of the potential consequences of the step he was about to take, all at his niece's urging. In some visions, he saw himself handcuffed, being shoved into a cell crammed with criminals. In others, he imagined taking a bullet to the head and his body being dumped in a ditch in Duque de Caxias, under a front-page photo with the headline:

"Cartel Renegade Awakes with Mouth Full of Ants."

Leme's drug boss, still sporting deep dark bags from a sleepless weekend, was jolted awake by the doorbell. It was his niece, carrying a black folder and handing it to the frightened dealer.

"Here's the introduction to your book, Uncle. Care to take a look? I think it's best you read it carefully. Because when it comes out the oven, you'll be asked to give interviews all the time."

18

Dr. Eugênio Batista is known for his arrogance and lack of respect aimed at colleagues with lesser degrees and, above all, nurses. There was nothing out of the ordinary in his screaming in the operating room.

"Hand me that fucking scalpel before this fucking pump I'm putting inside this butchered pig stops ticking."

The pump was the heart of the boy killed with the shrapnel launched by the biker's helmet—the same biker who was turned to pulp on Avenida Nossa Senhora de Copacabana. And the butchered pig was Joaquim Paranhos, plunged into the limbo of general anesthesia. Dr. Eugênio knew who the patient was but felt no need to mince words. Everyone in the room was his subordinate. He didn't tolerate strangers, especially those he deemed ignorant laypeople. Anita waited in the hospital reception and would only see the patient when he was released from the ICU.

"You wait here. I'll release the patient when I see fit."

He was about to add, "Go home and don't interfere," when he found himself confronted by two gray eyes. He shut up, frowned, looked away, and left the room as if he had seen a ghost. Or witch. He felt watched from head to toe and only found relief when he turned down the hallway toward the operating room. Maria Amélia consoled her adoptive mother.

"Don't be intimidated by this uneducated doctor. He is the best plumber available to change Daddy's pumping heart, but he's clueless about the mysteries of the human mind."

"Don't talk like that, my daughter."

"Just kidding, Mommy. It's just good for you to unwind a bit, isn't that right, Maria da Anunciação?"

The psychiatrist agreed with a smile. She had made a point of accompanying Anita and Maria Amélia to the hospital and hoped that, as a colleague, as a psychiatrist, she would be invited to attend the surgery. She wasn't. One of the subordinate doctors on the team was tasked with notifying Dr. Maria da Anunciação, calling her over for a private conversation:

"We know that as a colleague and friend of the patient you want to attend the surgery. But it is Dr. Eugênio's strict policy to not make any exception. Only those directly involved are allowed in the operating room. And perhaps our colleague could be of more service on the outside, giving support to his wife, who seems so distressed to me."

The psychiatrist swallowed the ban, but not without firing back:

"My dear colleague can tell the master surgeon that I'll stay outside, even though I could demand my presence from hospital management. And my worthy colleague does not need to lecture me on what I should do on the outside."

Dr. Anunciação left the room, almost slamming the door in the doctor's face, who followed with his head bowed. Anita watched the scene anxiously, believing that the doctor could have delivered some bad news. But Maria Amélia comforted her with a hug, her words seemingly directed more at the psychiatrist than her mother.

"It's nothing, Mommy. I can already guess. Dr. Eugênio will not permit the presence of Dr. Anunciação."

"You're right as always. Sometimes I think you have a crystal ball."

"And do psychiatrists believe in such things?

Maria Amélia's laughter to lift the funereal atmosphere of heart transplant day was heard across the hall.

Joaquim Paranhos' chest was opened up by two assistants under the watchful eye of Dr. Eugênio. He only involved himself in the delicate parts of the surgery, where his superior expertise was necessary. A divine gift, that's all it could be! He indicated the precise place where the assistants should make the incision to remove the old pump from Rio de Janeiro's Secretary of Penitentiary Administration. And as a precaution, he gave a little help to one of the assistants. A millimetric error could be fatal. Once the old heart was cut out, it was time to connect the patient's circulatory system to the artificial heart before the transplant. The assistant who seemed most nervous passed Joaquim Paranhos's huge heart with extreme care to one of the nurses who, if not a first timer, seemed never to have gotten used to the whole affair. With just a glance, Dr. Eugênio noticed his underling's unnecessary trembling and said in a falsetto voice, as if addressing a child:

"You don't have to be so careful with that shit. It's not even good for soup. Just drop it in the formalin."

And with the precision of a top expert, he received the boy's still-beating heart from two other seasoned surgeons on his team for the truly complicated task of joining it to the patient's veins, arteries, and nerves. A single look from him was all it took for the second team to step aside, allowing the two doctors responsible for preparing the organ for transplant to proceed. And although the two assistants moved to the rear, they remained alert, aware that any order from the surgeon would have to be heeded on the spot. Joaquim Paranhos was lucky, and everything went according to the best heart transplant manual, if there is any. After all the blood was drained from the donor's organ by the other two doctors on the team, the new heart, now properly connected, began filling with the patient's blood and beating independently. Dr. Eugênio took a step back so the two doctors could take care of the less complicated task of closing the patient's chest. He looked the whole team over and said:

"Phew, it's hard work being a human body plumber. But you can't deny we're good at it."

He should have said "I'm good," he thought, as he received the applause from all except the two assistant doctors, still busy stitching up the chest of Rio de Janeiro's Chief Jailer.

Now began the slow process of recovery. Joaquim Paranhos took six months leave, knowing little chance existed he would take up his post again. At home, where he once held sway, second only to his adopted daughter, the secretary on leave now embraced the role of tending to his wife's every wish and request. This was how—with a new heart and low on authority—he participated in the paternity farce, suffering the extra bitterness of having to betray his principles.

In agreement with Dr. Eugênio, the family doctor imposed a series of restrictions on the patient, such as no alcoholic beverages, cigars (don't even think about it), and most terrible of all, complete and definitive sexual abstention for at least six months. He should even avoid any excessive affection that could lead to an erection. At most, a little kiss on the brow, a pat on the face, a languid look of platonic love, with no erotic overtones. Joaquim Paranhos could not understand how Anita, fiery as she was, demanding sexual intercourse at least four times a week, had been enduring such abstinence with such good humor and joviality. Always vibrant and smiling, as if she were completely content. And the patient occasionally detected a knowing irony in Maria Amélia's glances. Particularly, Joaquim Paranhos felt a deep repugnance, originating from his new heart, whenever he had to meet his adopted daughter's uncle.

19

The critical six-month recovery passed. For a while, the media spotlighted the patient's political future quite prominently, speculating whether the Chief Jailer would go back to commanding the penitentiary system or retire to enjoy the privileges befitting a landowner's descendant married to a wealthy woman, the sole daughter of a Carioca couple with extensive offshore accounts. Finally, on the eve of the transplant's first anniversary, when almost no one remembered the case anymore, the definitive news came through an official press release from Guanabara Palace.

> The governor has decided today to appoint Dr. Alexandre de Albuquerque as Head of the State Department of Penitentiary Administration on a permanent basis. To date, Dr. Alexandre de Albuquerque has been exercising the position on an interim basis with outstanding competence, replacing the incumbent, Dr. Joaquim Paranhos Nogueira, on leave for health reasons.
> The governor appreciates Dr. Joaquim Paranhos Nogueira's commitment and dedication and hopes to count on his valuable cooperation in the future.

So died Joaquim Paranhos' professional career. And a new heart in an old man's chest might have many reasons to keep beating, but an acute depression of the recipient doesn't seem to help at all. For that's what happened. Despite expecting it, the governor's note struck him like a poisoned arrow. The final word that his professional career was over, that his political dreams of winning a seat in congress had evaporated, and that even his marital life would be reduced to sporadic sex, insufficient for a woman in the heat of her forties. The malaise only grew with Anita's pitying expression and Maria Amélia's intense stare, which, in a silence heavy with sarcasm, seemed to say: "My dear Daddy, you already did what you had to do. You're of no use anymore. You can die. I'll let you."

And die he did. One year, one month, and three days after the transplant, which the press had lauded as yet another victory for Dr. Eugênio Batista. The news of his death was consigned to the inner pages, under brief notes of little significance, the usual place for those now out of the limelight.

Former Secretary General of Prisons Dies

This morning, the former Head of Rio de Janeiro's State Department of Penitentiary Administration, Dr. Joaquim Paranhos Nogueira, died at the age of 62. He had been on leave for more than a year for health reasons after undergoing heart surgery. His body will be laid to rest today at the São João Batista Cemetery at 4pm. The governor issued a note stressing the merits of his late employee.

Apart from that, almost nothing. Dr. Eugênio Batista's team, which had access to experienced PR managers, pulled some strings with the newsrooms so the word transplant was replaced by surgery with no mention of the surgeon's name. The funeral was also discreet and barely reported. Anita, once again clad in black, was accompanied by Maria Amélia, Cleide, and Maria da Anunciação. Adamastor was also present, discreetly, blending in with the other mourners. He seemed weighed down, as one would expect at a funeral. But it was something else weighing on the dealer's mind. It was the book, which had entered its final stages and would be published in two weeks. No doubt a bombshell. One to launch him in style into a political career or destroy him once and for all. With just a glance, Maria Amélia perceived her uncle's concerns. She let go of her adoptive mother's arms, slowed her pace for her uncle to catch up, and whispered in his ear:

"What's with the burial mood. We're putting an obstacle into the ground"—and before finishing the sentence she looked clearly in Anita's direction—"an obstacle for all of us."

"Niece!" exclaimed Adamastor, revealing his discomfort.

"Your dearest niece knows what she's talking about."

She then quickened her pace, rejoining her adoptive mother and adopting the guise of an orphan at her father's funeral.

The following day, dressed in a light pink outfit, Maria Amélia headed to the Copacabana apartment, carrying the manuscript of the book along with the reviewed proofs and a preface signed by the Secretary of Security, Afonso Figueiredo. How was this possible? This is how the little witch pulled it off.

In a private moment with the governor, she requested him to set up a meeting with the Secretary of Security.

"Amelinha, what on earth could you want with my bluntest secretary?"

"Nothing too special, just for him to write the foreword to my uncle's book."

"Are you crazy, girl? The only thing on Afonso's mind is drilled order! It's far too risky, Amelinha. The opposition will seize on it immediately. Just think of the headlines in that tabloid that keeps making stuff up about me. They'll end up writing that my security secretary is in cahoots with a drug dealer."

"Leave it to me. I know how to soften up tough guys. And don't worry about the opposition and yellow papers. The book will ignite a wave of public acclaim. And Dr. Afonso will like it, I'm sure, even if he disagrees on some points."

"Amelinha!"

"Schedule the interview. Who knows, maybe I can drop by the secretary's office right now."

With a sigh of helplessness, the governor took the phone off the hook and called the Secretary of Security to say his aide wanted to talk to him:

"And does the governor know what about?"

"She'll explain. When can she come?"

"Five o'clock this afternoon. I have a hole in my schedule, but I can't do more than twenty minutes."

"Twenty minutes, five o'clock today. Is that enough?"

"More than enough."

If Maria Amélia had been any other aide, she might have felt intimidated upon entering the Security Secretary's office. In stark contrast to the governor's vibrant office, adorned with paintings of dancers, the secretary's lair was decidedly gloomy. Afonso Figueiredo didn't even look up, seemingly engrossed in a report. He merely nodded to Maria Amélia to sit in the armchair opposite him.

"Good afternoon, Secretary."

"Good afternoon. What can I do for you?"

"Write the foreword to my uncle's book."

"What are you talking about? What uncle?"

"Adamastor of Chapéu Mangueira."

It was only then that the secretary raised his head to get a better look at the insolent young woman sitting across from him. He initially wanted to yell but ended up softening his tone.

"Are you crazy! I'm the secretary of security. Drug dealers I send to jail. You are his niece?"

"I am, indeed. You do that very well, sending dealers to jail. Especially the small fry. The big ones always slip through, don't they? My uncle is renouncing his life of crime, and his revelations will be of great value to consolidate the Pacifying Police Unit project. I might even say we're presenting you with a golden opportunity."

"Young lady, I really don't have time and nor am I the foreword-writing type. In fact, I never wrote one."

"You don't have to write it. Just sign it if you see fit."

The audacity of this girl! For much less, Afonso Figueiredo would have already kicked out any subordinate. But the Security Secretary's congenital fury was being numbed by two gray eyes that never seemed to blink.

Maria Amélia continued:

"I know the secretary is busy and doesn't have much time to read the original manuscript. That can be handled by your trusted aides, of course. If it suits you, the foreword has already been drafted. Open to modifications as you see fit, of course. It's carefully crafted from every angle. At no point does it suggest the esteemed secretary sympathizes with my uncle's criminal past. On the contrary, the secretary is portrayed as a champion of the Pacifying Police, advocating for fighting drugs through education rather than repression. That aligns with what you've been saying in your speeches, doesn't it?"

"It's too much to ask, Miss. What about the governor? What does he think of this? Why didn't you ask him to sign the foreword?"

"Just between us, but politicians like the governor are all too eager to sign anything. It doesn't carry the same weight as a signature from Dr. Afonso."

A gentle breeze enveloped the secretary's ego, softening his usually authoritative voice as he pondered:

"I'll catch hell for this. Signing the foreword of a dealer's book, imagine that!"

"I've already imagined it. It will generate different headlines than riots in prisons and let's just say, the police's somewhat excessive use of force. These will be positive headlines; I can assure you. And good feedback on digital media."

"With me confirming that drug pusher is actually sorry and walking the righteous path?"

"Certainly not. If I may, I'll read the last paragraph of the foreword's draft."

The secretary made a sanctioning gesture, which was half the battle. Maria Amélia read:

"I don't know if the author is really sorry. I'm no psychologist or mind reader. The original manuscript reached my hands through people of extreme confidence, one of them the Head of the State Department for Penitentiary Administration, Dr. Alexandre de Albuquerque, who has credentials as one of the most active combatants in the front against drugs. What is important about this book, which I read and reread with extreme caution, is the meticulous way the author describes the drug world from the inside, opening new approaches to fight it. The book itself offers valuable insights. It falls solely upon the author to demonstrate that he has truly changed his life and embraced the cause of the favela's population within all the rigors of the law."

When Maria Amélia finished reading, she once again fixed her eyes on the secretary while waiting for the answer. He took a breath and said:

"No promises. But leave the originals and the foreword here. I'll answer when I have time."

"Thank you, Secretary. I'll be waiting."

She knew the secretary's vanity had been piqued. And vanity, after all, is every politician's Achilles' heel.

Maria Amélia didn't like being called Amelinha. This was a concession she reluctantly accepted to gain access to the corridors of power. Maria Amélia had her first meetings with the governor when her adoptive father was still Secretary of the State Department for Penitentiary Administration. From there, it was but a small step to seduction. And we are not only talking about intellectual seduction, with Maria Amélia talking politics as if she had a PhD in political maneuvering, but also seduction as it is commonly understood. Maria Amélia crossing and uncrossing her legs to expose her lace panties in the politician's field of vision. All this accompanied by a sly smile promising a thousand and one nights of pure pleasure. It was all a game and never got past that. Maria Amélia didn't want—or better, couldn't—be branded as the little plaything of old politicians. She wanted to be the forbidden fruit. Almost within reach but always unattainable. And Amelinha was present in all the governor's nights, even when he fucked his sixty-something wife in boring missionary.

In this web of influence, it is also worth remembering that the new head of Rio's prison system, Alexandre Albuquerque, had been Joaquim Paranhos' lieutenant, visiting Maria Amélia's home often. Moreover, he had been in that group with Joaquim Paranhos and Anita that met the girl who had just seen her mother gunned down. In short, the little witch's influence over the new head of the prison system had deep roots. And after Maria Amélia's visit, he was the first person consulted by the security secretary, who was also his old college buddy.

A savvy bettor would find the odds favorable for the security secretary agreeing to sign the preface of Adamastor's book.

20

Friday morning on Avenida Atlântica. Half past nine, still a bit early for those who just like to enjoy the beach, sprawled like drying meat on the sand. But not for the thousands of joggers, briskly walking from Leme to Posto 6 and back, hoping to shed their bellies and tone muscles in all the right places. Joining this merry-go-round, a significant number of cyclists rode along Atlântica's extensive bike path. Traffic was also heavy. The sun was weighing down without so much as a cloud to mitigate its rays, and the temperature, already hovering around ninety degrees, was an invitation to the general stampede toward the beaches. At the corner of Duvivier Street, near the Copacabana Palace Hotel, Camélia waited for a swarm of bathers to cross the street. She waited for the lights to flash so the slower ones would hasten their pace to cross over safely. At that moment, Camélia had all the patience in the world. She waited for the green lights that would launch the impatient drivers like race cars on a Formula One track. Camélia stepped on the road and was literally crushed, first by a Toyota traveling at forty mph, then by a Chevrolet pickup, and finally by an illegal minibus transporting bathers to the beaches further south. The body could only be identified in the afternoon because of her dental records. When Cleide, her husband, and Frederica were reached by the macabre phone call from the coroner, it was already four in the afternoon.

"No, it can't be her!" cried Cleide, whom the coroner's staff had advised against viewing the pieces to which her daughter's body had been reduced.

Astor, the husband, was forced to make the formal identification and did all he could not to throw up. Frederica, seemingly in a trance, embraced her mother and whispered:

"No, Mom. That's her. It's Camélia."

This certainty from the sister didn't come without reason. After waking up at eight that morning to meet Maria Amélia and head to Barra da Tijuca, she discovered a note with bold red letters under a crystal stone on her nightstand:

"Keep away from her!"

At that time, Frederica did not take the warning very seriously. She dismissed it as another bout of jealousy from her sister, who knew she was going to spend time with the enemy. But she didn't tear up the note. She folded it and slid it in her wallet, not even stopping to think that the red letters were Camélia's blood.

The young woman had been contemplating suicide for days and wanted to do it spectacularly so it would serve as a warning to her sister. She ruled out all traditional methods like poisoning, jumping from a building, or shooting herself, in the privacy of her room, away from the public eye. She sought an audience, to be featured in the evening news, become a headline in all tabloids, and appear in prominent newspapers like *O Globo, Estadão,* and *Folha de S. Paulo.* There is a taboo in the press, not only in Brazil, that suicides should not be reported. This is, of course, unless the circumstances are special, involving notable figures. The old newspaper *A Luta Democrática do Rio de Janeiro* was perhaps the best example of a tabloid entirely devoted to police matters. The more heinous the crime, the bigger the headline. Congressman Tenorio Cavalcanti, the owner of *A Luta,* boasted that the only time the newspaper deviated from crime reporting in its headlines was in August 1954, when it was compelled to print a political headline.

"Getúlio Commits Suicide with a Shot to the Chest"[4]

A Luta was in fact breaking two taboos with this headline. The first one, as we saw, pertained to the newspaper itself, which until then abstained from any political subjects in the headlines. The second pertained to the entire press not reporting on suicides, certainly not prominently on the front page. Beyond the political or economic status of the individual, another factor that compels the publication of such an extreme act is its spectacular and public nature. The gruesome scene on that sunny morning on Avenida Atlântica, where a young woman of Rio's high society was reduced to a shapeless mass on the asphalt, could not and would not be concealed.

---

[4] Getúlio Vargas was a politician who served as the 14th and 17th president of Brazil. He is considered the most influential Brazilian political figure of the 20th century. On 24 August 1954, while still in office, he committed suicide in the presidential palace with a shot to his own chest.

The trip to Barra da Tijuca was unlike the other frequent meetings between Frederica and Maria Amélia. And not because of Frederica. She had already forgotten her sister's note, in fact. It was Maria Amélia who wasn't at ease. She didn't touch her friend as she often did, even in public, and refrained from her usual teasing whenever she noticed Frederica's discomfort:

"Nitwit, this is our education. Later you'll have plenty of time to be the bottom or the top of a whole bunch of nitwits."

Maria Amélia sensed something off, a repellent force that hindered any intimacy with her friend. And for the first time she complained—she, who never got sick, who was always a step ahead of everything and everyone:

"I'm sorry, Frederica. Let's go. I'm not feeling well. I'm going home to rest."

"Okay. Let's go.

That's all Frederica said. Who was she to challenge her friend's request?

The morning before the suicide, Camélia had cut a cross in her hand with a stylus. She wrote the note to Frederica with a bloody cotton swab. Her sister didn't notice, but her father did. The hand marked with the cross remained intact amid the wreckage of Camélia's body.

Only a handful of newspapers presented the suicide hypothesis as an undeniable fact. Most chose to portray the death as another tragic incident in the city's chaotic traffic. This was followed by reports and statistics on traffic accidents, depicting the streets of Rio de Janeiro as among the world's most dangerous, not just due to muggings. Beneath a picture of a red light, one of the front-page headlines read:

"Death in Atlântica Avenue
Rio's Streets Can't be Racetracks!"

Camélia's funeral at the São João Batista Cemetery became a highly attended event. A long line of mourners proceeded, silent as the grave—pardon the inevitable pun. Maria Amélia didn't want to go, but she went.

More than anyone, she understood that even she couldn't always escape societal expectations. She approached Frederica, and with a meaningful look, suggested that her friend slow down and distance herself from her mother, whom she was comforting along with her father. Frederica consented and came to Maria Amélia's side, but they didn't touch each other. Asserting the authority she believed she had, Maria Amélia whispered in her ear:

"Throw it away!"

But for the first time since their friendship began, Frederica responded with equal resolve:

"I won't!"

She had no idea how her friend found out about the note, but she didn't bend this time. She then quickened her pace to rejoin her parents in mourning her late sister.

21

Frederica didn't expect a negative response, nor should she. First, there were no financial obstacles whatsoever. She could easily afford the study. Or to put it more succinctly, her father could. Second, the proposal for her anthropology masters was no doubt enticing: "Comparative Study on Beliefs and Rituals in the Urban Centers of the Americas." She had meticulously prepared the outline and sent it three weeks earlier to Penn State's Department of Anthropology, ranked among the best in the world. The answer came back positive, and Frederica packed her bags and left. Maria Amélia learned about it from Anita, who, in turn, had picked up the news from Rio's socialite grapevine. The relationship between the two mothers also began to show strain after Camélia's funeral. The consoling embrace between the friends had not been as tight as usual at the São João Batista cemetery. Sure, Anita gave a squeeze, but the arms on the other side remained almost limp, and their conversation lacked its usual intimacy.

"My dear, my dear, how terrible! A thousand times my condolences. You know you can count on me for whatever you need."

"Thank you."

That was it. Had Anita been even slightly more astute—possessing even a fraction of her adopted daughter's wit—she might have realized something was amiss. Yet, she chalked up the cool demeanor solely to her friend's emotional state. She didn't know that Cleide had gone through Camélia's room when she returned from the coroner. Despite her distress, she needed to understand why. The diary of the girl who had ended her own life offered a crystal-clear explanation.

She is to blame. The braided witch. She ruined my bond with my sister, bewitched her with her malice and cynicism. Even my mother seems to be totally enthralled by pigtails. I used to be happy, but she has draped a veil of misery over our house. Stay away from her. From her and everything under her influence.

For Frederica, spending at least two years in the United States emerged as the ideal solution to finalize her separation from Maria Amélia and to honor her sister's request, reiterated twice: once in her diary and once in the note written in her own blood. She carried the note in her wallet. Frederica hadn't told anyone about its existence, conscious that any slip-up could pique the interest of reporters hunting for suicide notes. The diary was also kept secret. Cleide didn't want to show it to anyone. Not to her husband. Not to Frederica. She wanted to spare them.

However, placing an ocean between the former friends wasn't necessary. Frederica's firm refusal during her sister's funeral had been the definitive, final severance. When Anita, in her holy gullibility, talked to her adopted daughter, she failed to understand what was going on:

"So, did you go to Frederica's farewell party yesterday?"

"No. Farewell for what?"

"Don't tell me you don't know your best friend is going to spend two years in the United States!"

"No. I didn't know. I have other concerns at the moment."

113

The security measures for a mere book launch were excessive, unimaginable for a literary event. The governor didn't want to attend at the last moment. Or, more accurately, Maria Amélia had dismissed him.

"It would be better if you stayed home. There will be a time for you and my uncle to share the stage. For now, it's wise to loosen the reins a bit. If pulled too tightly, they will snap."

"Amelinha. Sorry, for me you are Amelinha. You'll go far."

"Yes, I will. We will. Can't you smell Brasilia's *cerrado* already?"

The governor's broad smile looked presidential. Maria Amélia cut the euphoria short:

"But we can't be careless. See you tomorrow, Governor. I have to leave for a very important meeting to prevent too much strain on the line."

"May I ask where my top aide is headed?"

Maria Amélia replied with a sly smile:

"No, you can't. It's best you don't. Good aides are entitled to their own secrets."

Anticipation for Adamastor's book release surged as both the press and literary circles remained in the dark about the book's content. Maria Amélia made a point of it.

"Don't even think about leaking parts of the book or revealing excerpts. The title and author's name are enough. Keep them guessing and speculating. The more the better."

But she nevertheless demanded that her uncle use the appropriate channels still at his disposal to get an original copy into the hands of the drug lords a week before the release.

"We cannot and will not have unpleasant surprises at the launch party. Secrets are good to pique the curiosity of the press and the clientele. But it would be wise to eliminate any fishy smell for our cleaning product traders. They already have enough hot issues to handle as it is. We'll send them the original. And this is just between the two of us. The publisher's people don't need to know."

She smiled, smoothing the worried crease on her uncle's brow, who appeared oblivious to any irony at that moment. Maria Amélia was right, as always. Maybe the security measures, akin to those for Salman Rushdie's *The Satanic Verses* launch, were excessive.

The drug lords called upon lawyer Expedito Maciel to read and summarize the 360-page book. Above all, they sought an answer to what they considered a crucial question: does it mention names and addresses? It didn't. Nothing. No insinuations that could suggest anyone's involvement. However, Expedito Maciel noted that the book presented a thesis unfavorable to the drug trade, paving the way for operations by the pacification police and the boys and girls freshly graduated in social work. These people disgusted Expedito. But the book wasn't written by a snitch and Adamastor's corpse in a ditch in the Baixada wouldn't benefit the trade at all. Nevertheless, there was no use denying it, the book was favorable to the other position. Adamastor changed allegiances and should be banned from setting foot up on the hill. Especially Chapéu Mangueira.

At the makeshift headquarters of the *Terceiro Comando*,[5] nestled in the heart of Rocinha favela, the general command of Rio's drug trade convened to discuss the report. Around a massive table, they gathered, with Maciel at the center, intently poring over the original copy of Adamastor's book. The group was tense, their glasses of expensive wine barely sipped, much like the untouched roast suckling pig with farofa. Adamastor's replacement in charge of the trade on the Chapéu Mangueira hill was the most agitated of all. Not due to it being his first meeting at this level, but because he knew he'd face numerous questions and inquiries for having been his former boss' right-hand man for so many years. He spoke with the fervor that was expected of him:

"The bastard must be punished somehow. To me, he's a traitor, doesn't matter what he wrote in that shit. He's gone to the other side and it's going to hurt our business. Quiet quitters are bad enough, but depart while setting off fireworks and casting us in a grim light as you go ... As if the militias encroaching on every corner weren't enough, now we will be made sheep under the pacifying police forces' stick. Without

---

[5] One of the largest organized crime factions in Brazil.

punishment—I'm not talking about erasing the bastard—but without punishment things will get very bad for our side. Adamastor is preaching the end of our business in this damn book. The bastard says we're in a swamp. Swamp, my ass!"

We interrupt the meeting to recount an incident that happened moments earlier. The stronghold was secured at ten strategic points by the drug world's top snipers. At the main entrance, two thugs were wearing overcoats to disguise their AK-47s, on a day hot enough to melt asphalt. All the drug personnel in the favela were on alert. Orders had been issued that no outsider should ascend the hill that day, and if they did, they had to explain why and where they were going. The two guards could therefore hardly believe their eyes when this elegant young woman walked toward them naturally as if taking a stroll.

"And where does the young lady think she's going?"

The young lady pinned both thugs down with her gray eyes and spoke:

"The young lady is going inside. I've been invited. The sole guest. Dr. Maciel and the others are expecting me."

One guard intended to escort Maria Amélia by the arm, but instead, he simply followed her. She entered in time to hear the outburst of her uncle's former second lieutenant. Expedito Maciel explained the strange presence to the others with a gesture and whispered in the ear of the big boss sitting next to him:

"That's her."

She began speaking even before taking her seat:

"Our friend here is completely wrong. My uncle isn't causing you harm. Rather, he's showing you new potential avenues. He didn't invent the pacifying police force. He's not the driving force behind this increasingly open society that's moving toward legalizing marijuana and other soft drugs soon, maybe even cocaine. If you want to survive, you must dance to the new tune. My uncle will enter another circle, the true circle of power. The men here are just orbiting it and could be crushed anytime if circumstances so required. My uncle will be in a good position to help you, not harm you."

116

Armandinho, Adamastor's successor, looked poised to respond but was silenced by Expedito Maciel's dismissive nod. The lawyer, too, didn't utter a word to continue the meeting, as he was cut off by the commander gesturing with his hands for silence, then speaking in his tenor voice:

"What a feisty little thing! But I like it. Come here, girl. Sit next to me."

Immediately a chair was placed between the commander, affectionately called Dente Grande,[6] and the lawyer. Maria Amélia took her seat with the ease of someone mingling among the governor's secretaries. The tense meeting turned into a party when the young lady toasted the boss with a glass of wine. And the roasted piglet was consumed among the laughter and the jokes in what could be fairly classified as Adamastor's first book release.

22

Everyone was present, ranging from sensational tabloids to the so-called serious press, not to forget bloggers from every corner. Everybody looking for a connection between the drug-dealing and the political world under the spotlight of more than one TV camera. Maria Amélia blended in with the assistants. This was her uncle's night. His first five minutes of fame outside the drug world. Minutes that might stretch into hours, days, months, or even years of a political career, all meticulously orchestrated by his dearest niece.

Before he could sit to handle the autograph line, Adamastor was encircled by a sea of microphones.

Questions rained down:

"Are you definitively giving up the drug trade?"

"Of course."

"Aren't you afraid of reprisals? The *Terceiro Comando* doesn't forget ... Have you asked for police protection?"

---

[6] Big Tooth.

"I'm aware of the risks. But I didn't ask for police protection."

"What about all these armed guards here at the mall?"

"I'm not sure. You should probably ask someone else."

"There is talk of political courtship between you and the governor. Did it start before or after your decision to quit dealing?"

Amid the barrage of questions, Adamastor pretended not to hear this and moved on to a less controversial one:

"What do you want with this book?"

"First of all, to enlighten public opinion and contribute to policies that genuinely aid the impoverished populations of the favelas. I was a drug dealer. Everybody knows. Second, I want the book to serve as a milestone in my new life."

"Won't the law come after you?"

"I'm ready for it and prepared to face the consequences. I'm a newly-graduated lawyer. I'm well aware of the legal implications."

Adamastor was doing very well, but the sweat trickling down his temples wasn't solely due to the spotlights. There was nothing easy about this interrogation for him, despite being submitted for a week to a daily four-hour inquisition prepared by Maria Amélia. He felt a wave of relief upon seeing his niece approaching to guide him by the arm to the book signing chair.

"There will be ample time for interviews, Uncle. This is just the start."

"Niece? But aren't you also an aide of the governor?"

In response, Maria Amélia blasted the reporter with her gray eyes. The question had been expected, and her uncle's ties with the governor were bound to come to light eventually. But for the moment, it remained mere speculation. After helping her uncle to his chair, she looked at the reporter again, but this time donning a smooth smile.

The 2,500 copies printed for the launch weren't enough. However, the true measure of success emerged the next day with extensive press coverage. Headlines and opinions everywhere, including a none too flattering editorial in the newspaper with the largest circulation in Rio de Janeiro. Incidentally, the same newspaper where the reporter with the prying question worked:

Suspicious Connections and Hypocrisy.

In the book Adamastor of Chapéu Mangueira launched yesterday at Barra Shopping with his confessions of a drug dealer, he hints at previous links with the world of politics. Let's avoid naming the governor here to preclude accusations of a witch hunt. Indeed, the fact the author's niece is an aide at Guanabara Palace may be a mere coincidence. In the book, however, the author makes a point of not exposing anyone involved in the underworld, and he doesn't even make his regret explicit for having spent so much time in this illicit, illegal, and corrupting activity for our youth. It is clear the author wants to use the book to catapult himself into the political world. However, in our view, it is now up to the Justice system to delve into the matter, in possession of the general and theoretical information provided by the author. It must demand names and addresses of the main parties involved in the control of narcotics trafficking from Mr. Adamastor, who must prove with acts that he really left organized crime and wants to walk the line to defend the poor communities in the favelas. There's certainly no shortage of hypocrisy in our political sphere. So far, the book seems to offer only vague promises that can be interpreted this way, regardless of the signature of the hard-boiled Secretary of Security on its preface.

The impact of the editorial on Adamastor's mood was unmistakable on his face. He choked and nearly spat his coffee out at Maria Amélia.

"Relax, Uncle! I've read it. It's not that serious. This is more than expected."

"Not serious? That bastard is putting the law and all dealers in Rio on to me and you say it isn't serious?!"

"It isn't! Calm down," Maria Amélia smiled before proceeding.

"We went to war, Uncle. This was to be expected from the very beginning. Up on the hill, you shoot bullets. Down here, we shoot words. You need to get used to it. Remember Sarney. He seized what he deemed his during the military junta, played the democrat during the drum rolls protesting for free elections, became president, and even led the Senate. Imagine how much further he would have gone with me as his advisor!

This is just the beginning, Uncle. Read the other newspapers, see the exposure the launch managed to achieve, and drink your coffee, we have plenty to do. First of all, preparing your body and soul for this upcoming TV-interview."

"Will it work?"

"Of course, it will. Just finish your coffee and let's practice."

"I'm done."

"Then put this in."

Adamastor put the earpiece in while Maria Amélia stepped out and vanished into one of the adjoining rooms. From there, she began communicating with her uncle:

"Can you hear me?"

"Perfectly.

"Then let's go. Let's think of the most intrusive questions we can to test my barrage of responses. War is war and technology is here to help us."

In fact, the interview turned out to be like a firing squad, involving four renowned political journalists and Amado Cebelo, who perhaps can be best classified as a police reporter with zero moral backbone. Right off the bat, as soon as the host opened the show, he fired off the first question:

"Adamastor, do you think you will earn more in politics than selling cocaine and crack?"

Without hesitation, Maria Amélia relayed the answer directly into her uncle's earpiece. The repentant dealer faltered for a few seconds. But quickly, he regained his composure, as if mesmerized by the steady yet soft words his niece was breathing into him:

"Calm down, Uncle, relax, take a deep breath and let's go ... as we can see from the question, Amado Cebelo's perspective seems irretrievably mired in petty cynicism. But I won't shy away from the question. Yes, I will. I'm going to earn a lot more. If it's politics I'm getting into, as our dear reporter seems to know for sure. No matter which path my life takes from here, I'll earn greater respect from the community, enjoy more peaceful sleep, and ultimately, find more reasons to live."

"Months ago, when your book was still under wraps, there were rumors that you'd run for state deputy with backing from the underworld. Did you have any disagreements with your former colleagues?"

This time the question was posed by one of the political journalists.

"Rumors, speculation ... And I know there will be many more to come. I have nothing to say other than that I never intended to run for state representative. As for disagreements with my former 'colleagues,' as the esteemed journalist puts it. Yes. One and final disagreement. I'm not their colleague anymore."

"What about the secret deals with the governor?"

"What deals? If the governor has secret deals, with whomever, wouldn't it be better to address that question to him? I can assure you there are none involving me."

"Your niece is an aide to the governor. Is that just a coincidence?"

"My niece has her life. I have mine. If you don't already know, she is the daughter of the former Secretary of Administration of Rio's Penitentiary system, the recently deceased Dr. Joaquim Paranhos who the press called the Chief Jailer. A declared enemy of the drug world. This was the environment my niece was raised in, diametrically opposed to mine, when I was involved in drug dealing. Before my divorce from the drug world ... let's put it this way, we had little contact and the few times we met she always expressed her dissatisfaction with my former activities. As far as I know, she became an aide to the governor on her own steam. She holds a degree in psychiatry and is nearing the completion of her PhD. She has a degree and master's in political science and just finished law school. I'm currently very pleased to be reinforcing our family bonds. I won't conceal the fact that she was the first to read my book and she liked it very much. She never told me anything about her job as an aide to the governor. We'd never discussed politics before."

Fortunately, the makeup and bright studio lights somewhat masked Adamastor's flushed face as he echoed the firm, unemotional words fed by his niece. Maria Amélia's verbal barrage hit its mark, and at the interview's conclusion, even reporter Amado Cebelo greeted and commended Adamastor.

"Congratulations! You win! You can run for office and have my vote."

In a secluded, dark corner, Maria Amélia stowed away the transmitter resembling a cellphone and departed as discreetly as she had arrived.

23

It's rare for debut authors to sell twenty-five thousand copies on their first day in Rio and São Paulo's bookstores. A hundred-thousand in the first week. Naturally, the press played a role, with headlines and speculation highlighting the connections between the drug world and political circles. Maria Amélia realized it was time to distance herself from the governor, despite his seeming like the perfect launchpad for her uncle's career. With presidential elections in two years, the governor's name was among those most often mentioned. The idea had been for Adamastor to run directly for federal representative with the support of the presidential nominee. These plans had caused the former drug dealer sleepless nights for more than a week, intersected by nightmares in which he was placed inside tires and set alight while he heard his replacement in Chapéu Mangueira, in charge of the arsonists, scream that such should be the fate of snitches. After his third nightmare, he was taken aback at breakfast when Maria Amélia announced:

"I resigned yesterday. I am no longer the governor's aide."

"What are you telling me?"

"I resigned. Better for all of us."

"But wasn't it the plan exactly for me to run with his support? I don't understand anything anymore."

"Calm down, Uncle! We must go with the flow. Come on. The book's success is beyond all expectations. We'll soar on our own now."

"Niece, that's too risky."

"Nothing ventured, nothing gained! Now is the time to clear your name, Uncle. In the press and before the law. By now you must have read it. A pesky prosecutor is out there trying to get you. And don't be scared. All this was more than anticipated."

"Yes, but ... why move away from the governor?"

"Clearing a name is tough enough, even for someone who was just a cleaning products vendor in the favelas. Adding a politician like the governor into the mix creates a challenge beyond even witchcraft. We'll have to put some space between us, make no mistake. These meddling reporters will have to shut up. And we won't be staying neutral. When things start cooling down, we'll throw some oil on the fire. No, some gasoline."

"I don't understand!"

"You're going to expose some of the governor's scams, Uncle. I've got a pretty long list her."

"That's betrayal, Niece."

"Betrayal? You were never involved with the governor. The spotlights are for you. I'll stay in the shadow. I was his aide, not you. Don't worry about it, just be prepared."

24

"I don't get it, Amelinha."

"Like I said, Governor. I can't be your aide any longer. I'm very busy in college. I need to focus."

"But Amelinha, your future is here with me. It's time for us to embark on our great adventure to the presidential palace."

"I'll take care of my future. And all modesty aside, I do that very well. And another thing. I've asked you once, I'll do it again. Don't call me Amelinha. I don't like it. It belittles me. My full name is much prettier: Maria Amélia! Wouldn't you say so?"

"I don't understand. Are you upset with me? Did I do something?"

"What's this, Governor? You didn't do anything against me."

"And against other people?"

Maria Amélia gave a sly smile before answering:

"That's something for you to figure out. But here's one last piece of advice from an outgoing aide. You need to pay more attention to what they are cooking up in Minas Gerais and São Paulo. A trap is being set on the way to the presidential palace."

"Those two already ran out of steam. Don't worry about that. I have already secured the nomination."

"The governor is looking the wrong way. The enemy comes from within. I mean, they are much closer than you think."

"You scare me, Amelin ... Maria Amélia. Is an ally betraying me?"

"Yes. And I won't say any more. You are no fool."

"What will I do without you? We would make an invincible pair on our way to the presidential palace."

"Maybe we'll meet there? Goodbye, Governor."

The politician's look was still wistful.

"Goodbye!"

Maria Amélia told a half truth. There weren't two, but three enemies, as we already know. The governor had no idea, but the nagging suspicion the little witch had planted grew until, in a flash, it revealed the names of the two traitors: Alberto Peixoto and Afonso Figueiredo. But it couldn't be. The first was a childhood friend, they grew up together and he had always been in the governor's inner circle. He was present at all family gatherings, a companion during his youthful nights, and even now, in his escapades with young ladies selected by trusted madams. A confidant. Wait! Was there any secret between them involving the crooked paths a politician must take if he is ever to taste real power? He was the godfather of his daughter, more than that, the suspect's son was also the governor's godson. And, most of all, he was his private secretary, present at almost every meeting. The second one, born in Minas Gerais, was his Secretary of Security, in whom he had the greatest confidence. "It can't be," the governor thought. As the names sprouted in his head, almost out of nowhere, he couldn't see any explanation. However, the persistent notion kept insinuating small details that, though often overlooked, cumulatively bred distrust. For example, the childhood friend had been aloof in recent days and did not attend the inauguration of a school in Rocinha under the umbrella of the Unified Pacifying Police Force. The school was part of the governor's long game *en route* to the presidency. He advertised that he would train one teacher for every fifteen students in the state of Rio de Janeiro. This is almost the Cuban average, considered by UNESCO as one of the highest in the world. The school in Rocinha, as the governor hammered in countless speeches, would kickstart the plan. First in Rio and then in Brazil. That's what his presidential campaign managers would emphasize. Education for all, no child without school, zero illiteracy. And the friend did not attend the launch.

"Something's not right," the nagging thought would intrude again. Neither his friend nor the Secretary of Security, both of whom he had expected to make a statement emphasizing the link between the Pacifying Police Unit and the Schools-For-All Program, had done so. Why? The governor didn't have to wait long for an answer. Within a week it was plastered all over the headlines. The governor's shock was even greater when he read the name of the accuser. None other than his dear friend. And next to the newspapers in his office lay the resignation letter of his Secretary of Security. It was hard to read the newspapers scattered on the table, with his breakfast untouched. There they were, the conversations, the confidences spelled out. Everything he had said in strict confidence to his childhood friend, a native of São Paulo who had been visiting Rio's beaches since he was barely five years old. But he hadn't been able to shake off his origins. Among friends and acquaintances, and now also in the press, he was the *Paulista*, even though he had that honeyed accent loaded with *s-ess* pretending to be *x-ess*. Alberto Peixoto. The governor could hardly believe what he was reading. And on an impulse, he picked up the phone. On the other end of the line, the godmother answered. When she recognized the voice, she was at a loss for words.

"Governor?"

"That's right. Is your husband there?"

Under other circumstances, there would be a kiss here, a kiss there, inquiries about the godson, compliments about how adorable the goddaughter is, and other such pleasantries. The wife hesitated:

"Yes ... Well ..."

"Yes, or no?"

Startled, unskilled in the art of lying when caught red-handed, Daniela confirmed shyly.

"Yes."

"Please, I need to talk to him. It's urgent!"

Covering the mouthpiece, Daniela called to her husband, who appeared in a bathrobe with razor in hand. He muttered under his breath:

"Idiot, twat, did you need to say I was here?"

He took the phone from the woman's trembling hands.

"Yes, it's me."

"Is it true what I'm reading?"

"Of course, it's true."

"But we need to discuss this."

"I don't discuss these things over the phone. Besides, I don't think we have anything else to discuss."

"Just like that? Are we going to throw fifty years of friendship down the drain?"

"If the governor insists, we can make an appointment. As long as it's not in the palace. In a discreet place. Away from any aides."

"Tell me where!"

"The beach. There's drizzle forecast. That familiar spot in Barra. Just the two of us. Four p.m.?"

"I'll be there."

The scene could not have been any grayer. The cold rain had turned Barra da Tijuca into an immense wasteland devoid of a living soul, apart from the governor tormented by the specter of political exile. The angry sea, with its monotonous thunder, covered the sand in white foam, crashing in seven-foot waves. The governor arrived five minutes early, during which time he killed his double-crossing *friend* countless times in his mind. Perhaps the waves would pull him into a current, delivering him to a school of sharks. He even saw his buddy being ripped apart by a ravenous great white shark that would make Spielberg envious. But there he emerged on the sand, Alberto Peixoto, in one piece, sporting a well-groomed beard, and clad in a raincoat suitable for beachside discussions on a drizzly day. Some thirty feet from his childhood friend, the governor burst out:

"Bastard, why did you do this?"

"Let's skip the cheap insults. I could just pull a Jânio[7] and simply say 'I did it because I wanted it.'"

"Bastard!"

"I did it because you denied me access to the feeding trough filled to the brim with money from your overzealous educational project. Not one morsel, you kicked me to the curb."

"Bastard! What about the beach house?"

"Crumbs don't count."

"Bastard, filthy bastard!"

"So ... this is our discussion? Don't you have anything else to say?"

"Bastard, traitor, filthy bastard! What if I have a tape recorder on me?! Have you ever thought about that possibility? I'll take you with me to the depths of hell."

"I know you're not the type. You don't do the dirty work; you have others do it. If you had a tape recorder, you'd keep your mouth shut. You don't have one. You lack the audacity of those predestined to reach the top."

"Son of a bitch! Why? Why? I thought of you as my best friend."

"Friend, huh? But not when it comes to sharing power. My buddy up there, in the spotlight, and me here in the crowd, a private secretary, a jack-of-all-trades, an obscure follower of orders."

"This is an injustice!"

"Injustice, is it? When we were discussing the election campaign, my name came up for vice governor and you simply said you needed a name that could attract votes. You dismissed me on the spot, didn't even want to listen to me. Well, now, wouldn't you believe it! I'm running for vice. Not vice governor, but vice president. Of the Republic!"

---

[7] Jânio Quadros, president of Brazil from 31 January 1961 to 25 August 1961.

"Betrayal's price has really soared. You won't be elected! You'll end up rotting in obscurity!"

"You're the one headed for obscurity. I will be elected in the bosom of an unbeatable alliance that's taking shape as we speak. And that's not even counting the opportunist parties. There's going to be a headline-making surprise any day now. In honor of our former friendship, I'll give you the scoop. I am the vice president on the ticket of the alliance being forged between the PSDB and the PT."[8]

"Delusional bastard. Impossible!"

"Oh, impossible!? The convergence of both parties has been a long time coming. It is the new social democracy, you asshole! Anyone left out will miss the boat."

"With whose support?"

"Why, with whose support!? Bankers, industrialists, what's left of the unions. It's convergence, the only way to govern in the twenty-first Century. And you, forgotten, maybe even in jail."

"Fucking traitor, you're right, I didn't bring a tape recorder. I brought this!"

When he saw the revolver, Alberto Peixoto bolted, kicking up puffs of sand on the beach. The governor fired four shots, all of which missed their mark. He didn't miss the fifth, which he had reserved for himself, pointing the barrel of the gun at his own chest. He pulled a note from his pocket with his left hand, intending to hold it as he died.

Two stray surfers, searching for tsunami-like waves, rushed to the scene. They found the governor sprawled on his back in the sand and the secretary slumped on all fours, unable to keep running.

---

[8] The parties PT (center left) and PSDB (center right) have always been at odds in Brazilian politics.

25

On the morning after the governor reenacted Getúlio Vargas' suicide, Maria Amélia met her uncle for breakfast. When she arrived, the traditional chocolate cake breakfast he enjoyed so much was absent from the table. Instead, newspapers were scattered around, with their blaring headlines listing all the scams the governor was accused of. The editorial on Folha de São Paulo's second page maliciously added insult to injury.

Flunked for the Presidency

The state of Rio will not provide the Republic's new president. The governor failed his behavioral test. Beneath his well-publicized education plan, 'Zero Illiteracy,' lies a case study in corruption. The sums involved are certainly smaller than in the Petrolão scandal, but it is much more elaborate in its depravity. Slush funds, public bid scams, overpriced public works, and a lot of funds disappearing into the pockets of friends, sponsors, and the vultures of the infamous lobbies. Cases like the Dwarves-of-Congress and Mensalão have faded into history, while Operation Car Wash remains a divisive topic. None of them compared to the scheme set up by the governor, however. For each school built, two more could have been erected. The so glorified 'Zero Illiteracy' program is nothing but thievery. That the man behind this flunked for the post of president is not sufficient. The accusations about the shameful way he ascended to Rio's state government in collusion with his future Secretary of Communications, must also be investigated. In times like this, Justice cannot delay. The Supreme Court must act quickly to assure the nation that there is a real commitment to wash away the swamp in Brazilian politics. And the governor, if he still has a hint of scruples, should resign immediately.

Adamastor's face, as he read the newspapers, was a picture of terror. He already saw himself being fried in the same pan. Instead of walking the halls of Congress in some fancy suit, he saw himself surrounded by prison bars and the hardest criminals, not all of them convinced that he wasn't a rat. And from a clean source he knew that people from the underworld were involved in the governor's scheme, even though Adamastor himself remained out of the loop. Not entirely, by the way. The dearest niece was his impossible-to-hide link with the disgraced politician. With a taste of anxiety and wide-eyed with fright, Adamastor addressed Maria Amélia.

"Now what?"

"Now nothing. We wait for it to blow over."

"What are you saying, Niece? I'm toast. They're going to find a way to tie my name to the whole scandal. People from Rocinha are involved in this story."

"Calm down, Uncle. Scandals like these are to be expected. It seems you haven't actually read the newspapers yet. Two corpses surfaced in Rocinha. Bigwigs who until now had been considered untouchable. A crystal ball tells me they were linchpins in the entire conspiracy."

"My god, Niece! I'm in the line of fire!"

"No, you're not. You are in the line for fame, with a best-seller in hand."

"Yes, a best-seller lauded by the governor's allies."

"The intricacies of politics are a little more complicated, dearest Uncle. Right now, I am the only link with the governor that warrants greater care. Or rather, I was. I resigned in time when I sensed the bubble was about to burst. And for the press I've never been anything but a small fish. An intern, a pretty face adorning the governor's office. One trashy tabloid even insinuated I was some sort of Monica Lewinsky. Can you believe that nonsense! But there is more, something very much in our favor, so my sweet uncle won't have to lie awake at night. The foreword to your book was signed by Dr. Afonso Figueiredo, who resigned when he discovered the rot in government, to quote the newspapers. Your connection is with the healthy part, therefore, and that is the thread we are going to explore."

"What about this meddling journalist, Amado Cebelo?"

"Don't worry, he's eating out of my hand."

"What do you mean?"

"I had a talk with him. He's with us, don't worry. His type always gravitates toward the winners, even if he growls like a mad dog at the little ones, those under fire, small-time dealers, street prostitutes and politicians who lost their balance in the swings of power. He's on our side. He will be very useful in the campaign. Well, Uncle, for our best interests, I'm going to stay away for a few days. A month, perhaps. I'm travelling tomorrow. Soon, they'll forget all about the intern. The only problem is that my dearest uncle will have to fend for himself these days. Even contacts over the phone should be avoided."

"Are you suggesting that I'm already under surveillance, or wiretapped?"

"Being careful is one thing, Uncle. Paranoia is another. A month passes quickly. A strategic retreat. Interviews only about the book, about your unwavering desire to follow another path and help the needy in the favela. Don't advance any political project. Portray selflessness; you're the reformed drug dealer turned model citizen. The middle class loves that, and so do the poor. Even more so the owners of newspapers and television stations with their eye on print runs and ratings. Don't worry so much. *I shall return*, as general MacArthur said in a much worse pickle, with the bewildered face of an animal who had escaped kamikaze devils."

Maria Amélia fell silent when the Blue Danube playing on the radio was suddenly interrupted by an announcer breaking the news of the governor's suicide:

"He imitated Getúlio. He shot himself in the chest holding the note in his left hand."

And then the announcer read the note with a voice full of gravitas:

To the shame of my enemies, I leave the legacy of my death. It is of no consequence that I follow in the footsteps of the great champion of the labor movement. This will serve to mark, once again, that the enemies of the public, including individuals I thought trustworthy, will not rest until they destroy the ideals of well-intentioned people. People who

131

seek to eradicate the blight of illiteracy from our beloved Brazil and elevate our people from centuries of stagnation. I embrace death as a warrior in this ruthless battle against ignorance. History will vindicate me, now and forever.

Adamastor immediately added:

"Now what, Niece?"

"Now nothing, Uncle ..."

And she started laughing.

"What are you laughing about, dearest Niece?"

"The governor's consistency, Uncle. A demagogue even in death. He could have gotten there. He leaves behind a lesson: sometimes, curbing your greed can help you tread the path of power more safely. You must take it easy, Uncle. This alters almost nothing in our plan. We just have to wait for the headlines, the newsreels with the governor's blood and the frenzy on the Internet to die down and disappear. Like storms do."

26

The little witch was right. For a week, the suicide dominated coverage in print, broadcast, and televised media. And it flooded the Internet, of course. Who was involved in the governor's scheme? Was he wrongly accused? Was the private secretary accusing him innocent or guilty? What about the fired Secretary of Security? Did he know anything?

In the second week, as an investigative committee was set up in the Legislative Assembly, the story shifted to the inside pages, receiving only brief mentions on the front page. In the third week, only sporadic information appeared in some newspapers. By the fourth, the subject became past tense. By the fifth, past perfect. It had happened. Done! On to the next. After being sworn in, the vice president promised to clean everything up. This was mere lip service, as he too was implicated in the scheme. Progress stalled, with only the occasional report still mentioning the issue. And the show goes on!

But Maria Amélia was not done and decided it couldn't hurt to thoroughly dig through the scandal involving the governor. At the very least, there were lessons to be gleaned. She spent most of the night scouring Google for every detail on the matter.

And here it should be noted, who exactly was this now-deceased governor? After all, aside from securing a footnote in history by shooting himself in the chest like president Getúlio Vargas, the man didn't exactly distinguish himself from his predecessors. He failed to launch any significant projects, indulged in excessive demagoguery with unattainable promises, and engaged in the customary scandals that seem to be inherent on the path to power. Admittedly, the governor may have overstepped in this latter regard, perhaps even forgetting the uproar caused by Operation Car Wash. This is what Maria Amélia was trying to learn.

His name is (or was, at this point he's buried in the São João Batista Cemetery) Godofredo Francisco Campos. A man who learned the ropes dealing with the public and leading the masses as an evangelical minister. He had thought of aligning himself with former Governor Garotinho, but soon discovered that Edir Macedo's church offered better prospects. But how much better? These were prospects tainted by the label: Minister of the Kingdom of God. This exposed him to the pitchforks of a host of intellectuals, highlighting, among other things, the blatant cynicism of those claiming to operate under God's sanction. Godofredo felt he could do more than spend his life exorcising demons and invoking divine wrath for some loose change, while the big money went to the sect and its more esteemed ministers. After all, shouldn't the ultimate boss of all bad bosses set a positive example and fairly compensate his subordinates in this vale of tears?

His chance to leave his service to the Creator came during an exorcism in the sect's grand temple. He noticed a guy writing everything down on a small notebook, and from time to time, taking furtive pictures with his cell phone. "A journalist," thought the future governor, then thirty-five years old. At the end of the service, in which he purportedly expelled a demon

133

from an unemployed father, distressed because he couldn't feed his three starving children and his critical wife, Godofredo tapped the guy with the notebook on the shoulder:

"I see you're not a believer. May I know your intentions?"

The man invoked his constitutional rights as a citizen, a trendy move these days, meanwhile leaving the temple, fully aware that the officers and disciples of the divine hardly care about such things as the citizenship of mortal earthlings.

"It doesn't say anywhere that I can't write down what I want to write down and photograph whatever I please. The law is on my side."

"Take it easy, sir. I'm not looking for a fight. I know you don't believe. I know what you think of us: exploiters of people's good faith. Isn't that it? At least the man of the exorcism went home happy, relieved ..."

"And unemployed. And with no money to buy food for his children because he left what little he had here with you. How much was it?"

"Just ten reais, a mere trifle. We give a discount to those who really can't afford more."

"Is cynicism part of a minister's training? You look like a graduate."

"Spare me your insults. But here is the truth: if you want to write about the Universal church or about evangelical sects in general, I can be of real help to you. And I'll admit what you're likely already suspecting. I'm no believer myself. Maybe a little at first, just that tiny doubt I think everyone has."

"Shameless!"

"And you? You're a journalist?"

"I am, indeed. Any problems?"

"No, my friend. None at all. Do you only write about noble issues like this one? Exposing sects that exploit people's faith? Or do you mostly pen down what your boss tells you? Going around manipulating public opinion?"

They had already moved more than a block from the World Temple of Faith, walking beneath the palm trees lining Dom Helder Câmara Avenue. What would Dom Helder be thinking about this amongst the angels? Surely, he would be complaining, saying his name was not worthy of such a large avenue. Something suburban would be better suited. Edir Macedo would certainly agree. Because having a temple on an avenue with the name of a competitor in the market for souls just doesn't sound good. But why on earth are we digressing? Both men stood still for a few seconds. The journalist took in Godofredo from head to toe and was reciprocated with the same searching gaze. Finally, the journalist spoke, his voice now softened and reaching out to the interlocutor:

"All right, I think we can talk. By the way, my name is Armando Pereira."

"Pleasure to meet you, Godofredo Francisco Campos. Don't you think we should move out of this desert for a better talk?"

"Desert?"

"Yes, desert. There are even palm trees. And not one holy bar in sight on either side. Let's head back, I parked my car at the Temple. Let's go somewhere cooler. This could be a lengthy discussion, better had with a good beer in hand."

Armando Pereira accepted the invitation—which suited him well, having arrived by taxi. Both men headed to the Center, where infinitely more bars can be found than among the palm trees of Avenida Dom Helder Câmara. Perhaps it was the absurdly cold draft beer at Bar do Luiz on a sunny afternoon, with the temperature hitting ninety-nine, but the fact remains that one of the most Machiavellian plans ever produced in Brazilian politics was hatched there. As Maria Amélia scoured the Internet for details, she even felt a twinge of envy. To put it simply—not even the most conniving politician could find a flaw in it. In their conversation, Godofredo told Armando that he had long wanted to quit being a minister and go into politics. However, he didn't want to sever ties with the Universal Church. He wanted to leave through the front door, but with the necessary freedom to harvest votes from other religious and secular terrains. This is what he offered the journalist:

"I'll point you to all the Universal church's chicanery, minutes from secret meetings, how the money was raised for the construction of the replica of Solomon's Temple in São Paulo. I'll provide everything, but

135

strictly off the record. My name can't be involved. Consider me the 'Deep Throat' of your own Watergate story."

"And in return?"

"I want to be promoted. And not by you or by your newspaper. That would raise suspicion. I want to be promoted as the mentor of an advanced educational system such as has never been conceived in Brazil. Much more than Cristóvão Buarque's empty talk. When the word education comes up, it will be immediately associated with my name. Haven't you noticed? It's trending all over Facebook. Provide some education, and just like that, all of Brazil's problems are solved. I will set the stage to launch projects as soon as I get up there. Projects with the active participation of large industrialists and banks, who will be chomping at the bit to invest. Amid the applause of Facebook's mob and all those people who think they know the magic formula to deal with all the country's problems. First, here in Rio: at least one school per thousand inhabitants. Have you ever stopped to think how much money that will take? The money's out there, my friend. Enough to build schools and still leave room for a modest commission here and there—after all, none of us are made of stone."

"Aren't you worried about exposing yourself too much? After all, I am a journalist, my livelihood is revealing the scams of others."

"A calculated risk. Exposing a minor minister like me wouldn't be very profitable for you. And nothing ventured, nothing gained. Jokes aside, don't mistake me for a lunatic. However, the moment our eyes first met, I sensed our destinies were irrevocably intertwined, mine in politics, yours in professional activity. 'Take a chance,' a voice said, coming from I don't know where. I took it. Or rather, I'm taking it."

"I'm not sure how you plan to achieve this promotion of yours. That is, the promotion of this educational project I fully approve, when you said you don't want my help or that of my newspaper."

"I didn't say I don't want your help. Much to the contrary. I said: you and the newspaper shouldn't promote me in public. It needs to be done in a more indirect manner. Perhaps our public interactions should be infrequent, and if needed, even unfriendly. Let's think it through. Sleep on it. Nighttime can be a wise counselor for life-altering decisions. Don't you think?"

Armando Pereira agreed. And he wanted not just one night to think it over, but at least seven. One week was exactly the deadline for his piece on the evangelical churches. In this pressing issue, it was evident that Godofredo's assistance would be crucial. And so it was that both men arranged to meet again at the same place the following Saturday.

While browsing the Internet, Maria Amélia pieced the entire plot together from blogs of various leanings. For now, the mainstream press was silent on the matter: the hard evidence was lacking, a lot of upstanding people were involved. In the bowels of cyberspace, however, this business of supporting documents does not carry much weight. If people are saying it, it's taken as true, no questions asked. This is quickly followed by proposed punishments for robbing the republic, up to and including the death penalty. Maria Amélia's cursor hovered over the headline link: "Enough of the Shamelessness! The Full Truth Behind the Governor's Suicide." The text read:

Governor Godofredo Francisco Campos' scamming and swindling has been going on for a long time. It dates back to at least his time as a minister of the Universal Church of the Kingdom of God. And although he tried every means to hide this period of his life, he never broke entirely with the sect created by Mr. Edir Macedo. Indeed, the votes from the Universal Church, where the governor likely honed his skills in deception, are not to be overlooked. Today, we know from a reputable source that the governor, knowing full well of the risks, stepped into the world of politics through a Machiavellian deal struck with journalist Armando Pereira when he was writing a four-page report denouncing Universal's misdeeds in manipulating its faithful. And what do you know! The main data, the inside information, the details about the secret meetings, were provided to the journalist by none other than future governor Godofredo Francisco Campos. And in return for what, you may ask? For there appears to be no public connection between the governor and the journalist. On the contrary, Armando Pereira never wrote a single sentence praising the governor and has always worked, as we all know, for his staunchest opposition newspaper. Here we reach the epicenter of what could well be the most devious deal known in Brazilian politics, the plot hatched between both men: Godofredo would slip all the information about the Kingdom of God to Armando, and in return, he would activate a journalist friend at another newspaper to promote the future governor and his grandiose School-for-All plan. Antonio Felisberto, Armando's friend, worked hard on the task entrusted to him and was royally rewarded as Secretary of Communications, as we all know. Now, he is a defendant in the corruption case surrounding the Zero Illiteracy plan. We hope justice won't be delayed, as it often is when the criminal has been feasting at the table of the powerful.

Sex was at the heart of the rumors that led to the plot's collapse. What a surprise! Armando Pereira didn't breathe a word about the exchange of favors, not to his wife, his children, or anyone else. And he had warned his partner-in-crime at the time:

"Listen, Felisberto. Keep your mouth shut! I mean completely sealed, not a word to anyone! Not even to our beloved Ana. Not that I doubt her. But secrets of this size—you must know this as a journalist—cannot leave the circle of the people involved. To no one. Get that through your head."

"Leave it to me," Felisberto replied, as serious as if he were Rio's top expert in profiteering.

Yet, sure enough, he spilled the beans. Not to Dona Ana, the wife, who indeed only learned of her husband's misdoings after the governor's crazy act splattered everything on the front pages and evening news. Instead, it was in utter shamelessness, in a motel bed with three prostitutes—Estela, Margarida and Conceição—that Antônio Felisberto began speaking to himself, lulled by the whiskey cut with three lines of cocaine:

"We're geniuses. Me and my friend Armando planned the perfect con."

He realized he wasn't just talking to himself when one of the prostitutes asked:

"What con would that be, my hot piece of ass?"

The flattery was his undoing. It broke down all the journalist's defenses, who blurted out the plan to an audience of three prostitutes. Including Margarida, a law student who, naturally, had posed the question.

Estela and Conceição didn't even hear what the journalist had said in his pasty drunken voice, committed as they were to getting the secretary off, one with her hands, the other with her mouth. But not Margarida. Not only did she listen carefully to everything, but she also continued her questioning:

"He would receive the information, but it was you who promoted the governor?"

"Exactly, girl. But never mind. It's just political stuff, boring really. Now these boobs, these are exciting. I'm hungry, let me suck on them."

"You can suckle, honey. But tell me more. Is this how my lover got into the communications department?"

Something clicked in Felisberto's head. A belated click. The possibility of a politicized prostitute had not crossed his mind. Where had anyone heard of such a thing?

On the following Monday, his secretary entered to inform him that his new assistant was waiting.

"New assistant?"

"Yes, a Miss Madalena Feijó de Almeida."

"I've never heard of this person."

"Yes, you did, secretary. It's all settled."

It was she, Margarida, who didn't wait for a response and entered his office. Felisberto's mouth dropped open, but he quickly recovered, being himself a master of blackmail. To the secretary he said:

"You can go. And close the door."

Silence ensued as Margarida, or rather, Madalena, approached the secretary. She then sat comfortably in the armchair opposite the now apprehensive Felisberto.

"What do you want?"

"I've already said it, I'll be your assistant."

"My assistant, how exactly? You're skilled in something other than ..."

"Whoring? Is that what you mean? I am, indeed, even if in matters of depravity you know more than I do, don't you? For your government, I'm in my final year of law school, and I've documented everything."

"But you have no proof. The word of a prostitute against that of a journalist and now Communications Secretary."

"Do you want to take that risk? The scandal will be beneficial to me, promotion, I don't care. For you ... And what's more, it's not the word of one prostitute. There are three of us, remember? After all, you won't settle for just one, will you? But let's not lower ourselves. I don't ask for a lot. The fictitious position of Assistant so that I may promote myself as a future lawyer. Isn't that how whoring works in the political world?"

"What about the others?"

"The others are worldly women, professionals, they barely heard what you said. But don't get any ideas, they are my friends, accomplices, and they will confirm anything I say against you. You, not sir! That's how I'll address you privately, to constantly remind you that we're equals in both politics and in whoring. In public, you may be mister secretary, or the most dignified secretary, Dr. Felisberto, whatever you see fit."

The pact worked smoothly until the governor's suicide. If Dona Ana were to be jealous, it wouldn't be of Madalena. Her relations with Felisberto had become professional, or whatever you want to call it. The secretary never again felt an ounce of lust for his privileged assistant, who, in turn, was building her place in the sun in the world of politics and law. However, when the headlines about the governor's suicide multiplied, Madalena thought the best strategy was to throw more shit at the fan. And that's what she downright did! It was her blog spilling the beans on the governor's deal with both journalists. It also revealed new secrets she learned during her tenure as an assistant. She was spinning a web, ensuring it was designed only to ensnare the big fish. As a minnow, she should be able to escape easily. Madalena signed her blog with the same pseudonym of her working girl days, Margarida.

To those scrutinizing the situation and hunting the sharks funneling money from the public purse, Maria Amélia was also nothing more than small fry in this entire affair. Fleeing from these treacherous waters, the little witch was pleased to blend business with pleasure. She had long wanted to visit the city of the other Fiinha, the one we call Fiinha the First. She boarded a plane to Belo Horizonte, and from there it was an almost four-hour bus ride to Santo Antônio das Tabocas. It was no longer the city described in Tarquínio's account. It had sprouted vertically. Numerous seven- to ten-story buildings had risen, despite the abundant fields available for horizontal expansion. 'Onwards and upwards' seemed to be the new motto. Maria Amélia stayed on the seventh floor of the Hotel Central, from where she could see all the contours of the city. She responded to the receptionist's curious glances by explaining that she was conducting research for her university about the growth of the cities of the Midwest of the state of Minas Gerais because of the discovery of vast natural gas reserves in the São Francisco River basin. Of course, she said nothing about her actual biological father, even though he was already forgotten, remembered only by people past their sixties. It would do no good explaining troubled origins. Her credentials as a psychiatrist, a Doctor of Political Science, and a recent law graduate were sufficient. That was the reason, or the excuse, to visit the city. She told her interlocutors she planned to investigate the new legal and psychological intricacies arising from the sudden discovery of natural gas. Its effect on a city where, until a few decades ago, farmers were jokingly referred to as 'cow gigolos.' Santo Antônio das Tabocas remained one of the state's largest milk producers, and its braided cheese was renowned even in São Paulo and Rio de Janeiro.

The brief conversation with the hotel receptionist was all it took for the entire city to become aware of Maria Amélia's presence by the next day, the girl who had come to study the impact of the discovery of natural gas. Proof that the city was in the national spotlight, attracting scholars from Rio de Janeiro, no longer a provincial backwater in Minas Gerais. Santo Antônio das Tabocas' stock was rising in the country's political and economic scene. Such things, such dreams as govern the life of small towns in the interior.

141

By the next morning, the hotel reception had already received messages from the mayor and two councilors interested in talking to the researcher. Maria Amélia, who never engaged in anything without a plan, was prepared. She had all the necessary paperwork from the university to carry out the study. The mayor, the first to meet with her, was eager to know:

"Legal and psychological impact?"

"Exactly, Mayor. Business will now be conducted on another level. Petrobras and its partners, predominantly foreign firms, always have at least three lawyers present at any negotiation table. I doubt the local farmers, whose land will be expropriated for drilling, are accustomed to such practices. It is a new way of doing things and the whole city is entering a new era. All these changes are bound to have a significant psychological impact on the community. Of course, comparing this natural gas discovery in the São Francisco Basin to the California gold rush of the mid-nineteenth century is a bit of an exaggeration. In that case, the town of Sutter's Mill was virtually overrun by 300,000 gold seekers practically overnight, shortly after the discovery of the reserves was announced in 1848. And long before that, as you know, we had a gold rush right here in Minas Gerais, right at the beginning of the eighteenth century. Ouro Preto, Vila Rica, São João del-Rei and all the cities in the region are products of that era. It spawned a failed revolt by intellectuals and poets, ending with the hanging of a scapegoated dentist. And before that there was even war, the War of the Emboabas[9], as you're undoubtedly aware."

"Yes, yes," the mayor confirmed.

Maria Amélia smiled, before continuing:

"We are not expecting any wars or rebellions, of course. But a struggle is inevitable, no question about it. There are numerous interests at play. Additionally, there's the environmental impact, the pipeline construction, the drilling operations, and the influx of predominantly foreign technicians. I am almost certain that Santo Antônio das Tabocas won't be the same, Mayor."

---

[9] Armed conflict following the discovery of gold in the region now occupied by the state of Minas Gerais, in 1709.

Maria Amélia's words left a profound impression on the politician. That same week, he convened a meeting with the city councilors to discuss the much anticipated and highly sought-after impact.

As previously said, Maria Amélia mixed business with pleasure during her visit to Santo Antônio das Tabocas. The pleasure, of course, lay in exploring the land of Tarquinio and Fiinha the First, while simultaneously escaping the commotion in Rio de Janeiro. And the business? A *tête-à-tête* with the author of the blog that had exposed the rot in the governor's office at about 500 miles from its epicenter. Mary Amélia didn't have a shred of doubt that Madalena and Margarida were the same person. That's right, Madalena had also fled Rio's raging tide to Santo Antônio das Tabocas. Simply one more of those coincidences that smoothed Maria Amélia's way.

To the poor mortals of the town, Madalena was still the intellectually gifted girl who had made it in the hard battle for success, earning the privileged status of Assistant to a Secretary of Communications. Beautiful and adept at charming everyone, regardless of their looks, she had little trouble convincing friends and relatives that she had fallen into the secretary's clutches after passing a competitive examination at her law school with flying colors. She hadn't known about anything, God was her witness, she swore to her sister and friends, adding that she did not want to talk about it anymore, that she was in Santo Antônio das Tabocas precisely to escape the filthy swamp that had formed around him.

"A filthy swamp. And the secretary with that innocent boy face. I was already getting suspicious. He is a conman and, just between us, a womanizer like no other. He tried to make a move on me, but I didn't give him an inch. 'Get away from me because I know Dona Ana very well and respect her. That's not what I'm here for.' That's exactly what I told him the first and last time he came up to me with his loose hands. He never tried again. Certainly not with me!"

Before traveling to Santo Antônio das Tabocas, Maria Amélia reread Margarida's blog texts denouncing the Machiavellian scheme between the governor and both journalists, making sure that the information it contained couldn't be fruit of a fertile imagination, as no hard evidence was presented. Yet many facts and dates aligned with what she already knew in her privileged role as the governor's aide. It's someone from the inner circle, deeply involved in the whole affair—such were the whispers that would echo in the braided girl's dreams, waking her up in the morning:

"There must be some spectacular perversion at play."

Maria Amélia was selected as the governor's aide due to her exceptional merit and extraordinary talent. Madalena, merely a slightly above-average law student, had to have some ulterior reason behind her sudden hiring as an assistant. And this "something else," the voices in Maria Amélia's head would suggest, was tied to some form of perversion. Information of this caliber is not entrusted to aides, not even to aides endowed with talents found in few mortals. It is in revelry, in booze and sex, that many people open their mouths and say what they're not supposed to say. Maria Amélia printed a photo of Madalena and did some research in the vast fields of Rio de Janeiro's debauchery. She quickly located Madame Xavier's girls, and thus, the participants in the secretary's orgy. Two total simpletons. They were hardly aware of the governor's suicide, didn't read newspapers, and only followed soap opera gossip. Maria Amélia showed them the photo:

"You know her?"

"But of course. That is Margarida. Did something happen to her?"

"No, nothing happened. Don't worry and thank you very much."

Maria Amélia called Madalena's apartment immediately.

"Who is it? She is not here right now."

"I'm a friend and colleague, Maria Amélia. I need to speak to her urgently. We're in the same boat. I'm the governor's former aide."

Revealing herself to an unfamiliar voice was a calculated risk. But it also served to lend urgency to her call. On the other end, Madalena/Margarida's friend, who was looking after the apartment, hesitated briefly before responding:

"Madalena went on a trip ..."

"Where to?"

"I don't know, I think to her hometown in Minas Gerais."

"Ah, yes, the town with the church in the central square?"

"Santo Antônio das Tabocas."

"Thank you very much."

27

The beauty of small towns—or medium-sized ones, so as not to hurt sensibilities—is that you don't need to make appointments. You practically stumble on familiar people. And in the case of passing strangers, it's almost impossible not to bump into them. Which is how Maria Amélia didn't have to wait more than two days to run into Madalena, in the Choperia Central, the hottest spot around. Both women knew each other by sight, because the narrow circle of power is also a small town. Madalena got up to meet the former aide to the governor:

"I suppose it's not a coincidence you're here."

Maria Amélia smiled back and said:

"We need to talk. But not here with all the noise and prying ears. Introduce me to your friends first so we don't let on."

The prying ears belonged to the group of more than ten people, clustered around two tables, among whom Madalena was seated.

"Hi, guys, this is Maria Amélia. My friend from Rio de Janeiro."

"Oh, sit with us, pull up a chair ... Oh, aren't you the gas research girl?"

Maria Amélia accepted the invitation of the guy who seemed the most talkative and sat down beside him, right in front of Madalena.

"Beer?"

Maria Amélia nodded, and the guy signaled the waiter, who quickly brought over a glass of beer, topped with the recommended two fingers of foam. The big mouth continued:

"So, what a coincidence! You're our dear Madalena's friend over in Rio de Janeiro. Are you colleagues? You work together? Tell us about the wonderful city. I've never been. Can't wait to go."

Talkative, stupid, out of the loop on current events, Maria Amélia concluded about the cretin. Her concern was with another subject, twenty-eight to thirty, sitting next to Madalena and giving the little witch an inquisitive look through his glasses. She answered big mouth:

"Yeah, we're friends. It's been a long time since Madalena asked me to come and meet Santo Antônio das Tabocas. I heard she was here, so I decided to include your city in my research on the impact of the discovery of natural gas in the San Francisco Basin. It is very nice when you can mix business with pleasure!"

The bespectacled guy maintained a skeptical demeanor—no, it was more than that; he looked suspicious, almost incredulous. Maria Amélia decided to tease, nodded in his direction and asked Madalena:

"Is that your boyfriend?"

"What? Me dating Bartolomeu! Bartolomeu dates books. He is the city's intellectual. Can't you see?"

He attempted a smile, but his frown betrayed his dislike. As he stood up, he said:

"Madalena is right. My loves are calling me, and with them a pile of exams to correct. I have to go. Nice to meet you."

"It was my pleasure," Maria Amélia replied extending her hand.

Bartolomeu, the town's high school history teacher, clearly doubted the coincidence of the two women's meeting. As an avid reader of all the Carioca newspapers online, he was well aware of their activities in Rio de Janeiro. Maria Amélia realized the need for a private meeting with him, away from the distractions of drinks and idle chatter. The priority, however, the reason for the trip, was the private get-together with Madalena. After half an hour of pleasantries, she said she also had a certain love for books and work, so she needed to go back to the hotel. As she took her leave, she turned to Madalena and said:

"Stop by the hotel for coffee. Ten o'clock. Is that good for you?"

"Sure."

The morning was stuffy, but Maria Amélia dressed elegantly regardless. A blue silk ensemble down to the knees and fastened by a bow behind the neck. An attire for a breakfast at a five-star hotel. Madalena didn't dress down either, arriving in a gray taffeta dress with a plunging neckline and a flower-embroidered belt. Neither seemed to want to appear inferior to the other, in any aspect. And let there be no doubt. On a first date, when superficialities are the first things to be judged, clothing is essential. Witches know this intuitively, and Madalena was wasting her time on a competition she'd already lost. Let's see.

"Phew, so hot, worse than Rio, isn't it? Sit down, please. I'll just have some juice and fruit. I've long since cut bread from my diet. Wheat is poison, didn't you know? You want coffee?"

"No thanks. The regional coffee ... you wouldn't believe it. It's horrible! They brew it with a lot of sugar directly in the water, then strain it through a cloth filter that's been used multiple times. Of course, they have coffee without sugar here at the hotel. They use paper filters or those espresso machines or whatever. But even so, I won't drink it. I've long since given up on coffee."

"We're tied. So have I."

A few seconds of silence followed. It was apparent that both were trying to stretch the meeting as much as possible, to discover common tastes, things like that, the test of superficialities. One could almost say both attempted to establish a friendship. But this didn't prevent Maria Amélia from resuming the conversation after the brief silence, cutting to the chase, showing she was in control.

"So, Margarida, were you the one who hammered the final nail into the coffin of those notable political corpses in Rio de Janeiro?"

Madalena was visibly startled, wide-eyed, her mouth half open. Maria Amélia continued:

"No need for that frightened look. We both know you're Margarida, the blogger, and the one who overheard the communications secretary's confession."

"You're mistaken. My name is Madalena!"

"Keep your voice down. And try to smile, will you? Unless you want to cause a scene? Let's have a serious talk. I've already figured everything

147

out. I talked to your two colleagues of that meeting with the secretary. Madame Xavier filled me in. I'm not here to judge. In fact, I must admit I'm somewhat admiring."

"But, but ..."

"There are no buts. I mean, there are problems, sure, for both of us, and I think coordinated action can only be to our benefit."

"I'm respected here in town. What you're saying can destroy me."

"My dear Madalena, what I am saying can't destroy you. It's what you did that could be your downfall. I don't have the slightest intention of broadcasting what you do or don't do in Rio de Janeiro. This is the point: finding the best way to get us both unscathed out of this whole mess. No, more than that—we can capitalize on this situation."

"I don't see how ..."

"We've reached a place of respect in the political world, my dear. We are young and we have earned a place in the sun, among the powerful. That counts on a resume. Soon enough, this scandal will fade from memory, save for some politicians—mostly those with ulterior motives—who are always in search of capable aides. Make no mistake, we will be at the top of that list."

"Did you learn, or were you born cynical?"

"That jibe was unnecessary, my dear. I'd advise you not to go down that road with me. I am proposing we work together not only to disentangle ourselves from the scandal, but regarding our future among the powerful. Pardon my bluntness, but you don't want to spend the rest of your life as an ambulance chaser, do you?"

Madalena did not answer, stunned by her interlocutor. Maria Amélia continued:

"Well, we've already done the most important thing intuitively. We moved away from the scandal's epicenter. But that is not enough. Margarida must remain active, from here, without giving the game away. On her blog. When I said nail in the coffin it was more than figure of speech. The communications secretary and his journalist friend must be destroyed once and for all in their political and professional lives. No room for returns. The secretary in jail, Armando Pereira in total, complete and definitive ostracism. Spat out by his colleagues, banned from newsrooms. Indeed, a *requiem in pace* should be written on the governor's grave, not only for him, but for the whole case. The Pirate ship has sunk into the deep, leaving us, the survivors, with the treasure map. What do you think?"

"Oh, my God!"

"Yes, my God. Do you agree to join forces?"

Madalena signaled yes with a nod of the head, almost in shock. Maria Amélia, however, had one more question to ask:

"And the guy with glasses, Bartolomeu, is he your boyfriend after all?"

Madalena, snapping back to reality, quickly replied:

"Bartolomeu Esperidião, my boyfriend? Come on!"

"Bartolomeu what?"

"Esperidião. A traditional family here in town."

"So traditional one of its worthy representatives is serving a life sentence in Rio de Janeiro."

"Dear God, even that you know? Bartolomeu is his nephew."

"I want to meet him. As soon as possible. Today, for example. You can arrange that for me, can't you?"

28

It is time to find out how things are going in Rio de Janeiro. For example, how is Adamastor coping with the nosy journalists and opportunistic politicians constantly taking shots at him. But first, some more details on the governor's funeral. A dreadful affair—though, inevitably, every burial has a hint of terror. As Hemingway quoted John Donne: "ask not for whom the bell tolls." In the governor's case, there were no bells, no speeches, no litanies, and no candles. The church denies such rites to those who have committed suicide and politicians who have fallen from grace. Only a bit of weeping from the widow and some friends, the usual volunteers for the role of mourners. Hardly twenty people accompanied the coffin on a cart pushed by two employees dressed in black. The heavy silence of the ninety-degree afternoon was broken only by sobs and footsteps. The dead body was already begging for the dirt, despite having spent more than five hours in a morgue drawer at fourteen degrees. It had been released at four in the afternoon and the family thought it best to have the burial on the same day, at five-thirty, taking advantage of the last rays of pollution-blurred sunlight on the horizon. The governor's wake was gloomy. Politicians had fled from him as the devil from the cross, though some say the cross and the devil's spit make an inseparable pair. In addition to some family, because many opted not to show their faces, a group of journalists and photographers was present. And they gave the impression to be looking for material for the crime section. Absent were any former secretaries or protégés, perfectly exemplifying J. G. de Araújo Jorge's verse:

All friends are like migratory birds:
If the weather is good, they come.
If the weather is bad, they go.

Not a word, not a blessing was heard when the coffin made its final thump on the grave's bottom. Not one politician was there to endorse, however feebly, the few virtues the governor may have possessed in his fifty-three years of life. The widow, however, tossed in a red rose she had picked from the garden, where the governor used to spend his Sunday afternoons. His hobby, taking care of rose bushes. Two gravediggers completed the work, filling the six-feet deep rectangle. The governor was dead and had been buried for good, as the news would tell. The uproar, the harassment of the TV-reporters, and the tabloids' frenzy suggested that the politics section was overshadowed by crime news. The whole thing would last maybe a week, perhaps a little longer. But soon everyone would be satiated with the governor's corpse. The investigations into the Zero Illiteracy project scandal and the reporting on the time-consuming work of an investigative commission of the Legislative Assembly would be relegated to the inside pages. The little witch's best predictions were unfolding as she waited for the governor's corpse to be forgotten once and for all, circling in the higher spheres of Santo Antônio das Tabocas and scheming with Madalena to extricate herself from the whole imbroglio, taking as much advantage as possible.

And Adamastor? He managed well, thanks to his experience gained on the hill and the lessons from his niece. A pesty reporter from the seven o'clock news snagged the first exclusive interview with the reformed drug dealer. And she came in hot, spewing venom from her doll's mouth with the freshness of her twenty-five years:

"And what happens now with your connections with the governor and the Zero Illiteracy bribe gang?"

"Connections? Never had them. Who put that in your head?"

"Now, Mr. Adamastor, your book was prefaced by the secretary of security. Isn't that a connection?"

"As far as I know, Dr. Afonso Figueiredo resigned as soon as he learned of the misdeeds plaguing the government. The book simply caught his interest because he has similar ideas to mine, not the same, of course. But it's about a new approach to drugs. Haven't you seen the acclaimed UN report and the numerous interviews with former President FHC on this topic? Moreover, the former secretary's character is spotless."

"Okay, then how did the book end up in his hands? Surely with the assistance of your niece, who was an aide to the governor."

"I expected these insinuations from you. Maria Amélia, my niece, was an innocent victim of the governor's manipulations. And not just her. Until recently, the TV-channel you work for was defending the Zero Illiteracy project tooth and nail. These are things that excite young people. But I can assure you, at no time did I use my niece's services to get closer to the government. Even because she was shocked when she heard I was the Adamastor of Chapéu Mangueira. She never approved of my previous life. True, she was very pleased when she read the original manuscripts

151

and fully approved of my plans to change my life's course. But I was the one who took the risk of sending the original manuscript to the secretary before its publication. I knew I was treading on a minefield, and I didn't want him to write the foreword, but rather to give his opinion on the potential risks. As you know, it was in his power to ask for my arrest. That's the gamble I took. The foreword was a big surprise to me. You can ask Dr. Afonso Figueiredo."

"That is hard to swallow."

"Your problem, Miss. My conscience is clear. The mistakes I've made in my life are laid out in the book. I have no reason to lie."

"Do you intend to run for anything? City Council? Congress? State or Federal?"

"What an imagination you have! I'm still putting my life back together. Whatever I earn from copyright will go toward starting a business. A law firm, perhaps. You may not know this, but I have a degree and passed the bar."

"No political intentions?"

"Not now, no. As I said, I'm getting my life together. I left one world. I'm entering another."

The reporter gave up, thanked him for the interview, and motioned to the cameraman to stop recording. As she was leaving, she turned, smiled, and threw one last question at the ex-drug dealer:

"You swear you told the truth?"

"The truth, and nothing but the truth."

And he handed her his new business card, which read:

"Adamastor Leite Feitosa - Lawyer and Writer"

In Santo Antônio das Tabocas, Maria Amélia did not wait for Madalena to set up a date or casual meeting with Bartolomeu. She went to see him on the same day at the school where he taught. He was dismayed to see the braided girl at the entrance of the building and was already moving toward his bicycle when she approached him.

"Hey, I want to speak to you. We need to talk."

"Yes, but ... talk about what?"

"Are you Tarquínio Esperidião's nephew?"

"Yes, I am. Is that a problem? I've no involvement in what he did or didn't do."

"What if I tell you we're cousins? Just between us, no one else in town needs to know that. Not even Madalena. I'm Tarquínio Esperidião's daughter."

"You, his daughter? I'm sorry, but I already looked you up. Your father is Rio's former Secretary of Penitentiary Administration."

"A half-truth, dear cousin. Joaquim Paranhos Nogueira was my adoptive father. But my real, biological father is Tarquínio Esperidião."

"No way."

"And why not? I'm really his daughter. And therefore, your cousin."

"Nice to meet you then, cousin. But so, what?"

"Did you grow to be this cranky, or were you born like it? You sound just like my dad!"

"Miss Maria Amélia. It's Maria Amélia, right? I'm extremely busy. It's the exam season, and I really don't have time to spare. And I don't think you do either. You're doing research on ... what is it again?"

Maria Amélia fixed her gray eyes on the rude cousin and answered only after a few seconds, as if amending the words:

"The legal and psychological impact of the discovery of natural gas in the São Francisco Valley. But that's not what I want to discuss with you. I'm interested in your family. Anyway, in our family. Could I speak to a brother or sister of my father? Is anyone still alive?"

"One sister lives. My father, though younger than her, died three years ago. But what do you care to know? My uncle's life is practically an open book because of how much they've written about him when he committed the triple homicide. He even wrote a bizarre book himself. You've probably read it. I didn't waste my time on it; I've just heard about it. I don't know what Aunt Maria Amélia could add. That's right, Maria Amélia, the same name as yours. Coincidence."

"Yeah right, coincidence! Surely you know my father had an aunt with the same name who died at the beginning of the last century. So, yes, I'm more than interested in talking to my aunt, *our* aunt, Maria Amélia."

"What for? It's best to leave the dead alone and let convicted murderers serve their sentences."

"Bartolomeu, Bartolomeu! Your coldness, your pretended indifference, do not affect me in the least. You want to hide the excitement of having found a cousin with the same name as your aunt. And you play the role miserably. My father, your uncle, is also an object of study for me, psychiatrist that I am. Did you know he believes to this day that he was possessed by the other Maria Amélia, the one who had her chest blown out, when he had sex with my mother? And that I'm the product of that fuck?"

"That's complete insanity. My uncle is insane. He's always been. And so are you if you believe such nonsense. He should be in a mental institution, not a penitentiary."

"An interlinking insanity. Intertwining threads in a quilt woven with human lives. More than ever, I must talk to your aunt, my namesake."

"She's even crazier than he is, crazier than Tarquínio Esperidião. It's a waste of your time."

Maria Amélia's eyes shone.

"What do you mean?"

"Crazy. We've even thought about having her committed. She was shocked by Tarquínio's book. She thinks he's right, that he was possessed, like you just said ... when ... never mind."

"When what?"

"You just said it yourself. When he slept with the nurse who bore his daughter. I've never heard more nonsense. She went to all the spiritism centers around, even visited macumba sessions. She says she must contact her dead aunt. An obsession that has lasted almost a century."

"Take me to your aunt right now!"

A command, reinforced by her gaze, demanding instant obedience, as if she were the incarnation of Hera, with a thousand promises of revenge should it be ignored.

"Whatever you want. Follow me."

They walked along a poorly paved street, full of potholes caused by the rain. Bartolomeu quietly, pushing his bike, Maria Amélia imposing, commanding the show.

The house was not far from the center, one of the few still standing in the old style of the 1930s or 1940s. Next to it, a new building was already rising, and it was clear that the property would not withstand the wrath of the construction companies for long. Especially now, driven by the money promised by the natural gas reserves. Two windows faced the street, and a porch was on the left side. At the end of it, the front door. A typical farmer's residence from the last century, used mainly for weekends. The rest of the time was passed in the main farmhouse, which was usually bigger and more ventilated. In silence, Bartolomeu parked his bicycle, and they entered the porch through a small gate. There was no doorbell. Bartolomeu knocked on the door four times. A shuffling of slippers and a faint voice could be heard, already very close:

"Who is it?"

"It's Bartolomeu, Aunt. I have a visitor for you."

She opened the door and couldn't say a word. Just a deep sigh escaped her, as if she'd seen a ghost. Maria Amélia gazed at her with a knowing, sly smile, fully aware of why the other was so shaken. And she did more. She caressed the braids that fell over her shoulders.

If not for Bartolomeu's prompt intervention, Maria Amélia the Third would have collapsed right there in the doorway. Even faded saffron couldn't match the shade of yellow that spread across the woman's face. The nephew led her to the sofa in the living room and leaned her head against a pillow. Then he went to the kitchen to get a glass of water. Maria Amélia—perhaps out of malice—approached her, took her icy hands into hers, and looked at her with her gray eyes. The sickly figure let out another sigh.

"Don't be so shocked, aunt. Everything will be for the best. I'm here to protect you."

155

She nestled up next to her, gently shifting the old woman's head from the pillow to her shoulder, using her left hand, because with the right she took her aunt's hand and placed it on one of her braids. This is how Bartolomeu found the two, in a tender embrace, as old friends meeting after a prolonged absence.

"Your water, Aunt."

"No need, it's over."

The voice weak, but calm.

Maria Amélia shot the order to her cousin:

"Go away."

And both women remained there in total silence for more than half an hour. For one, it was a reunion with the aunt who had her chest ripped open by a 16-gauge shotgun blast so many, many years ago. The resemblance was incredible, to the smallest details. The braids, the gray eyes, even the dimple on the chin matched the blown-up photo framed in front of them. Even Bartolomeu, always incredulous, felt a little shiver when he first compared the picture on the wall to the girl hugging his aunt. For Maria Amélia, the one leading the show, this was another source of information in the search of her origins. She felt she had to pay another visit to Tarquínio Esperidão, taking with her the copy of the photo of the Maria Amélia who died so many years ago. The similarity was simply striking, a seasoned expert wouldn't have found any discrepancy between the facial features of Maria Amélia the First of the early twentieth century and the current one. This time, it wouldn't be a confrontational meeting with her father like before; it would be a family reunion, without the adoptive mother knowing. Maria Amélia's practical mind told her that things should not be confused, mixed up. Her past and her origins on the one hand, and her social and political pretensions on the other. The adoptive mother, navigating the superficiality of Rio's socialites, didn't need to know anything. Only a few chosen people should know. It wouldn't be hard to convince the cousin to keep the events of the afternoon a secret. It was in his interest, so as not to soil his fame as someone who had always adopted the *show-me-the-scientific-proof and-*

I'll-believe-it posture. If the aunt spoke, it would merely be the subject of further ridicule. No one gets rid of the label 'crazy' once its given. Lastly, Maria Amélia was eager to discuss her striking resemblance to the woman in the photo with another person: her colleague, psychiatrist Maria da Anunciação.

29

The meeting with her aunt was a fortunate coincidence, not something Maria Amélia had planned for. She had already read Tarquínio's book, but she thought it was pure madness. At that time, she was only eleven years old. She had postponed a more detailed study of the subject, planning to undertake it with Dr. Maria da Anunciação later. Now she was focused on *moving up in life*. For her, moving up meant getting closer to the center of power, infiltrating it if possible, and with a bit of luck, taking control. Perhaps this drive is hardwired into the human brain, a reflection of the innate survival instincts common to all species.

Perhaps Maria Amélia's greatest asset in pursuing her goals was her ability to keep things separate. The serendipitous discovery of her aunt and the murdered woman's portrait wouldn't derail her main plan, set in motion when she decided to travel to Santo Antônio das Tabocas: getting rid of the former Secretary of Communications and others implicated in the governor's transgressions who could sully her name. The anonymous and unsubstantiated accusations on Margarida's blog would serve only to cause a stir online, but in court or in Legislative Assembly investigations, they held little weight. She thought of suggesting to Madalena that she ask her two colleagues in the secretary's orgy to come out as witnesses against the journalist. They would be properly instructed in that regard. But what about the third prostitute? The accusations whirling around the Internet—Margarida's blog alone had reached five- thousand daily hits—mentioned three, by their aliases, of course. A major concern was the significant possibility that the former secretary had recorded Madalena's act of blackmail. In the Communications Department, he was notorious for recording everything in his office. In despair, ruined, the former secretary could well drag the up-and-coming lawyer out of pure spite with him into political and professional death. If such a recording existed, it would have to be found and destroyed. After that was done, the plan would be this: in addition to both colleagues, Madalena would have to convince a third in Madame Xavier's class to play her part. The testimony would be meticulously rehearsed under Maria Amélia's supervision and detailed guidance throughout. Three against one. No one would believe that such a competent and well-liked girl, known for her irreproachable behavior and modest attire at work, could be the prostitute the former secretary was talking about.

But the voice? Nowadays, even the smallest details can be isolated—the timbre, the pitch, the tone, and who knows what else. Even with sound editors that can be downloaded for free on the Internet. A voice can be like a fingerprint. Additionally, finding a prostitute from Madame Xavier's collection with the same allure as the model would be challenging. The plan could only go ahead if they could prove that Madalena's conversation with the secretary hadn't been recorded. And if it had, they would have to find a way to destroy it.

With all this on her mind, Maria Amélia set up a new meeting with Madalena on a bench under a pergola's shade in the town's central square. Even if an unexpected eavesdropper showed up—as they inevitably do at the worst times—the open setting meant they could easily spot any nosy onlookers approaching. If someone did come along, all they had to do was change the subject, make some small talk. And there was no danger of either running out of repertoire. Maria Amélia was first to arrive. She had scarcely opened Tarquínio's book—a copy borrowed from her aunt—when she saw Madalena coming. She had planned to reread some passages of the story, especially the one where Tarquínio describes that his body was possessed by the spirit of the murdered woman.

"Hey," Madalena said, sitting down next to Maria Amélia.

"Hey there. I spent a large part of last night figuring out how we can get rid of the former secretary, ideally without a scratch. You most of all. And this is the question: were you being recorded when you blackmailed that prick? I mean, is there any way you can confirm this? If you were, our priority is to destroy the recording."

"I already thought about that. In fact, the idea torments me. It's quite likely. He had a habit of recording everything in his office."

"Don't you have a way to check?"

"I don't know. I've become friends with his private secretary, Maria Aparecida. I really helped her with the exams she was taking to be a social worker. Do you think I should reach out to her?"

"Elementary, my dear Watson. Right now. Do you have her phone? Even better, her cell?"

"I do."

"Well, call and make an appointment. Let's go back to Rio de Janeiro. I'll finish the research today and we'll return tomorrow. At different times, under no circumstance on the same bus. And we go back incognito. We'll stay in hotels for a week. Different ones, of course. Hotels in the center or in Gloria or Catete, as far away from the fervor as possible. Tell Maria Aparecida to keep your conversation confidential. She'll understand. She must be nervous herself about what may spill onto her."

Mary Amélia caught the seven thirty a.m. bus, and Madalena took the one at three p.m. The former went to a simple three-star hotel in Catete, not far from Largo do Machado. The latter stayed in an establishment of similar characteristics, little more than two blocks away. They planned to use Largo do Machado as their meeting point. It's quite a busy area, full of tourists heading to see Christ the Redeemer. But specimens of the fauna found in the trendy spots of Zona Sul seldom venture there. They gravitate toward places celebrated in popular songs—Lebron, Copacabana, but certainly not Madureira or Irajá. And definitely not Largo do Machado or Flamengo Beach, which are seen as spots for the unfashionable with no access to power. They held their first work meeting on the evening of the same day in a small and discreet restaurant. During the bus ride, Maria Amélia devised a plan to approach the ex-secretary's former secretary.

"Did you already call to make an appointment with Maria Aparecida?"

Madalena nodded and Maria Amélia continued:

"This is the strategy: You must do everything you can to avoid appearing worried about yourself. Push yourself to the rear, a simple trainee who was employed a few months—four, right?—by the shameless prick's office. Show more concern for her, the long-time secretary, who's likely in the crosshairs of the press's light cavalry. I bet she must have been harassed by now. You will pat her on the back, console her, and thus show yourself superior. Then, casually, you'll steer the conversation toward the subject of the recordings."

"I'd thought about that."

"Great. Then go ahead. When will you meet?"

"Tomorrow. She invited me to lunch at her place."

"And no other ears will be nearby?"

"Only the maid's. But I'll be careful."

"Under the circumstances, you should be more than careful. It's human nature to step on those who once ranked above us on the social ladder when they fall from grace."

"You don't trust anyone, do you? I know Anastácia. She loves Maria Aparecida. She would never do anything to hurt her."

"Don-t buy that! Did you learn that in Sunday School? Don't step into any canoes without checking for leaks first. Let me rephrase: friendships have short legs in servile relations. So, don't say anything significant, not a word, in her presence. Anastácia, right?"

Despite her safety standards, Maria Amélia knew that sometimes they had to be broken. Consequently, she made two exceptions to her rule of secrecy about returning to Rio and staying in a budget hotel in Catete: Adamastor as an accomplice, and Dr. Anunciação as a calculated risk. Dr. Anunciação wasn't interested in the political world. She couldn't understand why Maria Amélia wasted her time on such things. Moreover, the psychiatrist despised gossip, practically ensuring she wouldn't go about revealing that the little witch was covertly staying in a hotel on a secluded Catete street. Maria Amélia only mentioned that she was laying low for a few days due to the commotion surrounding the governor's suicide. Since the psychiatrist asked her nothing else, she was soon making an appointment in the most appropriate place for a conversation without prying ears: her hotel room. Maria Amélia awaited Dr. Anunciação in the small hotel lobby, and upon entering her room, promptly took her great-aunt's photograph from her purse and tossed it onto the bed.

"What do you think of this, Dr. Maria da Anunciação?"

"Wow, have you been using Photoshop to give it that 1920s look?"

"Not at all. This is a copy of the photo hanging on the wall of Tarquínio Esperidião's sister in Santo Antônio das Tabocas. It's my great-aunt—the one whose chest was blown off by silver and gold pellets blasted out of a shotgun. Do you remember the stories he told you?"

"Of course, I do! But that's remarkable. I'll treat you more carefully, girl. Remarkable!"

"Yes, remarkable. I want to get to the bottom of this. I want to reread the report you wrote about Patient X, my biological father."

"Your biological father is Joaquim Paranhos Nogueira."

"Don't play dumb, Maria da Anunciação. You know very well that's not the case. My real father—though no one else needs to know it—is prisoner 3,029 in Bangu 3, Tarquínio Esperidião. If I recall correctly, you drew three conclusions about 'Patient X,' as you referred to him. Correct?"

"Correct."

"Well, I downloaded the article from the Internet just before you arrived. But the conclusions are what matter. Let's read them again carefully:

First line of interpretation: This case suggests we are dealing with one of the most extreme examples of obsession, where reality is overtaken by imagination. Following a prolonged schizophrenic episode, the deceased aunt developed such a potent persona that she began to dominate the researcher, ensnaring him in an imaginary realm that overshadowed reality. This isn't just a mere confusion between reality and imagination; it's about the complete obliteration of the former by the latter, the end of a schizophrenic process in which the healthy part of the mind lost the battle to the sick part, dominated by the aunt. And even at the prior stage, when the conflict was not yet resolved, the analysis of the patient's behavior already pointed to disturbances that put him on the plane of serious mental maladjustments. For instance, no rational individual would resort to such an absurd method as setting an alarm to ring every fifteen minutes as a way to combat insanity and dispel the aunt appearing in dreams. In this line of interpretation, we can only conclude that the patient's schizophrenic state has reached a point where hospitalization is more than advisable, if only because there is always the danger that the criminal fantasies—suggested, in theory, by the aunt—could be acted upon, which would transform the patient into a pathological case with a potential danger to society. This brings us to the paramount dilemma for all psychiatrists: whether to prioritize the patient's health at any cost or to protect society from the potential threats they pose.

Second line of interpretation: the patient does not believe in absolutely anything he reported. He consciously fabricated the entire fantasy to author the book about his aunt, using it as an outlet for his frustrations, stress, and unspeakable desires. The patient experienced catharsis. The coordinated nature of his accounts during the analysis sessions and the rigor of his fantasies' rationalizations suggests this is a real possibility. In this case, we are not faced with a schizophrenic, but rather a great actor who knows how to play the part of the mentally unbalanced very well to achieve his goals. But even in this second line of interpretation, the obsession with which the patient interprets his role does not allow us to place him in the admittedly ill-defined category of normal individuals. In one way or another, Patient X is an extreme case of obsession: obsession with the aunt who dominated him, or obsession with playing his part as obsessed with the aunt's life. In both cases, Patient X should receive psychiatric treatment.

There is a third line of interpretation, of course, but that one falls outside the scope of psychiatry: his aunt really was a witch and came back to dominate him. My background does not allow me to give this hypothesis any credence, but when discussing the case of Patient X with a serious researcher like Dr. Fábio da Mata, an expert in the study of paranormal phenomena, he stated that this possibility could not be ruled out.

After a short pause, Maria Amélia spoke intently:

"We must talk with this doctor Fábio da Mata immediately. Is he still alive?"

"He is, yes. But he's very old. On his way to ninety, I think, if not already passed it."

"Where does he live?

"In the Center. In an apartment building on Rua Buenos Aires. Perhaps the only one on the whole street. An old, refurbished law firm."

"Well, let's go. Right now."

Fábio da Mata was confined to a wheelchair. His caretaker was his spinster niece, Judite, who was around forty. Thin, bespectacled, with a hawk-like nose—whether she was single by choice or circumstance was anyone's guess. A witch as witches are depicted in most illustrations, with warts and pockmarks on her face. She looked after her uncle's extensive library, which occupied much of the apartment's living room and two bedrooms. It is perhaps the most extensive esoteric library in all Brazil, including practically everything that was ever written about witchcraft. Occasionally, the old man would spend an entire week engrossed in his books, never stepping foot outside the apartment. From time to time, he made brief excursions to Edifício Central, always wheeled by his niece, where he invariably browsed the area's second-hand bookshops. A widower for over ten years, he still typed on an old Remington typewriter, unless he was dictating to his niece on her laptop. Judite also scoured Google nearly daily for esoteric news articles, printing them out for her uncle, who shunned the use of computers. When lectured about this, he always replied:

"No. Not in this life. Maybe in others, who knows."

It was the niece who answered when Dr. Anunciação phoned to meet with Fábio da Mata.

"I don't know if today will be possible. He's very tired."

"Tell him it's about Patient X. He will surely remember. His daughter is here with me."

"Wait a minute." Judite covered the mouthpiece and spoke loudly to her uncle:

"It's Dr. Anunciação. She wants to meet you. It's about Patient X, do you remember that?"

The old man nodded. The story had made a deep impression on him at the time and remained etched in his memory.

"She wants to talk to you. She's nearby. She wants to come now, and the daughter of this Patient X is with her."

The professor's eyes twinkled. He nodded emphatically and exclaimed a resounding 'YES.'

"They can come. Tell them it's on the tenth floor. Apartment 1003. I am waiting."

Upon seeing such an old building, Maria Amélia commented:
"This one has an Otis."

And surely it did. The apartment was located almost directly across from the ancient, creaking elevator. Fábio da Mata himself answered the door when they rang the bell, standing with difficulty and leaning on a cane. He beckoned them to enter, settled back into his wheelchair, and fixed his gaze on Maria Amélia with the intensity of a lovestruck teenager. Maria da Anunciação broke the silence.

"This is Maria Amélia, Dr. Fábio."

"I know, I know. Please, come in, let's move to the living room," he said, addressing Maria Amélia as though she were a longtime friend, "Take my hand, let's go inside."

The living room, much like the two bedrooms and the hallway, was packed with books on shelves affixed to the walls. The old man briefly introduced his niece, requesting her to bring coffee for everyone, then continued in a voice that, while halting, now carried an almost firm tone, as if rejuvenated:

"You're privileged. Few people achieve what you have achieved. To be able to choose the time of one's own reincarnation. To conduct the show, so to speak. I know that Anunciação has her doubts ..."

"You seem to have none."

"And you do? Of course not."

Dr. Anunciação was dumbfounded. Her eyes flitted between the affectionate old man and the smiling little witch who seemed to relish the elder's warmth. Finally regaining her composure from the initial shock, the psychiatrist said:

"Dr. Fábio, Maria Amélia has something to show you. But as far as I can tell, there's no need."

Maria da Anunciação motioned Maria Amélia to show him the reproduction of the photograph. Dr. Fábio da Mata looked at it with no surprise and gave the photo back. With his gaze fixed on the girl, he spoke as though they were the only two in the room:

"It's you, in the other incarnation. I probably wasn't even born when this picture was taken. But now—we know, don't we?—you are much wiser now, you know what you want. Free from the torment of revenge. I see in your eyes that you have projects. Whatever they may be, know that you have my modest assistance. Always, in this life that is ending, and who knows, in the next reincarnation. Oh, here comes Judite with the coffee. Bring some cookies, too."

The coffee was taken in silence, as if everything had already been said. For Dr. Anunciação, the meeting felt endless, unable to contribute anything during that peculiar courtship, under their two gazes that rendered everyone else irrelevant. Not even Freud could have explained it, nor Jung. No reason. She was an intruder in another world. Both she and the old man's niece, who looked at Maria Amélia with something not quite akin to jealousy, but fear. Maria Amélia lowered her face, took Dr. da Mata's hand and said in his ear:

"I'll come back."

"Come back anytime. It's your house. No need to call ahead."

Maria da Anunciação only nodded her head in goodbye. As the elevator creaked its way to the ground floor, Maria Amélia turned to the visibly frightened psychiatrist:

"Remarkable, huh?"

"Remarkable? Terrifying, girl! I'm afraid of you. I can't explain it. Can you?"

Maria Amélia answered with a hint of cynicism:

"Explain what?"

In silence, they followed Rua Buenos Aires' narrow sidewalk to Avenida Rio Branco, where they took two taxis, one to the hotel and the other to the psychiatrist's house, who during their farewell still had the strength to say:

"I think this is the first time in my life that I find myself at a loss for words, not knowing what to say. I need some time to process what happened on Rua Buenos Aires before we can discuss it further. I'll call you when I feel fit."

"Okay. But don't overthink it too much. Life is beautiful, after all!"

30

One way to make life even more beautiful, as the thought sparkled in the little witch's mind on her way back to the hotel, was to always keep the sweet candy of power within arm's reach, ready to be indulged in at her whim. Doctor da Mata had described her as more serene and less vindictive, no longer haunted by the distant gunshot that had shattered her great-aunt's chest. Perfected, she was a perfected version, the reincarnation expert had noted. She would need to speak with him again, not just once, but several times, before he returned to João Ubaldo's perch of souls. She feared that disagreements would arise between her and the old man regarding the interpretation of *perfection*. She had no aspirations of becoming a kind and ascetic Buddha, living in isolated monasteries, punishing the flesh by denying it pleasure, despite Buddhism's aims to eliminate suffering. This might be well and good in the distant, far-off future, over countless reincarnations leading to Nirvana, to an existence that borders on non-existence, persisting even when the Earth is scorched by a decaying, dying Sun. And under no circumstances—she emphatically reminded herself—could she let herself be influenced by the example of a real or imagined Christ, the orchestrator of history's grandest masochistic display. Something in the little witch's head knew this went against human nature. She was certain that humans were merely the most developed animal on planet Earth, eternally bound to the primal instinct of avoiding suffering by all means and not accepting it as a form of redemption. Humanity cannot be saved by walking this path, by accepting martyrdom as a divine gift. "And don't get started on sublimation!" the little witch stressed, internally shouting down the clichéd counterargument. The great battle is always to avoid pain, to fight against it with all available means, even with death, if necessary, if the affliction can no longer be controlled. Make life beautiful and enjoyable, always, until someday—if ever—this is possible for everyone on Earth. This was the belief of wise old women in the era of matriarchy, always seeking the finest gifts from Mother Earth, though some paid dearly in the fires of the Holy Inquisition, during the zenith of male dominance. There were many risks along the way, like the political mess she had gotten herself into. But sublimate suffering? Never that. Redemption through pleasure, through success. She even mentally exclaimed to her neurons: "Down with pain!"

"We're here, Miss."

The taxi driver, having idled at the hotel door for over a minute, interrupted Maria Amélia's thoughts. She apologized, paid the fare, and headed upstairs to her room, shifting her focus to the earthlier matters that would enhance her life's beauty. The short-term task: get her uncle elected as federal congressman without succumbing to the storm caused by the governor's suicide. She called him and set a dinner date at a restaurant in Largo do Machado.

At the restaurant, Adamastor's surprise was evident.

"How are you here, my dear Niece? I thought you were going to spend quite some time in Minas Gerais."

"New developments have come up that require my presence in Rio de Janeiro. But I remain incognito. That's why I'm in a cheap hotel nearby on Rua do Catete. Three people know this, and you're one of them."

"New developments?"

"Yes, but it's best you don't know. You don't need to know. It would only add to the problems my dearest uncle is already facing. But I can tell you that my presence here is precisely to clear the ground, to pave the way for the election of Congressman Adamastor Leite Feitosa. From what I've read and seen, you've done very well."

"You saw the interview?"

"I did, indeed. With that nosy reporter. I saw it on YouTube. My dear Uncle, you're faring better as a politician than as a vendor of cleaning products in the favelas. The task now is to clear the field, clean up the mess, and bury it permanently in a deep grave."

"Explain yourself better, Niece. You scare me."

"Get everyone involved in the scandal out of the way. I mean, not everyone. Exception must be made for the two idealistic and talented young women who were snared by sly and corrupt politicians."

"Two? Is there someone else?"

"Don't worry. I'm referring to the assistant of the Communication Secretary. We've already made contact and, if everything goes well, we'll sail through it all. I'm meeting her today. What will you order?"

"I'll have this, Fillet à la Parmigiana with French fries and rice."

"That's horrible, Uncle! A fillet drowned in flour, alongside potatoes drenched in oil, and extra carbs from the rice, all adding to your waistline. And you'll also order a beer, of course."

"But of course, dearest Niece. No one is made of stone."

"Enjoy. If that's what makes life beautiful and delicious for my uncle, I won't say anything. But it's wise to be cautious, to avoid hastening your disincarnation."

"Disincarnation? That sounds like one of my dearest niece's special interests ..."

"Indeed, it is. I'll go with a fish fillet and vegetables. They're delicious, Uncle. You should give them a try."

"Thanks, but I'll have my parmigiana, my French fries, my rice, and this ice-cold and delicious beer."

"White wine for me. But back to our main topic. I don't want anyone, especially not my foster mother—our dear Anita, right, Uncle?—to find out I'm in Rio de Janeiro. As far as they're concerned, I'm still in Santo Antonio das Tabocas. If no one asks for me, all the better. My dear uncle should carry on as before. Keep things under wraps, but don't avoid reporters too much, it might raise suspicions. Just be natural. Stay the course, appearing to still be figuring things out after your book's success, neither confirming nor denying any political ambitions. A lot of people in Brasilia may not heed this, but as a general rule it's wise not to commit to anything you might have to backtrack on later. I can't stress this enough. Only speak out when you're absolutely certain and be cautious even then. When in doubt, resort to the conditional tense, but avoid sounding uncertain. The conditional tense with the scientific air of someone who wants to weigh all the data on the issue. What I'm saying is, lay low for now. Don't accept proposals, especially if they come as money, bribes, those trappings. Anything that could draw unwanted attention from star judges, the press, or blogs. Beware of administrative positions you may be offered. Best not to accept them. No entering politics through the back door. Look what happened to the governor."

"Don't worry, Niece. I won't make a move while the iron is hot."

"Great! But go ahead and eat. Parmigiana is barely tolerable when hot, and far worse when it's cold."

Soon after the work meeting with her uncle ended around nine in the evening, Maria Amélia headed to a nearby bar to meet Madalena, keen on getting the latest updates. Her accomplice was already there, sipping a vodka martini at a discreet table. She seemed calm. A good sign.

"So?" she asked immediately, skipping the pleasantries.

"Everything went very well, it seems. I was extremely careful, I'm sure she doesn't suspect a thing. Ah! By the way, she herself preferred that we talk alone. She sent Anastácia away as soon as the food was served. She is indeed terrified, feeling for the scoundrel who exploited her for so many years, could you believe it?"

"What about the tapes?"

"I didn't even need to mention it. She brought it up herself. She said the day of the suicide was pure turmoil, complete chaos. The secretary arrived late and asked her, almost shouting, for all the files on the hearings, while he frantically hit the delete key on his computer. 'Don't tell anyone, for God's sake!' she told me, adding that she heard the secretary ask Fernandinho, his computer technician, about the recordings of the hearings. The technician said he had destroyed them all, leaving no trace, including bringing a hammer to the hard drive where they were stored. 'Nothing was left?' the secretary had insisted. 'Absolutely nothing. All deleted. Unless you have copies on your laptop or at home.' She then seemed a little awkward, as if she was choosing her words very carefully. Finally, she told me: 'I'm sorry, Madalena, but I accidentally heard the secretary mention your name. He pressed Fernandinho on whether he had deleted the conversation you two had in private. Do you remember? On the day you introduced yourself to him.' I didn't let on. I pretended I didn't hear anything, but I was paying close attention to the conversation. Fernandinho was emphatic: 'It doesn't exist anymore. Deleted. Erased. And the hard drive destroyed, thrown in the trash, far from here.' I listened without saying a word and trying to act as naturally as possible."

Maria Amélia listened intently, not interrupting and not quite sharing her companion's excitement. Finally, she spoke:

"All right. We can be at least 90% confident that there's no remaining evidence of your conversation with that scoundrel."

"Ninety percent?"

"Yes. Someone as cunning as Antonio Felisberto isn't going to reveal all his cards. He may well have a personal archive at home or, who knows, in the safe deposit box of some bank. Your conversation with him was outright blackmail, plain and simple, my dear. These things are kept."

"Why are you always so mean?"

"Don't start with that, girl. The only thing missing is you putting on an innocent pout! I'm not being mean, just objective. Let's be straight today, so as not to regret it tomorrow."

"And what are we gonna do?"

"Indeed, what are we gonna do? Up until now, we've been playing defense. I think it's time to switch to attack."

"I don't understand."

"You'll need to enlist Maria Aparecida's help again. Ask her to call Felisberto to tell him you have a tape of the conversation."

"That's crazy! Aparecida won't get it. She'll become suspicious."

"Perhaps, but it's a risk we need to take. To her, it's just a tape. She doesn't know what's on it, and she never will. You won't tell her ... Will you?"

"A risk *I* need to take, you mean."

"Us! We're in the same boat, partner. The bastard will want to set up a meeting with you, and that's when you'll talk to him. A *tête-à-tête* where you'll have to be tough. You'll say you'll destroy the recording in your possession if he destroys his. If he has it, his reaction will be to negotiate. If he doesn't, he'll likely be rattled and resort to sentimental appeals, say that he is destroyed politically and that, with the tape, his family life will also turn into hell. I don't doubt he'll cry; crocodile tears he has in spades."

"That's crazy!"

"No, it's merely the best way to get out of this with barely a scratch. You most of all. Call Aparecida now. It's not ten o'clock yet. Come on. Use the payphone in Largo do Machado."

Maria Aparecida was surprised by the call, but as the good soul that she was, always wanting to help others, she promised to call the former secretary. The reaction was as predicted: a meeting with Madalena. At first, Felisberto tried to play innocent to his secretary, who he knew as very efficient, but not brilliant at grasping political tricks.

"Tape? What tape are you referring to? Have you heard it?"

"I don't know, sir. I have no idea."

"All right, leave it to me. It's better if Madalena calls me directly. Give her my new number. And don't worry. If you need a reference letter for another job, don't hesitate to ask. They're dragging my name through the mud, but I still hold considerable clout in this city. Get some rest. And don't worry."

The new number, a prepaid one registered under a different name, was only known to his closest friends or people with whom he could not lose contact, such as his faithful secretary. Madalena called him the next day at eleven a.m., and the meeting was set for eight o'clock in the evening. The former secretary would wait for her in his car, in this case a black Passat borrowed from a friend. From there, they would go somewhere where they could talk in peace. Felisberto's idea was to take her to a motel, not only to mix business with pleasure, if possible, but also to show that he held all the cards. Whores you take to the motel! Reduce her to her insignificance, show who was calling the shots. Because even in disgrace, a journalist and politician ranked above one of Madame Xavier's prostitutes. Easy prey, as soon as she stepped into the car, he would put her in her place and negotiate the lowest possible price for the tape's deletion.

At first, things went according to the former secretary's plan. Madalena went to the meeting place and stepped into the vehicle. But another car was parked less than fifty yards away, and at the wheel was a braided girl with a broad skill set, including driving through the maze of Rio de Janeiro's streets. The women had arrived half an hour early, and despite the heat, they kept the windows shut, making it difficult for them to be seen. In essence, wherever Felisberto went, Maria Amélia would be trailing him.

There were no greetings between the two. As soon as Madalena sat down beside him, Felisberto immediately asked:

"Where's the tape? I want to hear it."

"Take it easy, my dear, I know the ropes."

"I know that. But you must prove that you actually have the recording. How do I know you're not bluffing?"

"You must have recorded the conversation yourself. You know on which side the bread is buttered."

"It's irrelevant if I have a recording of your blackmail. Who would care about someone like you, a little whore? It's my reputation that is at stake."

172

"Look here, Felisberto. Your reputation, with all its skeletons, is filthier than any whore working the streets at Central do Brasil. I may have prostituted myself in the past, but I don't have to walk that path anymore. I am a trained lawyer, young, with a bright future ahead of me. Right now, my reputation is worth far more than yours."

Felisberto looked her up and down wanting to make his superiority explicit and said:

"Let's not argue in the car, a traffic cop could show up. Let's go somewhere we can talk more calmly. Let's head to that motel in Barra da Tijuca."

"Wherever you want. You can opt for the cheapest room, since we're only going to talk. Another thing: don't be irked if you notice your car is being followed. Because it's true!"

"Bitch!"

He then sped up, narrowly missing the car in front.

No words were exchanged throughout the journey winding down Niemeyer Avenue. Felisberto's anxiety was evident as he constantly checked the Volkswagen in his rearview mirror. At a glance, he noticed a braided girl behind the wheel, and it didn't take long for the gears in his brain to identify her as the governor's protege, the know-it-all aide. Maria Amélia also realized her mistake, she had come closer than she should and just as she was passing under a streetlight. She reasoned quickly, deciding to change the initial plan completely.

The brochure of the five-star motel they were heading to advertised *total privacy*. They also offered a unique and questionably legal option. The client and escort could present themselves masked and the payment could be made in cash. This is what Felisberto did. He pulled a black mask from his document case and stepped out of the car wearing it.

"What the hell is that? I'm not going into a room with you like that."

"I'm not going to expose myself, my dear. Cover your face somehow. You women always have some piece of cloth to serve as mask."

"I'm not going in!"

"You are! Use this shawl to cover your face ..."

"What the hell is this?" shouted Felisberto, seeing the braided girl standing next to him already wrapped in a veil that looked more like a burqa.

"What's the matter? Don't you like orgies? Well, let's do it, a mental orgy, an orgy of words, I want to see if you're really that good!"

Their retreat was complicated by the arrival of another car, its headlights illuminating their covered and masked faces. They went in. Felisberto paid the standard R$500 for a luxury room with a hot tub, and the three of them headed up to the second floor.

"Well, we can take off the masks now."

"You can remove yours, as you two are well acquainted. I'm not"—and, turning to Felisberto: "you didn't see me. You can't identify who I am."

"I can, you bitch. I saw you in the rearview mirror."

"In the rearview mirror? At night? Amidst all those twists and turns we drove through? Even the cheapest lawyer could dismantle your claim in any court. I'm not taking off my mask. Just as you aren't required to drop your trousers. Let's get to the facts. Leave it to me, Madalena. She has the recording. As for you, we don't know that you do."

"And what the hell could I do with a tape that would only serve to bury me further?"

"Very true."

"What do you want anyway?"

"Settle this matter. Bury it once and for all. Erase your hook-up with her and the others from the record."

"Erase how? It is on the Internet, in that blog written by the little two-faced saint over there."

"The blog stops. Its readers will forget and move on to something new. It's information without proof. The courts cannot use them. The big newspapers and TV networks didn't even want to touch it. It ends here. We'll destroy our recording as soon as you destroy any you have."

The former secretary put his hands on his head and exclaimed:

"How can I destroy something I don't have?! For God's sake!"

Felisberto's cry sounded like music in Maria Amélia's ears. He couldn't be such a good actor. There was the confirmation—99%, the little witch always included margin for error—that the bastard did not really have a recording proving the blackmail to which he had submitted. Calm and in control, showing she was the one calling the shots, ready for any arbitration if needed, the former aide to the dead governor said:

"All right, then. Orgy is over. You don't have the recording and neither do we. You forget about us, and we'll forget about you. You follow the path you want; we follow ours."

"And what proof do I have of that?"

"None. I mean, you have our word. You know you won't get more than that. We don't have it. I swear. On the leafcutter ant queen's ass."

"Fucking whores, whores from hell! Cunts! I'm leaving!"

"You can go. Gentlemen first."

The doorman looked surprised as the customer left the R$500 luxury room in less than ten minutes.

"Is there a problem, Mister? What about the girls?"

"No problem. And if there is, it's my own. The two whores will be down shortly."

31

The events on Rua Buenos Aires haunted Maria da Anunciação the entire night. Throughout her career working with the insane, from the docile to the volatile, she had always found a scientific explanation. Even for Tarquínio's case, which at the time had left such a deep impression on her, she had found sound scientific explanations. Until now, she had regarded Maria Amélia only as an extremely intelligent person, who would often make fun of the fantasies of her murderous father. The scene in Dr. Fábio da Mata's apartment had revealed a new Maria Amélia, taking on an exceptionality that went beyond any rational explanation. She needed to speak again with the reincarnation expert, privately, to resolve her growing doubts. The next morning, shortly after coffee, she phoned to make an appointment with the old man from Rua Buenos Aires on the same day. She didn't want to let the issue grow cold.

Dr. da Mata greeted her with an enigmatic smile, requesting his niece to give them privacy.

"So, doctor, you're convinced they exist now?"

"They who?"

"Witches. Aren't you here to talk about our little girl in pigtails?"

"Yes. And I'm not going to deny that I left here upset. I've known Maria Amélia very long, since she was born. I always considered her an exceptional, privileged person, but what happened here in the apartment exceeded all my expectations. You must forgive me, doctor, but what I witnessed was a scene of mutual fascination, some sort of energetic courtship, if I can put it that way."

Doctor da Mata merely smiled and motioned for the psychiatrist to continue.

"I've never seen anything like that in my whole life. And, once more, please excuse my bluntness, but she was clearly in control. That brat barely out of college reduced us to mere spectators of her performance. I tried to find a plausible explanation all night, but I confess I couldn't. I'm sorry, but my training does not permit me to accept the theory of reincarnation, even if espoused by a brilliant mind like yours. There must be a scientific explanation. There simply must."

The reincarnation expert remained silent with his benevolent smile. Maria da Anunciação continued without hiding her discomfort:

"Say something, please! We are both adults, with long years toiling in the most difficult profession in the world, trying to understand the intricacies of the human mind. She is barely out of her diapers; she shouldn't be schooling us as though we're novices fresh out of university. The roles are reversed. It can't be. I can't accept it, and worse, much worse, I can't understand it."

Fábio da Mata gently held the psychiatrist's arms, attempting to soothe her, and speaking with the tranquility of a soul that has experienced several reincarnations, or devil knows what:

"My dear Dr. Anunciação, you are mistaken. And although it's very difficult to accept, there is no escaping the evidence that our dear Maria Amélia is on a much higher plane than ours. Though she's young in this life, her experiences from past reincarnations far surpass ours. She embodies the spirit of the wise women who guided early humanity. She is above good and evil, as we understand it. Don't try to compete with her, we lack the faculty for that. You and I are just good professionals, diligent scholars. She's so much more than that."

"She can be mean sometimes. Cruel even. You could see the sheer delight on her face, aware that she had us completely under her spell."

"Evil, cruelty, kindness ... These are concepts deformed by our human, earthly perception. In the great Western religions—Judaism, Christianity, and Islam—faith rests on one God who, for the most part, is very cruel, in the image and likeness of his creators. And above all vindictive, one would say. The God of the Bible, and the Qur'an, does not forgive any doubts concerning his supreme authority. Jesus was perceived as a reformer who sought to temper the divine wrath of the Old Testament, yet even he showed no compromise toward non-believers. It's there in the Book of Matthew, Chapter 8, verse 12: 'But the children of the kingdom (the unbelievers) shall be cast out into outer darkness. There shall be weeping and gnashing of teeth.' So, the one God governing the entire universe—of which we and the most advanced science have only seen a tiny part—is imbued with human feelings, including the supreme vanity of punishing those who dare to doubt him and worship other possible gods. It's the foremost commandment on Moses's tablets."

"I thought you followed Kardecism, and therefore, Christianity."

"You thought wrong. Perhaps I lean toward materialism, viewing the soul as the quintessence of matter."

"Really, the doctor surprises me. I don't remember reading any of this in your books."

"And you wouldn't have read it. I did not dare write it. The concept is so disturbing, even if it goes back to Greek philosophers and has been entertained by modern physicists with an open mind and amazement at the possibilities opened by quantum physics, for example. I don't feel capable of unraveling what the human soul is. My only aim is to understand its manifestations on this small planet we call Earth."

"And Maria Amélia, could you write about her?"

"Oh, Dr. Anunciação, what vain vanity ... Let her go a bit. Don't try to compete with our little witch. It's best to enjoy the privilege of her friendship. I would say more, enjoy her teachings, enjoy living with such an exceptional being. I can't quantify it in formulas and graphs, but I'm certain she's a step ahead of us. We're still simple human beings. I get the sense that she's already transcended beyond that."

Dr. Maria da Anunciação returned home even more distraught.

32

After a week holed up in a cheap Catete hotel, Maria Amélia decided it was time to show her face. She had to return—as the cariocas say with their lavish modesty—to the buzz of the most charming semicircle on the planet: Copacabana, Ipanema, and Leblon. And don't forget Lagoa with its mansions. In essence, it was time to resume regular activities, enrolling in a Political Economy course, because Maria Amélia had decided she should collect degrees in the areas leading her to the center of power. She occasionally mused that the wheel of reincarnation had erred in its choice. She could have been born somewhere in Virginia, very close to Washington, with a Colombian American uncle selling cleaning products on the beaches of Miami. But let's not quarrel with fate. The reincarnation occurred in Rio, and for now, the target was that weird- looking building in Brasília: two cups without handles, one of them overturned, resting next to two towers. Niemeyer always liked to dazzle his admirers, but he didn't seem to care that artificial light had to be used inside his buildings, even if outside the Cerrado sun was roasting the rest of the Planalto Central[10]

---

[10] The central plateau region where Brasília is located.

reducing air humidity to less than 17%. Can anyone stand being inside that handle-less cup, overturned or otherwise, unless the air conditioning is cranked, and the environment has that nice smell of power? No need to blame members of congress for their continually missed Friday and Monday sessions because they are prolonging their weekends in milder lands, especially those with beaches, such as Rio's trendy semicircle.

So here we are. I mean, here they are. Maria Amélia in her Copacabana apartment, to the relief of the uncle seeking guidance in the labyrinth of his new life as former drug dealer and future influence merchant, the dangerous paths of those who have tasted the candy of power. Madalena shut down her blog after the encounter with Felisberto in the Barra motel and sent an email to Madame Xavier communicating that Margarida was properly dead and buried. No flowers were to be sent. And promising future rewards, she asked her to destroy all records of her as prostitute, especially the photos in the best *escort girl* catalogs of Rio de Janeiro. She struggled to find a job for a few months, spending almost all the money she had gathered in her four months as assistant to the former communications secretary. In the end, she got what she wanted: a paid—albeit very poorly—internship in a law firm on Rio Branco Avenue. The money was barely enough to pay rent on the apartment she still shared with both colleagues of her Madame Xavier days. She even considered temporarily selling her body independently, until she secured a better job. Maria Amélia talked her out of it.

"No way. Prostitution leaves an indelible mark on those who practice it. The doors through which we want to pass don't open to those bearing such marks. Except for back doors. You don't want to come in that way, do you? You need to find another place to live."

"How, on this pittance?"

"I'll pay the rent on a new apartment. I mean, my uncle will pay."

"How generous! I don't know how to thank you."

"You don't have to. We won't give you anything for free. You're going to work for my uncle. Public relations, for the time being. Then you'll have to burn the midnight oil on the political campaign trail, under my watch. Don't think it will be easy. I am extremely demanding."

179

"I'm very aware."

Maria Amélia's predictions came true. Two months passed and almost no one still remembered the Zero Illiteracy scandal, especially since it was restricted to the state of Rio and the worms of the São João Batista cemetery were already consuming the main culprit. Even better. Antônio Felisberto made the best decision for himself and others. He left the country. He landed a press office job for Petrobras in London and planned to spend at least five years there. He was considered a small fry in the proceedings running their course in Rio. His lawyer even painted him as an innocent victim of the suicidal governor's swindle. Could you believe it! His friend knew a friend, a Petrobras director, and used his reputation as good journalist to get him the job, which was sufficiently well paid for him to endure exile in the British capital. All this in the utmost discretion. A disappearing act not only in the interest of Felisberto, Maria Amélia, Adamastor and Madalena, but also a handful of other people suckling at the teat of the Zero Illiteracy cow. Armando Pereira also decided to get out and left as Washington correspondent for the newspaper he had worked for more than twenty years.

And in the end, there's nothing like one scandal to bury the other. The attention of the press turned to Minas Gerais in a case involving dairy. A variation of the Zero Illiteracy scheme, but now with the governor of Minas Gerais deciding it was time to give milk to all the children of his state. The anticipated corruption occurred during distribution, but on a scale that crossed acceptable limits. The scandal became known as *The Milk Tithe.* It worked as follows: producers undertook to provide anything from 2% to 10% of their production to the state's milk distribution center; in turn, this center provided one liter to all needy families in the state: the Milk Grant. The thing is that the center's director was a friend of the governor, and old college buddy. This guy decided he was also entitled to some suckling, taking 10% of the received milk and sending it, clandestinely, to a dairy factory, which in turn was owned by a friend of the friend. Ah, what a wonderful thing friendship is! But it was all leaked and the press had a field day with the headlines.

"Unprecedented Sucker Game"

"Little Kids Deprived by Suckling Sharks"

"The Milk Mates"

With so much spilled milk, the Zero Illiteracy scandal faded into a single note on the inside pages, if any. On the Internet, the buzz was gone for good. Maria Amélia decided it was time to go out in the field and launch her uncle's run for federal congressman in next year's elections.

"Now is the time, Uncle! Let's take the first opportunity to launch your campaign. And if none come up, let's create one, before your literary fame fades too."

The expected opportunity was served up by the competition. Ovídio Abreu, already maneuvering as the obvious candidate for the PMDB, invaded Adamastor's constituency: the favelas of Rio de Janeiro. It even looked like the guy had overheard the private conversations between uncle and niece and the little witch's cleaning products euphemism. The opponent struck with a jingle in hand.

> Ovídio Abreu, getting the favela clean
> With the peace force by his side,
> It's a winning team
> Make the hill a cleaner place
> A home to embrace!

He was going to sweep clean the dirt infesting the favelas once and for all. And he made a point of putting dirt in quotes, to make its meaning more comprehensive. In short, the future candidate was part of a movement, the so-called *Action Against Drugs* made up of some of the right's finest, feeding on the frustrations of the middle class after striking out in their last power grab. There were suspicions, as yet unproven, that the *Action Against Drugs* had links with the death squads that had set themselves the task of eliminating the drug bosses in the wake of the Peacekeeping Police.

181

The PMDB candidate denied any connection with illegal organizations, of course, saying he was only sympathetic to the *Action Against Drugs* movement, but that he had no affiliation or commitment to it.

Maria Amélia found Adamastor with frowns of concern. He didn't look like he slept well. His orange juice was almost untouched. He had taken only a sip of his coffee, leaving the croissants that were always part of his first meal. On the table lay the opened special section of the newspaper *O Globo* with a two-page article entitled:

"Ovídio Abreu Promises to Clean the Favela"

And the caption under a photo of the politician hugging the commander of the pacifying police read: "He's one of us."

"Have you seen this, Niece? Have you seen this?"

"Yes, I have. I read everything. I thought it was great."

"Great? The son of a bitch is stealing our agenda! He's going to syphon all the votes that should be mine."

"Keep your head, dearest uncle! He is actually giving us the opportunity to enter the fray. He stirred up our voting pool, giving us the chance to react. We'll go in with all guns blazing. I mean, you will. On the *Pinga-Fogo* show on Channel 2. That cute journalist who interviewed you when I was in Santo Antônio das Tabocas will be there. What's her name again? You must know. She has your business card, and you must have received hers, of course."

A slight flush came over Adamastor's face as he reached into his pocket pretending to search for the card.

"Oh, right, let me see. Ah ... I remember! Érica. Her name is Érica."

"That's it, Uncle! Érica! And you just failed your acting test. Have you ever seen a politician lose his cool because he was caught in a little flirting?"

"What are you talking about, Niece?"

"Come on, Uncle! You're going down that route with me? Don't worry. Mom Anita won't hear a thing. Unless you let it slip. But you won't, will you?"

A thought flashed through Adamastor's brain, the realization of the plain and simple truth: he was nothing but a puppet. Acquiescing, he accompanied his niece to the office, sat down and, like a good student, listened to everything he should do on Channel 2's *Pinga-Fogo*.

It goes without saying that Érica was the panel's main attraction, at least for the male audience and the interviewee, in particular. She was dressed in navy blue, her skirt at the knees, leaving her shapely legs on display. Her blonde, neatly straightened hair fell to her shoulders. The others were seasoned journalists, the youngest already bordering on fifty. Anita, who was watching the debate on television, certainly didn't like it when Adamastor gave two kisses on the interviewer's cheek that seemed to last longer than they should, denouncing a certain intimacy. Anita cringed, and had she had her stepdaughter's powers, she would find a way to burn that pretty young face with the same spotlight that was shining down on her. And the first question after the moderator's introduction came from Érica, dispensing with terms like *sir* or *esteemed guest* in a suspicious coziness ... This only served to further raise the jealousy of the former sheriff's widow.

"Adamastor, do you agree with Ovídio Abreu? Will you support his candidacy and the campaign to clean up the favela?"

"My dearest Érica ..."

Wait a minute, "my dearest Érica?" What kind of affections are these? Dona Anita's jealousy meter was beginning to show signs it was going to explode. And Adamastor went on, his voice sounding more mellow than it should.

"Dearest Érica ..."

Twice "dearest," but it wasn't meant to further infuriate the loving widow. It was to adjust the tiny earpiece and better hear the answers dictated by his niece. Unintentionally, he repeated the greeting for a third time again, replacing dearest by ...

"Dear Érica ..."

"That's enough! Adamastor is making a fool of himself for this little tramp. It can't be! He is very mistaken if he thinks he'll get away with this!" It goes without saying whose thoughts these were. But let's not further

183

interrupt the response awaited by thousands of viewers, whispered by the little braided witch sitting in front of a monitor in a room reserved for the interviewee.

"Not long ago, Rio de Janeiro endured the Zero Illiteracy scandal firsthand. It's what cheap demagoguery always leads to, promises everybody knows cannot be kept. What's even more serious about the cheap words mister... what's his name again? Ah, yes, Abreu, I forget his first name, but it doesn't matter ..."

"Ovídio Abreu," interrupted Érica, with an insinuating tone.

But what Anita saw was a charming peck directed at the interviewee. "Hussy!" she thought.

"Anyway, the favela doesn't need a broom, just as Brazil never needed Jânio Quadros' broom—remember?—or the empty promises of these populists who exude cheap moralism from every pore. What the favela needs is greater commitment to the everyday struggle against the causes of the dirt and ills of the communities: poverty, misery, starvation wages, all the social diseases afflicting Brazil, leading to one of the most unequal income distributions on the planet. The cleanup proposed by Abreu ... Sorry, Ovídio Abreu, as my dear Érica aptly reminded me ..."

This last "my dear Erica" hadn't been dictated by Maria Amélia, and upon hearing it, Anita almost threw a candlestick lying on the coffee table at the TV ...

"Anyway, this cleanup by Ovídio Abreu will hide reality, falsify the data on the issue. Do you remember the project to paint the favelas back in the 1960s? Most likely not. Memory is always short in these matters. They even wrote a samba at the time: 'Favela Amarela': *paint the favela / make of colored misery aquarela*. As it turns out, Ovídio Abreu isn't even original. It's an inferior version of the proposal from the former director of Tourism, a certain Mario Saladini, who wanted the tourists, at least, to see the beauty in the dwellings of Rio's miserable. Yellow as our flag. Ovídio, or whatever his name is, wants to clean. We want it too. Everyone does, except for those who like to wallow in the mud. But any cleaning effort must be underpinned by what we should call social justice."

Érica nodded, batting a languid look of approval.

"Bitch!"

The scream was followed by the crash of the candlestick against the television set. It startled the maid.

"What happened, Dona Anita?"

"Nothing! Pull the plug on this fucking TV. And then clean up as much as possible. But there is some dirt only I can clean."

She then retired to the bathroom, first to pee and then to examine her face thoroughly, stretching her skin to smooth out wrinkles.

She closed her eyes only to see Érica resplendent, her skin as tight as a drum. All that remained was seeing Adamastor giving her a French kiss. The mirror met the same fate as the television, struck by the shaver of the person responsible for such jealousy.

With tiny beads of sweat already percolating in the stuffy studio, Adamastor was now asked a question by one of the older journalists on the show. Short. Blunt. Cutting to the chase:

"Mister Adamastor! We just heard a candidate's speech. Are you running for federal congress? Are you Abreu's competitor?"

Maria Amélia's slow and steady voice in the earpiece was like relaxing music in the interviewee's ears.

"The esteemed journalist is in a bit of a hurry. As is this Abreu with his Jânio Quadros[11] complex. It's still March, candidacies can only be announced in July."

"That's not an answer. You're digressing. I repeat the question. Do you intend to run as a candidate? Are you affiliated with any party?"

"I'm sympathetic to the PSB. And I confess that I was probed about running for federal congressman. But it's still early days. I'm weighing the matter. I don't need to put up any false modesty. I know my book made a big impact on public opinion. A positive impact, with rare exceptions. That puts me in a ... let's say ... eligible position."

---

[11] Former president who used a broom as a symbol to sweep away corruption in Brazil.

"So, let's put it like this, there is a 99% chance that you will run in the next election."

This time the question was asked by one of the younger-looking journalists. He wore glasses, with his starting baldness showing off a large forehead. His question provoked laughter, and Adamastor himself surrendered to the banter.

"Our insightful journalist is exaggerating; 99% is the chance I will wake up tomorrow. But I won't deny it, there is a good probability."

Ah, probabilities! Little did Adamastor know that the odds were stacked against him enjoying a peaceful night's sleep, like someone who had answered all questions correctly. His head might well be crushed by a silver candlestick, already duly returned by the diligent maid to its place on the coffee table. Diligent because, if she wasn't, she would already have been kicked to the curb. Her jealous mistress was of the most demanding type, the kind that thought *you-can't-be-soft-on-these-people*. And it's a good thing Anita didn't watch the rest of the interview. Érica asked four other questions, and in the last one, she left no doubts about her preferences on all levels for the future congressman to be elected with the votes of Rio's favelados.

"I can already see Adamastor taking the vote. And if such a contest existed, he would be chosen the most charming congressman of the *Planalto*."

Had Anita heard this, she'd probably dispense with the candlestick and use a 12-gauge shotgun to blow out the brains of the siren on television and still have lead left for the repentant drug dealer.

33

There is not enough sex in this story. Or perhaps, to phrase it another way, some aspects have been inadequately explored or merely hinted at. Some of you may be under the impression that Maria Amélia, with her long braids and obsessive need to control everything around her, is a cold woman, lacking any erotic impulse. As far as the little witch goes, the subject of sex has so far only been lightly brushed. Some pages back, we saw that something more than simple friendship existed between Maria Amélia and Frederica. Remember? When our little witch told her former friend that they needed to undergo an apprenticeship amongst themselves before venturing out into the world to confront male masters fixated on one thing: penetration. More interesting things needed telling, and so we let the reader interpret and fantasize to taste everything that went on in the little witch's circle of girlfriends during her teenage years. I can assure you, remarkable things occurred, with her invariably in control, even in submissive roles, fully embracing her feminine desires in every aspect and position. But what the hell are we even talking about? We're not straying from the subject, in case that's your concern. All this has to do with the brainstorm that came over Maria Amélia shortly after Adamastor's successful interview.

On her way home, a new apartment she was leasing in Ipanema, the little witch was already plotting a strategy for her uncle's election campaign. The broom candidate would be playing for keeps and preparations for war needed to start immediately. One problem, above all, demanded the utmost attention: the drug trade. Open endorsement from drug dealers, if it were even feasible, would be more detrimental than beneficial. Just imagine Ovídio's screaming in the free election ads:

"Once a dealer, always a dealer! Adamastor of Chapéu Mangueira still gets his dues from his buddies. Don't vote for him!"

So where does the sex come in?

Patience, people. We'll get there. Politics first.

The drug dealers' influence in the favelas was undeniable, even after many had been occupied by the pacifying police. Before Lula launched his *Bolsa Família* program, the drug trade had already established a similar scheme in the favelas to aid poor families, provided they remained loyal, of course. Furthermore, the trade has been and continues to be a means to combat unemployment, offering many young locals the chance to become skilled in their *métier*, with most becoming drug runners or spotters stationed at strategic locations to monitor the actions of the BOPE[12] and the various outsiders climbing up from the city's lower parts. Somehow, these votes had to be secured for her uncle, maintaining an appearance of the drug dealers being at odds with politics, outwardly claiming opposition to all candidates, but pointing out under wraps that it was best to vote for Adamastor. Above all, a lot of people on the hill would have to get it out of their heads that her uncle was a traitor. With these thoughts in mind, Maria Amélia called the drug trader's lawyer early the next morning. She told him she wanted to set an urgent meeting with Dente Grande, the boss of all bosses of Rio's hills.

"Whatever you have to say, you can say to me. Dente Grande has no time," Expedito Maciel answered.

"He doesn't have time? I want to hear him say that. Don't test my patience, Maciel! You know very well he meets me whenever I want. Give me his new cell phone number."

"Are you crazy, girl? That number is just for us."

"Then call, now! Tell him the young, braided lady wishes to speak to him, she wants to set a date."

"I'll see what I can do."

"You won't see anything. You'll call now. You know very well Dente Grande won't forgive you if you don't. I'm waiting. He'll answer right away. You'll see."

And the little witch's cell phone did in fact ring in less than five minutes, with a gruff voice on the other end softening into gentleness.

"Hey girl! You want to have a chat with me? Let's set the date."

"Yes, let's. A discreet and intimate meeting, so we can talk at ease."

"Great! I'm at your disposal, girl."

"Here's what we'll do: you put on fancy asphalt clothes, and we meet at the Santos Dumont Airport to board the six p.m. flight to São Paulo. We go straight to the hotel and spend the night, discussing a topic that interests all."

---

[12] Battalion of Special Police Operations, equivalent to SWAT.

"Perfect! It's a deal. Let's go to the Maksoud. I'll have Maciel make the reservation on my fancy name."

"No such luxury is needed."

"But it is, girl. It will grease the wheels of our little chat."

The numerous police officers at Santos Dumont Airport wouldn't have had any difficulty recognizing Dente Grande, even in his fine attire. His unusually large and wide incisors, the reason behind his nickname, made him easily identifiable. However, with his stylish new haircut, well-trimmed beard, and imported gabardine suit, he looked just like any other executive living on the shuttle flights of the Rio-São Paulo air bridge. He just needed to keep his mouth shut and avoid his characteristic, Ronaldinho-like grins. A serious senior executive accompanied by his diligent secretary donning a pair of red Prada's, showing off a statuesque body tucked into a dark yellow dress with light brown stockings. And putting on a pair of braids, as usual. He carried a briefcase, presumably filled with documents to ensure business ran smoothly. When Maria Amélia arrived at the airport, Dente Grande appraised her from head to toe and whispered:

"I don't know if I can handle all this beauty!"

And she smiled with the certainty of the upper hand:

"Take it easy, Dente Grande. It's a short flight, but the night is long. We'll not want for subjects."

He didn't take it easy. He didn't even have time to be afraid.

He always made the sign of the cross when the plane took off. And the fear was bigger at Santos Dumont Airport with its short runway. He imagined the clunker failing to lift off, struggling until it crashed into the Rio-Niterói bridge. Nothing happened. That is, the Boeing took flight without trouble and the stewardess was already serving snacks with soft drinks while Dente Grande remained motionless, captivated by Maria Amélia, as if hypnotized. And maybe he really was. Who knows. He didn't even indulge in his usual fantasies about the plane grazing the roof of the Ibirapuera Shopping Mall upon arrival, skipping past other buildings in Moema before landing on the very short runway at Congonhas Airport, perhaps even shorter than the one at Santos Dumont. A single false move—as had happened before—would be enough for the machine to break apart and blow up, causing devastation until finally crashing near Nicolau Weber Square. Instead, the plane landed smoothly, without even a bump, as probability theory predicted with a huge confidence interval. Dente Grande said:

"My girl, I didn't even feel the usual nerves I experience on these flying contraptions. You've bewitched me!"

Maria Amélia said nothing. She just took him by the hand and led him to the taxi stand. Within forty-five minutes, a miraculous feat given São Paulo's traffic, they were already settled in a luxurious room at the Maksoud Hotel. Maria Amélia wasted no time undressing—first the shoes, then the silk stockings, skirt, and blouse, leaving only her panties, as she neither wore nor needed a bra. Hard breasts, full in the right way, which in this case meant fitting comfortably in Dente Grande's not-so-small hands. She put on the see-through negligee, courtesy of the five-star hotel. Now comfortable, the little witch opened her laptop, set it on a worktable with two armchairs, and called to Dente Grande:

"Toothy, come to work!"

Working was not really on the dealer's mind at that time. Upon their arrival, he rushed to the bathroom to relieve the urgent pressure building in his pants. He took a hot shower, dried off quickly and went to answer Maria Amélia's call, totally naked, showing off a penis that could well carry the same adjective as his teeth.

Maria Amélia smiled and put on a fake frown, speaking as if addressing a child:

"Work first. Then you'll have your treat."

"But girl, how can I work like this. I'm in a pickle. Save me!"

The witch closed the laptop, took off her panties and nightgown, and said with the air of a teacher, but without hiding her malice:

"Okay. You'll never get work done like that. It's half past eight. At ten-thirty, the fun ends and work begins. Come here, you shameless Toothy."

Let's forego detailing the intense hours that followed. Surely, everyone wants to know about the exciting discussion that happened next. Would the little witch really convince Dente Grande to support Adamastor, under the radar, and what arguments would she put forth. So what if it was suggested at the beginning of the chapter that we would talk about sex? But for what? The intention was only to show that Maria Amélia is more than a cold and calculating witch. She also has a well-functioning libido. Some boor, perhaps prone to sexist and prejudiced views, might even suggest she swings both ways. Or don't you know that her relationship with Frederica involved—more boorishness—some scissoring? For those desiring a detailed account of the two hours in the Maksoud room, we suggest turning to the Kama Sutra, the complete works of the Marquis de Sade, Henry Miller with his tropics and plexuses, or closer to us in space and time, Reinaldo Moraes' *Pornopopeia*. They have everything. Sex in all positions, use of all body parts, and even descriptions of the flavors and odors emanating from what the fathers of the holy church would call "fornication." Dente Grande, a born boor, wanted all of it. Maria Amélia, with her refinement, gave him everything she was asked for and some more, but always making clear she was the one running the show. Imagine for yourselves, therefore, the two hours of fucking in the Maksoud. Now, let's return to what concerns us for the remainder of the story. Maria Amélia:

"That's enough, my toothy. Let's take a quick shower and then get to work."

"I'm here for whatever my girl wants."

After emerging from the bathroom, Maria Amélia slipped into her panties and nightgown, then opened her laptop. Dente Grande came out shortly after, still naked, displaying his nearly erect member. Maria Amélia passed her sentence.

"Put on some underwear, or those shorts you wear in the favela to keep your feelings under wraps. Sit here. What I'm going to tell you is going to take all the cluck-clucks out of that turkey."

"You want to scare me, girl?"

"Not scare, no. Just open your eyes, and also those of your companions, to the reality you don't want to face. Your dealing days in the favelas are numbered."

191

"Say again, girl? Dealing is my bread and butter!"

"It's not me, dearest. It is the new reality you don't want to see."

"Those peacekeeping pig-fuckers—and whoever the hell else—will leave things just as they've always been. The cleaning is only for the fucking World Cup and Olympics. Dr. Maciel assured me. It's a passing wave. There'll be enough people wanting to smoke and snort."

"I agree. The drug market will continue, but not on a criminal basis, with this game of hide and seek between you and the cops. You must prepare for the new reality. Ditch those lousy shorts and start dressing in a suit and tie. You look very elegant bundled up in a gabardine, you know. You just need to refine your language a little. You'll attract a lot of rich ladies out there."

"Thanks. Thanks. But Maciel assured ..."

"Assured what? Maciel is a sneaky bastard who's getting rich off your money. And he's safe. Resting easy in his Copacabana apartment, shielded by the privileges that come with being a lawyer. Meanwhile, you're in the favelas, chained to the old methods. You'll be decimated by the BOPE and the UPP, both armed to the teeth for when the need comes to silence those who don't want to accept their pacification. Have you noticed that the banks are rising in the favelas? Just cross that fancy walkway built by Lula in Rocinha[13] and you'll find the branches of the big banks, Caixa Econômica and whatever. These people don't go out on a limb. They're going up the hill because they know the police are there to stay. It's the owners of financial capital, the bankers, who are in control, including of your trade. Their swindle makes yours look like child's play and they are well armed. You can't even begin to imagine."

"People will always be there to snort and smoke. The drug trade is forever, my girl."

"True. But the favela will no longer be the point of sale. Before long, marijuana will be legalized and sold in kiosks with mortadella sandwiches and guarana[14] on the side. Even cocaine will be accepted, although it may

---

[13] The largest favela in Rio de Janeiro with around 100,000 inhabitants.
[14] Brazilian soda.

be a decade or two before it is legalized. For years, the UN has been warning that repression isn't the solution to the problem. You of course haven't read the chorus of reports proclaiming the war on drugs is over, led by FHC. The distribution centers will move down to the asphalt, the city streets. Drug runners won't be needed in this world of cell phones, GPS and who the hell knows what more. You'll be left behind if you cling to the old ways. What's more, there is less misery. Technological progress not only allows but demands a fairer distribution of wealth. Drug dealers on the hill will be cut off, not because of the pacifying police and all the empty populism of the rulers, but because the greatest consumers live on the asphalt and will be happy to acquire their drugs with greater comfort and fewer risks down there. You belong to a bygone era, a past time. Get it, Dente Grande?"

"Hang on, girl. Hang on."

"Hang on what! I'm here to help, help you overcome this crisis and continue controlling the drug trade, in another environment and with other methods."

"Amelinha!"

"Don't call me Amelinha! I hate it. 'Girl' is fine. You can even call me Fiinha. That's how my real mother addressed me. It's a very long story. It's beside the point now. But Amelinha, no!"

"Fiinha. Okay. I like it! But listen. We know our business as it's always been done. We can't just change overnight. You're asking us to close down all our trap houses just like that. It can't be done, Fiinha. Fiinha. Yeah, I like it, I really like it. Look here, even Luizão liked it."

"Don't change the subject, Dente Grande. You call that turkey Luizão? Settle down."

"My Fiinha, my girl, don't be angry with me. I should be angry with you."

"Angry for what?"

"You want me to shut down all my trap houses."

"I don't want you to shut down anything. Put out the fire in that turkey and pay attention. I'm saying things are changing. I want to help. That's the reason we're here, isn't it?"

"But I'm not sure what to do. The higher-ups won't get it. So, what exactly does my Fiinha want"

"It's nothing too complex. Just stay out of next year's election for now. Sit tight, abstain, let the people on the hill vote as they please."

"We don't give a damn about those slimy politicians!"

"Then great! You'll convince your thugs on the hill to stop blocking my uncle from coming up. He's running for Congress. He has to visit the hill because he can't win without their votes."

"Fiinha, that's too much to ask. Adamastor betrayed us. He switched sides. The men won't take it. If he stays down there, okay."

"My uncle didn't betray anyone. Come on, he bailed from a sinking ship, which you should do as soon as possible. The favela vote is essential for his election. You don't have to endorse him. In fact, you'd better not support him at all. We'll take care of the campaign. You guys stay put."

"The men won't accept it."

"You have the strength to convince them. Aren't you the top dog of Rio's hills? Exercise your authority!"

"And what do we get out of it?"

"A congressman who'll facilitate the drug trade's transition to the asphalt. Above all, a congressman ready to denounce any arbitrary action by the police on the hills. You'll see my uncle didn't betray you. On the contrary, he is opening the doors to a clean exit. But all this has to happen behind the scenes."

"I'll take it to the men and Maciel. But it's going to be a tough sell."

Maciel. That lawyer was stuck in Maria Amélia's throat. She would have to make him come to heel. But most of all, she convinced herself that she needed another night's work at Maksoud with the boss of all bosses, mixing business with pleasure. And to wrap up the first round of talks, she said:

"Alright. Go talk to your guys. And now, come here. I want a taste of that turkey."

34

Maria Amélia decided it would be best for them to return on separate flights to avoid the risk of being seen together. Even in his clever disguise, a more attentive reporter or, worse, a cop, could recognize the drug boss, accompanied by the niece of Chapéu Mangueira's former capo. Dente Grande objected:

"You wouldn't believe it, but I'm terrified of going on those flying contraptions. And the landing in Santos Dumont, Jesus! The thing has to make a turn. The wing almost touches the ground. Jesus on the cross!"

"You should be terrified of a police bullet, of the non-stray variety. One with an actual address. Let me know if you change your cell number."

In Rio, a very urgent problem awaited Maria Amélia: the pandemonium that had become her uncle's relationship with her adoptive mother. Each time Adamastor tried to call, Anita slammed the phone down without a word. It was now the third day, and the phone in the mansion's living room was out of order. And Maria Amélia was not on hand to calm Anita's spirits, occupied as she was in a private meeting with the drug boss at the Maksoud. Also not available was Anita's former best friend and confidant. The estrangement between Maria Amélia and Frederica had concomitantly triggered the cooling of Anita and Cleide's relations. This gradual cooling eventually led to a complete rupture. Cleide would no longer answer Anita's calls, which first occurred almost daily, then weekly, until one day Cleide answered:

"Yeah, it's me."

"Finally! I've been trying to reach you for a while."

"What do you want?"

"Talk, why, what else! I don't get it, Cleide."

"I don't have time!"

A long silence followed. And although Anita was not the most discerning type, she understood the friendship had died for good with that dry, impersonal "I don't have time." She told herself that her friend and confidante had simply changed with the daughter's suicide. A pent-up bitterness that couldn't be shared with fair-weather friends. Of course, this is not how Anita reasoned it, and she certainly didn't suspect that the adopted daughter could be behind the story. She never called Cleide again, and her other second-tier friends weren't enough to vent such accumulated jealousy.

The uncle's call for help reached Maria Amélia while she was still in São Paulo:

"Your mother has hung up on me about 200 times already. I don't know what to do."

"Yes, well, what did you expect, Uncle? You and Érica flaunting it like that. In front of the TV cameras. And then that lovebird-gaze farewell. You met her later, didn't you?"

"My dearest niece. I need help. Don't judge me. I love Anita."

"Yeah, yeah ... Leave it to me. She listens to me. Please take it easy with Érica. Be more discreet. I think it's time for a real wedding, in a nicely decorated church, with all the bells and whistles people love so much. You and Mom Anita. Me as maid of honor. It's going to be beautiful."

"But first, you need to clear things up for me. For God's sake, my dearest niece!"

Maria Amélia went straight to her adoptive mother's house, without even stopping by her apartment in Ipanema. She didn't ring the bell but opened the door with her key and entered, calling out:

"Mom Anita! Mom Anita!"

Anita hurried over, and embracing her adopted daughter, began crying so loudly that her sobs could be heard outside. The tears wet Maria Amélia's shoulders, and she was tempted to say: "Stop being a fool, keep your high school dramas to yourself!" Instead, she caressed the crying woman's hair and comforted her:

"Don't cry, Mommy. Don't cry. There is no reason for so many tears."

"He doesn't love me anymore. Your uncle doesn't love me anymore. He wants to trade me in for that shameless little hack."

196

"That's not true, Mommy. In politics, you have to play nice with everyone. That's what happened. I agree that Érica may well have ulterior motives, but my uncle adores you. So much so that he is desperate about what is happening. He says it's a blow to his heart every time my mommy slams the phone in his face. And listen, he told me, in tears, that he wants to marry you as soon as possible. That he has no eyes for other women. He swore it."

"Oh, he doesn't? So, what did I see on TV? What the entire city of Rio saw!"

The crying became convulsive. Maria Amélia drew her closer and continued stroking her hair, in silence, until the crisis subsided, leaving only soft sobs, like a passing thunderstorm. When at last silence reigned, the little witch blew into Anita's ear:

"He loves you. You and no one else. I assure you. And you know I'm never wrong. This is your Fiinha talking. Uncle Adamastor adores you."

"You swear?"

"On the leafcutter ant's ass," passed through Maria Amélia's mind, but what she voiced was more in line with the soothing tone needed to placate a betrayed woman.

"I swear! I can already hear the wedding march. The church full of people, the cream of Rio's society attending the wedding between the Planalto Central's most dashing deputy to be and the most beautiful widow in all of Rio de Janeiro. You're not meant to be a widow. Remember, it's been a year since Dad Joaquim passed. He wants your happiness, wherever he is. I dreamt about him, did you know? 'Maria Amélia, tell your mother to be happy and I'll share in her joy.' With that serious voice of his. Mom Anita, Dad Joaquim signed the release on your happiness."

She went a little overboard and sobbed at the same rhythm as her adoptive mother. Next time, Anita wasn't going to slam the phone in her lover's face, for they had a high-profile wedding to plan.

35

In matters of love and politics, everything was proceeding smoothly for the former cleaning products vendor from Rio's favelas. However, a prosecutor stood in his way. For Dr. Almeida da Fonseca, Adamastor's book was essentially a written confession, fully admissible in any court. Consequently, he issued an indictment just two months prior to Adamastor's planned campaign launch.

"Now what?" he asked his niece, visibly distressed.

"Now, Uncle, we take advantage of the trial, use the press to bring public opinion to our side and forge ahead."

"That's not going be easy. What about the Clean Slate Act? It is still in effect!"

"Rotting in low-paid public employment is easy, but not at all exciting. Don't worry. You've got two lawyers ready to give this Almeidinha a reality check. My sweet uncle's name will be so spotless that not even the Clean Slate Act will be able to touch you."

"Two?"

"Madalena and me. We've already drawn the line of defense. I'll stay more in the background, leave the talking to Madalena, who is finishing her master's degree in criminology. But there's an issue, Uncle. Madalena runs rings around Érica. And you, with your inability to see a skirt tail without losing it, cannot disrupt the show. Mom Anita will be present at the trial, remember. And as you know, Uncle, just as Nélson Gonçalves famously sang in his baritone voice, jealousy is the monster of society."

"Come on! All I can think about is getting out of this. But is Madalena experienced?"

"She is. And I am even more. Don't worry. We'll take this Almeidinha by surprise."

"Surprise? Surprise how?"

"Accepting the complaint. Pleading guilty."

"My dearest niece, you want to scare me to death? I'll go to prison!"

"Please, Uncle, I've had to endure enough drama lately. After all, what is that book you wrote? A declaration of your drug dealing? It's spelled out right there."

"You wrote it, Niece."

"But I didn't sign it. It's your name on the titlepage. We discussed this issue plenty. It was a risk we accepted. Now, we must ride the wave and surf our way to victory."

"I take the blame. Then what?"

"Then comes the question of sentencing. A former drug dealer openly admits to his past crimes and pledges to follow a righteous path from now on. Public opinion will cheer. People in bars will be saying, 'I wish those politicians would do the same! If he runs, Adamastor's got my vote.' In the legal sphere, the higher courts have accepted the jurisprudence that a spontaneous confession, even if partial, is a mitigating circumstance. And that's mitigation with a capital 'M,' especially when public opinion is in favor of the accused. Actually, Uncle, we should thank this Almeidinha. He's giving us the boost we need to launch your candidacy."

"And my life behind bars!"

"My dearest uncle ... It's petty to not want to take any risks, and the petty always lag behind. If you even go to jail, it won't be for more than a month. Other punishments are more likely, such as fines or community service. The latter would be great. And once the sentence is served, no Clean Slate Law will be in our way."

"Oh, Niece, I wish I could share your optimism! I don't mean to be blunt, but it's my ass on the line!"

"In line to Brasilia, my dearest uncle. Next year, you'll be sitting in one of the seats in the chamber's assembly. Leave it to me. Leave it to me and Madalena. We'll tell you precisely what to say during the trial."

The trial was an additional shock for Anita, fresh from the trauma of Adamastor's flirtation with Érica in front of the television cameras. All her thoughts were on the wedding. At the very least, she wanted something sumptuous with the Candelária Church as setting. And beneath her worries about Adamastor's trial was another dilemma: whether or not to invite Cleide. She consulted Maria Amélia.

"Yes, send her a dry and formal invitation. She's not coming. Better that way."

"It's a shame, we were such close friends. You're still in contact with Frederica, aren't you? She must know what happened. Try to find out for me, my daughter."

"Frederica? She's in the United States now. Let them be, Mom Anita. We don't need them. Don't dwell on it."

"Throw away a friendship of so many years, just like that?"

"It's like cleaning the house. Sometimes you have to discard things that once seemed essential but are no longer needed."

"You scare me sometimes, my daughter. Cleide was my best friend."

"Was, you say. Was. She's not anymore."

Maria Amélia pondered that Rio de Janeiro was full of women like her mother, keen on forming cliques, gossiping, and meddling in others' affairs.

"You're right," she finally said. "Her daughter's suicide turned her heart bitter. Unfortunately, we can't do anything. Forget her."

Problem solved. Anita decided to mail Cleide a formal invitation, sending it for the sake of sending. But what about the case against Adamastor? How would her friends react? How would the news reverberate in the upper echelons of Rio society she found herself in? Help, Maria Amélia!

"Don't lose any sleep over that, Mom Anita. Uncle Adamastor is already one of us. He is no longer a cleaning products vendor in the favelas. He's riding high, the author of a best-seller, poised to win a guaranteed spot in Congress. The trial will help his rise. Focus on the wedding and drop that worried expression—it doesn't suit you."

"Oh, my daughter, what would I be without you?!"

Any mind reader would have picked up, "The same fool, but filled with nothing but nonsense." Maria Amélia said goodbye to Anita with a long assertive hug and took a taxi straight to her uncle's apartment in Copacabana. The newspaper headlines demanded her presence. One of them cut to the chase:

"Prosecutor Asks for Adamastor's Preventive Detention"

"Have you seen this? Have you seen this, Niece?" exclaimed the former drug dealer as soon as Maria Amélia arrived, skipping the usual peck on the cheek and fanfare of her visits.

"I have seen it and read it. Everything, my dear, frightened little uncle. And just like you, I also read the presiding judge's prompt denial, arguing there was no other choice. Look here, read: 'Given that the defendant poses no danger, I refuse the request for preventive detention, recalling that the accused confessed of his own free will and has shown a willingness to cooperate with Justice on several occasions.' Uncle, things are going our way. We have nothing to complain about. Have you read the editorial of the largest newspaper in the city? If not, read it"—and she pointed out the text with her finger.

Waste of the Prosecutor's Time

Out of duty, prosecutor Júlio Almeida da Fonseca asked for the preventive arrest of Adamastor Leite Feitosa. But he knew in advance his request would not be granted in any court. And neither will be any attempt to convict the defendant, other than to a pro forma sentence, at most, community services. Adamastor's actions are commendable. He had the courage to give up his life of crime voluntarily, even going public with a book about it called Social Lessons from the Drug World's Gutter. If only more politicians had the guts to come clean about their dirty deeds, like Adamastor did. Public opinion has already absolved Adamastor. Much of the press has done the same. Now it's time for the judicial system to follow suit and pave the way for Adamastor to pursue his newfound path of righteousness.

Maria Amélia clapped when her uncle finished reading the editorial.

"Do you think that's good enough, Congressman Adamastor Leite Feitosa?"

With a look of relaxation, he replied:

"I truly hope so. I'll be praying to the Virgin Mary for it."

"Well, Uncle, I can assure you that both your defense lawyers aren't virgins."

And she laughed as she hugged the still frightened, but in the future surely acquitted candidate.

A little more than a month after this conversation, Adamastor was indeed acquitted, perhaps not fully, but certainly symbolically. The prosecutor was actually just going through the motions. The evidence presented was right there in the defendant's own book. Without any new evidence, the accusation that he had been involved in the punishment of snitches during his drug-dealing days was dismissed as pure speculation. Nothing. Except for some notes in the tabloid press. Adamastor's reputation as the big shot in Chapéu Mangeira was always that of a *good* dealer. Peaceful, resolving misunderstandings with a talk. His maid, Alzira, testified to this:

"I've never had a better boss. He gave me everything I wanted, even helped educate my boys. Agenô is completing some course ... I'm not sure, Senai or something."

Fantastic. A Robin Hood, leaving his adventurous past behind and pledging to walk the path of law, alongside the sheriff's ex-wife. The judge handed down the sentence:

"A week of volunteer work at the LBA. Function: distribute warm clothes to homeless people in Rio de Janeiro."

Maria Amélia couldn't have planned it better. All in full view of the press.

"Wait a minute! Get your face closer to that elderly woman. Just like that, perfect!"

For once, the tabloids featured a front-page photo unrelated to any crime. The condemned Adamastor, his cleanly shaven face almost touching the dirt-streaked cheeks of a homeless woman on Praça XV's sidewalk, as he handed her a blanket.

After serving his sentence, the PSB's state committee unanimously endorsed the repentant dealer's candidacy for federal deputy. Everything absolutely compliant and according to plan. And we haven't even touched on Madalena's brilliant performance, guided by Maria Amélia. In the audience, someone smelled something fishy watching that strikingly beautiful woman defend the former drug dealer tooth and nail. Who could this have been?

36

In the speech launching his candidacy aired during the free electoral ad time, Adamastor made an additional pronouncement:

"I want to announce that I'm leaving the single life and committing my heart to this wonderful person by my side. We're getting married on the thirtieth."

And he kissed the cheek of the Sheriff's widow, wearing her black dress with golden weave, sparkling like the stars in the firmament. Snap, snap, snap! The next day, the pictures of candidate and bride appeared on some front pages and virtually all social columns and gossip blogs. A sea of likes on Facebook. Cleide was going to miss a huge wedding. Speaking of Cleide, what about Frederica? Is she still in Arizona? Working on her master's thesis: "Comparative Study on the Beliefs and Rituals in Urban Centers of the Americas." Yes, in that her research is not yet complete, but no, as she's currently in Rio de Janeiro on vacation. The day she arrived, she hugged her mother and asked:

"Have you been to that house?"

Cleide understood immediately and answered:

"No. I never set foot there again."

"Great!"

And they shared a complicit look. The father, who cared little for his wife's relations with the socialites, merely shrugged, as someone without a clue. The day after her arrival, Frederica called Maria da Anunciação:

"Good morning, Dr. Anunciação. I'm Frederica, the twin sister of your former patient Camélia. Do you remember?"

"Of course, I do. How are you doing? What can I do for you?"

"I'd like to meet you, not exactly as a patient. But you can schedule it as an appointment. It's a touchy subject ..."

"And does this matter pertain to a certain braided person, by any chance?"

"How did you guess? Yes, indeed, I wanted to talk about her."

"Come this afternoon. I'm canceling one of my less urgent calls. It will be my pleasure to receive you. No appointment. I think we have a mutual interest in this matter. Four o'clock?"

"Perfect. I'll be there. Four o'clock."

Meanwhile, in the proscribed house not far away, Anita, Adamastor, Maria Amélia, Madalena, in her capacity as electoral campaign manager, three representatives of the PSB's state leadership, and a few other friends, raised their champagne glasses to the new candidate. Maria Amélia was first to make the toast, saying:

"To my dearest uncle. See you in Brasilia!"

"In Brasilia!" the others answered in unison.

Anita, however, didn't really care one bit about Brasilia or any of the political chatter. Her thoughts were on Candelária's decorations with white carnations and red roses everywhere. And she in a dazzling pale pink dress and 1920s hat. Maria Amélia's suggestion. All guests, men and women, dressed *a la vintage*. She dreamed of an epoch-defining wedding that would cause waves on social media, shine on television and blogs, make the front pages, and then spread over the pages of the weekly magazines. She wouldn't settle for less, she wanted to be on the cover of Veja under the title "Wedding of the Century." With just the right subtitle to make the socialites drool:

"The Envy of Gatsby"

Poor Cleide, who wouldn't attend. Or would she? No, of course not. She had received the invitation, torn it up without a second thought, and tossed it into the trash can. Just like that, without a word to her husband or Frederica, who was enjoying the last weeks of her vacation.

Frederica arrived at Dr. Anunciação's office at four. The secretary had been dismissed. The psychiatrist was waiting for her in person. They greeted each other with the traditional pecks on the cheek, sat side by side in comfortable armchairs in the waiting room, and started the conversation. The psychiatrist spoke first:

"You were friends for a long time, right? Best friends ..."

"We were. And I deeply regret it. I should have listened to my sister, poor thing. She saw through it all, from the start."

"All of it ... And what exactly did your sister see?"

"You know perfectly well. The braided hag—I can't call her anything else—just dominated me all the time. The same way she dominates all around her. She seems to have attracted Camélia's accident at the school gate."

Frederica started sobbing.

"My sister told me, and I didn't believe her. Just before the car hit her, she saw the mocking smile on the braided hag's face, as if looking forward to what was about to happen. My poor sister ..."

The psychiatrist took her hands, trying to comfort her. Frederica continued:

"And there's more. Something I never told anyone. I'll tell you but you must keep it a secret."

"That's what we psychiatrists do most: keep secrets."

"My sister left me a note on the day of her suicide. This one, which I've kept with me ever since. Written in her own blood."

Maria da Anunciação read it aloud:

"Keep away from her!"

"Yes, 'keep away from her!' But there was no need, she drifted away from me. Thanks to my poor sister."

"What do you mean?"

"I found the note on the morning of the suicide. I didn't take it seriously. I went to Barra da Tijuca with the braided hag, for another of her so-called 'lessons' on dealing with men in the future. Lewd and indecent! And not just with me. The entire class. All like little bitches trained to satisfy all her impure desires. Disgusting tramp! Sorry, I feel sick just remembering. But that day in Barra da Tijuca she didn't want anything to do with me. It was the first time I saw her complain about being unwell. We left. It was as if my presence bothered her. At my sister's burial, the wretch came up to me and hissed in a commanding tone: 'throw it away!' I said I wouldn't. And she walked off, forever, I pray to the heavens."

"The note. She told you to throw it away? But how did she know?"

"You tell me. How did she know? Can that wretch read thoughts? Is she in league with the devil? Back at the university, in Arizona, I spoke to a handful of witchcraft experts and two of the world's most renowned parapsychologists. They didn't tell me anything I didn't already know."

"Did you show them the note?"

"No, like I said, you are the first person I've shown it to."

"Well, you should have shown it. Do it next time. It may be painful, but you need to face the problem."

"Maybe I will. I'm afraid of betraying my sister's memory."

"On the contrary. But I have a proposal. You're still in Brazil for a few more days, right?"

"Two weeks."

"Great! We are going to pay professor Fábio da Mata a visit. He has a rather interesting theory about reincarnations. He is convinced that Maria Amélia is the reincarnation of an aunt who passed away in the early 1900s. It would be interesting to see his reaction to the note. Are you up for it?"

"I don't know. I'm skeptical about these things and need to think it over. I think I've heard of him from your paper, 'Patient X,' if I'm not mistaken."

"Exactly. That's him. Shall we? I can call him right now and we can make an appointment. He lives downtown."

"I have to think it through. I'll call you tomorrow. Poor Camélia, she tried to make me see and I turned a blind eye. I can't forgive myself!"

They said goodbye. Frederica stressed she would call the next day.

In the mansion once owned by Rio's former Secretary of Penitentiary Administration, not far from the psychiatrist's office, something was humming. A bee in the widow-bride's bonnet. It was withering the carnations and roses in Candelária's decoration and pushing the wedding march off track, as a slipping needle of an old record player. And it was Madalena who was going up to the altar in her wedding dress. Come on! Anita just couldn't swallow that a beautiful girl like that was merely the groom's innocent campaign manager. She wanted her to be the stereotypical college nerd: skinny, round glasses with black rims, flat like an ironing board, skinny arms, bad nails, stinky armpit ... And, if possible, no twat or any other penetrable orifices. Anita complained to Maria Amélia:

"I really don't like that girl, that Madalena, speaking to Adamastor every day. Your uncle is such a womanizer ... if I don't keep an eye on it ..."

"What's this, Mom Anita? You don't need to worry about Madalena at all. I vouch for her."

"I don't know, Fiinha. I have to be careful."

Maria Amélia smiled and said:

"Mommy, if you're worried about Madalena, sleep easy. I never told anyone because it doesn't matter, we must mind our own business and live as we choose, right? Madalena doesn't like men. She's a proud lesbian."

"A *dyke*?"

"Call it what you want. I'm not prejudiced. She even has a steady girlfriend. Don't worry. Nothing goes up that thicket."

"I'm relieved. That shameless hack was more than enough. I've already spoken to your uncle and I'm counting on you to help keep that little hussy away from me. I'm capable of making a scene. Kick up a fuss bigger than the Flying Circus."

"Stay cool, Mom Anita. Stay cool ..."

But Madalena's lesbianism was nothing but one of the witch's fabrications. An extreme sexual appetite is what she really had. In the lean years, when still one of Madame Xavier's girls, she took the greatest pleasure in most paid fornications. Now, free from financial constraints and to fuck whoever she wanted, Madalena managed three boyfriends and already had her sights on two PSB leaders. And she had big eyes for

Adamastor, of course, while also perfectly aware that a simple flirtation with the candidate would be like killing the goose with the golden eggs. More than Anita's jealousy, she feared the other, the one controlling everything and everyone. So even though she didn't like it, Madalena wasn't at all surprised when Maria Amélia told her bluntly:

"You'll pretend to be a lesbian every time you're in the presence of Mom Anita. You should even hit on me when Mom Anita is around. Of course, I'll scold you for it, lightly. But what I really want you to do is invite one of your former colleagues, maybe the chubby one from the day Felisberto opened his beak. You'll invite her into the committee office, close the door, and start a make-out session. Kisses, palpations, little fingers wherever you want. Then, at the right moment, when things are really hot, you call my cell. I'll open the door in the company of Mom Anita, and I hold it open just long enough for her to see the trailer."

"You are asking too much, Maria Amélia."

"Too much? Rubbish. Spare me your false decency. You've done a lot worse than that, sex with nasty, smelly customers. It'll be just once. Mom Anita will be appalled, and I'll tell her that you won't give any more shows like that after I speak to you. Once and done. And another thing. Keep your nymphomaniac advances for when you're not here. Not a glance, not one begging look at Uncle Adamastor. I want you to establish a reputation as a demanding bore here on the committee. Imitate Sigourney Weaver's toughness in *Working Girl*, but don't even think, however lightly, of playing Melanie Griffith's overflowing naivety, throwing your charms to everyone. But most of all, put out the fire between your legs, thinking that my uncle is some Harrison Ford available to everyone on the female staff. Are we clear?"

"All right, all right. But you don't have to tread on me like that. I accept. I'll perform the show," sighed Madalena, dissatisfied with the sacrifice that was required of her.

"And I hope the *performance* is impeccable."

But during the act, there was a little snag. As Maria Amélia walked toward the office with Anita, waiting for the phone to ring, Adamastor joined them.

208

"Oh, you two are here. Wait for me. I have to get some papers from Madalena."

And he opened the door just as Maria Amélia's phone was ringing. He froze for a moment, closed the door, and turned to the other two as someone who had seen what he ought not.

"What is it, Uncle?"

"Nothing. I'll come back later. Let's get some coffee."

"Later? I want to see what alarmed you so. Come, Mom Anita."

And she opened the door just in time to see Madalena and her former colleague trying to pull themselves together, one wearing her panties, the other trying to erase the lipstick stains that were going down her stomach. Anita, stunned:

"Oh! What's this? Oh, my God!"

Maria Amélia, harsher than Sigourney Weaver:

"What a disgrace!"

She pulled Anita by the arm and left, slamming the door.

"How horrible, I never thought Madalena had come to this point. Go meet Uncle Adamastor. I'll go back to straighten Madalena out."

"Straighten her out? Fire her, you mean."

"Easy, Mom Anita. Being a lesbian is no crime, it is not a reason for dismissal. Of course, being discreet is key to anyone running a political campaign. Such a scene will not be repeated."

Maria Amélia went back into the office, leaving Anita red-faced and at a loss as where to go. When she closed the door, she smiled to both women, still troubled by the plan's outcome, and said, clapping lightly:

"Excellent! Worth it! The addition improved the sonnet. Matilda, you're excused. You can go now. You've got talent, girl! Go be an actress, it's better than whoring around. And you, keep your head cool. I'm going to soften Mom Anita up now and remind my dear uncle that firing an employee for lesbianism is a very bad look."

Said and done. In the small restaurant across from the committee, Adamastor and Anita discussed the event heatedly. In fact, they had already decided on Madalena's summary dismissal.

"By today," Adamastor said to Anita as Maria Amélia joined them.

"Today what?"

"Madalena gets the boot."

"Are you crazy, sweet uncle? Fire her for what?"

"You have to ask? After the scene we saw you ask why?"

"Yes, I do. We fire Madalena and she flies to the press the same day. I can give you a heads up on some of the following headlines: 'Fired Because of Bigotry'; 'Gay Movement Accuses Adamastor of Discrimination'; 'Gays in Campaign against Former Drug Dealer' ... Nobody wants that, right, Uncle?"

"But it's a scandal!"

"Easy, Mom Anita. I've already spoken to Madalena. Her friend will never set foot here again. She promised the utmost discretion henceforth. Her sexual preferences are not our concern. What we're interested in is this feisty thing's efficiency. We're not gonna lose her. The incident is closed! Isn't that right, Congressman Adamastor?"

The candidate, who still had an election ahead of him, merely acquiesced and nodded yes. Anita still said:

"I don't care if you say I'm bigoted. But I would fire her."

Maria Amélia kissed her on the forehead and whispered in her ear:

"All the better. One less worry about our sweet uncle."

The next day, Frederica phoned Maria da Anunciação as promised, telling her she agreed to meet professor Fábio da Mata. And on that same afternoon, they went knocking on the door of the reincarnation specialist. The niece opened the door, informing them that her uncle was waiting in the living room before returning to the kitchen. The professor greeted them with a sly smile.

"What an honor to have you back. It is a pity you didn't bring our dear Maria Amélia. Who is the young lady?"

"Frederica. It's Maria Amélia we want to talk about. Frederica was her friend. She is currently studying in the United States."

"Was? Not anymore?"

"No, in all honesty, not anymore. She has something very interesting to show you. Show him, Frederica."

She took the note out of her wallet and placed it on the small table in front of the old professor. He looked at it, picked it up, examined it more closely, and returned it to Frederica.

"I feel the immense emotional charge of the one who wrote it. And it looks written in blood. Was it?"

"Exactly, professor. Tell him, Frederica, tell him."

"My sister, Camélia, wrote it on the morning of her suicide. Because of her."

"And *her*, let me guess, that's our dear Maria Amélia."

"Exactly."

A deep silence followed, the kind that never seems to end. Noticing that Frederica was blocked, dissatisfied with the interlocutor's admiration of the hated braided hag, Maria da Anunciação decided to take the floor and explain everything.

"Years before her suicide, Camélia was run over at the school gate, shortly after our *dear* Maria Amélia's gaze pinned her down, as if she knew what was about to happen. After the accident, she lost the vivacity she enjoyed with Frederica, her twin sister. She went from being a brilliant student to a mediocre one, with no appetite for study, while Frederica became the best friend of our *dear* Maria Amélia. I think the professor has a clear picture now. But there is one more detail: on the day of Camélia's funeral, our *dear* Maria Amélia, unaware of the note's existence, came up to Frederica and whispered in her ear to throw it away. Throw what away? The note, of course. How did she know? There's much more to the story, but the professor has more than enough understanding in these matters. What does the professor say?"

"What do I say? Very simple. Both of you are mired in a sea of hate. Maria Amélia cannot be blamed for what happened to your sister. She just foresaw what was about to happen. Her privileged mind fished out a lint from the immediate future, as parapsychologists say. The note? How did she figure it out? Maybe you don't realize hatred can permeate objects.

Most don't. But someone capable of commanding her own reincarnation sees things that surpass the most fertile imagination. I'm sorry for your sister, but you can't blame Maria Amélia. Dr. Maria da Anunciação knows this, and if she doesn't, she should. Or, at least, she should be sceptical and seek explanations that go beyond the closed, so-called scientific standards. There is more between Heaven and Earth than academic certainty. There's too much hatred in you two. I smell it in the air."

Frederica began to cry while the psychiatrist, wounded in her pride, tried to argue.

"Excuse me, professor, but I don't hate anyone. I just want to understand, comprehend, if at all possible within the parameters that have always guided my studies. And the professor, forgive me if I offend you, seems himself totally bewitched. Unfortunately, we have to leave, the climate is not conducive to a rational discussion."

"It isn't, indeed. When you're calmer and have reached all the limits of rationality, come back. My door is open."

"Thank you," said Maria da Anunciação, pulling the sobbing Frederica by the arm.

Already on Buenos Aires Street, she said firmly:

"Crying's no use. Unfortunately, it didn't work out. He's more bewitched than I imagined. Maria Amélia has him under complete control. But there is another person who can provide us with useful information. When do you return to the United States?"

"I'm still here for ten days."

"Great! Then I can make a new appointment."

"And with who?"

"Tarquínio Esperidião. My old patient."

"The cursed woman's father, the killer rotting in prison?"

"Yes, him. And he hates that cursed woman more than the two of us put together."

37

Maria Amélia decided the election campaign should kick off with a rally at Chapéu Mangueira Hill. She was aware of the risks. But the benefits were huge, they would pay off. It would be the best way to immediately counter Ovídio Abreu's offensive, as he could count on the support of a couple of bigwigs controlling the pacifying police. Take the bull by the horns. Walk up the hill where her uncle once ruled as a drug boss with a slightly more substantive proposal for social inclusion than the typical, hollow favela-sweeping promises smelling of *déjà vu*. "Former Drug Dealer Returns to Hill and Says Work and Education Outweigh Election Eve Moralism." She anticipated such comments in several newspapers, and she would pull her strings to make it so, of course.

One remaining obstacle was Adamastor's replacement, his former underling Armandinho. In his eyes, her uncle was a traitor that couldn't ever set foot on Chapéu Mangueira again. "Only over my dead body," he would boast several times to his capos, although he knew many did not agree. Worse yet, Armandinho was unwise enough to blurt it out loud and clear, in one of his delirious small boss tantrums:

"He won't come up here! He can climb Rocinha. Dente Grande will let him up."

The phrase "poking the bear" almost fits, but Dente Grande saw himself more as a tiger than a bear, and he wouldn't allow nudging with any stick. Armandinho was summoned to a meeting in Rocinha, with the observation that if he did not go willingly, he would be taken. He went and defended himself with talk of autonomy:

"We agreed that as long as we followed the security rules, we would have autonomy to manage our respective areas. Preventing a traitor from ascending the hill falls under my jurisdiction. You have to support me, otherwise our discipline becomes a free-for-all for those snitches."

"Listen here, Armandinho. Fuck your autonomy. The matter has already been settled. You were already warned not to stick your nose in it, pal. I'll let your nitwit antics slide. This time! Don't show your face on the hill for a while. Take a vacation. Tonho Duck Foot will take your place. Go to Crateús and don't come back until after the election. Go visit your family. Leave now. Today, if possible. Adamastor goes wherever he wants. He minds his own business, we mind ours. We're not going to get involved in this fucking election."

"Well, that's ridiculous!"

"Ridiculous? You waking up with a mouth full of ants is bad for all of us. Don't push your luck, nitwit! My patience is wearing very thin. You've been warned, nitwit!"

Fortunately, Armandinho's survival instincts spoke louder than his wounded pride. The next day, he boarded a Gol plane to Recife. Had he woken up with a mouth full of ants, that would have been a major setback for the plans of Adamastor and his niece. It would be hard not to associate the execution with the candidacy. Dente Grande took it upon himself to call Maria Amélia.

"All clear, Daddy's little heartthrob. Your uncle can go up."

And he ascended with the expected pomp and circumstance. The only reason the turnout wasn't higher is that the area at the end of the Ary Barroso Avenue ramp couldn't handle such a crowd. A couple of thousand people let's say. In Maria Amélia's reckoning, more than enough to bring the first free TV ad to fruition. With symbolic imagery, of course, marking the end of her uncle's more than one year-long banishment, prevented from going up there where he had once been king. Without a target on his back, he could walk up the hill freely and enjoy the view he enjoyed so much. Once elected to the federal congress, however, his new domains would extend beyond the views from even the Babylon or Rocinha summits. As Adamastor ascended the Ary Barroso, he noticed with unease that the shacks' walls, the lampposts, and other surfaces were plastered with his opponent's posters: "Ovidio's broom will clean up the favela," "If you like filth, get out," "Congressman Ovídio," "Clean favela with Ovídio." And there was the opponent's image on all the posters, as some Jânio Quadros reincarnate.

214

Maria Amélia caught her uncle's worried look. She smiled.

"Are you scared of the man with the broom? Don't fret. Give me the speech. I'm going to make some small adjustments to the introduction."

In just a few minutes, she made changes to directly counter the opponent's promised broom sweeps. Adamastor began the speech on the improvised stage at the end of the long zigzag uphill, next to Anita and with Mary Amélia and Madalena behind him:

"I don't need to introduce myself. Everyone knows me here. And I will continue to be Adamastor of Chapéu Mangueira. But a new Adamastor. An Adamastor who is no longer here to sell the illusion of drugs. An Adamastor who proposes a journey toward freedom from poverty and unemployment and away from the glaring inequalities between asphalt and hill. I didn't bring a broom. Favelados aren't filthy. (Applause). Favelados are poor and face discrimination. Have you ever seen the news of a nice apartment in Barra da Tijuca being invaded by BOPE? Without a warrant? No. Of course not. Yet this is what happens on the hills of Rio de Janeiro almost every day. Invasions! Complete disregard for the right to sleep peacefully in your own home, even if it is a shack. There is a widespread belief that favelados are some second-class citizens who don't enjoy the full rights of the suits below them. It bears repeating. Favelados are not filthy. You don't need a broom. You need a job. You need a school. And, above all, you need respect. I'll fight together with you for all of this. That is what the new Adamastor of Chapéu Mangueira promises you ..."

Thunderous applause. But let's pause the speech here, which actually continued for another three pages. Despite the good reception on the hill, Maria Amélia was more interested in the newspaper and social media coverage the next day. While the favela vote was crucial, winning over the intelligentsia and the progressive middle class was equally important. She thought a lot about all this while writing the speech. She refrained from making concrete promises that were impossible to keep. But, above all, she was very happy to frame her opponent as a simple broomstick distributor. The headlines, the radio and television news would inundate all hills and favelas with Adamastor's speech, which purposefully contained more accusations than promises.

With the exception of the pro-Ovídio tabloid, almost all newspapers welcomed Adamastor's speech and gave it heavy prominence. This was echoed by all the television news shows. In the most famous one, the host exchanged a knowing look with his co-presenter and said:

"Adamastor Leite Feitosa once again didn't run from his past as dealer. He introduced himself as Adamastor of Chapéu Mangueira, stating very accurately that favelados aren't filthy, they don't need a broom. He undoubtedly won a point over Ovídio Abreu, whose proposed sweeps are both out-of-turn and outdated. Let's wait for the opinion polls."

Was she satisfied with this? No, Maria Amélia wanted more—much more. See her uncle exceed the vote count obtained by Tiririca in 2010, without being a clown.[15] Even Paulo Coelho would have to say that the whole universe was conspiring for the braided witch's beloved uncle. After reading all the newspapers, she said to the select audience at the Lagoa mansion, smiling and oozing with cynicism:

"We couldn't be happier. We're knocking it out of the park! But let's not even think of letting our guard down. The price of freedom is eternal vigilance. A quote from the old UDN brigadier or from Thomas Jefferson, the abolitionist with a handful of slaves on his plantations, who knows? Our vigilance is more restricted. We just need to stop Ovídio's broom from taking flight and sweeping the favela votes with it."

Madalena attempted a mistimed joke:

"And brooms fly?"

"You look like you read Harry Potter. You should know that they do."

A few seconds of awkward silence followed, because the tone of Maria Amélia's reply was no joke. Anita was the first to speak:

---

[15] Tiririca famously campaigned as clown with the slogan *"Vote Tiririca; Pior do que tá não fica."* (Vote for Tiririca; It won't get worse than it already is.)

"I'm sorry, but I don't get any of this political talk. My daughter said so and I believe it: Adamastor will win and be the best and most beautiful congressman in Brasilia, I'm sure. If you'll excuse me, I have a date with my friends in Barra Shopping. See you later."

She kissed Maria Amélia on the forehead and Adamastor on the mouth.

At the mall she met someone she didn't expect: Frederica. Both were standing in front of a shoe store when they came face to face. Too close for either to pretend not to see the other. Anita said:

"Frederica? What a pleasure!"

"Good afternoon, Dona Anita."

"None of this Dona nonsense. How are you? And your mother?"

"Fine. We're fine. Will you excuse me?"

"Wait a minute. Tell me more. You are studying in the United States, aren't you?"

"I am!"

"Will you be here next week for my wedding? I sent an invitation to your mother."

"Mrs. Anita, I'm sorry if I'm rude, but I don't feel comfortable pretending nothing has changed in our relations."

"But that's what I don't understand. What changed? Why did it change?"

"Ask your adopted daughter."

"My daughter, you mean? My lovely daughter whose best friend you were?! I don't understand. Please explain. I want to know what happened."

"I have something to show you. Actually, come with me. I'll make a photocopy to satisfy your daughter's curiosity."

They went to the Saraiva bookstore and Frederica took a color photocopy of Camelia's note. She handed it to Anita in a sealed envelope.

"To satisfy her curiosity. Goodbye, Mrs. Anita. And please don't call my mom anymore. Friendships end, haven't you been told?"

217

Maria Amélia was still in the Lagoa mansion when Anita returned from the mall much earlier than expected. Visibly shaken, she did not even kiss Adamastor or caress the face of her adopted daughter. She also didn't share any details about her shopping adventures or conversations with friends. She walked in empty-handed and went straight to her room.

"Excuse me, I have a headache. I'm gonna lie down a bit."

Maria Amélia followed her, certain that something serious had happened.

"I'm sorry, Mom Anita, but this isn't just a headache. Something happened. Something that really upset you. Actually, I've never seen you this way. Not even during those silly bouts of baseless jealousy. What happened?"

"Your friend sent you this. She said it would satisfy your curiosity."

"My friend?"

"Yes, Frederica."

Maria Amélia opened the envelope and read it, her expression growing even tenser than her foster mother's. She put the note back in the envelope and murmured under her breath:

"Bitch!"

"What is it, my daughter? What's the matter?"

"Let's burn this now. Let's go to the kitchen. We will burn it until nothing is left."

"But what is it, what is it?"

Anita followed Maria Amélia into the kitchen, who took a silver platter out of the cupboard, placed the envelope on it, soaked it with alcohol, and set it on fire.

"What was it, Fiinha? What was it?"

"A suicide note from the deceased, telling Frederica to stay away from me. Jealousy, Mom Anita! Jealousy! She blamed me for them growing apart."

"How absurd!"

"Exactly, Mom Anita, absurd. I, you, we did everything to help them, gave them every kind of support. And this is how they repay us. With spite.

218

But let's forget it. We have two important tasks: a wedding and an election. Look, there's nothing left. Even the ashes were swallowed up by the exhaust. Some things need to be extinguished."

Lies. Maria Amélia was lying to herself. The original note was still intact, kept in a golden heart-shaped pouch Frederica always wore close to her chest. She wouldn't even take it off to sleep or shower. Not at all. And yet it had to be destroyed. It was an inadmissible indictment.

Anita felt a chill down her spine, seeing her daughter's fear for the first time. The faint echo of Tarquínio's curse, warning that she would regret the adoption, rang in her ears. She closed her eyes to ward off the evil thoughts. Maria Amélia sensed the growing doubt in Anita, as if she could see it materializing. She hugged her, stroked her face and hair. They sat in silence for more than five minutes. When she spoke, Maria Amélia's voice was soft but firm:

"Mommy, nothing can come between us. Not the envy of the living or the spite of the dead. Our bond was sealed when you wiped away my orphan tears in the penitentiary. Not even if you had given birth to me, would there be such a strong seal. Don't be shaken by such hatred."

Anita, in tears, pressed Maria Amélia close and exclaimed with a surge of maternal emotion:

"My Fiinha. My Fiinha."

38

The wedding day arrived and even nature was feeling generous, radiating her warmth under a clear blue sky. The Candelária was adorned with white carnations and red roses to receive the cream of Rio de Janeiro's society, all clad in suits and dresses from the 1920s, the time of silent movies and the automobile's invasion of the streets. The guests were paraded in those vintage cars and Louise Brooks hairstyles in a procession that brought traffic to a halt on Primeiro de Março Street. Buses were parked aside, as their passengers watched the colorful convoy pass, accompanied by a festival of horns and applause, even from about a half-dozen beggars on the sidewalks. The cars, more than 300, had been borrowed or rented from collectors across Brazil, an operation costing more than 500 thousand reais. Enough money, at the very least, to elect a state assemblyman, a newspaper would print the next day. In front went the groom in a light grey tuxedo and hat of the same color with a wide dark gray band. Al Capone style. A provocation? Justified in the name of elegance, most social columnists would agree the next day. And so Adamastor went alone, stylish, behind the wheel of a 1926 Bentley Speed Six whose color almost matched the driver's clothing. A Cuban cigar stuck in his mouth only for show, because he did not smoke. Fords, Mercedes, Alfa Romeos, almost everything produced in the effervescent twenties of the last century. And in the procession's rear went the bride in a stunning pale pink dress, seated in the back of a 1938 Ford Model A, shining as if it had just rolled out of the factory, just for her. Its light beige color contrasted with black mudguards and two headlights reminiscent of Fernando Pessoa's glasses. Everything blindingly shiny, driven by a uniformed chauffeur in cap, goggles, and gloves, in the muggy heat at the end of a sunny day. In the car just ahead of the bride, a Model T, Maria Amélia sat behind the wheel, perhaps imitating Fiinha the First, who also drove an identical car belonging to one of her uncles, without ever having taken lessons. (More details in the book *A Witch in the Window*, right now we have a wedding to attend.)

Next to Maria Amélia, also in the front seat, went Madalena. The driver's dress was black and transparent at the top, and the passenger's was pleated blue. But it was Maria Amélia's hat that stood out the most, dark gray and ornamented on the right side with an immense red rose. The braids thrown forward in an X. In short, a faithful reproduction of Fiinha the first's photograph hanging on her aunt's wall in Santo Antônio das Tabocas. That is how she led her adoptive mother down the aisle, holding hands to give her to her uncle. The bride's light pink dress, needless to say, was entirely overshadowed by the adopted daughter in black, who captured everyone's attention with her piercing gaze.

As anticipated and desired, the wedding had huge repercussions. It featured on all the evening news shows, and the next day headlines and blog posts abounded: "Show of Luxury and Wealth," "Rio's Finest Back to the 1920s," "Return to the 1920s at Adamastor and Anita Xavier's Wedding," "Adamastor Wedding has 1920s Car Show." There were also critical pieces, writing about the wedding's exhibitionism and extravagances.

One note was particularly scathing:

Adamastor of Chapéu Mangueira Marries in Al Capone style

It is strange to see the former dealer, Adamastor of Chapéu Mangueira, today running for federal congress, marry the widow of Rio's former Secretary of Penitentiary Administration. And it is telling that he showed up at the Candelária ceremony wearing a suit and hat imitating Al Capone. Sure, everyone was adorned in 1920s fashion. One was even dressed up as Rudolph Valentino in the role of the Sheikh. But come on, not one of his aides could recommend to the groom that an Eliot Ness impression would be better? Or that such exhibitionism doesn't go well with a candidate asking for the votes of the poorest, in the favelas?

The note caused some wrinkles of concern in Adamastor. But Anita was profoundly irritated by a short and blunt comment in a social column:

"Wedding or Carnival?
Never were so many peacocks seen in one place."

The next day, before the honeymoon trip to Paris, Maria Amélia went to the Lagoa mansion to have breakfast with the newlyweds, certain that she would have some work appeasing them because of the unfavorable news. Anita was furious:

"Have you seen this, Fiinha? Have you seen this? Read! 'Never were so many peacocks seen in one place.' We don't deserve that!"

221

"Mommy, there is no such thing as bad publicity. While you're outraged by this nonsense in an irrelevant rag you fail to see the positive buzz in most newspapers, on television and the Internet. And just wait until you see the stories in the weeklies. The wedding will go down in the history of Rio's social life."

"I hope so!"

"Smile, silly. Look here, this wonderful photo on the front page."

"I'm worried, Niece. I fear all this could have a negative impact in the favelas. Luxury and wealth. And we need the poor vote, as this newspaper very well reminded us."

"My dearest uncle. Poor people like voting rich. When they look in the mirror, they want to see a lucky, successful person. When they vote, they think: 'I will not choose another loser like me.' Oh, what about Lula. Well, Lula never presented himself as a nobody, but as a person who came from nothing and became a leader, his reflection in the mirror transformed into reality. Or perhaps he's like Narcissus, seeing his reflection in the murky waters of politics, but with his feet firmly on the ground so as not to be submerged by the mud. That's a good example. Yes, we'll get a lot of flak. From self-appointed moralists, from young people immersed in fleeting idealism. But when all is said and done, human nature prevails, which is to always evolve, always improve. And for the individual, improving means having a shot at getting everything you want. In a word, get rich. A poor candidate doesn't show the formula to get rich. So, the masses almost always vote on those who have enrichment *know-how*. Do you see, Uncle? This is no talk for on stage. It's between us. They can say whatever they want, but politics is the art of manipulation. After murdering Caesar, Brutus addresses the plebs as an honorable and wealthy citizen and convinces them he did it for the well-being of all and the Roman Empire. Then comes Mark Antony, before the same plebs, and shows that the murder was a heinous act against the Empire. The plebs waver. Whoever manipulates them best, wins. Shakespeare's *Julius Caesar* is a political science class. I recommend reading it before moving to Brasilia. Or at least watch the 1953 movie. We're moving into sticky, booby-trapped terrain.

A swamp. Don't fret about this marriage news. People love pomp and circumstance. The wedding's glamour will not cost votes in the favela. But it may attract some from Mom Anita's friends, from the inhabitants of the mansions around Lagoa and the penthouses of Leblon and Ipanema."

"Oh, my goodness, Fiinha. You're amazing!"

"Realistic, Mom Anita. Realistic is the word."

"Yeah, but I still don't like this Al Capone story. We should have thought of that. An Eliot Ness hat would even look good on me."

"Eliot Ness?"

"He was just a hard-nosed cop, Mom Anita, like Dad Joaquim. From the movie *The Untouchables*, starring Kevin Costner. Remember? Nonsense, Uncle. Al Capone suits you better. Stylish. It's the sense of humor of someone who has nothing to fear or a clean conscience. As far as I know, a costume has never taken a vote from anyone."

Thanks to Maria Amélia, Adamastor and Anita were able to travel in peace to Paris, where they would stay at the Ritz for a week. Enough time. Perhaps even too much, considering the election battle was about to reach its peak. Ovídio, broom in hand, would certainly make his speech throwing Al Capone's hat and the freely flowing money into the plebs' face.

Maria da Anunciação, meanwhile, had pulled her strings to get the interview with Tarquínio Esperidião. It wasn't easy. At first, he did not want to see her, judging her to be one of the little witch's friends and defenders. After much insistence, he took the psychiatrist's call.

"What do you want?"

"A conversation of mutual interest, to clip the wings of someone you know very well."

"Clip the wings? As far as I know, you're one of the hag's fans."

"Maybe I was. I'm not anymore. And I want to introduce you to a former friend of hers, in fact her former best friend, who today addresses her as you just did, hag."

"And why didn't you say that straight away? Just make an appointment with these bureaucrat fuckers at the penitentiary. I have plenty of time."

The phone call was on Wednesday and the meeting was set for the following Saturday, the eve of Frederica's return to the US. A rainy morning, and Frederica did not believe she would get anything useful out of her visit, certainly nothing that would at least compensate for the vexation of being searched by malicious eyes and restless hands touching what they shouldn't. Good thing it was a policewoman, but she couldn't help but express her discomfort, almost saying out loud, "indecent!" when her breasts and vagina were groped at length. The psychiatrist's search went much faster, with the policewoman intimidated by the visitor's steady eyes. Tarquínio was waiting for them in the visitor's room, handcuffed.

He dismissed introductions:

"What do you want from me?"

"Good morning, Mr. Esperidião. This is Frederica, who I told you about over the phone."

He looked her up and down and said:

"So, you were the little witch's best friend, were you? And what happened? What scam did she pull?"

"It is a very long story, Mr. Tarquínio. Tell him, Frederica."

Frederica told him everything. The friendship after the initial skirmishes at school, Camelia's accident, her suicide, and the note left by her sister. When at last she finished, she was trembling, deeply moved, on the verge of tears.

"It's hanging here on my neck. I always have it on me."

A few feet away, the guard pointed to his watch, indicating that visiting hours were about to end. Dr. Anunciação made a sign asking for a few more moments.

"Miss, I don't think you should walk around with that. Don't throw it away. That's what the witch wants, right? But keep that note in a safe place. Don't walk around with it."

Maria da Anunciação interjected:

"And why not?"

"Because she wants to destroy that note at any cost. And destroying it together with the person who carries it wouldn't make the slightest

224

difference for her. With that around her neck, that girl is attracting all the evil the witch has. Keep it in a safe place, but away from you. I know who we're talking about."

"Your daughter, isn't she?"

"No, no, and no. She's not my daughter. I've explained all this to you, Dr. Anunciação. Don't provoke me. She's not my daughter. She generated herself."

"What I know is that you, imprisoned all these years, haven't thought of much else than neutralizing your daught ... I mean, Maria Amélia's exceptional powers ..."

"The witch. You can say it. That's what she is."

"Have you reached any conclusions?"

"I wish! What about you? This young lady here, if you play it carefully, maybe she's a way to finish her off before she does us."

"You scare me. But I'm not taking it off. It stays here in honor of my poor sister."

"Then don't say I didn't warn you."

Tarquínio was interrupted by the guard, who came to end the visit. Both women left in silence, Frederica still deeply moved, clutching the message written in her sister's blood to her chest. It was only after a long time, already back in the car in the city, that Frederica spoke.

"Why does he want me to take it off?"

"That man is obsessed, as you saw. He firmly believes that his body was possessed by the other Maria Amélia, the dead one, when he had sexual relations with my former assistant, Sister Patricia, the mother of the living Maria Amélia."

"The hag!"

"Yes, the hag. It's only natural the note's existence upsets him. Perhaps it's overkill, but it wouldn't hurt to put it in a safe place, as he suggested. Maybe for your own peace of mind."

"No, the safest place is with me. I will not betray my sister. It is an amulet that is already part of me. I won't take it off."

"Okay. You don't have to fight me. I spoke as a psychiatrist, to reassure you. Habits of my profession. As a friend, I respect your wishes. Keep it on you."

In Paris, drowning in the luxury and wealth of a champagne-drenched honeymoon, Anita didn't hear about any of it. Adamastor didn't tell her, following his niece's recommendation, who had told him about the accident in Aterro do Flamengo.

"Don't say anything, Uncle. Mom Anita would be upset. By the time she comes back, the information will have left the news. Time is the best medicine to cope with tragedies. My suggestion is that you come, as arranged, and leave Mom Anita in Paris for another ten days. You have a lot of friends out there. She'll like it."

At first, Anita twisted her nose at the proposal. She wanted to enjoy her husband's company for longer. If it were up to her, the honeymoon would be endless.

"Endless. Just the two of us. We could even do like John Lennon and Yoko Ono, seven days without getting out of bed."

Adamastor pondered that he needed to return to Rio de Janeiro. The political campaign, with the beginning of free ad time on television, demanded his presence.

"It's going to be a lot of work, my sweetie pie. I won't have time for anything else. You'll be bored. You still have lots to explore here with Valquíria. You'll return to Rio with an MBA in Paris. You'll be your friends' envy."

"But what I want is your tight hug. That's all."

"We'll have plenty of time. But first, the work, my sweetie pie."

The angry girl pout was her sign of acceptance. Adamastor boarded an Air France flight to Rio de Janeiro, still in time to read the latest repercussions in the press of the scene of fire and blood in Aterro do Flamengo.

At eleven o'clock in the morning, a twenty-two-year-old man drove his Land Rover against traffic up the Aterro do Flamengo in the direction of Centro-Zona Sul, after ingesting a couple of whiskeys mixed with cocaine.

First, he grazed a crowded bus, which overturned leaving four dead and at least thirty injured. Many cars crashed in an attempt to avoid the collision, among them another bus, which skid off the track and left another ten passengers injured. Finally, the Land Rover collided head-on with an Audi A4, which was coming at more than fifty miles per hour. The vehicles exploded and caught fire, completely burning the bodies of the young man and the other vehicle's driver. With one exception. The Audi driver's right arm was ripped off during the crash and thrown about fifteen feet away.

"Folly, Death, and Fire at Aterro," a headline read a few minutes later on the homepage of the site of one of Rio's main newspapers. But it is the text that concerns us most:

> The Galvão Cerqueira family has once again fallen victim to Rio's traffic madness. Anthropologist Frederica Galvão Cerqueira was one of the five fatal victims of the accident at Aterro do Flamengo. A Land Rover driving the wrong way collided head-on with her Audi. Both bodies were burned, with the exception of Frederica's right arm, which was torn off during the collision and greatly facilitated the body's identification. The Land Rover's driver was identified as Alberto Sampaio, a diagnosed schizophrenic and drug addict ...

One detail did not make the news: Frederica's hand was closed, holding the amulet she wore on her chest. The forensic experts were at a loss to explain how this was possible. She would've had only fractions of a second to react between the moment she saw the Land Rover flying toward her and the impact. Still, in a reflex, she had grasped the amulet the instant her arm was torn off by an iron bar. The arm was collected without any reporter seeing it.

During the burial of what remained of Frederica—for the worms, only one arm—Cleide Galvão Cerqueira could not shed a tear. Numbed as someone who has lost everything, and perhaps, expects nothing more. She walked with her head held high beside her husband, his head bowed, tears streaming down his face. Immediately after came Maria da Anunciação, visibly shaken. Cleide's eyes shone with hatred, tempered with restrained despair. She had nothing to lose, but maybe something to do. Hanging around her neck, she carried the amulet with her suicidal daughter's note.

39

Nobody should blame Maria Amélia for the accident. After all, her only concern at the time was her uncle's election; all her efforts were focused on that. She wasn't even slightly concerned with otherworldly matters. Frederica was undeniably a closed chapter, long archived in the past. When she stumbled upon the news while browsing the Internet, just a few hours after the accident, she felt a fleeting moment of compassion, a passing flash. But she didn't have time to waste. A potentially explosive election campaign was around the corner, after all. Ovídio Abreu made his first appearance on the free electoral TV slot going all out against Adamastor, the extravagant drug dealer who had squandered a fortune on a wedding party.

> Is this the champion of the favelas? A self-confessed drug dealer embraced by socialites with nothing better to do, teaming up with pseudo-intellectuals in defense of drug liberalization, as if marijuana and cocaine were soft drinks? No! We must reject those who ignore the need to clean up the slums, to sweep away drug dealers and organized crime once and for all. We stand with the Pacification Police. We stand for a clean favela. I count on your vote!

Upon arriving at campaign headquarters, Maria Amélia expected to see her uncle hunched over newspaper headlines, nervously biting his nails because of the comments surrounding his opponent's speech. She was wrong. The accident at Aterro do Flamengo was what worried him most. He feared his niece would be too shocked, sidelined from the campaign trail for perhaps an entire week. As soon as she arrived, he said to her:

"You can go back home, Niece. You must be in shock."

Pretending not to understand, she replied:

"Uncle, are you talking about Ovídio's speech? We'll dismantle it in the blink of an eye."

"Haven't you heard about the news? The crash at Aterro."

"Oh, yes. On the Internet. It was truly tragic."

"Wasn't she your best friend?"

"Yes, she was. Poor thing. Uncle, disasters happen every day. There's no point lamenting what can no longer be changed. Shake it off and get rid of that mournful look on your face. Focus. The task at hand is to use heavy artillery to destroy Ovídio, broom and all."

"Alright, Niece. Whatever you want." But to himself, he thought, "My God!"

Maria Amélia entered Madalena's office, and the two of them began crafting Adamastor's speech for the free airtime. It turned out like this:

No introduction is needed. Everyone knows his name: Adamastor Leite, PSB candidate for federal congress. And it's no secret that he had ties to drug trafficking. Even Ovídio Abreu, who lives under a rock, knows that. However, the candidate Adamastor Leite is a different person. Not someone who is repentant, but someone who has evolved, who has become aware, who changed. He doesn't deny his past. And he is willing to be held accountable by the law. He proposes a different future. A future where dignity and respect prevail in the favelas, and where homes are not unlawfully invaded by law enforcement without judicial authorization. Isn't the law for everyone? So let the law be upheld. Dignity and respect. Not the harsh sweep of a broom tainted with cheap moralism.

After reading the text, Adamastor found it peculiar. He didn't quite understand the third-person perspective.

"It's a trick, Uncle. Old, but sometimes it works. You can only use it at the right moment and with great caution, so as not to appear arrogant, like dictators and kings. In this case, you're taking a critical position, speaking from the outside as if you were an observer. And observer means voter. These are questions your opponent will definitely ask and your enemies will thoroughly exploit. If you speak in the first person, most likely out of habit, people will expect a *mea culpa*, and that's something we need to avoid. I said it before, and I'll say it again: asking for forgiveness is an act of pusillanimity. What you did was change direction. But without lamenting the past. You will likely get votes from those wanting to stop all drug trafficking in the favela and the nostalgic who benefited from Adamastor's food baskets in Chapéu Mangueira. Do you see, Uncle?"

"More or less, Niece. But I still have one doubt. We didn't say anything about the wedding party. Ovídio is going guns blazing, denouncing the excessive spending."

"One thing at a time, Uncle. Let Ovídio rant for now. Enjoy playing the role of prince charming. When the time is right, we'll address the issue. After all, seconds are precious in free airtime. There's no time for distractions."

When Maria da Anunciação went to offer Cleide her condolences, she told her that they needed to talk. The grieving woman nodded in agreement, and the psychiatrist said she would call her the following week. Before that, however, she wanted to have another conversation with Professor Fábio da Mata. That same afternoon, she gave him a call:

"Professor, we need to meet. Can I come by this afternoon or tomorrow morning?"

"Come whenever you want. But I believe you'll be wasting your time if the subject is what I think it is."

The atmosphere was tense. The professor was first to speak.

"It seems my esteemed colleague is still poisoned, intent on blaming Maria Amélia for what occurred."

"Perhaps even the esteemed professor will have some doubts when he learns what happened on the morning of the accident. Frederica and I went to prison to speak with Tarquínio Esperidião, your dear Maria Amélia's father. Upon learning she was wearing her sister's note close to her heart, he warned her to remove it, fearing it could bring harm. Does the professor have anything to say?"

"That the deceased, my esteemed colleague, and Mr. Tarquínio were consumed by hatred. Yes, he is right. A suicide note written in one's own blood is not something to wear near the heart. It carries a great deal of hatred. It attracts misfortune, and I think that's what happened. There was even a coincidence. She died almost like her sister, a victim of a car accident."

"But who or what attracted the tragedy? Could it not have been the person most interested in destroying the note?"

"No, Dr. Anunciação. Maria Amélia does not concern herself with such things at the moment. And, moreover, she had already forgotten about her old friend. Don't try to blame her. A criminal investigator would not find a motive."

"Not a criminal investigator, perhaps, but the professor might. Let's not be naive. The note had a huge impact on your protégé."

"Yes, my protégé. Don't think I take that as an insult. I like the idea. Although it would be the other way around. I am the humble protégé of the one who managed to guide her own reincarnation. At the time, Maria Amélia felt that the note was driving her away from her friend. She tried to prevent that from happening. The other did not accept, and Maria Amélia simply continued on her path, allowing the other to follow her own. The hatred and resentment remained with her, along with the blood note hanging around her neck. Do not blame my girl in braids."

"*My girl in braids*? Is that what you call her now? Has the bewitchment reached such a degree?"

"Dr. Anunciação, you are blind. And if I may say so, without meaning any insult, you seem envious for not possessing as broad a perspective as my girl in braids."

"I believe we have nothing more to discuss on the matter. Our perspectives clash."

"Yes, ma'am, they clash. Nothing you say will convince me that my girl in braids is a bad person. It may well be she has a different view of what is good and evil. She is on a higher plane than our narrow moral view of the world."

"Goodbye, professor."

"Goodbye, doctor."

Maria da Anunciação had wanted to tell him that Cleide still possessed her daughter's suicide note. She had even wanted to arrange a meeting between the three of them. She left, dazed by the idea that maybe witchcraft did exist, that there could be some truth to the bizarre visions of many of her patients. One thing she knew: if Maria Amélia were a witch, she was an evil witch. And, therefore, she had to be extremely careful. The following week, she went to Cleide's house. Two concerns tormented her: not arousing Maria Amélia's vengeful wrath and not discrediting herself in front of the Brazilian Association of Psychiatrists. She exercised great caution during the conversation:

"Cleide, I see you still have that note around your neck."

"I do. And that's how I'll find my daughters, hopefully soon."

"It may be a cliché to say this, but life goes on. I know the pain you carry is immense at the moment, no words can soothe it. But one day you will overcome it, and when that happens, I think you should take the note off your neck, keep it, yes, in a secret place, but don't carry it with you."

"What are you talking about? I don't understand."

"That note carries a great emotional burden."

"Are you asking me to forget? I lost my two lovely daughters. I have nothing left, Maria da Anunciação. Nothing. Absolutely nothing. I'll carry it on my heart until I die, which I hope is very, very soon."

"I'm going to tell you something I haven't said yet."

"Say whatever you want, nothing else matters to me."

"Just before the accident, Frederica and I visited Maria Amélia's biological father in prison. And he warned Frederica about the danger of carrying the note around her neck."

"Are you telling me that wench could have caused the accident? That she killed Frederica, just like she killed Camélia? The murderer?!"

"I'm not saying that. I can't make such an accusation. Nobody can. No court in this world would accept such an accusation. I just think we need to be careful. It's not something a psychiatrist should say, but some phenomena we can't explain, phenomena that transcend the boundaries of our known world."

"And is there anything we can do to put an end to her and her whole kind? Anything? Do you have the answer, Maria da Anunciação?"

"No, I don't. And I don't even know if that's the way."

"Then we have nothing more to talk about."

The psychiatrist felt it was time to step back. Several minutes of silence followed. Finally, she said:

"I'm leaving, Cleide. You're right, our conversation doesn't make sense anymore."

"No, it doesn't. Come back when you have an answer to my question. Goodbye!"

"Goodbye."

40

Paris is a party. Especially for those staying at the Ritz, unconcerned about the euros they'll spend on a dinner with champagne at L'Ambroisie. Anita returned to Rio bursting with stories, eager to share everything she'd seen and enjoyed. She didn't let anyone else speak; she cared little for the election campaign. If Adamastor lost, all the better. They would have more time to enjoy life. Perhaps they could spend a six-month season in Paris, enjoy some time skiing in the Alps, have a chalet just for the two of them. They could live an endless honeymoon; her family's wealth would never run out.

"I fit right in. Even Estelinha, who's lived in Paris for ten years, was impressed. I spoke exclusively French. It was great. It's such a shame you had to return early, my love. Let's go back to the City of Light!"

"I'm glad you liked it so much, my dear."

"Mom Anita, Uncle is practically elected. No way he'd lose now. You've already discovered Paris. Now you'll discover Brasília."

"Oh, my daughter, don't say that! Yuck! I'm not going to that beachless desert. No way. Your uncle will have to live on a plane. I insist he be here every weekend, at the very least. Do you hear me, *cheri*? Every weekend, holidays, religious days, and any free time. Rio. Forget Brasília. And what's new around here? I haven't talked to anyone yet."

"Nothing too interesting, dear. No news. Just politics, which you don't care about, right?"

If not for Maria Amélia's training on how to control the rush to his face when lying, Adamastor would have turned into a ripe chili pepper. Maria Amélia smiled in approval, content with her uncle's choice to omit any mention of the accident in Aterro do Flamengo. She would find out soon enough, but the more time passed, the better. Bad news dissipates with time, just like everything else. Anita should vent all her emotions, recount all her adventures in Paris, and only then, *en passant*, learn about the tragedy from a friend. "Oh, how dreadful!" she would then say, but without being knocked out, and, above all, without getting obsessed about the talents her adoptive daughter was rumored to possess. Anita was still talking about her Parisian adventures in bed with Adamastor when the jet lag hit her. She turned to her side and said:

"*Bonne nuit, querridô.*"

It was only on the third day that she heard the news, during a phone call with one of her friends:

"Oh, dear, you didn't hear? It's terrible! Cleide is beyond consolation. In fact, she's been behaving quite strangely lately. She didn't cry during the funeral, you know, she was so distraught."

Anita confronted Maria Amélia and Adamastor:

"Why didn't you tell me?"

"We didn't want to burden you with it, Mom Anita. We thought it best not to disrupt your happiness. Besides, there was nothing you could do. It happened. An accident."

"I'm going to call Cleide. I have to call her. She was my best friend, after all."

"Mom Anita, you used the verb in the right tense. She was. And she has shown more than once she is no more. Don't call. There's too high a risk of being treated poorly."

"But why? Why?"

"Because that's how it is. Don't call!"

This was one of the few times Anita disobeyed her adoptive daughter's commands. When she found herself alone in the mansion that afternoon, she called her former friend. The husband answered the phone.

"I'm so sorry for not calling sooner. I was traveling and only just heard the news. It's just horrible! I don't know what to say. Can I speak to Cleide?"

"Best not, I think. She's still in shock. I appreciate it, but I think it's better not. I'll tell her you called."

Cleide took the phone from her husband's hand:

"I won't accept any condolences! Go talk to your daughter, she's probably overjoyed."

And she hung up the phone.

On the political-electoral front, things were developing marvelously. Money flowed into the campaign, even from the drug trade, disguised as donations from the favelas' merchants. Dente Grande became convinced that Adamastor as congressman would be of great value in the new times announced by Maria Amélia during their passionate lovemaking until dawn. Adamastor was voted in with the highest tally ever obtained by a federal deputy from Rio de Janeiro. Ovídio also got elected, but by a narrow margin, thanks to the votes from sentimental moralists and the far right, which was also interested in cleansing the favelas. Not with brooms, but with rattling machine guns and rifle shots. Maria Amélia decided to move with her uncle to Brasília, knowing that its foxes were far more cunning than Rio's Ovídios. They arranged to promote Madalena and make her the uncle's official aide, while Maria Amélia would continue as Richelieu, without a salary, pulling the strings of her puppets. No one could accuse Adamastor of nepotism. On the contrary, Maria Amélia was not only a great professional in the fields of law and psychiatry, but also had access to her adoptive family's immense wealth, of which she was the sole heir. Rich, intelligent, beautiful. Want more? There's more. She possessed exceptional powers. Just ask Professor Fábio da Mata in case of doubt. Or maybe Dr. Maria da Anunciação, who at this turn of events had become a friend and confidante of Cleide, meeting her at least twice a week. What were they talking about? Guess!

However, Anita's behavior appeared somewhat unusual during this period of change. She didn't like being away from her husband for an entire week, but deep down, without consciously admitting it, she found a certain relief in maintaining some distance from her adoptive daughter's overpowering presence. During her sleepless nights, Cleide's biting comment from their phone call continued to echo in her ears, just like her last conversation with Frederica at the mall. She didn't want to admit it, she made every effort not to accept it, but the truth was she had begun fearing her daughter. And in that realm between sleep and wakefulness, she still heard the incarcerated father's curse:

"You'll regret it. The little witch is no good. I'm here in prison because of her."

But it is Brasília that concerns us now. In Adamastor's eyes, the city was a spectacle, a thousand times more exciting than Paris with its wide avenues designed for military parades: Arc de Triomphe, La Defense, and whatever else. There, everything is made for the pomp and circumstance GIs like so much. Yuck! Brasília is more modest. The Esplanade of Ministries and the 250-yard span of the Eixo Monumental are wide, but not very suitable for parades. They are better for popular demonstrations on the medians between the six lanes on each side. It's not an issue, Brazil doesn't even have missiles to flex its military muscles. Why have a parade? One thing that caught Maria Amélia's eye was the discrepancy between Brasilia's architecture and its sidewalks.

"Pay attention, Uncle. When we look up, Brasília is beautiful, marvelous. But if we look down, it's a sorry affair. Broken sidewalks, even right at the entrance of Congress. Pity that it's a local issue, we won't have time to deal with it. Well, it isn't even just local. Even in São Paulo's Faria

Lima, with its majestic buildings housing the most powerful banks on the planet and star-packed hotels, the sidewalks are broken and poorly maintained. Rio's Atlântica Avenue, with its iconic wave-patterned pavement stones, stands as the exception to this trend of poorly maintained sidewalks. Despite being just an imitation of Manaus during the rubber boom era, Avenida Atlântica's sidewalks blend perfectly with the majestic hotels, from Leme to Posto Seis."[16]

"You're right, Niece."

He spoke for the sake of speaking. To give a response. In reality, Adamastor was thrilled. And in this state of near ecstasy, uncaring about such mundane matters as sidewalks, Adamastor entered Congress for the first time to assume his role as Federal Deputy for Rio de Janeiro. Three impeccably dressed women watched the ceremony from the gallery. One seemed a bit apprehensive, even gloomy. Maria Amélia had picked up on the adoptive mother's change in behavior some time ago. And she knew perfectly well why. As much as Anita tried to hide it, Maria Amélia learned of her meetings with Maria da Anunciação. The first meeting had happened shortly after the phone call to Cleide, and it was initiated by the psychiatrist, in the week following her return from Paris:

"You can come to my house whenever you want."

"No. Not your house. I prefer somewhere else. Can it be at my office?"

"Dr. Anunciação, you scare me. But alright. When?"

They scheduled the meeting for the next day's afternoon. Maria da Anunciação started speaking right away:

"I won't beat around the bush. The subject is your adoptive daughter, and I'll say it straight away: she is malicious, harmful, dangerous."

"How can you say such things to me, just like that? You're talking about someone I've raised since she was seven, with all the love, care, and affection a mother could give. Don't speak about my daughter like that!"

"Oh, Anita, you knew very well what this was about. Why did you come? Because you suspect too. It's impossible that after so many years,

---

[16] Leme and Posto 6 are at the extreme ends of Copacabana Beach.

you still haven't noticed the coldness, the calculative nature, the lack of compassion in your dear Maria Amélia."

"I'm leaving ..."

And she burst into tears. The psychiatrist continued sternly:

"Yes, go ahead and leave. And if there's any sand in your garden, bury your head in it. I won't conciliate. Your Maria Amélia harms people. Think about your friend Cleide, who lost two daughters."

"It was an accident!" Anita shouted amidst her tears as she stormed out, slamming the door.

That night, she couldn't sleep, feeling like a bug stuck in the web of a spider with cold grey eyes like her adoptive daughter's.

Adamastor failed to comprehend the depth of his wife's distress, who just a few days ago had been happily recounting her adventures in Paris. He asked:

"What's wrong, dear?"

"Nothing. It's just girl stuff. Frederica's accident has affected me deeply, and I couldn't even offer my condolences to Cleide. It will pass ... I hope it passes."

It didn't pass. Anita fell into a cycle of depression. It wasn't hard for Maria Amélia to find out that she had visited Maria da Anunciação's office. The psychiatry world is small, just like any professional group. News travels fast, and Maria Amélia had a great informant who, despite being confined to a wheelchair in downtown Rio de Janeiro, knew everything that was going on, with the support of all available means: telephone, Internet, television, and, of course, visits. Some of those visits, at least once a week, were from Maria Amélia, his girl in braids, the privileged one who guided her own reincarnation. During their last visit, Professor Fábio da Mata had told her:

"Be careful. Envy is the mother of most harm people inflict on each other. It's not for me to tell my girl this, you're much wiser than I am. A psychiatrist we both know is scheming things. She can't stand being surpassed. When she asks her mirror who's the brightest psychiatrist in Rio de Janeiro, do you know what it answers?"

"Oh, professor, I don't deserve such praise!"

"Yes, you do. False modesty is a weakness of inexperienced souls, which you certainly are not."

"Let Maria da Anunciação rant! Her and Dona Cleide. They blame me for the accident with Frederica. Did the professor know?"

"Yes, I did. It's the envy of one and the hatred of another. It's the suicide note that carries the curse. They are blinded. And when the blind fight, they shoot in all directions. No innocent person remains unharmed. You must be very careful."

"Mom Anita has already been hit, professor. She no longer has the courage to look me in the eyes. She's distant, unrecognizable. Maybe I have to resort to extreme methods to cure her. I still have doubts."

"Don't. Follow your instincts. Your strength lies in your instincts, detached from the moralism and concepts of an imperfect world."

The shock treatment Maria Amélia imagined was quite straightforward. Lay all the cards on the table. Let Anita know that she was aware of the accusations against her, that she knew about her encounter with Maria da Anunciação. And so she did the day before Adamastor's inauguration.

"Mom Anita, what's going on? Lift your head, look at me! It's Maria Amélia, your daughter. Don't you remember?"

Anita promptly burst into desperate tears and clung to the other woman in an awkward embrace. Maria Amélia gently caressed the hair and face of her adoptive mother, attempting to wipe away the cascading tears. But Maria Amélia sensed their bodies touched without any cushioning. Their auras no longer resonated with each other; the symbiosis was breaking, and the engine of their relationship was short on lubricant. Nevertheless, she spoke with affection yet determination.

"Don't let them poison our relationship. Maria da Anunciação is spiteful, envious, and Cleide is blinded by pain. People who suffer can't help but be bitter. Come back to us, Mom Anita. Go back to being the joyful woman you've always been and know that your daughter will be by your side no matter what."

After a few minutes, they released each other from the embrace. Anita tried to look her daughter in the eyes but broke down into convulsive sobs. Maria Amélia led her to the bedroom, helping her lie down.

"Rest, Mom Anita. Empty your mind of all negativity, and sleep."

Up until now, I have strived to be a faithful narrator, and it is not my place to justify any of my characters' actions or intentions. But now Maria Amélia is demanding that I justify, to you, reader, the next steps she had planned to resolve the issue with her adoptive mother. I won't engage in that. I yield my keyboard so she can explain herself in the first person:

"Mom Anita is poisoned. Incurably poisoned. Her stay in Paris was too short. She needed at least another month of parties and socializing before confronting the news of the disaster. I also underestimated Maria da Anunciação, let my guard down, allowed her to interfere. Mom Anita's psychiatric condition is quite simple: acute depression. She exhibits all the symptoms. With medication, the right antidepressants, her condition can be improved, but a cure is doubtful. Personally, I don't think it's possible. Her unlimited trust in me has been shattered. I own my mistake, but it's not in my nature to cry over spilled milk. A depressed Mom Anita is of no help to anyone. First and foremost, she won't help herself. From now on, she'll become increasingly unhappy. She won't help the people around her. Uncle Adamastor will be greatly affected in his affairs as rookie backbench congressman, and he will have to go to great lengths to achieve the goal we set, which is to lead the party. And that's not to mention the sexual problem. My uncle is in the prime of his fifties and wants to make the most of it. Depressed, out of sight for an entire week in Rio, Mom Anita can no longer quench his ardor, his desire. Depression is contagious, especially between the sheets. I've already seen my uncle looking at Madalena like a child eyeing a treat. It wouldn't surprise me if they've already slept together. You can't prevent what is human nature. The conclusion is obvious: Mom Anita's life no longer has meaning. Not for her, suffering from acute depression in a situation that only tends to worsen, not for Uncle Adamastor, not for me, transformed into the target of her suspicions. And one thing I know, don't ask me why, but I know. If I wish for her to die, she dies."

Maria Amélia's wishes are left in suspense, but the fact is that Anita's depressive condition worsened, displaying some classic symptoms: loss of appetite, nighttime insomnia and daytime drowsiness, headaches, and a complete lack of interest in everything around her. This was her state during Adamastor's inauguration, detached from the excitement of the new congress members, all eager to savor the sweet candy of power. Adamastor was one of the first to be called for the oath, which is done in alphabetical order. Shortly after being elected, he had traveled to London for a tailor-made suit. He swore:

"I promise to uphold, defend, and comply with the Constitution, observe the laws, promote the general welfare of the Brazilian people, and uphold the unity, integrity, and independence of Brazil."

Applause followed, applause because he deserved it. Madalena's frantic applause, accompanied by a languid look of pleasure; Maria Amélia's applause, crowning a victory that belonged to her more than anyone else; and Anita's three rhythmic claps, obligatory, her gaze lost somewhere in the Chamber of Deputies. Maria Amélia embraced her. Another uncushioned embrace. Their auras now repelled each other

Sixth Part

-

LAGOA'S LITTLE PARLIAMENT

41

They say that fire and gunpowder shouldn't be kept together. And Madalena was the gunpowder to Adamastor's fire. Or vice versa, if you prefer. Every day, several hours a day, in the same office. Most of the time alone. Could anyone endure that? Put yourself in Adamastor's shoes, spending his weekends with a constantly complaining, perpetually unenthusiastic woman. Unlike most, he dreamt of Mondays when he could take the eleven a.m. flight and be welcomed at Juscelino Kubitschek Airport by his faithful and smiling chief of staff. In the past few days, they walked hand in hand to the waiting official car. Another daily presence in the office was Maria Amélia—the super-assistant with no defined position, no salary. And Maria Amélia didn't meddle in the relationship between her uncle and his chief of staff. Actually, she did meddle. She was the one who consented their imminent intimacy. Anita, meanwhile, was definitely filed away as a lost cause. Adamastor was apprehensive at first. He was afraid of getting involved with a lesbian, still remembering, with some disappointment, the day he caught her with her friend in the office. Once, as if meaning nothing by it, he casually mentioned it to his niece.

"Incredible. I'm not prejudiced, far from it. But it's a shame such a beautiful woman like Madalena is a lesbian."

Maria Amélia burst out laughing:

"Uncle, Uncle ..."

"What's so funny?"

"I'm laughing at my sweet uncle who's dying of desire for his chief of staff."

"Me? I'm a faithful husband, Niece."

"Oh, really ... What if I tell you something? Madalena isn't a lesbian."

"She isn't? Then she swings both ways?"

"No, my dear sexist uncle. She only likes one thing."

"What do you mean? I saw it with my own eyes. And so did you."

245

"It was all performance, Uncle. Pure acting. It was my idea. So Mom Anita wouldn't interfere. In addition to being beautiful and hot—wouldn't you agree, Uncle?—Madalena is also talented. The three of us make an unbeatable team, we'll cause a stir in the Chamber's plenary. And if you want to mix business with pleasure, go ahead."

"And your mother? I don't understand what's wrong with Anita. She came back so happy from Paris, and now this never-ending depression."

"It's really a difficult and sad situation. Even I, as a psychiatrist, don't know what else to do except continue prescribing the usual antidepressants. I think she dreamt of having you all to herself in Rio de Janeiro. She was disappointed. She thought you wouldn't be like Dad Joaquim, who only cared about his profession. She was already experiencing intense feelings of alienation. Dissatisfied, she fell into depression."

"The disaster with Frederica also seems to have really affected her."

"Yes, it did. Both things, Uncle. You'll have to be very patient with her. But don't stop living. Keep doing what you've been doing. Dedicate the weekends to her, but don't forget to live your life in every other aspect."

"Wise, Niece. Wise."

On that same day, Adamastor planted a kiss on Madalena's lips after locking the office door. The aide's tongue almost reached the congressman's throat.

To rise to his party's leadership, Adamastor needed to show his worth, present projects, participate in committees, and, above all, seize every opportunity to speak in the plenary. He entered with his good looks, his ease of communication, his slick tongue honed in Rio's favela. Everything to make it very far, with the best aides of the Planalto Central by his side. Efficient and beautiful aides. In no time, not a single congressman remained unaware of Maria Amélia's almost daily presence in the halls of Congress or the meetings in which her uncle participated. One of them once tried more intimacy by calling her "Amelinha."

"Not 'Amelinha,' congressman! Maria Amélia, please!"

She had cultivated a reputation for being both beautiful and fierce. Especially if anyone dared to make indecent proposals to her uncle, a novice in the political arena. One of Adamastor's first projects was to require that all municipalities in the country maintain enough primary schools to serve every inhabitant aged seven to fourteen. The federal government, in turn, would be obliged to provide the necessary funding to the municipalities that could prove they lacked resources. Come on, what did you expect? Nothing is created, everything is copied. Even more so in the world of politics. A project inspired by the "Zero Illiteracy" scheme of Rio's former governor, as you can see. A governor who himself imitated president Getúlio Vargas with a bullet to the chest. And it's clear that the major beneficiaries would be the favelas and small resource-deprived towns. The construction of such a large number of schools, many in remote areas where oversight is very hard, would of course require a significant, not-to-be-underestimated amount of money. Suppliers, construction companies, and even bankers interested in financing part of the project were buzzing with excitement. And the office door of the author who drafted the bill was the first they knocked on. There were three of them: the owner of the Agricultural and Livestock Bank of Minas Gerais; a supplier of construction material, also from Minas Gerais State; and a well-groomed lawyer. All three asked Madalena to leave, indicating that they felt more comfortable having a frank conversation with the congressman, alone. The lawyer started the conversation:

"First of all, we want to congratulate the honorable congressman for presenting a project that elevates the entire political class. Your Excellency went from defending education for all, in theory, to proposing something concrete to make it a reality ..."

The door opened and in walked Maria Amélia, who sat beside her uncle without even greeting the visitors.

"Gentlemen, this is my niece, Maria Amélia.

"We know who she is," the lawyer continued, "but we would very much like to speak privately with the honorable congressman. Could we ask the young lady to excuse us?"

"No chance! Whatever you have to say to my uncle, you can say to me as well. That's how we operate. As a team. And it's best to record the entire conversation to facilitate our understanding. We believe in maximum efficiency here. And transparency. A bunch of journalists out there are dying to know about these private conversations with deputies."

"I don't know if your niece speaks for the honorable congressman. Does she?"

"Yes, she does. We have no secrets."

"Well then, we'll leave it for another time. Good day, honorable congressman."

And the trio left, not daring to raise their heads, knowing they were being stared down by the congressman's niece.

Adamastor slapped his forehead.

"Oh, my dearest niece!"

"Your dearest niece won't let you engage in any cheap fuckery, not today, not tomorrow, not ever."

"This is business, Niece. Not cheap fuckery."

"Business?! Those three are well-known. The worst kind of lobbyists. What were they going to offer you? What's the commission? Political support if you favored their bid? We don't need any of that, Uncle. You're married to one of the richest women in Brazil, and besides you, the only heir is me. We don't need these cheap kickbacks. And even if we did, it's wise not to accept them from shady players like that. Do you know what the journalists call them in the hallways? The give-and-take trio. I wouldn't be surprised if the Federal Police is already on their tail. I've told you before, and I'll say it again: we're much more ambitious. Get that in your head. And the higher we rise, the greater the control of civil society. Doesn't uncle read the newspapers? Doesn't he browse the Internet? The process of democratization that Brazil—and arguably the entire world—is undergoing ensures that politicians are more accountable to groups forming and communicating at the grassroots level. Don't grow a tail to be stepped on, leaving a trail of fraud. That is, if you don't want to move beyond being an obscure federal deputy. And remember: many haven't

248

forgotten about Adamastor of Chapéu Mangueira, who made his living selling cleaning products in the favelas. You're still in the process of cleaning your record and need to be more careful than the average person. A paragon of honesty, as honesty is conceived in this hypocritical world. If that trio steps back in here, please show them the same door they came through."

Adamastor answered his niece with a sigh of consent just as Madalena returned from her lunch break. She realized an argument had taken place, and that once again, Maria Amélia had triumphed. She didn't get involved. Instead, she tried to break the tension, resorting to the weather:

"Ugh, I can't stand this dry air in Brasília! Did you see? Humidity at 17%, worse than the Sahara Desert. If I can, I'll go to Rio this weekend."

"But please, go alone. In Rio, you're answerable to Mom Anita."

"I don't know what you're talking about."

Maria Amélia responded with a glance, shooting her a piercing look from head to toe. And if Adamastor had a tail, it would have been tucked between his legs as he left:

"I'm going to have a cappuccino."

Anita was gradually wasting away. Lack of appetite was one of the most striking symptoms of her depression. Over the weekend, Adamastor went straight from the airport to the mansion in Lagoa and remained holed up there until Monday morning, listening to his wife's laments. He would rather stay in Brasília, in his room with the humidifier running, gently caressing his efficient aide's hair, among other little things. The weekend belonged to Anita, however, as stated in the first and only article of his niece's decree.

"Sweetie, let's go to the movies. There's a Woody Allen movie playing."

"I don't feel like it. You go if you want. I have a headache, I feel nauseous. No desire for anything."

"What can I do?"

"Nothing, Adamastor. Nothing."

"What did I do?"

"Nothing. You didn't do anything."

"Then who has caused you so much harm?"

The response was convulsive crying. Adamastor placed Anita's head on his lap and let her drain her reservoir of tears.

That afternoon, Maria Amélia visited her adoptive mother. She asked her uncle if she could have a few moments alone with her. With her eyes, Anita even begged her husband to stay in the room, but she couldn't put her desire into words. Maria Amélia addressed her adoptive mother almost like a professional:

"I see you're not taking your medication. Why are you refusing your medication? Mom Anita, don't you want to improve?"

"You know I don't need medication. You know why I'm like this."

"Do I, Mom Anita?"

"Yes, you do. There's nothing worse in this world than a mother losing her daughter. Where is my little braided girl? Oh, dear God, where is she?"

"She's right here by your side, Mom Anita. She never left you. Please don't tell me that you're still in touch with Maria da Anunciação. Don't let yourself be poisoned. Look into my eyes, it's me, Maria Amélia, your Fiinha, remember, your Fiinha."

"Which one?"

"Mom Anita! The only one. The one who loves you with all her heart."

She sat on the bed and began stroking Anita's hair, pulling her head onto her lap. They remained in silence for over ten minutes, only the sound of a tear-choked breath could be heard. The one sitting, gently caressing the other's hair, didn't make a sound. Her gaze was fixed on the wall, detached like a judge from the emotional aspects of a case, her verdict already decided.

Although sultry and promising an afternoon storm, Monday morning arrived like a blessing for Adamastor. He had the maid bring him a hearty breakfast in bed, while Anita, beside him, barely drank a cup of tea and nibbled on a biscuit. He got up, kissed his wife's forehead, and said to her:

"Take care! Let me know if anything comes up. I'll come whenever you need me, even if I have to interrupt a speech in the plenary."

Anita responded only with a look, perhaps wanting to convey, "He learned to be a populist even with his own wife."

Upon boarding, Adamastor noticed that Maria Amélia was on the same flight. They sat together.

"Uncle, Anita's condition is serious. I fear she won't be able to get through this."

"What do you mean, Niece? It's just depression, right? It should pass, shouldn't it?"

"It's acute depression, Uncle. And I'm afraid there are other complications."

"Complications?"

"Don't be so startled, Uncle. One patient at a time. In Anita's case, the main complication is the psychiatrist."

"I don't understand. Aren't you taking care of her?"

"No. And it's best this way. There is too much personal involvement. It doesn't work. The problem is that I don't trust the psychiatrist she chose. Aren't you aware she visits Maria da Anunciação every week?"

"So what? As far as I know, Dr. Maria da Anunciação is your friend and colleague. I've never heard you criticize her professionalism."

"Well, you're hearing it now. And we were never really friends. But the truth is that she's poisoning Anita's mind against ... guess who? Your own niece."

"I can't believe it!"

"Believe it. And the worst part is that we can't do anything."

"Yes, we can. You stay in Rio de Janeiro. Madalena and I can handle things in Brasília."

"Can you, Uncle? Do you have the armor to resist the smooth talking from lobbyists and the sniping from opponents? From what I've seen— and my dearest uncle must forgive my frankness—you're swimming in Brasília like a little duckling in the water, an easy target for the Planalto's snipers. This matter has already been settled. My workplace is now in Brasília."

"But what are we going to do about Anita? I've heard suicide is one of the risks of acute depression."

"That's true. But you're not going to take a leave from your mandate to look after Anita, are you? As for me, I believe a certain distance is beneficial. We've always been so attached to each other. It's better for her to fight off the poisoning without my direct assistance. The problem is Maria da Anunciação! She's the cause. She's the one poisoning Anita against me."

"I'm sorry, Niece. I don't see how to solve the problem. And I can't understand why Dr. Maria da Anunciação is so against you."

"Perhaps envy, Uncle. Envy goes hand in hand with pettiness."

Maria Amélia fell silent for a few moments before continuing:

"Maybe a new trip to Paris. She really enjoyed it and became such good friends with Suzana, who has a beautiful apartment in the *Quartier Latin*. You are the one who should convince her of that, uncle. Call her today. And dedicate the entire next weekend to convincing her. We need to distance her from Maria da Anunciação's bad influence."

Upon arriving in Brasília, Adamastor went straight to the Chamber of Deputies. The corridor to the main area connecting the offices and the committee meeting rooms was empty, except for a few journalists, early-morning lobbyists, scattered visitors, and some deputies, perhaps eager to show their commitment. Seeing him hurrying toward his office, one of the journalists commented to his group:

"Look at Adamastor setting a bad example. Clocking in at half past eleven on a Monday morning. If he keeps this up, the rest of the gang will have to follow suit, fulfilling their duties with the populace."

But the deputy's haste was primarily driven by his overwhelming desire to embrace his chief of staff, who awaited him with equal eagerness. They greeted with a kiss on the lips. Earlier, at the airport, Maria Amélia had said she would go to her apartment first. She lied. She took a flight back to Rio de Janeiro, firmly decided to speak to Dr. Maria da Anunciação on that same day. She arrived at the office unannounced and asked the secretary if she was seeing any patients:

"No, but Dr. Anunciação asked not to be disturbed for the next thirty minutes."

"Thank you," Maria Amélia replied as she opened the door to the office without knocking.

The psychiatrist looked up with alarm, still holding the phone, murmuring:

"Call me later. Something came up"—and to Maria Amélia: "What's this, barging in without even knocking?"

"I'm not here to discuss formalities, Maria da Anunciação. I'm here to tell you to leave my mother alone. Stop turning her against me."

"And who put that idea in your head? I don't pit anyone against anyone. That's not my style."

"Go pose for your clients, doctor. Not for me! You are poisoning Mom Anita, yes, you are. Just like you poisoned Cleide's mind. You and that crazy father of mine. Here's what we're going to do. You will cease all contact with Mom Anita today, come up with whatever excuse you want ... travel, illness, I don't care. Otherwise, I'll report you to the Brazilian Association of Psychiatry for unscientific practices. Just imagine when our esteemed colleagues find out that you're accusing me of being responsible for the suicide of someone I had no contact with and for the misfortune of another person because she wore an amulet around her neck? That won't sit well with our colleagues, Maria da Anunciação. Do you want to be discredited at the end of your career? Do you?"

"You have no proof of any of that."

"Oh, you want to play games? Great. I like games. Ever since I suspected you of filling my adoptive mother's head with nonsense, I began recording all phone calls at the Lagoa mansion. Legally, doctor. The mansion is mine too. I can do whatever I please there. And you said a lot of things over the phone to my mother, enough to bury your career as a psychiatrist."

"This is blackmail."

"Call it whatever you want. And it's already too late to press your recorder's button. Are you losing focus, Maria da Anunciação? That's the

253

first thing you should have done when I entered. But you didn't. You lost your composure and didn't. Now it's too late. What are you going to do?"

"I never thought your cruelty would reach this far."

"Cruelty? Come again, Maria da Anunciação? Defending oneself against slander is cruelty? Is that what they taught you in college? Focus, doctor, answer my question: what are you going to do? Will you do as I demand, or will you continue poisoning Mom Anita?"

"Compassion. Have you never heard of the word? Aren't you even the slightest bit concerned about what's happening to Anita?"

"Emotional blackmail, doctor? At a time like this? My relationship with my adoptive mother has always been an example of mutual love. Until you and that crazy Tarquínio poisoned it."

"And who'll take care of Anita?"

"That's none of your business. We've said what needed to be said. I have other things to attend to. Goodbye, doctor. Make use of that phone at hand. Call Mom Anita right now and tell her you can no longer be her psychiatrist. Give whatever excuse you want."

Maria Amélia left, leaving the office door wide open and the psychiatrist sitting in her chair, at a loss for words. The secretary approached, frightened, and closed the door, choosing not to say anything. On the way to the airport, a Plan B began taking shape in the braided girl's mind, in case Anita couldn't be distanced from Maria da Anunciação's influence. There was the possibility to send her mother to Paris, but that wouldn't guarantee to keep her away from the psychiatrist. It could even facilitate contact through video conferences and other wonders of communication in this digitized world. Plan B would have to be a more definitive solution. But before putting it into practice, she thought it would be best to pay a visit to her biggest admirer. The taxi was already on the Linha Vermelha Highway when she notified the driver.

"You can turn back. Drop me off in the city center, on Buenos Aires Street."

The taxi driver was about to say something, perhaps complain, but he gave up when confronted by two gray eyes in the rearview mirror. When

254

Maria Amélia finished her conversation with Professor Fábio da Mata, it was past four in the afternoon. Leaving his apartment, she hailed another taxi to the airport, caught the first available flight, and arrived in Brasília just after six in the evening. She went directly to the Chamber of Deputies, arriving before the end of the voting period, and therefore, in time to show everyone that congressman Adamastor Leite Feitosa was not alone but protected by his black-braided and gray-eyed guardian angel.

42

Maria Amélia told Professor Fábio da Mata about everything, including her conversation with Maria da Anunciação. He listened silently until the end.

"You did well. In fact, you always do everything very well. But you know what? You didn't really tell me anything new. I think we've already discussed the matter. Dr. Maria da Anunciação's plotting goes way back. I am aware. And I'm convinced she'll back down. She is very vain, and the Brazilian Association of Psychiatry is her sanctuary. Deprived of her church, the doctor succumbs, her zest for life dissipates. These are the weaknesses of inexperienced souls. But, as always, you're right to be concerned. Only God has 100% certainty, and we're not 100% sure he exists. So, it's best to always keep a card up our sleeve. I have a suggestion. Bring your adoptive mother over for a conversation. Your influence over her is still significant, despite all the poison she's been exposed to. She seems to me like a very inexperienced soul. Perhaps her second or third reincarnation, at most, if not the first."

Maria Amélia approved of the idea but decided to wait a bit. She wanted to give Maria da Anunciação a few days to comply with her demand. Then, Professor da Mata's alternative would present itself naturally. On Tuesday morning, she found her uncle in the office with a face that looked like he had swallowed something sour. In other words, he was exuding concern from every pore. It could have been because of the major debate scheduled for early evening in the committee analyzing one of his amendments to the political reform proposal. But it wasn't.

"What happened, Uncle?"

"It's your mother, Niece. She just called me. She's desperate. She said she's at her wit's end. Dr. Anunciação called her and said she can't see her anymore because she herself is sick and going to the United States for treatment. Your mother wants me to go to Rio today, no matter what, or she might do something crazy."

"You're not going anywhere, Uncle. You can't miss today's debate. I'll go instead. And don't look so spooked. This is good news. Mom Anita is finally free from that venomous snake. Don't worry. I already have an excellent replacement. The greatest connoisseur of the human soul in Brazil, I would say, perhaps even the entire world. And I'll try hurrying back today to witness the debate. Oh my, I could use a flying broomstick."

Soon after lunch, Maria Amélia was already on board a Gol Boeing 737 heading to Rio de Janeiro. She landed at Santos Dumont Airport and immediately hailed a taxi to the Lagoa mansion. A deep silence filled the house. The head of the household staff, let's call him the butler, informed her that Anita had woken up in a highly agitated state and had called her husband before falling into a deep sleep. He feared she had taken an excessive number of barbiturates. Maria Amélia entered the room and saw that her adoptive mother was truly in a state of collapse, a sign she had overdone her medication.

Gabriel, the butler, informed her that the family doctor had seen her two hours before, assuring them everything was under control and that the patient would likely sleep for a while longer. Over the phone, the doctor told Maria Amélia that Anita had indeed taken an excessive dose of Valium but showed no signs of intoxication. If the intention had been suicide, Maria Amélia thought to herself, her adoptive mother had chosen the wrong medication. If she truly wanted to die, she would have taken a potent barbiturate based on malonic acid, not the already discredited Valium. She measured Anita's blood pressure, checked her pulse, and left the room, informing the butler that everything was in order and that she would indeed sleep a while longer, as the doctor had said. She then entered the spacious room that had once been Joaquim Paranhos' office and called Professor Fábio da Mata. They arranged to meet the next morning. Maria Amélia bid farewell to the butler, informing him that she would return the following morning.

"Don't worry. She will really sleep for another two or three hours. Oh, one more thing! You don't need to mention I was here."

From the mansion, she made her way to Galeão Airport to catch the first flight to Brasília. Under no circumstances did she want to miss the committee meeting discussing the amendment to the government's latest political reform proposal. The amendment's author: Congressman Adamastor Leite Feitosa. In other words, she herself.

On the flight, Maria Amélia saw a stewardess approaching with a glass in one hand and a bottle of champagne in the other, accompanied by a pilot, who greeted her with a bow:

"Dr. Maria Amélia," the pilot said, offering her a glass of champagne, "please accept this in honor of being our most frequent flyer on the Rio-Brasília route in the past three months. You outshine everyone." And he presented her with a caricature depicting her as the giant in seven-league boots with one foot in Brasília and the other in Rio de Janeiro.

She smiled, showed the caricature to the other passengers, and sipped the champagne to a round of applause.

The political reform had been dragging on for a long time, and what little progress had been made only served to reinforce the existing political parties, without encouraging greater ideological commitment or fostering a more democratic internal structure. Maria Amélia tried to explain all of this to Adamastor, who feared getting involved in such a mess. His niece was well aware of the risks, but she also understood that daring steps were needed before the leap in her uncle's career. She had crafted three amendments to the government's reform proposal, and one of them was slated for debate on the very evening that had seen her shuttling between Brasília and Rio in three separate flights. All part and parcel of life as a super aide. The amendment under discussion focused on the nomination process for candidates in executive and legislative roles at municipal, state, and federal levels, and it mandated that parties hold conventions involving the participation of all their members.

"I've already heard they're gearing up for a fight, Niece. Some newspapers are already saying that we're injecting more bureaucracy when it's time for streamlining; that parties have their leaders, and it's these leaders who should choose the candidates. We're trying to complicate things."

"Yes, and you'll have to challenge all that. I expected this. Take notes. Point out that they are conflating greater democratization with increased bureaucratization. More bureaucracy means more cumbersome requirements. Such as demanding too many documents to pursue any cause, as was done until recently. ID card, voter registration, birth certificate, and what the hell else. It took them a long time to realize that one document was enough. A meeting of party members to decide on the candidate list doesn't fall into the realm of bureaucracy. It represents the greater democratization of choice, making it more difficult to broker deals over dinner tables and in hushed conversations. That's when my dear uncle will truly pick a fight with the chieftains still practicing politics as in the last century, with their closed-door meetings, Benedito-style, who thought a meeting of three was already an assembly. Candidates benefit from the common election fund, so it is only fair—are you taking notes, Uncle?—that the decision isn't monopolized by a select few leaders. Eradicating secret agreements won't be possible, of course, but they'll become more challenging to arrange, and the candidates will be more representative. Put on your armor. The old leadership will kick up a fuss. But those starting out in politics now, accustomed to greater scrutiny, dealing with the Internet's daily criticism, for example, will support the measure. And the chosen candidate enters with the advantage of truly representing the group they defend. The amendment is quite likely to be rejected in this first attempt. But the seed will be planted. And the sower's name will make headlines, and waves in the blogsphere. That's what we want right now: raise the issue. My dear uncle will be known as the enemy of backroom politics and defender of internal party democratization. You must be persuasive. The debate needs to go beyond the committee rooms and catch the media's attention. This is of utmost importance."

At seven-fifteen the next morning, Maria Amélia was aboard a jet to Rio de Janeiro. By nine, she was already at the Lagoa mansion. She found Anita awake, in a robe, sitting on one of the sofas in the grand living room, her hair disheveled. Upon seeing her daughter, she immediately asked:

"Where is Adamastor?"

"Good morning, Mom Anita. Uncle is in Brasília, his place of work. How are you?"

"Do you need to ask? I want your uncle here, today, now!"

Maria Amélia approached and kissed her mother's cheek, but the gesture was not returned:

"Mom Anita, I know you're feeling this way because of Maria da Anunciação. She's not the only psychiatrist in the world. There are plenty of them here in Rio de Janeiro. I'll take you to someone who can really help you."

"I don't want to."

"Please don't behave like this, Mom Anita. Please. Look at me. It's me, Maria Amélia, your Fiinha. At least give me a chance to show you that you're mistaken, that you're being poisoned. Professor da Mata, whom I want to take you to, is Brazil's foremost expert on mystical matters, like the ones troubling you. I'm not asking much. Just that you listen to me this time. For the love that has united us for so many years. Please!"

With her head down, doing everything she could to avoid the gaze of her adoptive daughter, Anita remained unyielding.

"I won't go. I already know who he is."

"Oh, you know? Maria da Anunciação told you?"

"Yes, you know she did, and I wouldn't be surprised if you're behind her illness."

"Look, Mom Anita. Lift your head up. Like this."

Maria Amélia gently took her adoptive mother's chin, lifted her head and confronted her with her gray eyes. A whirlwind of thoughts raced through Anita's mind as she saw before her the seven-year-old girl with braided hair, vulnerable after witnessing her mother succumb to a gunshot to the chest. She tried to lower her head, but she couldn't, even though Maria Amélia had already removed her supporting hand. Anita burst into tears.

"Let it out, Mommy, just let it out. I'm here to protect you, always, against anything and anyone, if necessary."

Within a minute, Anita found herself in Maria Amélia's embrace, crying profusely, while the latter maintained a distant gaze, as if not sharing the same emotional wavelength. Before three hours had passed both women were facing Professor Fábio da Mata in his apartment on Buenos Aires Street. Maria Amélia thought it best to leave them alone, so she asked the professor's niece to show her some books from the soul specialist's library in the bedroom. Fábio da Mata took Anita's hands and began talking.

"Yes, Mrs. Anita. Dr. Maria da Anunciação is right when she says that our dear Maria Amélia is exceptional. Indeed, she carries within her the accumulated wisdom of several reincarnations. Envy, however, the mother of most evil, causes people to only see malice in the extraordinary powers of privileged beings. You should really be proud to have this unparalleled figure by your side, your daughter. Let's get straight to the point. She has nothing to do with the tragedy that befell your ex-friend's daughter, much less with her sister's suicide. The cause may well have been envy from one and hatred from the other. No one can cease to be good, no one can cease to be intelligent, no one can cease to be exceptionally gifted just so others won't feel envy. Maria Amélia is not guilty of anything. She only feels one thing for you: love, so much love."

And Anita wept, not convulsively, but with tears of acceptance, a trait typical of those with less experienced and more fragile souls. Maria Amélia returned from the bedroom, and upon hearing the sobs, embraced her, alternately stroking her hair and wiping away her tears. She then looked at Professor da Mata, not with her mesmerizing eyes, but with the tenderness of the most compassionate of souls.

43

After temporarily resolving the issue with her adoptive mother, Maria Amélia flew back to Brasília to assist her uncle in calming those anxious about losing power in their territories. Fiefdoms? She decided her uncle should go on the attack immediately and proclaim, right at the beginning of his speech, that it was high time to put an end to the electoral corrals, not literal, physical ones, but rather the digital kind. She even coined a phrase related to the former Senate president: "Sarney Never Again!" In her heart, she was perfectly aware that even the amendment proposing party reform was nothing more than a Band-Aid within the broader political reform. Politics would continue to be, as always, the art of manipulation and the dance of interests. They were going to lose the battle, she and her uncle, but take a step forward to win the war. She was aware that even the most forward-thinking left-wing parties were bastions for a privileged minority, the new nobility. Ultimately, they might be engulfed by one of the democratizing waves that run through the course of history, sometimes with the force of a tsunami, but more often as mere ripples unable to alter the game's rules. "If Professor da Mata is correct," she mused, "it will take several lifetimes to achieve that." The goal was much more modest for now. Secure her position in the halls of power, from where she could influence the hurried commuters at the subway and bus terminal at the far end of Eixo Monumental. It was a striking contrast. On one end, power; on the other, the shapeless masses; and between them the ministry buildings and cathedral conceived by Niemeyer, the most atheist of Brazilian architects. Maybe manipulation has no creed? No, Maria Amélia concluded, manipulation does have a creed—the creed in oneself. And from another perspective, it is also true that all creeds lead to manipulation.

Maria Amélia didn't want to set up her own residence in Brasília. At least not for now. She always had a room reserved at the Royal Tulip Hotel, from where she could use binoculars to see her uncle's new residence on the other side of the lake, on the Ministers' Peninsula. She went there almost every day to have breakfast, even though the journey, skirting a large part of the lake, took about an hour. She would take a taxi because an own car in Brasília didn't appeal to her either; she didn't have time to waste, and during the cab ride, she would devour newspapers and consult her laptop. The morning after the debate, she followed her routine to the letter. She found her uncle nervous. The amendment had been rejected. He felt guilty, having failed to persuade anyone.

"Did you see, Niece? It couldn't be done. We lost."

"But we won, Uncle. Look at the headlines, check online. Take this one: 'Adamastor declares war on the oligarchies.' We're on the front pages, Uncle. That's what matters to us right now. The spotlight."

Through one amendment after the other, one project after another, all of them leaning left, or rather, progressive, Adamastor established himself as one of the most influential members of congress in Brasília. But everyone associated him with his niece; quite a few tried to avoid her when they had any proposals that went a little off the tracks. Most notably, lobbyists avoided her like the plague. They secretly referred to her as "*Trançuda*," Adamastor's Braided Wench. Maria Amélia set the fight against corruption as one of the fundamental goals of her uncle's career.

"We can't give an inch in this matter, Uncle. I've said it before, and I'll say it again. Civil society has made great progress. Demands are growing stronger. You can't reach the top today without adhering to certain rules of conduct. And it's not just the pressure from civil society activists and the myriad of blogs on the Internet highlighting politicians' slip-ups. There's still the traditional press, the hypocritical press, associated with interest groups, always eager to dig up any dirt on those opposing their ambitions. Rectitude is needed, not out of moralism, but political survival. Irreproachable behavior—upright, honest, incorruptible—these must be the adjectives linked to Deputy Adamastor, once a drug dealer, now a crusader against corruption. This gets better ratings than anything else. And votes, lots of votes. We can't let our guard down for a minute. The enemies are keeping a close eye, with heightened vigilance. One misstep, and everything goes down the drain. Remember the *caçador de marajás*, the famed hunter of big-time swindlers? President Collor de Melo failed miserably because he didn't adhere to the standards he set for others. And a judge ..."

Adamastor made a timid attempt to contest:

"Well, a handful of corrupt individuals did get away with it."

"Did. That's the right tense. I don't need to spell out the corruption reigning this country since the beginning of colonization. Rui Barbosa, the Republic's goody-two-shoes, once stated in a speech that, in the face of such villainy, it's embarrassing to remain honest. The exchange of votes for a pair of shoes, the old electoral strongholds herding voters like cattle. The governor of São Paulo Ademar boldly proclaiming that he stole but delivered. Many politicians in recent history lost their mandates for much less. Numerous ministers have fallen, and two presidents faced impeachment in this century. Indeed, some corrupt individuals manage to dodge the allegations and navigate the legal tangle to escape. But you, my dear uncle, wouldn't want to gamble with that risk, right? And the higher you ascend, the more scrutinizing eyes will follow from below. Come on, the world evolves. Slowly, but it evolves."

"Alright, Niece! Alright! I promise I'll act like a paragon of honesty."

The major political showdown in the second year of the legislature was occurring within the party. Adamastor ran for party leader against his friend and, to some extent, mentor from the old socialist guard. To supplant him, they needed to dismantle his reputation for integrity. Adamastor hesitated:

"I can't do it, Niece. Gonçalves was the first to welcome me into the party, the one who helped me most and still does. Shouldn't we wait for him to recognize his issues and resign of his own accord?"

"Look at you, dear uncle, hesitating. Gonçalves messed up. He took bribes! We know that. The accusations are all over the Internet, and it's very likely that the tabloids are set to publish the story by this weekend. Sure, go and talk to him. But to demand his resignation as member of congress. Tell him you're doing it as a friend, show him the stories on the Internet. Do it today or at the latest tomorrow. The firing squad on the other side is already locked and loaded. I'll accompany you to the meeting if my dear uncle doesn't feel comfortable."

And so, they went.

"These are baseless accusations. My conscience is clear. I didn't receive any bribes. We must resist the police state, these wiretaps, this nosy infamy. You too, Adamastor? Is this your way of repaying me?"

"I believe you, Gonçalves. But it's not about that. Our adversaries are poised to strike, and we're certain they possess undeniable evidence."

"So, you believe them?"

"I didn't say that. I said they have evidence; how it was obtained, whether it was fabricated, no one knows."

"No one knows, you ingrate?! I know! They were fabricated! You're not sure? You want my job, don't you?"

"Let's not make it personal."

"Indeed, let's not. My uncle is right. The deputy must resign and admit his mistake while there's still time to protect the party and the socialist idea, of which the deputy claims to be a great defender. Show an act of nobility to your comrades and yourself. Save yourself from the ordeal of an impeachment."

Valdomiro Gonçalves turned to Maria Amélia with hatred, pointing his finger at her, intending to expel her from the room. He stopped in his tracks, taken aback by the intense gaze of his colleague's assistant.

"That's right, Deputy. Spare yourself. You know it. We all know it. The allegations are true."

"Well, I, um, think my niece ..."

"Oh, Uncle! The deputy knows he violated a fundamental code of conduct. For the good of all—the party, his colleagues, his friends, and even himself—there is no path other than resignation. And it better be soon! Before he becomes the cover story of a magazine that is probably ready for print."

264

Congressman Gonçalves dropped his finger and began to weep uncontrollably. He nodded in agreement. Maria Amélia, with the same steady voice, still gazing intently at the parliamentarian and certain of her advantage, suggested:

"If the congressman wishes, I can help draft the resignation statement."

It was more than just help. She wrote it; the deputy merely contributed with his signature. The next day, it made headlines, and the tabloid had to find a new cover story to avoid beating a dead horse.

Resignation Statement of Deputy Valdomiro Gonçalves

Given the allegations against me that also implicate the Socialist Party, my lifelong dedication, I hereby resign from my position as deputy. This brief statement is not the place to defend myself against these allegations. I will address them in court, when the time is right. I step down now to allow the PSB to carry on its work without more disturbances. The voters who entrusted me with three consecutive terms are aware of my dedication to the socialist cause over the past twelve years. I make way for others to carry on the struggle for a more just society.

Valdomiro Gonçalves
Federal Deputy

44

In Rio de Janeiro, Anita's behavior was becoming increasingly bipolar, posing a danger to everyone around her. It appeared she had stabilized after her conversation with Professor da Mata, though she could no longer express unconditional love for her adopted daughter. Although their talks were quite friendly, with frequent use of the beloved nickname "*Fiinha*," they no longer had the former depth and spontaneity. Their auras repelled each other, and words ringed hollow. To make matters worse, Anita started having constant nightmares again in which Cleide showed her daughter's suicide note while screaming:

"She's to blame! She's to blame! She's to blame!"

And following each nightmare, she would spiral into depression, refusing to eat, insisting on Maria Amélia or Adamastor's presence, pulling them away from the political arena in Brasília. Medications were no longer having an effect, and Maria Amélia knew her adoptive mother's progressive poisoning was the cause. Mental poisoning, the seed of suspicion planted in her mind by Maria da Anunciação. The week when Adamastor assumed his party's leadership in the Chamber, he received a phone call from the butler of the Lagoa mansion, reporting another crisis of the wife, a bad one. It was a Wednesday morning, and Adamastor did what he wasn't allowed to do. He went to Rio de Janeiro without informing his niece. He merely left a message with Madalena. Needless to say, Maria Amélia was livid. Before he could take a taxi at the Galeão Airport, Adamastor's phone rang.

"What's this business of traveling on a Wednesday, leaving the caucus rudderless at such an important moment?"

"Don't be angry, Niece. It's Anita. She's in crisis. She said she wants to see me today, without fail."

"What, are you now a psychiatrist? Do you even know how to handle her condition?"

"She's my wife. I have an obligation to be by her side."

"Oh, come on, Uncle! Spare me the melodramatic guilt trip. I was born immune to it. Where are you?"

"I'm still at the airport."

"Great. Take a plane back then. The schedule won't have to be canceled."

"But, Niece, I can't. Anita needs me by her side. The crisis will pass, and I'll come back shortly, if possible, even today."

"Yes, you can! You won't alleviate Mom Anita's crisis in any way; she requires special care. Professional help. And that's my job. You come, and I'll go. I've already left some notes with Madalena about your speech this afternoon and annotations for the debate on party reform. You'll only make matters worse in Rio. Madalena just told me my fare is booked. I'm going. You come back. We'll cross paths in the air."

And she hung up the phone, not giving her uncle the chance to respond.

In New York, a world away from Rio, Maria da Anunciação was reconnecting with former colleagues from her days as an intern at the United States Psychiatric Institute. What actually interested her most was reaching out to the leading figures in the field of paranormality. During these almost obligatory travels, she had promised ... no, sworn, to go to extreme lengths in her battle against Maria Amélia. Nearly everyone she spoke to recommended that she go to Arizona to talk to Dr. Steven Adams, recognized as a leading parapsychologist in the country, also an expert in shamanism and witchcraft. The name wasn't unfamiliar; she recalled reading about him in specialized journals and remembered Frederica talking about him. Before traveling to Arizona, she decided to pay a visit to the headquarters of the American Society for Psychical Research, located in an old mansion on 73rd Street in west New York. This was not an easy decision. In academic circles, the society's reputation was questionable, with their hands-on activities deemed at odds with legitimate scientific research. To this day, for example, their website has a form where people with premonitory experiences regarding the 9/11 attacks can come forward. For staunch psychiatrists—a group Maria da Anunciação still theoretically belonged to—this seemed like a promotion of charlatanry. At the headquarters, she was warmly received by a colleague, a woman nearing eighty, who eagerly listened to Maria Amélia's story.

"The doctor has stumbled upon a priceless research opportunity; perhaps we can finally uncover conclusive evidence of supernatural powers, which parapsychology so desperately needs to be accepted by that bunch of academics who can't see beyond their own noses?"

Maria da Anunciação let out an awkward little laugh, knowing the shoe would have fit perfectly not that long ago. However, she concealed her embarrassment from her conversation partner. She was pleasant throughout the conversation, and in the end, she not only obtained

Professor Steven Adams' address but also a letter of recommendation. As they said their goodbyes, the woman held Maria da Anunciação's hands and told her:

"You won't believe it, but Steven was my student. I always knew he would go far. The girl's case—what's her name again?—will greatly interest him. Let's shut up those high-and-mighty academics."

Maria da Anunciação held her tongue. In the past, she would have overwhelmed the elderly woman with a flood of scientific counterarguments.

The next day, she traveled to Arizona, where an undoubtedly unpleasant surprise awaited her.

In Rio de Janeiro, shortly before Anita's latest crisis, Maria Amélia used a servant-free weekend at the mansion to thoroughly search through her adoptive mother's computer. Not everyone knows that deleted files, such as emails, can be easily recovered. When a file is deleted, it actually continues to occupy space on the disk to expedite performance. Only the first bit is modified informing another file can overwrite it if needed. Recovery is relatively straightforward for anyone with basic knowledge of computers. In fact, several software options are available on the Internet—many of them free—that perform the task with great ease. Maria Amélia just ran a file recovery program from a USB drive, and within minutes, practically all the emails recently sent and received by Anita were at her disposal. She had no trouble finding what interested her:

Dear Maria da Anunciação,

I hope you're feeling better. As for me, things are still not going well. I'm still struggling to grasp what's happening. I could never have imagined, truly never, until recently, that I would have doubts about my adoptive daughter. But I do, there's no denying it anymore. Even worse, despite the fact that it depresses me deeply, sometimes to the point of leaving me bedridden for days, I prefer to remain in this state than be completely under her control while displaying a false tranquility. I can't resist her gaze; I think it's worse than being hypnotized. I feel like I'm just a puppet. She managed to take me to

Professor Fábio da Mata, you know, and he almost convinced me that she is a good person, that the evil is caused by the envy of others. I know she'll return this weekend and hypnotize me once again, convince me. I fight, I fight, I swore not to surrender, but it's extremely hard. And it doesn't matter if I try to pretend, she senses it. I've been living as if I have two personalities lately. One believes in my daughter, capable of showing some joy, and the other is irreversibly depressed, doubting if life is even worth living. I don't know what to do. I miss you dearly.

Warm regards from your friend,
Anita.

And the answer:

Dear friend,

I would love to be close to you, but unfortunately, I can't. And be certain of this: she is the reason behind it all. I'm being blackmailed. She's threatening to expose me to the Brazilian Association of Psychiatry for practicing witchcraft. Imagine that. It's the classic case of the pot calling the kettle black. I think she's more dangerous than we thought, and that's why we need to be extra cautious. For instance, don't store my address in your inbox and make sure to delete all our emails. The ones you send me and the ones I send you. Under no circumstances can she know we're in contact. We need to find a way out. By the way, I'm sending a long email to Cleide so the two of you can get in touch. It's very important that this happens. But with extreme caution. Nothing should even remotely arouse her suspicions. You will receive a phone call from Cleide soon.

Warm regards,
Maria da Anunciação.
PS: Don't forget to delete this email.

Armed with the information she needed, Maria Amélia closed the laptop and went to the spacious living room to watch television while waiting for her uncle and adoptive mother. They had been out shopping at the mall and planned to dine together at a restaurant that evening. When they arrived, Maria Amélia gave Anita a sly look, as if to say, "I know what you think I don't know." She then smiled and asked:

"Did you buy out the entire mall?"

"Don't exaggerate, Niece. Anita only bought one of the floors."

The laughter was discreet, forced. It was as if Anita wasn't comfortable in her own skin. Maria Amélia approached her, kissed her forehead, and stared at her with a smile, but at the same time, there was a hardness in her gaze, like a boss feigning kindness while letting an employee go.

"Let's have fun today. Eat well and enjoy ourselves. The three of us."

The heat in Tucson was intense as Maria da Anunciação stepped off the plane at the airport. With no time to spare, she skipped the obligatory tourist trip to the Grand Canyon on her itinerary. She went straight to the hotel to freshen up with a long shower before taking a taxi to the university, where she had a scheduled meeting at five o'clock in the afternoon with Professor Steven Adams. When she entered the parapsychologist's office, however, the psychiatrist noticed that he looked at her with a mixture of mockery and cynicism. The surprise was delivered after the usual introductions:

"Dr. Anunciação, I'll be traveling to Brazil next month. It seems our subject of study is exactly the same. Quite the coincidence, isn't it."

"I don't understand. I haven't even mentioned the topic I wish to discuss with the professor."

"But it's about your colleague Maria Amélia and her extraordinary abilities, isn't it?"

"Professor, you surprise me."

"The first time I heard of her was from a Brazilian student named Frederica, if I recall correctly. A rather troubled young woman. Later, I contacted Professor Fábio da Mata. We have been corresponding frequently for almost a year now."

"Ah, so the Professor must know practically everything."

"Know everything? Nobody knows that, dear doctor. However, I find myself almost entirely in agreement with Professor da Mata. Nevertheless,

I still have to go to Brazil to see for myself. I'm eager to see those eyes reputed to hold such power. It could be a significant breakthrough for parapsychology, don't you agree?"

"Professor da Mata must have told you that my relationship with Maria Amélia is strained. We used to be friends, but I have become convinced she is evil."

"Evil? I'm not sure I can agree with you, colleague. That's not Professor da Mata's opinion, in any case. And as you're aware, concepts like good and evil don't really hold much weight in scientific discourse."

"I'll be frank. I don't want to continue this discussion; it's pointless. To the professor, Maria Amélia is just a subject of research, nothing more. And, more than that, even without meeting her, the professor already shows evident admiration for her. She ceased being an object of study to me a long time ago. It might sound unprofessional, but I see her as a malevolent entity who has hurt many, myself included. Our discussion has no further purpose."

"What a pity, doctor," as he spoke, he retrieved a folder from a drawer, "a real shame. Together, the four of us could have made a formidable team. This is your article on Patient X, an impressive piece of research."

"Thank you very much. But I won't be a part of it. I want nothing more to do with her."

"You don't? Didn't you come all this way specifically to talk about her?"

"I'm not interested in understanding her exceptional powers. My interest lies in combating them. Can I ask you one thing before I leave?"

"Of course."

"Please don't mention our meeting to Professor da Mata. To anyone, if possible. Pretend I was never here. Good afternoon, professor."

The next morning, she took a flight back to New York with a sense that her enemy's tentacles had a much wider reach than she could imagine.

Meanwhile, across the Atlantic, Maria Amélia was on the phone, insisting on Adamastor's immediate return to Brasília. For the first time, however, he hesitated and didn't heed his niece's call. Forty minutes later,

271

he arrived at the Lagoa mansion to find his wife in bed, her hair disheveled, as if she were truly a madwoman from an asylum. He pressed her against his chest, tried to fix her hair, and leaned closer to her mouth to better understand her murmurs.

"I can't bear it anymore. I can't bear it anymore."

"But what's going on, Anita? We have everything we need to be happy. What is happening?"

Her response came as a convulsive sob, broken by her words:

"I was so naive, I can't believe I allowed myself to be deceived for all these years."

Adamastor continued holding her tightly in his embrace, unsure of what to say. He really couldn't offer her any professional help, and deep down, for some unknown reason, he didn't want to delve deeper into the matter and hear the name of the person who had deceived her for so long. Anita gradually calmed down and eventually fell asleep in his arms. But sleep also has its traps, and it wasn't long before Tarquínio Esperidião's voice echoed through the mist of her dream, shouting at the top of his lungs:

"She's a witch. You will regret it!"

Upon returning to the living room, Adamastor found his niece, still clutching her briefcase.

"Fantastic, Uncle. The party leader, absent from an extremely important Wednesday debate, attending to a woman with psychological issues in Rio de Janeiro."

"It's not just some issue, Niece. Anita is truly disturbed."

"Well then, let's call it a major issue. But you don't have the right medication. You don't know how to handle this. Go back to Brasília. Go discuss tomorrow's agenda with Madalena, at least. Don't worry, I'll take care of Mom Anita."

Filled with a deep sense of remorse (some say anticipatory remorse helps ease future guilt), Adamastor obeyed his niece's order, this time to the letter, aware that discussing the agenda would take up the entire night, interspersed with kisses and hugs.

Anita woke up feeling slightly relieved and called out:

"Adamastor, where are you? Come here, dear."

When she opened her eyes, she saw Maria Amélia by her bedside. She wasn't surprised. She simply asked for her husband once again.

"He went back to Brasília, Mom Anita. This is a very important week. He can't be absent from the debates in the plenary and the discussions with his colleagues. I'm here to help you. Look at me, relax."

And she looked like an obedient little lapdog, even resting her head on her daughter's lap, knowing there was no way out. The day before her crisis, Anita met with Cleide for the first time since their friendship had soured. They chose neutral ground, a discreet café at Barra Shopping. Before speaking, the two hugged and wept together for more than five minutes. They sat down, ordered two cappuccinos with chocolate, and drank them slowly without saying a word. Cleide was the first to say something, showing the amulet with her daughter's note hanging around her neck.

"It's here with me. Only death can separate me from it."

And they embraced once again. It was a meeting filled with tears.

In the living room, Maria Amélia directed the butler to ensure Anita took her antidepressant pills as scheduled. She returned to the bedroom, kissed her adoptive mother's forehead again, and whispered in her ear:

"Everything will be fine, sleep."

And she slept. In strict obedience to her daughter's order, with the extra reinforcement of the Valium brought by the butler.

Maria Amélia decided to return to Brasília, but feeling that Anita was a lost cause and almost certain that a meeting with Cleide had taken place. During a spell of vigorous turbulence in the plane, Maria Amélia concluded that the die was cast; that there was no other way. As the plane bucked like an untamed horse, she pondered over all the variables—the obstacle that the adoptive mother represented for her uncle's career, Anita's own suffering, the danger of interference in her professional life. After much deliberation and calculation, she deduced that her adoptive mother had exhausted her role in this incarnation. And aware of the power of her thoughts, she resolved that it was time for Anita to die.

45

Anita died three months later, during the parliamentary recess in July. She seemed calm, but it was deceptive, partly motivated by Adamastor's presence. A keen observer would have noticed the stiffness in her face, even when she smiled. Whenever her adopted daughter appeared, it worsened. As if she wasn't in her own body, or as though she wanted to evaporate and disappear. Maria Amélia's gaze made her nauseous, a feeling she tried to conceal, knowing she was irreversibly under her control. She relaxed a bit in the presence of Adamastor and the staff, people she considered less knowledgeable about the ins and outs of human nature. However, Maria Amélia saw through it all, aware of her adoptive mother's secret rendezvous with Cleide. Anita was like a volcano, ready to burst. The eruption unfolded at Barra Shopping, the exact site of their clandestine meetings. The three of them—Anita, Maria Amélia, and Adamastor—were walking near the Lacoste store window, while Cleide approached from the opposite direction. Maria Amélia and Cleide collided at the corner. Or rather, they crashed into each other. Maria Amélia managed to maintain her balance, but Cleide fell to the ground and while she attempted to hold onto something, she ripped off the pendant from her neck, dropping it at Anita's feet. Anita picked it up and tried to hide it behind her coat. When Cleide realized who had bumped into her and felt the absence of the pendant with her daughter's note, she fainted. While being cared for by the shopping mall's emergency team, Maria Amélia shot Anita a piercing gaze with her gray eyes and ordered:

"Hand it over!"

Trembling, unable to disobey, Anita handed her the amulet. Not in her hands, though. Maria Amélia opened her purse so the object could be thrown inside. She went to the bathroom, but before entering, she called over a teenager nearby.

"I want you to do something for me. Can you?"

"That depends."

274

"It's very simple. Do you see this locket in my purse? Take it, open it, and remove the piece of paper inside. Then tear it into tiny pieces and flush them down the toilet."

"Are you crazy or something?"

"Maybe. But a crazy person full of cash. Here's a hundred bucks to do it and then vanish."

After the girl completed her task, she returned the locket to Maria Amélia, who then replaced the note with another slip of paper inscribed with the same words. This time, however, the words were written with a red CD marker. The reader may wonder how she knew what was written on the note since as far as we know, no one had told her, let alone that it was written in red—the red of Camélia's blood. Besides her seemingly exceptional powers, Maria Amélia also always proved to be an exceedingly cautious individual, preparing things in advance to be used at the right time. Ever since sensing Frederica held something repellent on the morning of Camélia's suicide, Maria Amélia had exerted all her power to first uncover, and then destroy the thing that had so disturbed her. Ultimately, the weakest link was Anita, as expected. In the throes of a crisis, moments before bumping into Cleide, Anita was in despair. Under Maria Amélia's dominant gaze, she tugged at her hair and exclaimed:

"It's horrible. The note is horrible. It's written in her own blood."

"In her own blood? Oh, Camélia's note. And what exactly did she write, Mom Anita?" Maria Amélia asked, her eyes fixed on the sick woman, who responded emphatically, without even trying to avoid the hypnotizing gaze:

"Keep away from her!"

"And what type of paper did she write on? Did you pay attention?"

It was a cross-examination demanding an exact answer.

"A page from her diary's notebook, I think."

The puzzle had been solved. Both Camélia and Frederica used the same type of notebook to write their diaries. As she gently stroked her adoptive mother's hair, trying to calm her, Maria Amélia concluded she always had to have a similar note on her. She couldn't disregard the chance of the amulet falling into her hands, or of someone she controlled.

Upon leaving the restroom, Maria Amélia noticed Cleide seated yet gasping for breath. She wouldn't have to be taken to the shopping mall's clinic. Anita, standing beside her friend, barely noticed Maria Amélia's return before she handed her the amulet. Simultaneously, Cleide clasped her neck in panic and exclaimed:

"My God, where is my amulet? Where is it?"

"It's here, Cleide. You ripped it off accidentally. Here you go."

"Oh, thank God!"

She opened it, made sure the note was still there, and put it back around her neck. From a short distance, Maria Amélia watched, unable to conceal her satisfaction.

The journey back home was tense. Anita hurried along with cold hands and a restless gaze, pulling Adamastor along as she tried to put as much distance as possible between herself and Maria Amélia, who was calmly following behind. Feeling temporarily free from her daughter's gaze, she whispered in her husband's ear:

"I would love to have some alone time with you tonight, a day and night just the two of us."

"But we are, my dear. Let's head home—today and tonight are ours."

Anita whispered almost imperceptibly:

"And what about her?"

"My niece? Well, she's part of the household. We can act as if we're alone."

Perhaps it hasn't been mentioned yet, but Maria Amélia's keen ear was yet another one of her qualities, picking up sounds in all their nuances, in addition to her ability to read people's lips. So, Anita's whisper and her uncle's reply did not escape her notice. She slowed her pace, and when they were about thirty feet away, she shouted:

"Goodbye, lovebirds! See you tomorrow."

Maria Amélia realized that her adoptive mother was deeply affected by the scene of her fainting friend and the lost amulet, which had stirred up all her suspicions. She deduced that the proposed private time was anything but romantic in nature, but rather inspired by fear and apprehension. She also believed her mother intended to lay all her suspicions bare to her uncle, attempting to involve him in the plot against her. Something had to be done or something had to happen before Adamastor was poisoned too. But what? How? In such a short period of time? Since nothing else could be done, objectively, Maria Amélia decided it best to celebrate the day's victory—the destruction of the cursed suicide note—with a night of pleasure. She called Dente Grande:

"Hello, my blackie! Are you up today?"

"My whitey, today I want to die tangled up in your braids!"

On her nearly three-hour flight from Tucson to New York, Maria da Anunciação was seized by a premonition that there was no escaping Maria Amélia. She began to think of ways to come out with the least amount of physical and moral injuries. Should she confront the battle directly with Cleide and Anita at her side? Too risky. Both of them were weak, or inexperienced souls, as Professor da Mata would put it, with Doctor Adams' agreement. The three of them would fall into the opponent's first trap. Staying in the United States for longer meant definitively giving up her professional career. Even though she spoke English well, it fell short in the fiercely competitive field of psychiatry. She had no intention of winding up in a psychiatric ward or a city social service office, doling out Valium to every patient. Her select clientele, who paid handsomely for thirty minutes of catharsis, were in Brazil, specifically Rio de Janeiro. She had to go back. Take the bull by the horns? No. None of that. No bullfighting. Something more civilized. A pact between souls with a history of past harmony. She decided to return to Rio the same week. The first thing to do was to schedule a meeting with Professor da Mata, and through him, try to reestablish a connection with Maria Amélia. If she couldn't beat her, she might as well join her. Or, at least, appear her ally. What she truly felt, however, even if her conscious mind didn't fully accept it, was that "join" didn't quite cover it. Submit was more accurate.

After arriving in Rio and learning of Anita's death, Maria da Anunciação felt relief before any pity. Anita was the biggest obstacle to reconciliation, the stumbling block. The prospect of confronting Anita, perhaps the most naive soul she knew, to admit that everything she had previously claimed was false, seemed unthinkable. How could she ever admit that the adopted daughter was, as Professor da Mata would put it, a soul of higher evolution, worthy only of admiration? There was still Cleide. But the bonds of friendship and personal involvement with her were weaker. She could simply dismiss her as a patient, or alternatively, downplay the Maria Amélia phenomenon in their consultations and conversations, act as she had always acted before, the psychiatrist following scientific canons, fighting against everything that smelled of paranormality and other obscurities not identified in laboratory research. Breaking with Cleide would be much easier. And Anita was dead, thankfully, her subconscious told her (slightly censored, let's say). Perhaps she was poised for a less naive reincarnation, one with a bit more savvy.

But we haven't disclosed how Anita met her end yet. She didn't even make it to the house alive after the collision between Maria Amélia and Cleide. In fact, shortly after Maria Amélia's farewell, Anita clung to Adamastor, collapsing in his arms. As the congressman screamed in despair, someone called an ambulance. She didn't reach Barra Hospital alive. The vessel couldn't withstand such anguish, despair, and helplessness, and burst, flooding a large part of her brain. By the time the ambulance arrived, she was already dead. Desperate, the former drug dealer's first reaction was to call his niece. In vain. Maria Amélia had her cellphone off, driving her BMW and lost in thoughts about all the things she and Dente Grande were going to do that night.

46

Anita's funeral took place the morning of the next day. Cleide intended to attend but changed her mind at the last minute. She didn't have the strength, she felt she didn't, to face Maria Amélia, all dressed in black, supporting her uncle, who was truly in a state of misery. Adamastor's eyes were swollen from a night spent sleepless and weeping, tormented by remorse, remembering the nights of delights in Madalena's arms while his wife wasted away in solitude, abandoned in Rio de Janeiro. During the wake, in a moment alone with Maria Amélia, he tried to unburden himself:

"Niece, I am to blame! Anita probably knew about my relationship with Madalena. I'll never forgive myself. Please, niece, forgive me for being so thoughtless with your mother."

"Straighten up, Uncle. Tragedies are not undone by lamentations. What happened, happened. You weren't to blame for Mom Anita's depression. She chose to live in a world of fantasies. Or, let me put it another way. Perhaps she had no other world than the repetitive and boring life of high society. She was the one who didn't want to go to Brasília, she decided to stay alone in Rio de Janeiro. And also, anyone can have a stroke, at any time. But you should cry for your loss today. Really cry! It's good for you. But don't let yourself be tormented by the feeling of guilt. That's a weed that must be uprooted."

She didn't say it, but while still looking at her uncle she thought: "This is just self-indulgence, confessing in hopes of being forgiven. And he directs it at me of all people! A month, at most, and Mom Anita will be a distant memory, and life will go on with Madalena and the scheming in Congress."

She pulled Adamastor by the arm:

"Come, the others are waiting."

Adamastor atoned for his guilt for the rest of the week in a hotel on Avenida Atlântica. Given his superstitions and paranoia, he could no longer bring himself to sleep in the Lagoa mansion, which now had become Maria Amélia's residence and office. In no time, it would also become the meeting point for politicians from all corners, engaging in the intricate maneuvers and whispered conversations that lead to power. The following Monday, Adamastor traveled to Brasília and was received at the airport by Madalena, whom he only pecked on the forehead. He would have to atone for a few days longer before the long-awaited kiss on the lips.

Within the mansion's vast spaces, the party hall was modified. At the center, a round table, inspired by King Arthur's perhaps, surrounded by about thirty chairs. In the right corner, a desk with electronic gadgets: a computer, a video projector aimed at a screen, two landline phones, and a security monitor overseeing all rooms in the house. One of the cameras, for instance, was placed right above the round table. As the meetings around the large table and political scheming at the desk became frequent, it didn't take long for the mansion to become known as *"Parlamentinho da Lagoa,"* Lagoa's Little Parliament. Adamastor never felt comfortable there, neither at the round table nor at the desk.

"Niece, there are too many microphones, too many cameras. It's scary."

"Afraid of being wiretapped, Uncle? Just like all those deputies, you seem terrified of eavesdropping. Consider this setup like a vaccine. An anti-wiretapping vaccine. And it also serves as public relations. It proves we discuss things here openly. Haven't you seen Folha's editorial?"

She was referring to the main piece, mentioning the meetings around the round table. The title was already flattering:

"Everything in the Open at 'Parlamentinho da Lagoa.'"

And just like that, the name stuck. Adamastor still had doubts, however. His time in Congress, along with conversations with old political foxes, had made him far more suspicious than in his dealing days. During these discussions, he learned some of the rules governing the lives of politicians: Don't discuss anything serious over the phone; Whenever possible, always say "Maybe" instead of "Yes" or "No." In short, be cautious. Extremely cautious, like a soldier crossing a minefield. Were such a thing possible, he would be Benedito Valadares reincarnate, for whom a talk among three already meant an assembly. His niece's round table didn't inspire fear, therefore, it inspired terror. And he still couldn't understand: how could everything be laid out in the open? She herself had taught him that politics is the art of bargaining, of agreements that demand the utmost secrecy during the negotiation phase. Could his niece be wrong for the first time? During a weekend stroll over the Avenida Atlântica promenade with Maria Amélia, he decided to touch on the subject again:

"But it's very difficult to open your heart with so many people and in front of so many cameras. I still don't understand this whole 'Parlamentinho da Lagoa' thing."

"Uncle, it means *putting your cards on the table*. Politicians don't open their hearts. And they only show their cards when forced. You still haven't grasped the spirit of it, right, Uncle? This stays between us. Let's put it like this: the round table is a piece of propaganda, Uncle. It puts us in the limelight. It makes us a reference for what is being debated in the country, it piques the curiosity of journalists and the public, it presents us as open-minded politicians. It's a second channel for debates, where I can also participate directly. Lagoa's little parliament is already a reality. More than that. It's a mandatory meeting point, a multi-party club to discuss everything, at least what is being discussed openly. And it's in our hands."

It would have been more accurate if she'd said "in my hands," but let's chalk it up to a use of the royal 'we.'

"I'm glad to hear that, Niece. I was afraid it would be a place for negotiations."

Maria Amélia stopped and stared at her uncle.

"Look at me. Who do you take me for? Being naive is already a hindrance to survival in ordinary life. In politics, it's suicide."

Let's take a step back in time to witness the moment of Adamastor's first kiss with Madalena following Anita's funeral. The period of abstinence lasted twenty painful days, without either of them taking the initiative. Madalena didn't visit the congressman's residence all this time, choosing to remain in her own room at the same hotel where Maria Amélia was staying. In the office, their greetings were reduced to a curt "Hello," "How are you?" "Everything in order?" No touches, no hurried caresses when they found themselves alone. Adamastor flew to Rio for the seventh-day mass. Alone. Maria Amélia told him that attending archaic ceremonies like Catholic mass wasn't part of her concession. She joked with Adamastor:

"I won't go, Uncle. The church's saints don't suit me."

"And what should I tell people if they ask?" he inquired.

"Nothing. You don't need to say anything. If they ask, simply say: 'I don't know.'"

During mass, Adamastor did something he hadn't done in years. He received communion. During his confession the day before, in Brasília, he lingered on the issue of marital infidelity, but the priest was more interested in his parliamentary activities.

"My son, you are a congressman. How have you defended God's people?"

"All my actions are in accordance with the Church's doctrines, Father."

Generalities. The priest wouldn't settle for that:

"And what about this bill to remove crucifixes from public buildings and offices? You'll vote against this project, won't you, my son?"

"It's not against the Catholic religion, Father. It's out of respect for other religions."

"Do not deflect from my question. Denying the Lord's presence is a mortal sin. 'God above everything,' wasn't that a lesson from your catechism? How will you vote?"

"Father!"

"I am not the one judging! He is. For or against?"

"Against, Father. I'll vote against."

The answer was delivered in a faint, weak voice. False, the priest might surmise, but he preferred to leave it at that, knowing from experience that limits still exist when pressuring someone with voting rights in Congress. He absolved him with a long sign of the cross, implying that the marital infidelities were merely trivial sins of the flesh.

The following week Adamastor had time to enjoy the rest of his suffering and contemplate that the priest, already past his seventies, might be wrong, that God, in His omnipotence, wouldn't punish anyone with hell because of a symbol. A day before his awaited kiss with Madalena, he sought to confess again, this time to Maria Amélia.

"You confessed and let a priest tell you how to vote? Sweet uncle, I know you were raised as a penitent, but at least choose which bucket you vomit your weaknesses into. Father Vicente—that's who you confessed to, right?—is known throughout Brasília as a leaky bucket. Everything spills out. Fortunately, it was only that silly bill on symbols. It won't pass anyway. At least not now. Our culture, and not ours alone, is deeply influenced by symbols. It's even more pronounced in the United States ... What else did he inquire about?"

"Concerning politics, just that. The rest was about my personal life."

"I see. You told him everything about your escapades with Érica and your romance, I love that word, with Madalena. You've cleansed your soul, haven't you, Uncle? Even Mom Anita would forgive you, assuming she can forgive anything from up there."

"Niece, don't say it like that. May Anita's soul rest in peace."

"Amen! Is that what you want me to say? Please, Uncle, from now on only confess your private sins. Discuss your political matters with me first. Well, if you intend to go any further. The choice is yours."

Maria Amélia's indifference regarding Anita hurt Adamastor deeply, but he lacked the will or the strength to object. And he was relieved she didn't pressure him to vote against the anti-crucifix law. When alone, he cried like a child, evoking the deceased's name and asking for forgiveness a thousand times. Drenched in tears, massaged by guilt, his senses captured a message in Anita's carioca-accented voice in the electromagnetic sphere—or whatever sphere it may be:

"You are forgiven. Life goes on."

As soon as he arrived at the office the next day, he closed the door, planted the long-repressed kiss on Madalena's lips, and whispered an order in her ears:

"Pack your things. From today on, you'll be living with me."

After hearing her uncle's confession, Maria Amélia traveled to Rio de Janeiro. She had a meeting scheduled with Maria da Anunciação. It had been arranged through Professor da Mata. The proposal had been for Maria Amélia to go to the doctor's office, although the other party had a stronger vested interest. So much was clear. She didn't shy away from sarcasm when rejecting the proposed location when Dr. da Mata passed on the message:

"Tell her, Profesor, *la distancia es la misma. Que venga el toro. Mejor, la vaca.* I'll be waiting for her at the Lagoa mansion at five o'clock in the afternoon."

Professor da Mata burst into laughter, something he hadn't done in a long time. Then he said, seriously:

"I'm glad you two are reconciling."

The meeting was brief, lasting less than ten minutes. Gabriel escorted Maria da Anunciação to Maria Amélia's workspace, where she was waiting comfortably in the armchair behind the desk. Maria Amélia didn't bother to stand up or offer a more formal greeting. She immediately said:

"So, Dr. Maria da Anunciação, what do you want?"

The psychiatrist swallowed hard at the word "doctor" pronounced with a tinge of contempt and replied, defensively:

"Reconcile. I want to reconcile with you."

"Mom Anita is dead. Maybe I should blame you for not following psychiatric standards. It was you who poisoned her mind against me. I have evidence."

"I know I didn't act appropriately. I apologize."

"Very well. You're forgiven. I don't hold grudges. But, changing subjects, how are your sessions with Cleide going?"

"Cleide is no longer my client. I told her I'm in no condition to treat her obsession. Besides, she doesn't want treatment anymore. She claims she's cured and knows what she wants from life."

"To destroy me. That's what she wants. Maybe she told you how, back when you were partners."

"No, she didn't tell me. You don't need to worry. She's desperate, but she's weak. She couldn't move a finger against anyone."

"What's this, Maria da Anunciação? You're a psychiatrist, and you know full well what people with nothing to lose are capable of. Don't hide anything."

"I'm not hiding anything. Poor Cleide. She's broken."

"And wearing a talisman around her neck, waiting for the right moment to strike. Fine, I'm prepared for whatever comes my way. For today, I believe we have nothing else to discuss, right?"

"I don't think so. Good afternoon and thank you."

"Gabriel will show you out."

Already inside her car, Maria da Anunciação felt she couldn't drive. She was stunned, her head spinning, sensing she had entered an irreversible path of submission, yielding to the other woman's dominance. She had the urge to open the car door and scream everything she truly felt about Maria Amélia into the streets. But she held back. She sensed being watched by two gray eyes from one of the mansion's windows. She gathered herself, and finally, started the car and drove back home.

In the "Parlamentinho da Lagoa," Maria Amélia managed, after some trouble, to persuade her party and some allies to support two proposals for political reform. One of them involved putting an end to mandatory voting, which was still in effect since being established in the 1934 Constitution. Maria Amélia argued to the group of twelve gathered in the little parliament:

"The problem at the core of mandatory voting is that it reeks not only of the past, as a relic of the Getúlio Vargas era, but also of the nauseating smell exuded by paternalism. Abolishing mandatory voting aligns with the same struggle that allowed women and illiterates to vote. Moreover, optional voting allows us to gauge the level of interest in society and the confidence it places in its leaders."

"But casting null or blank votes is already an option. In my view, this is sufficient mechanism to measure social engagement."

"No, it's not! The weight represented by 60% not showing up at the polls is greater than the equivalent in blank and null votes. It's clearer. It stands out more. And it shows more respect for the voter's will, if that's what my colleague considers important. Mandatory voting presupposes that voters are incapable of independent will, treating them like children

285

who need to be led by the hand. It's ridiculous and contradictory to punish someone for not exercising a right. In fact, this is the crux of the matter. Is voting a right or a duty for the deputy?"

"Both. A right and a duty."

"Duty? That might apply to your employees on the soybean plantations in Mato Grosso. It's a right, colleague. Voting is a right. A person who doesn't vote merely waives a right, voluntarily submits to what is decided by the others who did vote. The notion of duty is very much to the liking of dictatorial regimes, and the word is stale from being shouted in military orders."

Maria Amélia stood up and saluted the soybean planter.

"It's a duty to the country! To the fatherland!"

Before responding, Maria Amélia shot her opponent down with her gray eyes:

"Good heavens! Look, everyone, the deputy's flaunting his patriotism like a membership card!"

"That's right! I'm not ashamed of my patriotism."

"Then keep your membership card. Let's focus on the voting issue. Voting is a right, and all arguments around its imposition, the incantations of duty to the homeland, are based on a view contrary to the rights of individuals, of citizens, if the deputy so prefers," and she smiled, anticipating some backlash for deliberately using the feminine form '*cidadã*', before emphasizing, now addressing the whole audience:

"It's not a duty. It's a right!"

"And how will people be called upon to fulfill their duty? Everyone crying for their rights, no one fulfilling their duty. Is that what you want?"

"Voters are not like your employees on the soybean plantation, deputy, subjected to working hours that exceed the limits of labor legislation. Perhaps you and many other colleagues are under the influence of Kennedy's speech when he came up with that cheap: 'Ask not what your country can do for you, ask what you can do for your country.' Bullshit, as his fellow countrymen would say. But I will answer your question directly. In a society where all demand their rights, there's no need to remind anyone of their duties. But this isn't our biggest concern right now, and we won't belittle our colleague's patriotism, so esteemed in military barracks. It's the other amendment that we'll have to move heaven and earth for to force it down Congress' throat. But it wouldn't hurt to always defend the end of mandatory voting whenever an opportunity arises. With the other, more pressing amendment, we'll also be pioneers, aligning with the progressive factions of civil society that demand greater control of political activities."

"I'm not sure I can get on board with this. Count me out."

"That's your right, Deputy. Just remember, when this bill becomes a celebrated law, don't come saying that you were one of its defenders from the very beginning. If I can, I'll expose you right away."

"Don't threaten me, Maria Amélia!"

"I'm not threatening you. I'm warning you. Informing you. Shall we move forward with the project or not, folks?"

A general agreement was reached among nods and a few interventions to address some details. The typical case of so many meetings. Someone says something—often redundant—just because they have to say something. After the meeting, Maria Amélia took the soybean planter by the arm and whispered in his ear:

"You're in the wrong trench, wouldn't you agree?"

When they were alone, Adamastor, unable to hide his nervousness, said to Maria Amélia:

"Niece, you were very harsh with Dr. Alfredo. He is our ally."

"Ally up to what point, Uncle? Something tells me he can't be trusted. Maybe he's just here to gather information. To me, he's on the other side of the fence."

"Even so, don't you think you went a bit too far when you ridiculed his patriotism? Accusing someone of being unpatriotic is serious. Very serious."

"Uncle may have a small point there. But don't worry. We won't expose ourselves further on that terrain. Oh my, just look at the worried wrinkles on uncle's forehead because of some criticism of that man's exaggerated patriotism. You might be right. But just between us, what is a country, after all? What is Brazil? Nothing more than an outlined territory where people live within a framework of traditions, rules, and laws. Any one of us could've been born in Bolivia, France, Bangladesh, or some island in the far reaches of the Pacific."

"How do we explain that to the voters?"

"Well said, Uncle! How are we going to explain that to voters? Not all at once, of course. I'm not out of my mind to advocate for political suicide, nor am I dealing with inexperienced teenagers who want to save the nation with slogans. But we need to start laying the groundwork for the emerging new world. It's pretty obvious that the planet we live on is nothing more than a spaceship with limited resources, sailing in an immense ocean. Perhaps an infinite ocean. And all it does is orbit a fifth-rate star. And what's worse, it's full of obstacles. But let's go no further. No detours, or else my dear uncle will go haywire. We won't tell the voters directly that the concept of a homeland doesn't exist, obviously. This will happen gradually. One step at a time. For now, to begin with, we'll just make it clear that voting isn't a duty; it's a right. Having a right is appealing, it's positive. Duty implies sacrifice. It's negative. I'm sure the project to end mandatory voting has a lot of popular appeal. In fact, everyone agreed on that. The other proposal is much more delicate. Much more. And we have to force it down Congress' throat."

"True, Niece. Wouldn't it be better to give up?"

"No. I've already said we must push forward. It's a proposal championed by numerous NGOs and progressive groups, who find it absurd to hand the rulers a blank check for a four-year stint. Impeachment is an option, but not only is it usually traumatic, it also prevents a more direct involvement of the voters. In the European parliamentary system, there's a chance of the government falling if it loses its majority, which helps to somewhat correct this distortion, if you will. But it's just slightly better than the absurdity of presidentialism ..."

Maria Amélia paused, smiled, and continued:

"I'll probably have to be reborn again before this becomes possible. But we can start pulling the strings right now, leading the way. We might be stirring up a hornet's nest. Ever read Sarney's *House of Fire Wasps?* Forget it. Ideas proposing mechanisms to hold rulers accountable won't find much favor in Brasília. Rest assured, Uncle. The backlash against our proposal will clearly come from within Congress, from the not-so-small group accustomed to the perks of high-ranking positions. We may well lose in Parliament. For now. But we'll win in the streets. I'm even prepared to be reborn again and wait."

Somewhere deep in Adamastor's subconscious, a censored thought lingered that could roughly be translated as follows, even though he wasn't fond of reading Bakunin: "My dear niece will need to be far less authoritarian to live in the libertarian world she proposes." He refrained from making the sign of the cross to dispel the thought because he knew that would only irritate her further.

The proposal, the reason for so many discussions and censored thoughts, and which has not yet been fully explained, was as follows: 1) Introduce a system of popular initiatives with the aim of removing elected officials from the Legislative and Executive branches at all levels—municipal, state, and federal; 2) Call for a new election if the proposal obtained signatures equivalent to at least two-thirds of the votes obtained by the respective elected official—be it a city council member, congressman, senator, mayor, governor, or president; 3) To remain in office, the elected official would need to obtain more than 50% of the votes in the new election. The proposal did not sit well with practically anyone. In meetings without Maria Amélia's presence—which were extremely rare—the Socialist Party had already decided the bill could not be presented. She was perfectly aware. She knew her uncle had made commitments to the others in those party meetings where she was absent. Still, she feigned ignorance, as if completely unaware, fully conscious that Adamastor endured sleepless nights, feeling he was betraying his niece. And on occasion, more than once, she gave her uncle a sly look, as if she knew it all and granted him forgiveness.

Once, during one of the long weekend breakfasts at the Lagoa mansion, Adamastor dropped a hint to see how his niece would react. He recounted one of the criticisms he had heard during a meeting she had not attended:

"The proposal you're so passionate about mirrors Switzerland's system of popular initiatives, doesn't it?"

"Well, well. They're going all out against your beloved niece when she's out. The popular initiative system in Switzerland may be more comprehensive than in other countries, but it still exudes the nauseating smell of patriarchy, chauvinism, if you prefer. Even today, in Appenzell Innerrhoden, for example, the voting is carried out in public squares, imitating the practice of ancient Greek cities. And do you know how they used to vote not too long ago? On a very festive day, the gentlemen would assemble in the public square and raise their swords—yes, swords—to approve a proposal! The women stayed home, often with a knife in hand to chop onions for the soup, one of their country's national dishes, I presume. Did my dear uncle know that Switzerland only granted women the right to vote in 1970? That even in 1990, during the open-air voting in Appenzell Innerrhoden, known as the *Landsgemeinde* in their dialect, the women's vote was rejected by a gang of old men raising their hands? Progress, right? They replaced the swords with their hands, perhaps because it would be challenging for such an old bunch to lift anything else. No, Uncle, we're not trying to copy the Swiss system. The popular initiative is already established in Brazil, defined in the Constitution and regulated by law since 1998. Wake up, Uncle, the 2010 Clean Slate Law is the result of a popular initiative. What we want is something much more comprehensive, a popular mechanism to control the government. Voters with the power to fire those who deceived them after being elected. But don't get upset. I know it won't pass for the time being. It's just to stir up public opinion in our favor."

Adamastor listened in silence. To lighten the mood, Maria Amélia patted her uncle's head and joked:

"Uncle, uncle, this niece of yours really messes with your head, doesn't she?"

Adamastor smiled. A yellow smile if it'd had any color.

But her uncle's weak attitude wasn't what really concerned Maria Amélia. It was the realization that her achievable objectives in this lifetime couldn't be pursued within the framework of the current political parties. The Brazilian Socialist Party (PSB) had already served its purpose: electing her uncle. The other parties were all the same. The Workers' Party (PT), forged at the end of the military dictatorship, used to have an original proposal, but it had become bloated with the candy of power and indistinguishable from the rest. Maria Amélia even sensed a pact brewing between PT and the PSDB (Brazilian Social Democracy Party). During a meeting in Lagoa's little parliament, she raised the issue:

"I challenge any one of you to explain the difference between PT and PSDB in the post-Lava-Jato[17] era. Not the superficial details. A fundamental difference in political objectives. Both are social democrats. More precisely, they represent the new social democracy, whose most notable champion is the former British Prime Minister, Tony Blair. In the old social democracy, represented, let's say, by Willy Brandt and Harold Wilson, the main concern was responding to the so-called socialist world, which was socialist only in name. They created the blessed welfare state as a defensive measure against more left-leaning movements, most of which looked to the countries of Eastern Europe, or worse, Maoist China as their models. The new social democracy emerges, precisely and not just coincidentally, with the downfall of the Soviet Union and its allies in the East. It, too, is defensive, but now trying to present an alternative to the advancement of right-wing neoliberalism, with its capitalist development-at-any-cost mantra. The problem is that in their eagerness to be a valid alternative accepted by the consumerist masses, they more often than not end up practically resembling what they aim to replace: unchecked neoliberalism."

A brief silence followed Maria Amélia's exposition, and she took the opportunity to touch a sore spot and reach the intended point:

---

[17] Operation Car Wash is an infamous, and ultimately failed judicial operation against corruption that degenerated into lawfare against the opposition.

"And the worst part, my dear colleagues, is that the Socialist Party is following the same path. These are worn-out formulas, all these parties can be said to be part of the left-wing. They no longer respond to the challenges of the new world."

The *parlamentinho* was made up of astute individuals, so all sensed that Maria Amélia's proposal was about creating a new party. Yet another "ism" in the mix? But the truth is that nothing substantially different had been invented after the nineteenth century, except for resorting to very fleeting matters to name parties. Someone could suggest the Witch Party or the Braided Wench Party, for example. But who would dare? Maria Amélia's speech made another thing clear, in case you, the reader, haven't noticed yet. She was the one making the proposal, not her uncle's advisor. A young woman aspiring to stretch her own wings in the skies of the *Planalto Central.*

47

Despite stumbling on his Rs, Professor Steven Adams' Portuguese was quite reasonable when he disembarked at Galeão Airport on a swelteringly hot Monday. It struck a customs officer as odd that he was carrying three large suitcases for just a one-month stay. And suspicions increased when the suitcases were opened.

"What the devil is this?" the guard questioned.

"It's not the devil. They're devices for measuring telluric energy."

"Telluric energy? Look here, guys, this gringo is bringing telluric energy devices. Anyone know what the hell that is?"

Two other guards approached to examine the situation. One of them asked:

"And what are you going to do with this stuff?"

"I already said. These are devices for measuring telluric energy. You must have heard of parapsychology, right?"

"Oh, that crazy business with objects moving on their own."

"More or less. Well, these devices are for that purpose."

"Right, but that's not very well explained."

"I have a letter from the Brazilian Consulate with a list of the devices. You can keep it; I have a copy. When I leave, I'll take everything back. There's no smuggling involved. None at all."

"Damn it, has anyone read the letter?"

The first guard carefully read the list with the consulate's stamp and passed it to his colleagues.

"Look, the gringo is a professor. We'd better ask."

One of them stepped aside, made a call to the customs office, and returned shortly after.

"You can let the gringo go. They said he's a nice guy."

Professor Steven Adams stayed at the Copacabana Orla upon a friend's recommendation. After navigating the initial customs confusion, he next encountered the taxi driver's reluctance.

"What the hell is this? That's not a suitcase; it's more like a crate. It won't fit in my cab. Wait for a van."

He ended up waiting for more than twenty minutes. The first thing he did at the hotel was take a long bath, and only then did he call Professor Fábio da Mata. Their meeting was delayed until the next day because Maria Amélia was preparing an important intervention by her uncle at the plenary. She would board a flight to Brasília at ten o'clock Wednesday morning, and the meeting was scheduled for two o'clock in the afternoon at the professor's house. Maria Amélia had enough time to stop by the Lagoa mansion and take a shower. She arrived half an hour early to have a more relaxed talk with Professor Fábio da Mata.

"What does this gringo want, after all?"

"Your reputation is already spreading around the world, girl. He's extremely interested and intends to conduct a series of parapsychological tests with you. I'm not really a believer in such devices. It's very hard to measure impulses of different natures. Be that as it may, science, as it is currently conceived, will only accept these kinds of experiments, even if reluctantly. That doesn't mean working with him wouldn't be worthwhile. I think the exchange of experiences between the both of you can be very enriching."

It was Professor da Mata's niece who answered and greeted the American visitor when the doorbell rang. The visitor mistook her for Maria Amélia and enthusiastically extended his hand.

"Nice to meet you. We'll have a lot to talk about."

Judite took an embarrassed step back, looked down, and replied, barely touching the extended hand.

"Pleased to meet you as well. However, I think there's been a misunderstanding. I'm not who you're looking for; I'm the professor's niece."

Surprised, Steven Adams responded:

"Oh ... And is *she* in?"

"Yes, sir. She's in the living room with the professor. Follow me."

The American froze in the doorway, pierced by the smiling gaze of the person he had crossed an ocean to meet. Several seconds passed without anyone saying a word before he composed himself enough to greet Professor da Mata, as protocol demanded. Then, his legs trembling, he approached Maria Amélia as she stood up.

"You can't imagine what an honor it is to meet you! It's a pleasure, truly."

She responded with a mischievous smile:

"Let's not overdo it, doctor. Professor Fábio has already spoken highly of your expertise. I understand you've already met our colleague, Maria da Anunciação."

"Oh, yes. She sought me out at the university in Tucson. But please, call me Steven. Please, no titles necessary. Just Steven."

"Very well, Steven. Was your conversation with Maria da Anunciação fruitful? We're also close. She and I are also on a first name basis. No titles."

Had the American not been so captivated, he might have detected the sarcasm and cynicism in Maria Amélia's remarks. But he couldn't take his eyes off the face framed by two braids. His response was evasive, downplaying his discussion with the psychiatrist:

"Nothing out of the ordinary. I didn't learn anything new. May I use 'você' when addressing you?"

"You can and should. Things of our language. In the United States, 'you' is universal. Here, we have these formalities. In Portugal, 'você' is a sign of respect. Did you know that? But I digress. Professor Fábio said you want to conduct some tests, some measurements."

"Yes, yes. If it's not too much trouble."

"What trouble? I'm an open book. Or maybe I'm a window to another world, as Professor Fábio likes to say ..."

She turned to Fábio da Mata, who remained silent.

"... but the professor is prone to exaggeration. I'm hardly a third of what he makes me out to be."

"She's more! Much, much more!" raced through the American's mind, feeling a lump in his throat, a weakness in his legs, the state of lethargy of someone completely captivated by two gray eyes.

48

The American's equipment was installed in one of the empty rooms of the Lagoa mansion. Mansions always have empty rooms, especially when the owner is a single woman spending most of her time in Brasília. Although unfurnished, the room was kept clean with a single portrait on the wall. Fiinha's picture, the other one, Maria Amélia's great aunt, who was murdered with a shot to the chest in the early twentieth century. At first, Steven Adams didn't want to accept the offer. He'd rather leave everything at the hotel. But Maria Amélia was emphatic:

"No way. It's in my house. I have room to spare. There's no need for you to stay in a hotel. The guest room is already prepared. You can check out of the hotel today."

"But, Miss Maria Amélia ..."

"Drop the 'Miss,' please. Just Maria Amélia is plenty."

"Alright. Maria Amélia, but I'd rather stay in the hotel."

"And why is that? I have a huge house with four permanent servants. I spend most of my time in Brasília, and you're staying in a hotel when you came here to work with me, or experiment on me, call it whatever you want. Today, you settle into the guest room or any other room you prefer."

The mischief screamed from the last sentence, especially since Maria Amélia's eyes were fixed on the American, filled with insinuation instead of hardness.

"Yes. Ok. I'll need to call a large taxi."

"No taxis. My driver Alberto is at your disposal. He'll fetch your paraphernalia."

"Paraphernalia?"

"Your devices, your measuring tools."

Once in the mansion, Steven said:

"Can I ask you something?"

"Steven, let's drop the formalities. Didn't you come here to ask me things? Ask whatever you want."

"The picture on the wall. The clothes are from the early twentieth century. Any reason why you dressed like that?"

Maria Amélia replied with a smile, one might say with a touch of wickedness:

"But, Steven, that's not me. It's a photo of my father's aunt. The one murdered with buckshot to the chest."

"It can't be. It's you!"

"No, it's her! But go get your things. I'll tell you the whole story later. We'll have plenty of time to talk. Alberto! Take the professor back to the hotel."

One person, however, really didn't like the idea of Steven's lodging at the Lagoa mansion: Dente Grande. He had known for some time that the girl with braids was beyond his control, but he refused to accept another man, especially a *gringo*, staying in her house. What upset him even more was the directness with which Maria Amélia informed him of the new situation over the phone:

"Hi, Dente Grande. We won't be seeing each other for a few days, maybe months. I have a professor visiting from the United States, and we have a lot of work to do."

"But how am I supposed to live without my girl?"

"Figure it out, Dente Grande. Emotional blackmail won't work on me. Jealousy? Cut it out. You've heard the song '*Ninguém é de ninguém*' on an old record? Sung by Cauby Peixoto? It's a thing of the past, smelling of mildew. In this case, I'm the one who has no owner. Maria Amélia. Plenty of girls are eager for your slong in the favela."

"You're breaking my heart."

"I could do without that. Not even Cauby's records are that corny anymore. Don't make a fool of yourself, Dente Grande. Let's put it this way: our relationship is on hold indefinitely. A kiss. Goodbye."

And she hung up the phone. If anything irritated Maria Amélia, it was whining.

Dazed by the silence of his cell phone, Dente Grande filled his immense lungs to shout.

"Motherfucking gringo!"

The cry was heard across the favela. But it was the insult of someone throwing in the towel, the final buck of the horse before accepting the reins. Although we shouldn't compare people to horses. Should we?

After arranging the equipment in the room with the portrait of the other *Fiinha*, Adams was led by one of the employees to the spacious meeting room where Maria Amélia awaited him at her work desk.

"Everything in order?"

"Yes, thank you very much. It was very kind of you to give me so much space."

"Forget about it. But what do you think after closer observation?"

"I don't understand the question?"

"The portrait, Steven. The portrait of my father's aunt. Take the book he wrote. It will also help you improve your Portuguese."

"Ah ... interesting."

"What's interesting? The book or the portrait?"

"The book is interesting. The portrait is extraordinary. You know, now I understand better why Professor da Mata is so convinced that you're a reincarnation. I must confess, I don't really personally believe in such things; it's not the focus of my research. I believe in energies, in flows unknown or poorly understood by science. Reincarnation goes more toward the spiritual, religious side, I would say."

"We agree completely, Steven. But it's almost impossible to deny there is a connection between me and my father's aunt. Read the book, it's not very long. You'll see the resemblance is not merely physical. We share many attributes. Maybe it's an extratemporal connection. It's even difficult to describe. A phenomenon for which I'm unfortunately sure we won't find measurable evidence accepted by the scientific community."

"That's true. I agree. But that's why we're here. Trying to make progress, step by step, sometimes too slowly."

"Awaiting the big leap. The breakthrough, as you say, right?"

"Yes, that's it. Who knows, maybe you're the key?"

"Well, here I am, dear Steven. Discover me. Every way you can."

The American felt a shiver down his spine. Especially with the insinuation emphasized in Maria Amélia's voice and facial expression, which couldn't be any clearer. Still, he remained planted in his seat until he was guided by two arms and felt a passionate kiss on his lips. That very night, they slept together, not in the guest room, obviously. When he woke up the next day, he found a note from Maria Amélia saying breakfast would be served in bed and that she had traveled to Brasília. She would be back in the evening.

The schemes in Brasília, which were already ongoing in Lagoa's little parliament, centered around the creation of the new party in which Maria Amélia wanted to play a central role without the need to rely on her uncle. Adamastor had hoped his niece would put forth his name to preside over the new organization. He was wrong. She proposed that the new party be led by a collegiate committee until a convention could be held with the power to elect the board. And the name? Ah, the name! This question sparked heated debates and ended up being deferred to a new meeting in the *parlamentinho*. Many didn't want to give up the name "socialism" or anything reminiscent of it. Maria Amélia wanted something new, something capable of making an impact that could awaken voters from their apathy, tired of so many promises. But what? A name came to her just before the Gol jet touched down in Santos Dumont airport, while she admired Rio's contours. *Redentor.* Redeemer Party. But the jolt of the wheels hitting the ground awakened her from her reverie. "*Redentor?* *Redentora* maybe!" And she smiled to herself, the sarcastic smile of self-criticism ready to demolish anything resembling narcissistic exaggeration.

On the way home, as the taxi seemed like it was about to take flight on Aterro do Flamengo, a new name sparked in her mind: "*Nosso Partido*" (Our Party).

"NP," simple, and at the same time vague enough to be filled with any program or ideology. It's what Maria Amélia had been looking for a long time. And it also brought people together, she thought, it united. She came up with a subtitle to please the majority in the *parlamentinho* still attached to old formulas and names: "*Nosso Partido*: for a socialist and democratic platform." The meeting at the *parlamentinho* was held that same evening, and she decided to invite the American to attend.

"Colleagues, this is Steven Adams, a parapsychologist. Don't be alarmed. My X-ray eyes can attest he is not a CIA agent and is here only because I insisted heavily."

Smiles, some forced, revealed a sense of suspicion hanging in the room. Even Adamastor couldn't quite grasp the American's presence. But it was Alceu Pereira who spoke up expressing a timid resistance. He was competing with Maria Amélia's uncle for the nomination to lead the new party.

"But will our friend Adams understand anything? It's not only the language barrier, there's the entire political context he surely doesn't know (unless he really is a CIA agent, he thought). It will be very tedious for him."

Maria Amélia stared him down.

"Oh, Alceu, don't worry. If Steven gets bored with our chatter, he can leave whenever he pleases."

"If it's such a bother, I can leave right now."

"It's hard even to detect this gringo's accent. There's definitely a whiff of CIA in the air," Alceu thought, unable to hide his discomfort, but Maria Amélia was determined to have her guest stay, and she quickly put an end to the matter and moved on to the topic at hand:

"So, colleagues, as we agreed, today's subject is the choice of the new party name. I have a proposal. Simply: '*Nosso Partido.*' What do you think?"

A moment of silence followed. People shifted in their seats, clearing their throats. Even Adamastor, who was already privy to the proposal, chose not to speak. Maria Amélia waited for a reaction and measured the time on her watch until the pause had reached thirty seconds. And seconds are slower than snails in such cases. Then she spoke:

"Nobody wants to speak up? Do you all like it that much? Or have you lost your tongues? Speak up, Alceu. Your nose has more twists than my braids."

Laughter, but awkward, embarrassed, forced laughter. Alceu cleared his throat.

"Well, if Alceu cleared his throat, it means he wants to speak. Go ahead, Alceu."

"Forgive me, colleague Maria Amélia. But '*Nosso Partido*' sounds like something from the countryside. The name of a club, *Our Club*, or a parish newsletter. Something like *Our Newspaper*. But as the name of a party, a serious party with national aspirations, it doesn't seem very appropriate to me."

He looked around and felt he was supported by the majority there. The support was restrained, however, and when his eyes met Maria Amélia's, he felt like a condemned man about to be shot. He wasn't entirely wrong.

"See here, colleagues, Alceu is a sophisticated man. He despises the simplicity of the countryside, perhaps even forgetting that it still represents a share that cannot be disregarded. '*Nosso Partido*' may be compared to

300

everything he said. But that's precisely where its strength lies. Simplicity. '*Nosso*' is a word that not only feeds the dominant sense of ownership in the human soul, but it also induces collectivism, sharing among a group, be it of goods or ideas. Our Party. The leaders and active members, but especially all the sympathizers who form the voting majority, will feel like participants in something that is ours, that belongs to the entire group."

Alceu cleared his throat again, but when he spoke, his voice had no fervor, no punch:

"But it's a bit vague. '*Nosso Partido*'? Our Party for what?"

"For carrying forward our proposals, Alceu. Our ideas for the transformation of society, for something that can destroy the dominance of financial capital once and for all and open the doors, so to speak, to a new socialism untainted by the authoritarianism inherited from last century's practical Marxism, with its Leninist, Trotskyist, and goodness knows what other formulas."

Alceu ventured:

"Stalinist?"

"Ah, colleague. Stalinism can't even be seen as a Marxist offshoot. If anything, let's say it was just an aberration of Leninism. But all right. '*Nosso Partido*' may indeed sound a bit vague. Maybe it requires a subtitle to at least satisfy those who can't yet let go of old formulas. How about: '*Nosso Partido*: for a socialist and democratic platform'?"

"That sounds like a good solution," Adamastor volunteered so as not to miss a good opportunity to say something that could please both the Greek girl in braids and the defeated Trojan. Alceu, however, was still in a contentious mood and retorted:

"Why not simply 'Socialist Democratic Party'?"

"Because it's an old, outdated formula. Voters are tired of repeated formulas. '*Nosso Partido*' is new. If it catches on, and I'm sure it will, the subtitle won't even be remembered, even if it should be our goal: create a platform for a new type of democratic socialism. Which, by the way, is nothing new and has been tried without much success."

Another participant, who knew from experience that all of Maria Amélia's proposals ended up being approved, wanted to end the discussion:

"I suggest we put the proposal of our colleague Maria Amélia to a vote. '*Nosso Partido*: for a socialist and democratic platform' sounds very good to me. Who's in favor?"

Everyone raised their hand, except for Alceu, who became the target of everyone's gaze.

"All right. I'm outvoted. Let it be '*Nosso Partido.*' And I hope it yields results, that it convinces."

"Have no fear, Alceu. My crystal ball assures me of future successes, with the ramp to the presidential palace at the end of the line. You'll see."

Maria Amélia's had an almost mocking tone. But two people sensed she was serious, that she truly had the ability to see the future. One of them was Alceu, deep down already convinced that they were all mere puppets in the braided girl's hands. The other person, in case you haven't guessed yet, was Steven Adams, once again certified of his host's exceptional powers, more than that, of her persuasive ability to keep everyone around her under her control. Including him.

49

Dente Grande couldn't sleep. In his convulsive insomnia, sheets soaked in sweat, he saw the gringo tossing and turning in the mansion's bed, holding his braided girl and doing things he didn't even remember doing. They say the combination of jealousy with imagination is one of the worst poisons for a tormented soul. And he remembered, with renewed hatred, that Maria Amélia had never allowed him to visit the Lagoa mansion, arguing you shouldn't play with fire in politics, let alone sex. His fury increased as facts confirmed he wasn't just a pleasure object for the little witch, but also a puppet, a servile campaigner to gather votes from the scum in the slums. He felt the urge to kill them both; to enter the mansion hooded as a robber and blast them with his long-barreled .38 revolver. First, a shot to the gringo's testicles, restraining the unfaithful girl by her braids to force her to witness her partner bleed to death. And then he'd put the .38's barrel in her mouth and fire, deaf to the girl's screams, never again to be her obedient little dog. He jumped out of bed and shouted for the entire favela to hear:

"I'll kill them!"

His cavernous voice startled the on-duty Pacifying Police guard at his post, who was dozing off on a stool. He jumped up to call the sergeant, who had also been awakened by the shout:

"Did you hear that? That's Dente Grande."

"That's not for us. I'll call the BOPE; the motherfucker won't get away this time."

A squad equipped with an armored truck was climbing up the favela in less than ten minutes under the command of Captain Justino, who had sworn to St. Jude Thaddeus never to betray his wife again if he let him put an end to Dente Grande. He gave the order to his men:

"The perp is here. This time he won't escape, even if we have to search every shack. There's only one way about it. If he shows his face, start blasting. Even if in doubt. I mean, start blasting no matter what."

"But, Captain, the Pacifying Police Colonel said we should exercise restraint. Only shoot as a last resort."

"That's just a cock-and-bull story. And who's leading this platoon? Me, damn it! The order is to pump him full of lead. I don't wanna see that scumbag enjoying the five-star treatment behind bars. I couldn't care less about those criminal-huggers and their bleeding-heart speeches on human rights. We're supposed to pump him full of lead, damn it! With the grace and help of St. Jude Thaddeus, who hates criminals."

Dente Grande sensed he had made a huge mistake by shouting with his distinctive booming voice in the middle of the night. Even worse, he should have stayed in Rocinha with its one-hundred-thousand-plus people, where searching every shack and building would have been impossible. He filled his shorts pockets with ammunition and ran out shirtless into the narrow alleyway. He stopped, realizing he didn't have many places to go, like a fox cornered by a pack of crazed hounds. In Rocinha he could at least have made a dash for Tijuca Forest. If those sons of bitches hadn't already found his escape tunnel, that is. A modern-day Leônidas, given the circumstances. He and his trusty .38 revolver against BOPE's assault rifles, pistols, and armored vehicles. Hide? Where? He felt his life was hanging by a thread. In a flash, he had a crazy idea. He returned to his shack, put on the wig with straight hair—the same one he had worn when he traveled to São Paulo with Maria Amélia—and dressed in the same sharp suit. He took fake documents identifying him as Valdomiro Pereira da Conceição, a pastor of the Kingdom of God, exchanged the .38 for a Bible, and set off on the alleyway that would take him to the Mirante da Paz, where he could take the elevator down to the General Osório subway station in Ipanema. In less than five minutes, he was approached by five heavily armed UPP policemen.

"A high-hat in the favela at this hour?"

"I'm Pastor Valdomiro of the Kingdom of God."

Now speaking with a soft voice, he pulled out the documents with the pious composure of a preacher, or a seasoned drug dealer skilled in eluding the police. He got lucky. The Pacifying Police sergeant from the platoon was part of the Kingdom of God flock. He looked at the documents, bowed, and asked:

"A thousand apologies for the disrespect. Where is the pastor headed?"

"To the Mirante da Paz walkway. I still want to catch the last subway. I got delayed attending to one of God's children who is not long for this world."

"We'll escort you there. The walkway is closed by order of the BOPE. The criminal Dente Grande is on the loose. Didn't the pastor hear him shout?"

"I did, indeed. Horrifying! It sounded like something from the devil."

Dente Grande mentally thanked the little witch for giving him the elocution lessons that allowed him to disguise the distinctive booming voice that marked him as the boss of the hill.

And so he went, escorted by two helpful policemen to the walkway, down the elevator, through the long tunnel with stairs and escalators, and to the platform heading to Copacabana. Walking in silence between both policemen, Dente Grande pondered on the best way to take care of the little witch and the gringo. Then, he remembered a detail: "Fuck, I don't have my piece!"

The solution was his lawyer and "Jack of all trades," Maciel. When he felt safe on the subway after bidding farewell to the policemen, wishing God would aid them in the difficult task of ridding the hill of criminals, he took out his cellphone and called Maciel. Fortunately, the subway car wasn't too crowded.

"I need help immediately."

"I'm just hearing the news. Wait a moment, and I'll call you back."

"I want to talk now ... Motherfucker! He hung up!!"

A couple sitting nearby were taken aback by the pastor's swearing. Dente Grande looked at them and said:

"Sinners like him can really get on our nerves. They even make us swear."

And he went to a more secluded seat at the back of the subway car, awaiting Maciel's response. An experienced lawyer doesn't take calls, on his own phone, from clients pursued by BOPE and, who knows, the entire Rio police force.

Dente Grande, who didn't put down his cellphone, answered at the first chord of his device's ringtone, "*Bonequinha Linda*":

"Motherfucker!" he shouted, not caring about the other passengers.

A guy like Dente Grande isn't easy to understand. Capable of behaving with the composure of a Franciscan when pretending to be a pastor to fool the police on this tail, and now attracting so much attention on the subway. The couple got off at the first station, Cantagalo Hill, which very well may not have been their intended destination. On the other end of the line, using one of the few public phones available, Maciel said:

"Stay calm, Onofre!"—he used Dente Grande's real name—"The entire Rio police force is after you. It's on TV, everywhere. At times like this, my phone is most likely tapped. What do you need?"

Dente Grande felt it was time to restore common sense and spoke, almost in a whisper, but with the firmness of someone accustomed to giving orders.

"A fire stick. I slipped away from the heat and I'm safe on the subway. I'm heading to the bar. Listen up: you roll in by cab and deliver the package pronto."

"But ..."

"No 'buts,' damn it! Bring me the package. You know very well where the emergency heater is kept."

Maria Amélia was surprised when the phone rang. Only friends and acquaintances had that number, and they all knew she hated being bothered after ten p.m. It had to be an emergency. She answered the call.

"Yes?"

"A thousand apologies for calling you at this late hour. It's Maciel."

"To begin with, who gave you this number?"

"Let's set formalities aside. I am the lawyer of our mutual friend, and I know everything about him. You must have heard about the ongoing manhunt on the news. I have information that might be useful to you, to give you a heads-up, so to speak."

"Cut to the chase. I don't have time for lawyer games."

"He's heading your way. Armed."

The all-night bar-restaurant with self-service in Copacabana was one of the joints where Dente Grande would meet his lawyer during emergencies. There, Maciel handed him the Taurus .38 inside a folder, and the drug lord took a taxi to the Lagoa mansion, still disguised as a pastor. He stepped out of the taxi when close and walked to the entrance. In addition to the three security guards and high walls with electric fencing, there were two fila dogs, sharp-toothed beasts. They were vicious to any intruder but melted with joy when their owner petted them. Forcing an entry was no option. Dente Grande simply pressed the doorbell. He was going to seek asylum, cry that he had nowhere to go. Once inside, he would unleash his silenced .38, leave the dogs some poisoned meatballs, and on his way out, acting like an ordinary visitor, he would kill the three guards by surprise.

Everything had to be done swiftly; there was no time or opportunity to execute his dreamt-up revenge. A shot to the butler's head as soon as he opened the door, then he would find the room and kill both of them the same way. Everything clean and silent. Dente Grande had never been to the mansion, but his scouts had apparently provided him with all the details on how the security system worked, with special attention to the pair of fila dogs.

He rang the doorbell.

One, two, three times. On the fourth call, one of the guards approached the gate with his hand on his .45 pistol:

"What do you want?"

"I'm a friend of Dr. Maria Amélia. She's expecting me."

"Name?"

"Onofre."

"Onofre what?"

"Arruda. Talk to her. She's expecting me."

"I already did. You can come in but put your hands on the wall. My colleague will frisk you."

There was no way out. The security guard pointed his pistol at him as the gate opened. The second guard quickly opened the folder, finding the silenced .38 and the meatballs wrapped in newspaper. The third guard went to the mansion's door and was given instructions by the butler on what to do. He was surprised, but passed on the message:

"He can come in, unarmed."

Once again, Dente Grande felt no match for his braided girl. He entered, pretending to be the drug lord hunted by the entire police force of Rio de Janeiro. In fact, he didn't need to pretend; he was indeed that very person, only disguised as a pastor of the Kingdom of God.

The butler, not hiding his irritation at having to work so late, led him to the room where Maria Amélia awaited him, wearing a nearly transparent robe that showcased her sculptural figure. Dente Grande shivered with fear of succumbing once again to the allure of the braided girl.

"And what do you come to my house for, armed with a silenced .38 and meatballs for my beloved angels? And with the entire police force on your tail! Oh, Dente Grande!"

"My girl, please forgive me, but I've nowhere to go."

"True, you don't. And you came here with the worst intentions. No, no, don't bore me calling me 'my girl.' You're in a dire situation, with no one left to trust. I've warned you time and again that you needed to change your ways. You and everyone else involved in this business now smell of the past. Wake up, toothy! And there's more. You can't escape the heat this time. I already knew you were coming here, armed and furious. Leaks in your organization, in your gang. It also won't be long before they know you're here, and that's not good for either of us. The BOPE folks are itching to give you a bullet-riddled send off, you know. You're no Corisco,[18] and that rusty .38 isn't a Beretta, with the firepower to go out in a blaze of glory. Surrender while you can, right now. I shouldn't, but I'll help you. You wait here, and I'll make some phone calls. Then, you sneak away, take a long stroll to the taxi stand at Bogari Street with Humaitá Street and wait for a patrol accompanied by reporters and representatives of human rights organizations. There you go. That's how you'll be safe from the BOPE shooters."

"And if I talk?"

"Talk about what, Dente Grande?"

"About our fucks, the hustles to score votes for your uncle in the favelas."

"Blackmailing me at this point? Don't push your luck. The patrol might not come with reporters, but with itchy trigger fingers."

"That's why I doubt."

"You're in no position to have any doubts. Look over there ..."—she pointed to the corner of the room where the three security guards stood, their .45 pistols drawn and the pair of fila dogs beside them. She remained silent for a few seconds and then continued, mocking the fugitive.

---

[18] The nickname of a *cangaceiro* executed by the police in 1940. Cangaceiros were outlaws in Northeastern Brazil in the early twentieth century.

"Oh, you have Saint George's sword?"

She was referring to the two gray amulets hanging around the drug lord's neck. She then got up and went to her room to make some phone calls. She didn't start from the bottom; she went straight to the top of her contacts, calling the governor. The governor's aide answered:

"The governor is in his quarters and asked not to be disturbed except in case of extreme urgency."

"Well, this is one of those cases. Go call him."

The governor's aide timidly knocked on the door, and the furious governor interrupted his little game of "will they or won't they" with his wife.

"What's going on? Who is it?"

"It's Dr. Maria Amélia. She says it's urgent, very urgent."

"Well, hello, doctor ..."—and then his voice softened—"what a pleasure. But what's the matter?"

"There's big commotion in the city, with the entire police hunting Dente Grande. The word is that BOPE is going to execute him."

"On whose orders? Not mine."

"Then do the following. Call the Secretary of Security and instruct him to send a patrol to the taxi stand on Humaitá Street, near the entrance to Bogari Street. The drug lord will be waiting, unarmed. In the meantime, I'll alert the press and human rights organizations, so they can witness the operation."

"Aren't these things best done discreetly?"

"No, they aren't. Your government will be lauded by the media for arresting the most wanted criminal in the entire city without firing a single shot."

After making a few more phone calls, Maria Amélia returned to the room and said:

"You can go, but don't do anything foolish. The men are waiting for you at the agreed location."

"What guarantees do I have?"

"None, Dente Grande, none. Your life is in the hands of fate. Take this chance or die. And leave your cellphone here. You don't need to communicate with anyone else tonight."

"I'm no longer the girl's stud," whispered the worms in Dente Grande's brain, "now I'm an *encumbrance*, I forget where I heard this word, but I've heard it. I'm in her way. An entry to be erased. No way I'm going. They're waiting there, fingers on the triggers. I wasn't born to become a bullet-riddled sieve at the foot of a hill where only fancy people live. No way I'm going."

And so, he didn't. Without a gun on his waist, he felt like a lost child on a deserted beach. Worse still, he didn't have a cellphone to communicate with anyone. He made a risky decision and took a taxi to Expedito Maciel's house, knowing he was the traitor who had called Maria Amélia. He would catch him by surprise, without any notice. Maciel didn't know he had the keys to his building's front gate and apartment. If the doorman suspected, he would come up with any excuse, claiming he was a guest of the lawyer, or silence him with a punch to the face as a last resort. That was the plan. He would enter, knock out Maciel, take all his available belongings (there had to be weapons!), and escape in the lawyer's car using alternative routes with little likelihood of encountering police barriers.

Think again! It was a foolish move by Dente Grande, driven by desperation. Four BOPE officers were waiting for him there. As soon as he put the key in the front gate, he received a single rifle shot to his forehead. A trembling Expedito Maciel placed a .45 pistol in the dead man's hands, as instructed and coerced by the police. The doorman, who should have stayed quiet in his corner, stood there watching everything. One of the officers, seeing Maciel's trembling, put on gloves, kicked him aside, and fired three shots of the .45 pistol at the doorman, who died without knowing why. Then, he used Dente Grande's finger to pull the trigger. Since they had already killed one, a quick calculation revealed that it was better to eliminate the other. Maciel died with a .45 shot to the chest. Minutes later, the journalists who had gone to Humaitá were redirected to the scene on Figueiredo Magalhães Street, and the BOPE officers told the story of how they had to resist Dente Grande's murderous rage.

Through the radio, Maria Amélia heard the news while in the arms of her pet American.

"What happened? Did they kill another drug dealer?"

"Yes, they did," she replied, and as if speaking to herself, "fate decided, and if it did, it's for the best."

"What?"

"Nothing. Let's turn in. I want you!"

Seventh Part

-

THE CANDY OF POWER

50

Maria Amélia slept like someone who had just rid themselves of an annoyance. Steven Adams, not so much. He suspected her involvement. From the mansion's bedroom window, he had witnessed all the security guards' commotion and Dente Grande's arrival, just before he was executed in Copacabana. And he didn't understand why Maria Amélia had told him not to follow her to the living room.

"Stay here, read. I'll be back soon. It's a matter that doesn't concern you."

She was hiding things from him. Which was fine. After all, they merely had a relationship that was professional, above all. Two liberated individuals who knew how to enjoy the perks of combining business with pleasure. She didn't have to explain past, present, or future lovers to him. It wasn't jealousy that tormented him, therefore, even though he would prefer not to share her with anyone else, if possible. What he felt—and which now manifested with great intensity—was fear of the creature sleeping like an angel by his side. Fear of her power of manipulation, with him as one of the manipulated. Even worse, as he shuddered at the thought, she seemed to have the ability to simply get rid of people when they no longer suited her. Would his turn come?

Steven Adams' fears grew the following morning during breakfast. Maria Amélia was cheerful and smiling, reading the news about Dente Grande's death as if it had happened in China. Still, he mustered up the courage and commented:

"Horrible thing that happened yesterday."

"Here in Rio? That happens every day. You're talking about the news of the dead drug dealer in Copacabana, right?"

"Yes, terrible! Do you think he really resisted? Some say he was lured into a trap."

"Possibly, Steven. But since when do you care about such things?"

315

The American didn't answer, he just shrugged as if he didn't really care about the matter. He did care, though. And that little bug that had kept him awake all night was whispering in his ear that Maria Amélia was deeply involved in the case. Steven called Professor da Mata from Santos Dumont Airport, where he had left Maria Amélia for her flight to Brasília.

The old man wasn't surprised by the phone call, as if he had been expecting it, and he willingly offered to meet.

"Come right now. Let's talk over a hot cup of coffee."

Hot and bitter. The customary greetings were brief, given Steven's eagerness to address the matter.

"The professor must be wondering: is this about Maria Amélia again?"

Da Mata's smile suggested he had no doubts it was.

"The professor is surely aware of the commotion in the newspapers and on TV surrounding the death of the drug dealer nicknamed Dente Grande. Well, I am certain Maria Amélia is involved. He was at the mansion hours before being killed. I know, I saw through the window, I was there. I confess I am afraid."

Professor da Mata closed his eyes for a moment, as if weighing the American's words. Then he clapped his hands on his knees and said:

"My dear Steven, you're not telling me anything new, but I'm disappointed to see that even my noble colleague hasn't grasped that our Maria Amélia is above such petty matters."

"Petty matters? A murder!"

"Yes, petty matters! I know very well of Maria Amélia's contacts with the criminal, her relationship, if you will. She told me about it, just as she told me this morning over the phone about Dente Grande's visit to her house. There are no secrets between us. And you know what? Your time in Brazil has expired. You've already learned what you came to learn, and frankly, you don't have the *cacife* ... do you know what 'cacife' means? You don't have *what it takes* to be with the braided girl, to share her whole life. In fact, to my knowledge, no one is worthy of such a privilege. Perhaps you were too fascinated by her beauty, her gray eyes, everything surrounding her, and failed to grasp the main point. Maria Amélia is one

316

step ahead of us all, above norms and etiquettes. Yes, my dear Steven, that's how it is. Maria Amélia sails on different seas, beyond the crude understanding of many. And she is shielded, even though she doesn't want it consciously. It's true: any obstacle to her goals is eliminated. That's the power of someone who controlled their own reincarnation. Please don't take it personally, I don't mean to offend you. But the best you can do is pack your bags. You've already concluded that all your parapsychological apparatus is not enough to unravel the mysteries of the braided girl."

"I'm not sure if I can agree with the professor on all of this. So, this is a farewell then?"

"Yes, Steven. It's a farewell. And good luck. Honestly, I hope the knowledge you've gained will be useful in your studies."

"Goodbye, professor."

Steven arrived dazed at the Lagoa mansion, but it didn't take him long to decide he should return to the United States. Immediately. Without prior notice, without waiting for Maria Amélia's return from Brasília. He packed his bags, gathered his equipment, and called a travel agency, inquiring if any seats were available on a flight to the United States. There was one to New York. Expensive, but available. And off he went, leaving only a note for Maria Amélia.

My dear,
I've gone away. Professor da Mata can explain the motive for my sudden decision. A big kiss goodbye,
Steven.

Maria Amélia wasn't surprised. In fact, she liked the decision taken by the American. She felt relieved, foreseeing that he would soon become a burden in her life. It was time to focus on the plan to make "*Nosso Partido*" the largest political organization in the country, and the American had no role to play in that. Like Dente Grande, Steven was just a distraction that needed to be set aside, for now.

317

51

Adamastor was struggling with the new, unspoken rules that had come to prevail in Lagoa's little parliament. The work there was driven by a much higher goal than the continuation of his political career. He was no longer the figurehead, and Maria Amélia was no longer the hidden force propelling him. The niece had emerged from the shadows, from her role of advisor, openly taking center stage in debates and decisions. The title held no official status, of course, but everyone referred to her as "*presidenta do parlamentinho*," the president of the little parliament. That this would soon become official was widely foreseen. *Nosso Partido*, which in a few months was going to test its mettle in the congressional elections for the first time, now had a *presidenta* at the helm, putting the uncle on par with the rest of the rank and file. Adamastor dreamt of being chosen to run for senator from Rio de Janeiro, and one can imagine his disappointment when his name wasn't even included in the list of possible party candidates. Three names of former PSB politicians were put forth, but all withdrew from the race when Maria Amélia straightforwardly announced in one of the little parliament's sessions:

"Ladies and gentlemen, I've decided to run for the position of senator. The competition is going to be fierce, and we cannot afford the risk of losing."

Adamastor and the other three contenders chose to lower their heads, avoiding the confrontation with those two gray eyes that stared them down with the arrogance of one who makes the decisions. There was only one reaction. A timid one.

"But our colleague could get burned."

"Yes, I could! In a fight, there's always a risk of getting burned. Does our colleague have a better name to stand against the heavy fire the other parties are preparing?"

He didn't. And even if he did, it would be very hard to challenge someone who appeared just a breath away from slamming her hands on the chair to emphasize her determination and audacity. From the little parliament, the proposal was taken to *Nosso Partido*'s first national convention, held fifteen days later in Brasília. The approval was unanimous.

Adamastor, however, couldn't hide the look of frustration and disappointment on his face. Such a state of mind did not go unnoticed by Maria Amélia, and knowing what it was about, she broached the subject on the day they were returning together from Brasília to Rio de Janeiro.

"Don't put on a sour face, my dear uncle. A second term as congressman will do you good. You'll run to fill my position in the following elections."

"Aren't you going to seek reelection?"

"No. I've other plans. But let's leave it at that for now."

Even before her name was approved, with six months left until the elections, Maria Amélia kicked off her electoral campaign in such a covert manner that no electoral judge could condemn her for premature advertising. From her own pocket, she had massive posters put up all over Rio de Janeiro, showing only a banner with the picture of two gray eyes. Her eyes. And a single word: "Trustworthy!" With the help of friends and activists from *Nosso Partido*, it didn't take long for the poster's image to become a social media sensation, where comments like these could be read: *Trustworthy and beautiful. I wish I had those inspiring eyes. I would vote for those eyes. Hypnotize me, please. I dream of meeting the owner. Show yourself, we're waiting...*

Amidst the numerous comments repeated abundantly on Facebook, Instagram, Twitter, and who knows what platforms more, one of them went in the opposite direction:

"Those are the eyes of a witch!"

An opponent who recognized the owner of those eyes? Unlikely. The most probable suspects were a bitter lady mourning the deaths of both her daughters and a man rotting away in prison, consumed by thoughts of revenge against that distinctive gaze. Let's discard the first option—neutralized, lost, without even the support of her psychiatrist, who had laid down her weapons, knowing she was no match for the owner of such seductive eyes. Indeed, the statement's author was Tarquínio, who had vowed to do whatever he could to disrupt the little witch's plans, no matter what they were. It hadn't taken him long to find out. The news of her candidacy had spread across all media, days after the posters appeared. While watching television in the prison mess hall, Tarquínio saw the poster's impact and decided to remove ambiguity, adding another sentence with an appropriate exclamation mark:

"Those are the eyes of a witch! Don't vote for her!"

Some things haven't been properly explained, however. How could Tarquínio, confined in a prison with strict discipline, have access to the Internet? Or even use a cellphone and communicate with someone capable of posting on social media? Let's clarify that. For some time now, Tarquínio had changed his attitude in prison, aware that sooner or later he would need the help of fellow inmates as well as the facility's staff and guards. And that's how, little by little, he transitioned from being a grim and isolated individual to a popular figure, helping other prisoners communicate in writing with their relatives, especially with their girlfriends. His reputation as wordsmith quickly reached the guards and prison staff. One of them was addicted to dating websites and enlisted Tarquínio's services to impress potential dates. A *quid pro quo* was established. The guard set up social media accounts for Tarquínio under the handle "*Juca Justiceiro*" (Juca the Avenger). In each subsequent post, more details were added, always beneath the image of two eyes:
"I know what I'm talking about. I know the witch who owns these eyes, and I know what she's capable of."

And in the next days ...

"The initials of the witch's name are M and A. The embodiment of falsehood. Don't vote for her. When she shows her face asking for votes, I'll reveal who she truly is."

Three months later, with the start of the electoral campaign, a new poster—this time featuring a full-body image of Maria Amélia—replaced the old one. Beneath the image was the caption:

"Maria Amélia for Senate. The woman with the trustworthy eyes. *Nosso Partido.*"

No critical remarks surfaced on social media. Someone or something had silenced Juca Justiceiro, and you probably already guessed who. Indeed. Maria Amélia had called the prison to schedule a meeting with Tarquínio on the next visiting day. She received a call back, saying the prisoner didn't want to meet with her.

"Then pass along a message for me, please. Tell him I know very well who Juca Justiceiro is. And whoever is assisting him should get ready."

Well-acquainted with the witch's tricks, Tarquínio wasn't the one who became uneasy. It was Genivaldo, the guard, who spent several sleepless nights. When he finally had the chance to talk privately with Tarquínio, he was trembling.

"What should we do?"

"Nothing. Juca Justiceiro is dead. May he rest in peace!"

"But the lady said she's going to find out everything. The warden is summoning all the staff—one by one—to investigate the case. I'll be called in later this week. And she'll be there. They told me you get hypnotized by her eyes. I'm scared!"

"Then call Pedro!"

"This ain't no joke, Mr. Tarquínio. It ain't about just losing my job. The warden said the culprit will be thrown in with the inmates for at least a week, and you know very well what those brutes tend to do."

"You knew the risks when you got involved. Buck up, man! We'll think of a way out. And my first piece of advice is this: don't lower your head when you're called. Lowering your head signals guilt, but in this case, you need to avoid the witch's gaze. Try to fix your eyes on the warden's face. And act normal. Don't give anything away, man. Don't look like you've seen a ghost. Put on an innocent face. I'll think of something. Let's find a way to meet tomorrow."

A lost cause, Tarquínio reflected as he watched the guard skitter, almost like a rabbit being chased by a pack of dogs. He won't resist, his thoughts continued, he'll crumble at the first eye-to-eye with the witch. Screw it! His problem. Mine is to find someone in here who can help me. The wench is going to do everything in her power to prevent that from happening. On second thought, I'll have to talk to her again. Whatever, I can't be screwed over more than I already am.

"Dr. Maria Amélia, the prison warden is on the line."

"Thank you. Yes? Oh, so he wants to meet now? Make him wait. First, let's find out who helped him ... Thank you, warden. We'll see each other this afternoon to continue with the interviews."

The attitude was more than suspicious. He slouched in the chair as if it couldn't contain him. With his gaze lowered, the stiffness of his hands was evident, his mouth dry and bitter, as if his liver shared in the agony of knowing he was lost, releasing all the accumulated bile.

"You don't need to answer anything, Mr. Genivaldo. Your name is Genivaldo, isn't it? I just want you to lift your head and look me in the eyes."

It took all the effort his anguish allowed him to follow the order, delivered slowly, firmly, with each word articulated. And as his eyes met Maria Amélia's, the guard almost fainted. He would have turned whiter than a candle had he not been of mixed race. In less than ten seconds, as if shot by her gaze, he lowered his head and began to sob.

"There's no need to say anything, Mr. Genivaldo. We already know"—and addressing the warden—"There's no need to continue the interviews. We already have all the information we need."

"In my office, thirty minutes. This could get you fired on the spot and slapped in a cell. No severance pay. You can start packing your bags. And we ain't done, pal. I want a written confession. And if you got buddies in on this, I want names."

52

Maria Amélia's triumph could not have been more overwhelming. She got 79% of the vote, a unique case in the history of Rio de Janeiro and Brazil. Her entry into the Senate was nothing short of triumphant. Dressed in a black pantsuit, sleeves reaching her elbows, and red Pradas that would make Meryl Streep envious. And the braids tied at the ends, forming the V of victory. The audience, packed with admirers, rose as if she were a queen entering the ballroom of some Versailles. The senators also stood up, opening a path until she made her way to the podium, where she had been chosen to read the oath of office. The other newcomers entered in silence, some even with heads bowed, as if overshadowed by their colleague, who gazed down on all from the podium before reciting the oath without even looking at the text.

"I promise to uphold the Federal Constitution and the laws of the country, to faithfully and loyally fulfill the mandate that the people have bestowed upon me, and to uphold the unity, integrity, and independence of Brazil."

It's quite possible that such an ordinary and repetitive text has seldom met such thunderous applause. The senators and the audience, all on their feet, were still excited when the other newcomers approached the chairman, as tradition dictates, and simply said:

"So I promise."

Maria Amélia's face was glowing. One could almost see a light radiating from her gray eyes, as if the sweet candy of power she was savoring gave her added energy.

Far away from there, in a foul-smelling cell, the situation was quite different for Prisoner 3,029. We already know that he had been forced back into the isolation of his early days in captivity. But there was a significant difference. Initially, Tarquínio had decided freely and spontaneously that he would not share the long years of his sentence with anyone. This was no longer the case. Time had taught him that when you spend most of your time between four walls surrounded by barred fences, the best thing to do is to make the most of the moments when social interaction is possible. From his initial isolation, he had risen to the position of perhaps the most popular prisoner among the personnel of the detention facility. Some even addressed him as Dr. Tarquinio or Master Tarquínio. All of this came to an end overnight, buried along with Juca Justiceiro, who didn't survive the clash with someone so much stronger on social media. Now, the prison guards and even most of his fellow inmates saw him as a pest to be avoided. By order of the warden—who in turn followed a recommendation, guess from whom?—no staff member would converse with Tarquínio except for what was strictly necessary for maintaining order within the establishment. And always accompanied by a colleague. Conversations were limited to at most two minutes; any longer and the employees were subject to punishment. Moreover, Tarquínio was forbidden from basking in the sun in the courtyard alongside other inmates. On sunny days, he would get some yard time alone, isolated from everyone. With nothing else to do, he returned to his writings, in a desperate attempt to find a way to destroy the witch who'd caused so much misfortune.

That's how he heard over the loudspeakers that he had a visitor. Could it be the wench with the gray eyes? No, it wasn't. It was an elderly gentleman who didn't know him personally but had important matters to discuss with him.

Feet chained and hands cuffed, Tarquínio was dragged before Dr. Fábio da Mata, who awaited him in his wheelchair. Sitting uncomfortably and facing the visitor, Tarquínio made no attempt to hide his wary gaze. He remained silent, refraining from taking the initiative, letting the other speak first. Fábio da Mata played the expected part. He looked the prisoner up and down for some time. Finally, he spoke:

"Mr. Tarquínio Esperidião, I am Professor Fábio da Mata. I don't know if you've heard of me, but I can assure you that I'm well acquainted with your story. I followed the entire process of your internment at the Jacarepaguá Rest Home, where you were treated by Dr. Maria da Anunciação. I know everything. And today, I am sort of a confidant to your daughter, Maria Amélia."

"Hold on a moment, mister. I didn't quite catch your name, nor do I care to. My daughter? No. I have no daughter. Are you talking about the witch?"

"I understand your bitterness, Mr. Tarquínio ..."

"You understand nothing, and I don't care if you do. If you've come to deliver a message from that wench, you're wasting time. Yours and mine."

"I think you should listen to me, it's for your own good. It's a peace offer."

"Peace? Oh, the witch is scared. She wants peace!"

"Mr. Tarquínio, I can grasp your resentment. But I tell you sincerely, it's an uneven battle. Maria Amélia stands far above us all. If she so wished, she could crush you like a cockroach whenever she pleases. And you're well aware of this."

"That cursed wench!"

"That blessed woman, I would say. Or, if you prefer, that woman with powers far beyond ours. You're swimming against a powerful tide."

"And if I drown that's my problem. You can tell the witch that the war will only end when one of us is vanquished, erased from the realm of the living."

"If I were you, I would consider her offer."

"But you're not! Guard!"

"Please, Mr. Tarquínio. Grant me at least five more minutes. You won't regret it."

"Five minutes. Alright. I have no commitments, after all," and he laughed between clenched teeth, like a hungry hyena observing the skeletal figure of the old man in his wheelchair.

Tarquínio's hysterical laughter, as if he wanted to exorcise the dark humor from his imagination, made Professor da Mata lower his eyes, not wanting to partake in the immense hatred exuded by the prisoner's sarcasm. Several seconds of silence ensued before the old man could respond.

"She's offering you freedom: commutation of your sentence and the possibility of parole. That's what Maria Amélia is proposing."

"And in exchange for what? My silence? My submission to her whims? The crimes I committed, as you very well know, were dictated by her, that damned wench, the witch from the depths of hell. As long as I'm alive, even behind these accursed bars, I can think of nothing but destroying her. The other one had her weakness; she will have hers too, and I will find it."

"Mr. Tarquínio. Maria Amélia transcends our narrow-minded view of good and evil. Even I can't tell you why she's offering you ... let's say, a light at the end of the tunnel. Perhaps she has a purpose. I can only tell you this, accept it. You know very well it's your only way out."

"Guard! Guard! Take me away from here. The interview with this decrepit cripple is over. Get out of my life. I won't speak to a witch's mouthpiece."

Kicking and screaming, Tarquínio was dragged back to his cell, while a guard pushed Professor da Mata's wheelchair into the adjoining room, where Maria Amélia awaited. She had been eavesdropping, thanks to a microphone attached to the professor's coat lapel. Seeing the old man's tense and apprehensive expression, Maria Amélia responded with a smile of someone quite satisfied with how the interview had unfolded. Tarquínio's reaction showed he was lost, desperate, unable to envision a new plan to satisfy his obsession with destroying her. And it was likely he wouldn't live much longer, consumed by old age that was evident in the wrinkles and blemishes on his skin and his powerlessness against a supremely powerful enemy. But he was still alive. Hatred is a hearty sustenance.

53

Maria Amélia was one of the eighteen female senators, interspersed among sixty-seven male colleagues. Yet, no one spoke of Senator Maria Amélia. They referred to her—on the senate floor, in hallway conversations, and even among people on the streets—as *The Senator*. Given the emphasis with which they spoke, surely the capital letters are warranted, or perhaps, even all caps: *THE SENATOR.*

The most hardened reactionaries—from the rural bench to members of the religious bloc—expressed an uncommon respect for her, or at the very least, kept their distance. Some almost begged for forgiveness when they were chosen to challenge one of her propositions or statements. Always in high heels of vivid colors, just like her dresses, preferably alternating between red and black, Maria Amélia asserted herself, standing out in any moment and circumstance, swinging her braids tied at the tips. Yet there were exceptions within the Senate. One of them was the evangelical bishop Tamarinho Junqueira. Instead of referring to her as "The Senator," he called her "The Witch." In the beginning, Maria Amélia didn't mind; she even found it amusing, watching the grotesque figure of the senator gesticulating at the podium and pointing a finger at her.

"Don't be fooled by the witch's slender figure. Friendly, elegant. Satan, too, disguises himself to corrupt souls and establish his empire. This house will be cursed as long as she's here, sullying and tarnishing it."

"A point of order, senator: this is the Federal Senate, not an evangelical church for your cheap sermons."

"Distinguished colleague, from what I see, you're another one deceived. In fact, everyone here seems to be. It's her enchantment; I will prove with facts that she uses witchcraft to get where she wants to be. But by the time this chamber realizes, it might already be too late. I trust in the Almighty God to prevent that from occurring."

In the bishop's repeated attacks, Maria Amélia realized that someone was feeding him with information about her life. Someone who knew her intimately, someone who despised her from the roots of her hair to the soles of her feet. And there could only be one such person. It became apparent that the bishop was in touch with Tarquínio. Perhaps Maria Amélia had been mistaken, possibly for the first time, in assuming that prisoner 3,029 was entirely isolated, unable to communicate with the outside world.

Even within such stifling seclusion, Tarquínio managed to gather snippets of information here and there, snatched from conversations in the distance, from TV during meals, about the bishop's onslaughts against Maria Amélia. He decided he would have to meet him, equip him with information. He wrote a personal letter, taking care not to mention the daughter's name in order to evade the censorship.

To His Excellency Bishop Tamarinho Junqueira:

I wish to join the flock of the Kingdom of God and would be immensely grateful if Your Excellency would grant me the honor of a visit. I recognize it is much to ask; Your Excellency's time is precious, especially to spare a few minutes for a repentant prisoner. However, perhaps I might be able to offer valuable information to assist Your Excellency in your struggles within the Senate. I humbly beseech you for a glimmer of hope. Your Excellency will not regret it.

With all humility,
Tarquínio Esperidião
Gabriel Ferreira Castilho Penitentiary—Prisoner 3,029."

In normal circumstances, Tarquínio's letter would've been lost among thousands of similar requests sent to the bishop-senator every day. The astuteness of one of his aides tasked with reading the correspondence and filtering those deserving of attention proved invaluable. The aide was familiar with Tarquínio. He had read his book *The Window*. He went to see the bishop, who was in Rio de Janeiro, in his mansion by the Lagoa, less than 500 yards from his arch-enemy's residence. Seeing the aide approach, the bishop furrowed his brow; he was savoring a Jack Daniels and didn't wish to be disturbed.

Embarrassed, the aide lowered his head and murmured:

"It's very important. It's a very important letter."

"Let me see," and he snatched the letter from the trembling secretary's hands.

"What? You brought me a letter from a prisoner, some Tarquínio ... whatever-his-name-is, claiming it's 'very important'?! Explain yourself, or you're fired on the spot!"

Nearly stammering and with his head down, the aide replied:

"Tarquínio Esperidião is the real father of Senator Maria Amélia, the witch. And he hates her; I read the book he wrote."

"What are you telling me? That she's the illegitimate daughter of Dr. Joaquim Paranhos Nogueira?"

"The prisoner Tarquínio claims she isn't. A deal was made because Dr. Nogueira's wife wanted to adopt the girl."

"Complicated story. Check into it. And schedule this meeting immediately. Make it a priority. Forget the rest of the appointments. It goes ahead of everything."

The bishop downed the bourbon in one go and savored it, almost convinced that God was assisting him.

Short, stout, with beady eyes—that's how the bishop looked, rubbing his hands against the cold of that misty morning in the prison's visiting room. When Tarquínio approached, escorted by two burly guards, the bishop stood up and opened his arms. He wanted to embrace the prisoner and anoint him right there as a new disciple of the Kingdom of God, in front of a few tabloid photographers and the staff members, all excited by the presence of the senator. Tarquínio spoiled the bishop's plans.

"No hugs. I'm not here to join any church. Let's get to what matters. You hate the witch, and I hate her even more. You want to destroy her, and I want to send her to the depths of hell. Let's focus on that."

"Respect the senator. Address him properly," one of the guards escorting the bishop interjected, forcing Tarquínio to sit down with such force that the chair nearly broke.

The prisoner, having one of those days where he couldn't care less about the consequences, retorted:

"And if I don't address him as 'Your Excellency,' are you going to send me to jail, buddy? I'm already here."

The bishop made a calming gesture toward the guards, then motioned for them to step away. He didn't want any witnesses to the conversation.

"Alright, Mr. Tarquínio, it seems we're on the same page. I'm not here to convert you. Is it true you are her father? The witch's father?"

"I'm not the damned father of that cursed thing. She took possession of my body herself to fornicate with the woman who bore her. I was merely used for my seed, and as for that other poor soul, let's just say she was nothing more than a rented womb for the devil."

"What are you telling me?"

"The truth plain and simple, Bishop."

"But it's on record that Dr. Paranhos acknowledged paternity."

"Bullshit! That silly wife of this was bewitched by the little wench on the day I shot a rifle round into the chest of her birth mother—or should I say, the coerced, unwilling mother."

"And you killed her why?"

"An accident, Bishop. I actually meant to blow the witch's head off while she sat in the woman's lap. If you don't believe me, check the newspapers from back then. It's all there, and it's one of the reasons why I'm locked up forever."

"And what can you offer me?"

"Nearly twenty years of isolation thinking only of one thing: how to destroy her. I have information from the very day that damnation was born."

"Seems one meeting won't be enough, then."

"No, Bishop. Or would you prefer I call you senator? Whatever suits you. I'll give you the full dossier. Everything on that damned creature."

The agreement between the bishop and prisoner 3,029 didn't seem to hinder Maria Amélia's plans. Despite the impassioned speeches crying out against her from the heavens and the earth, the senator from the Kingdom of God couldn't even begin to overshadow Maria Amélia's prestige. The meetings at the small parliament in Lagoa, almost every Friday and sometimes extending into the weekends, showed that the ambitions of the braided lady were far from being exhausted.

"And this pastor, what should we do about him? I still have many friends who could make things difficult for him, see if he backs off."

"Uncle, seriously? After over six years speaking on the house floor, you still haven't grasped that the battle is now fought with words. The machine guns of people like Dente Grande have been silent for quite some time now. Restrain yourself and don't repeat what you've just told me to anyone else."

"But he seems to know a lot. Isn't that dangerous?"

"Life is dangerous, Uncle. The end awaits us after every heartbeat. Of course, he knows a lot. It's no accident he visits Bangu 3 Penitentiary more than once a week."

"Tarquínio Esperidião?"

"Who else? My dear old daddy, naturally. Let's pay him another visit. Actually, you do it. Who knows, maybe he'll accept that offer he can't refuse from this dear brother-in-law."

"Me, visit that bastard, my sister's murderer?"

"Yes, sir, this very week. Do you want me to set it up? I can call the prison warden right now."

What is the best way to convey the sense of "*desprezo*" (contempt)? According to the Houaiss dictionary, there are numerous synonyms to choose from: disdain, depreciation, indifference, scorn, and so on. It even advises looking into synonyms of "*repulsa*" (repulsion). Amidst these options, "*menoscabo*" (disregard) stands out as the most fitting to portray Tarquínio Esperidião's expression, uncomfortably seated during the visit from Congressman Adamastor Leite Feitosa.

"So, the little witch's dear uncle has come to deliver another message? Waste of time, Congressman. Or should I address you as house manager of the Chapéu Mangueira crack house?"

With a demanding gaze, urging the guards to step back, Adamastor whispered:

"It's not exactly a proposal, bastard. It's a challenge."

"A challenge? This is getting interesting. Spit it out."

"Senator Maria Amélia challenges you to a face-to-face with a revolver on the table. All you have to do is pick up the gun and fire. Isn't that your dream? To kill her, to destroy her?"

"Interesting. And how do you propose we get a revolver on this table inside a prison? Did she make arrangements with the warden?"

"It won't be here. It'll be outside. If you manage to fulfill your grim wish, she'll have a fake passport and money in her purse for you to leave the country. If not, you'll submit, never again interfering with her plans or advising her adversaries."

"Where should I shoot her? In the face? In the heart?"

"Bastard!"

"And how does the witch plan to get me out of here?"

"Don't worry about that. Is it yes, or no?"

"I'm in."

The smirk on Tarquínio's face as he was led back to his cell suggested he greatly relished the challenge. He even risked a small beating by turning around to shout:

"Hey, Chapéu Mangueira! Tell the witch I have some terms of my own. I won't make her wretched life easy."

It wasn't the possibility of being set free that most appealed to Tarquínio. Most likely, he would be exiled to some unfamiliar country, aged and without the vigor to start anything anew, perhaps in a situation as oppressive as life in prison. But what brought him immense satisfaction was the knowledge that Maria Amélia was worried, that his revelations—first through the Internet and now through the pastor-senator—were thwarting her schemes, whatever they might be. Now, it was time to get down to business. That is, to set his mind to work, delve into the prison library and all the other resources at his disposal to overcome the little witch's glare and put two bullets in her, one in each eye. That was how he wanted to do it. Blow out both eyes. Maybe that might even strip her of the power to reincarnate, so in the future, she wouldn't disturb the peace of regular folks like himself, Tarquínio Esperidião. Shatter her brain, shut all doors, ensuring she would never again lord over other mortal beings. The cursed wench must have her weak spot, and he would discover it. He had plenty of time and even more determination, as he couldn't think of anything else. Much like Aunt Lena in the previous incarnation, who dreamt of unveiling the power of the braided witch, the first Maria Amélia. Yet, even with a lot of time at his disposal, he had to be swift. Maria Amélia's message indicated she was in a hurry and likely had a fully orchestrated plan to free him. In her position, with the extra powers the devil had granted her, almost nothing was impossible.

Upon hearing from Adamastor that Tarquínio had accepted the proposal, Maria Amélia reacted almost automatically. Without showing any emotion. She said:

"Excellent, it's high time to solve this problem once and for all."

Adamastor, with a timid and ill-timed comment:

"But isn't it dangerous?"

The response was a withering glance from a person who knew every move in the game.

The new meeting between Adamastor and Tarquínio took place the following week. The prisoner handed the congressman a written list of demands:

My conditions:
1) A minimum of 15 days of grace in the new setting before the encounter.
2) Full permission to prepare the setting, with any necessary financial assistance.
3) A commitment that no third person will be involved.

Tarquínio overlooked the fact that a third person, the messenger, was already involved. This was also one of Maria Amélia's concerns.

After reading the demands, she instructed her uncle:

"Go back and tell him I accept. He can do whatever he pleases, even use holy water or any kind of charm, it doesn't matter. And Adamastor,

I'll say it again: mum's the word, no one else should know about this except the three of us. Don't you dare tell anyone! Anyone! No excuses. Be extra careful around Madalena and in your chats with the other floozies you're fooling around with. And with your drinking buddies. To no one—are you hearing me clearly?—to no one will you utter a word about this."

"What's this, Niece? I'll be as silent as the grave. But what if Tarquínio spills it?"

"Drop the 'niece.' This is gravely serious. Word cannot get out. Tarquínio has every interest in keeping his mouth shut. If he talks, the whole thing collapses, and it will be just the word of some prisoner everyone thinks is crazy against a senator of the Republic."

Once again, she fixed him with a piercing stare, silently conveying that Adamastor would pay dearly for any slip-up. Not the look of a beloved niece.

What Tarquínio didn't know was that Maria Amélia's plot had been in motion for a long time, even before she was elected senator. Two years earlier, she had drafted a bill that was introduced by Adamastor in the Chamber of Deputies, proposing a house arrest regime for convicts who reached the age of eighty. The bill didn't garner much attention from the media and continued its course until Maria Amélia, now a senator, rallied the *Nosso Partido* caucus to get it approved.

"With this, we'll show our human side. Brazilians have a soft heart," she said in one of the sessions of Lagoa's little parliament.

It was no coincidence that the bill was scheduled for discussion within a month by the time Adamastor presented the proposal to Tarquínio. Through conversations and backroom deals, it was clear that the bill would be approved and signed into law. In two months, Tarquínio would turn eighty, the machinery of events running smoothly without hiccups. Well, the only hiccups were in Adamastor's troubled dreams, in which he now harbored only one feeling for his niece: fear.

54

The day was hot and rainy. The morning sun and first raindrops caused warm and stifling steam to rise as Tarquínio walked out through the prison gate, ready to take the first breath of freedom after twenty-five years of captivity. All his belongings fit into a small suitcase. He held the notebook, in which he'd penned his investigations about Maria Amélia, under his arm as though it contained the secret to saving his life. His face betrayed no emotion, and he didn't acknowledge the guard who had escorted him out and wished him well on his journey. Setting his suitcase down, a tag revealed his destination: a home for the elderly in Bonsucesso, in the north zone of Rio de Janeiro. There a small room awaited him, likely as cramped as the prison cell, but equipped with a television and a computer. He had heard tales of the Internet, and yearned to explore cyberspace, much like how children today navigated it even before they learned to read. The TV and computer were concessions he had secured from the senator. Tarquínio was eager to dive into this new world, which he had only heard of in passing conversations in prison corridors or the mess hall, where inmates were allowed to watch shows chosen by the prison administration.

Maria Amélia's black car picked him up, driven by a chauffeur whose face clearly displayed his displeasure at serving an inmate branded as a cruel and heartless murderer.

"Sir, it's best if you sit in the back. It's more comfortable. That's the usual way."

"Well, with me, it's different. I'll sit up front. Have you been working for the witch for long?"

"I don't know what you're talking about. I'm one of Senator Maria Amélia's drivers."

"The witch—yes, that's who I'm talking about. Didn't you know? Now, lift that head and look at me!"

"Excuse me?"

"Excuse my ass! Just take me to that fucking nursing home already. Damned witch!"

Both remained silent for the entirety of the journey, and Tarquínio barely spared a glance at the landscape that passed by along the Via Amarela. Instead, he chose to review the notes he had compiled about hypnotism techniques. Some time ago, Tarquínio had adopted a more scientific approach to combat his primary foe. He integrated findings from thorough laboratory experiments to decipher—or at the very least, attempt to decipher—the devilish power radiating from Fiinha's eyes. Something that broke through the mist of mysticism, transcended the stories and tales that have been with humanity ever since primates marveled at the sunrise, bewildered by its origin. He was resolute in his decision to face his nemesis with every resource available to him, most crucially, something to counteract her potent gaze.

His reception at the Sacred Heart of Jesus nursing home wasn't exactly festive. The matron embodied the perfect stereotype: tall, plump, wearing a gray dress with a bunch of keys hanging from her waist—just as one might expect of a nursing home administrator. It was a deliberate display that there would be no privacy, that she could enter any room whenever she pleased. She sized up Tarquínio from head to toe and said:

"Mr. Tarquínio Esperidião, your room is ready. We have rules to follow in this establishment. The private television and computer are exceptions made at Senator Maria Amélia's insistence, who, by the way, is covering all the extras. But that's where it stops. Here, you're the same as everyone else."

The recently released inmate's gaze was dripping with sarcasm. He cleared his throat, rubbed his hands, and replied:

"No, ma'am! Or is it miss? What's your esteemed name again?"

"For you, I'm Sister of the Good Shepherd."

"Oh, so where are the sheep? Look, miss—miss, is it? I'm an exception, whether you like it or not. Your little speech doesn't play for someone who's been locked up in a Rio de Janeiro prison. And you, miss ..."

"Don't call me miss! It's Sister of the Good Shepherd!"

"Alright. Sister of whoever, you're not going to go against the senator's wishes, are you? Tone it down and have someone change the lock on my room. Do it today. I'll keep the key. Send the bill to the senator."

"You're disregarding all the rules! You're very insolent!"

"Yeah, I'm very insolent, and psst, don't spread the word, but they say I'm dangerous too. But it's not true; I only do crazy things when the witch orders."

"Merciful Jesus!"

"Alright, miss ... sorry, Sister, you're well protected. This Jesus is the good shepherd, right? Don't be scared, I'm in my 'harmless madman' phase. Nothing's going to happen. May I proceed? Where's my room? I need some rest. I want to sleep for at least 15 hours straight. Is the mattress soft?"

Dumbfounded, the Sister of the Good Shepherd pointed to one of the many doors in the vast corridor and handed a key to Tarquínio. From the nearby cafeteria, she noticed that their confrontation had been watched by several residents and, worse, by a few of her subordinates, surely pleased to see the shrew challenged. She went into her office, took a deep breath, picked up the phone, and dialed.

Cut! There's been an oversight with you, dear reader. An important event hasn't been revealed: something that took place between the approval of the home confinement bill for those over eighty years old and Tarquínio's exit from the penitentiary. It's likely that Senator Maria Amélia had nothing to do with it, merely a coincidence, even though she undoubtedly benefited from it.

Adamastor noticed that he was losing weight for no apparent reason, except for a light but nagging headache. His private doctor had made that annoying "hmm, hmm" and instructed the congressman to go to the hospital for a brain scan. I bet you've already guessed—spot on! They found a tumor the size of a large marble. The biopsy was conducted that very day, and the result was crystal clear: cancer.

"And is there a cure? What can be done?"

In response to this tentative question, the specialist confirmed Adamastor's worst fears, first clearing his throat as if that could soften the blow of what he was about to say:

"Very little, Congressman. The condition is highly advanced, and due to the tumor's location, the risk of surgery is substantial. The likelihood of survival is minimal."

There followed a pause, which felt eternal for the patient, as if he were trying to forget everything he'd just heard. He even pinched his lips compulsively, as if trying to wake up from a nightmare. But he didn't wake up; he continued to hear the doctor:

"We can attempt radiation therapy and chemotherapy to halt the tumor's growth. I advise you to step back from your parliamentary activities and rest. Morphine will be needed when the pain becomes too intense."

"When the pain becomes too intense. This fucking doctor," thundered through Adamastor's mind, "didn't even use the hypothetical 'if.' When. It's just a matter of time." Then he instinctively asked:

"When?"

The response hit him like a heavyweight knockout punch:

"A few weeks."

Three weeks in fact. In his quarters at the Lagoa mansion, Adamastor became a frail figure, bones almost breaking through the skin. He didn't want to go to a hospital and had all the necessary equipment and devices transferred to his room—three nurses and a doctor available twenty-four hours a day. Maria Amélia visited him every day, even when she had to charter a private jet after the Senate sessions. For Adamastor, these visits were the best moments of his agony. His niece's gaze was far more potent than morphine; it eased his pain, brought him a sense of tranquility, and perhaps even resignation. During one of these visits, a month and two days after the cancer diagnosis, Maria Amélia conveyed to her uncle with her eyes: "The time has come."

And time had come; the private game between father and daughter would have no other witnesses, just as Tarquínio had insisted.

"Senator, it's from the Sacred Heart of Jesus nursing home. The caller didn't want to identify himself but said you'd know who it was. It's a man's voice."

"Transfer the call to my private phone."

The phone was in a small, completely soundproof room. There were a metal detector and electronic devices at the door. This was where Maria Amélia had her private conversations and phone calls. Wiretaps, in this case, would only be in the form of hairpins, and she didn't use those in her braids.

"Look, I don't want to stay in this hellhole of a nursing home with crucifixes everywhere and some hag of a Sister trying to shepherd me. In a week, I'll be ready to meet you, for our *tête-à-tête*!"

"See you in a week then, Daddy!"

"Don't call me Daddy, you witch from the depths of hell!"

And he slammed down the phone. In the small room designed for conspiracies, a red light indicated another incoming call.

"Who is it?"

"It's from the nursing home again. The director wants to speak with the senator."

"Go ahead and transfer ..."

The voice of the Good Shepherd's Sister sounded agitated, or perhaps it would be better to say, trembling.

"He's insane, senator. I'm scared. My authority is at stake; he refuses to follow any of the rules."

"Calm down, Sister. He's all bark and no bite. He won't risk going back to prison. Mr. Tarquínio knows what he wants; he won't cross the line. Besides, I'm already arranging another place for him. Just one more week. One week. Simply accommodate his demands and let his provocations go in one ear and out the other."

"My authority ..."

"... will be restored and rewarded, Sister."

The word "restored" almost went unnoticed, but "rewarded," emphasized in each syllable, deeply touched the director's spirit.

After arranging his few belongings in the cabinets, Tarquínio sat at a small, varnished desk that predated the Internet. He began to flip through his notebook. After about fifteen minutes, having underlined a few sentences and jotted down some notes on a piece of paper, he left his room and went to the communal phone in the hallway.

"Yes, this is Mr. Tarquínio Esperidião from the Sacred Heart of Jesus nursing home. I want to buy a computer with all available features, the most advanced model you have, and I want it delivered today. Also send a technician who has the time to teach me how to operate the contraption. Understand?"

"Are you joking? We don't have time for that."

"I'm not joking, sir. I'm dead serious, and money is no object. I can pay double, triple, doesn't matter ... Son of a bitch, try hanging up on your mother's face, bastard!"

Tarquínio then phoned Maria Amélia's office.

"She's in Brasília, Mr. Tarquínio."

"Doesn't matter where she is. Tell her this: I just called a fucking computer store, and those sons of bitches thought I was joking."

"I don't understand."

"You heard me, miss, or whatever you are. Write this down, it has to be delivered today."

"Can't you be a bit nicer?"

"Save nice for your grandma! A secretary, especially a witch's secretary, has no right to complain! Call those bastards at Rio Branco Informática and place an order for a top-of-the-line computer, with all the available features. And I want a technician available the entire day. I'm pressed for time, I want to learn how this thing works today, if possible. One more thing. I repeat: I want that computer today! Are we clear? As for that outdated piece of junk in my room, it can go to any old idiot in this fucking nursing home, or shoved into whatever crevice the Good Shepherd's Sister prefers."

In a state of shock, the secretary called Maria Amélia, who was in Brasília. The secretary's complaints went in one ear and out the other. The senator simply replied:

"Fulfill all his requests."

It was four in the afternoon when the Rio Branco Informática van arrived with the delivery, a state-of-the-art computer featuring an efficient voice command system instead of a touch screen. The technician was a stocky man with glasses and a little mustache, looking more like a bookkeeper from the inkwell-and-quill era. Tarquínio looked him up and down before spitting out his venom:

"Can you actually teach me how to operate this crap? You look pretty timid."

The technician managed a strained smile and responded:

"I'm the best the company has."

"Ooh la la! I can only imagine the rest. How do you turn it on?"

Tarquínio didn't want to admit how fascinated he was by the wonders of the new computer, a far cry from the older models replete with mice and other cumbersome accessories that he had encountered before. He had little to learn; he simply had to speak to the machine to tap into the wealth of information available through search engines. After just a few hours, he felt confident enough to begin his research and dismissed the technician:

"You can go now, shorty."

On the second day, driven by his eagerness to consume all available knowledge about witchcraft, sorcery, hypnosis, and other paranormal powers, he realized that the information offered was superficial. He couldn't delve deep into any subject unless he either paid for it or gained access to university websites and research centers. The basic dishes were freely available on Google, but the prime cuts were tucked away in exclusive corners of cyberspace, often at a steep price. He subscribed to every service that appeared, naturally forwarding the bills to the senator's office.

After spending five days immersed in a world of information, reading and taking notes for nearly fourteen hours a day, Tarquínio felt ready to set the stage for the ultimate challenge. He aimed to arm himself with every possible weapon—from the latest hypnosis techniques and strategies to resist seductive powers to superstitions rooted in folklore. To his existing knowledge, accrued during his captivity, he added a smattering of spells from macumba, candomblé, caboclo traditions, and sesmaria folklore. He even had the eyes of a braided doll pierced by an old Haitian he met in prison, a voodoo specialist. He also kept a copy of Psalm 90 in his pocket. In what he saw as a life-or-death duel, he felt that every available weapon should be used without prejudice. During the few hours he slept, no more than four a night, he was plagued by nightmares. In his dreams, Maria Amélia would remove needles from the eyes of the Haitian doll and thrust them not into a doll but into Tarquínio's own eyes. He would wake up drenched in sweat that seemed tinged with red, the twin stabs feeling palpably real. Even after pinching his cheek to ground himself, the smell of blood lingered.

It was ten in the morning on a cloudy and hot day—one of those stifling, hazy days that turn Rio de Janeiro into a giant sauna. Maria Amélia arrived at the nursing home wearing a red silk dress that revealed the contours of her body. The Good Shepherd's Sister, dressed in her ceremonial apron, personally opened the door for her, with assistants lining the entrance hallway on either side. She curtsied, and her subordinates followed suit. Maria Amélia smiled, gestured for them to lift their heads, and asked, with a touch of cheekiness:

"How is our patient doing?"

Apprehensively, the Good Shepherd's Sister replied:

"This week, he has forbidden us from entering his room. We have complied, in accordance with the esteemed senator's instructions. He has received numerous deliveries—plants, and a variety of odd items. Would the senator like someone to accompany her?"

"No need. This a private meeting"—and looking first into the eyes of the superior and then at her subordinates—"Resume your normal routines. I'll call if I need anything."

At the sound of knocking on the door, Tarquínio asked irritably:

"Is it the witch? If so, come in. And lock the door."

Maria Amélia wanted to burst into laughter, but she restrained herself to just a smile, countering with her preferred weapon: indifference, and mockery in the face of the weapons wielded by her enemy. There were no real surprises for her. After all, almost every arrangement in the room had been carried out by people under the senator's command, as she was the one footing the bills. Just a few hours earlier, one of the technicians, under the pretense of inspecting the large mirror that covered an entire wall, had checked for hidden cameras and microphones.

"But you didn't have to go through so much trouble to receive your daughter. What a beautiful flower bed! And you took care to put rue right in the center, surrounded by sansevieria, dieffenbachia, and pepper plants. The seven miraculous herbs! And that magnificent mirror at the back!"

"Stop talking and tell me, where's the gun and my new documents?"

"Calm down, Daddy!"

"Don't call me Daddy, you wretch!"

"They're here, in my purse."

"Show me, I want to check. And put everything on the table."

"Calm down, calm down, a little patience."

Slowly, Maria Amélia took a Smith & Wesson .32 revolver from her purse. She emptied the six bullets into her hand and gave the gun to Tarquínio for inspection.

"I want to check the bullets too."

"You can examine them, but first give me back the gun."

After a few seconds:

"Is everything in order, Daddy?"

"Let's get on with it, then!"

Tarquínio positioned himself directly in front of the mirror, despite his skepticism about the belief that witches and sorcerers dislike mirrors because they reflect their true appearance rather than the disguise they wear. He also recalled the tale of one of Fiinha the First's sisters, who supposedly won a staring contest once because the witch was dazzled by her own gaze, reflected in a cracked lens of her mother's glasses.

Maria Amélia double-checked that the door was locked. Calmly, she loaded the bullets into the cylinder and placed the gun equidistantly on the table between the two competitors.

"I'll snap my fingers, and then we'll begin."

"No, I'm the one who will snap!"

Maria Amélia spread her arms in agreement.

Tarquínio snapped his fingers.

One didn't have to be a wizard to see that Maria Amélia wanted to lose the game. Her intense gaze was clearly more focused on the mirror than on Tarquínio's eyes. She showed a frustrating indifference. Tarquínio stood up, walked calmly to the table, picked up the revolver, and channeling Juca Trindade—the man who had fired a 16-gauge shotgun into the first Fiinha's chest at the beginning of the last century—aimed the gun at the senator's heart and pulled the trigger.

Click.

Surprise.

Click, click, click ...

Apprehension.

Click.

Nothing.

He turned the gun toward his own mouth and fired the remaining round.

Click.

He slumped back into the chair, his mouth twisted in spasms typical of someone suffering a stroke. Calmly, Maria Amélia took the gun from Tarquínio's hand and returned it to her purse. Only then did she open the door and call for help.

"Hurry, Sister! Mr. Tarquínio is unwell! Get a doctor and contact the São Vicente Clinic in Gávea immediately. Tell them to send an ambulance right away, and make sure to mention it's a request from Senator Maria Amélia. Hurry up!"

Treated promptly by a top-notch medical team, Tarquínio survived. However, he lost his voice, his left side was completely paralyzed, and a constant dribble of drool flowed from the corner of his mouth, diligently wiped away by one of the nurses hired for round-the-clock care.

The Sister of the Good Shepherd said:

"Senator Maria Amélia is a very generous woman. We have instructions to do everything and anything to ensure that Mr. Tarquínio receives the best care possible."

While we can't be sure if Tarquínio could hear such praises for his arch-nemesis, his gaze remained vacant and distant, incapable of meeting even the humblest person's eyes. Nor can we say with certainty whether Fiinha had malicious intent when she specifically advised the Sister of the Good Shepherd to keep Tarquínio's room exactly as he had decorated it, emphasizing the importance of the vase with seven herbs and the massive mirror dominating the wall near the bed's headboard. And who will ever know what gnawed at Tarquínio's insides as he sat in his wheelchair, his body slumped to the left, his eyes as lifeless as those of a dead fish, staring endlessly into a mirror that reflected his pathetic form? The nurses seemed to prefer leaving him that way, facing his grotesque reflection, even during mealtime when they spoon-fed him soup three times a day. One can only speculate that he wished for death to end his suffering sooner rather than later. Then again, maybe not. Perhaps his true desire was to muster enough strength for a counterattack. And occasionally, even if the nurses failed to notice, his eyes seemed to flash with an increased brightness, as if he had discovered the braided witch's Achilles' heel

Eighth Part
-
RENEWAL

55

Maria Amélia had always trusted the roll of destiny's dice during decisive moments, but this time, the outcome surpassed her expectations. I don't know if any readers believe she genuinely managed to make a Smith & Wesson revolver misfire six times or if she would willingly expose herself to such danger. The revolver was real, but the bullets were not. They were perfect imitations, commissioned by Adamastor shortly before his aggressive cancer diagnosis, and meticulously crafted by an artisan in Campina Grande, Paraiba—a city infamous for its ability to counterfeit Swiss watches and anything else human ingenuity might devise. Inducing a stroke in Tarquínio wasn't part of the plan either, just as she hadn't intended for the police to gun down Dente Grande. However, fate, as was often the case, consistently exceeded her expectations. Her intent, or more accurately, her plan, had been to convince him that the bullets were indeed real, leading him to the conclusion he should have arrived at long ago: that there was no competing with her, and he should give up and live the rest of his life wherever he pleased. For that, Maria Amélia was willing to pay all expenses. Perhaps it was a miscalculation, but it was a calculated risk, nonetheless. The hatred Tarquínio harbored after so many years of captivity was immeasurable.

Fate had willed it so, for the better. Paralyzed and unable to speak, reduced to a shell in a wheelchair and cared for by a team of nurses funded by her, Tarquínio transitioned from being an obstacle to becoming an asset in his daughter's political ambitions. There was the Good Shepherd's Sister, proclaiming the senator's benevolence.

Although confident in her abilities, Maria Amélia never neglected practical considerations. Her first course of action was to dispose of the fake bullets, discarding them into a Penha neighborhood sewer on a stormy night.

She also got rid of the Smith & Wesson revolver, which had belonged to Adamastor. She could have kept it, stored it in her room at the Lagoa mansion. Given Rio's reputation for violence—amplified by the media—it wouldn't have been out of the ordinary for a senator to own a weapon for self-defense. However, keeping a firearm would clash with her political stance advocating the complete disarmament of the public. This position was far more progressive than that of a Workers' Party senator, who suggested tripling the sales tax on weapons. For either proposal, owning a gun at home was politically untenable. To dispose of the revolver, she employed a simple yet effective method: On a dark, rainy night, she drove to a desolate area between Barra da Tijuca and Jacarepaguá. There, she dug a hole two feet deep with a shovel and buried the revolver. She returned home, taking care to ensure she had not been observed. And, if by some miracle someone were to discover the buried weapon, which was less likely than winning the lottery, the revolver was registered to Adamastor, not her.

Day after day, seated in front of the vast mirror in his room, Tarquínio felt like a train passenger, forced to travel backward, continually witnessing the same recent past without being able to glimpse what would come next. The past, his life, slipped away from his scant memory, impaired by the stroke; everything moved too quickly and appeared distorted. It was like a bullet train tearing a straight line through the desert, revealing only a past reduced to sand. At times, he felt as though he had died, only to be roused back to life by the nurse forcing the daily soup down his throat. Even worse was when the Good Shepherd's Sister came to feed him in person out of sheer spite. She said nothing, didn't assail him with the litany of curses buzzing in her mind; she merely fixed a mocking gaze on the paralyzed man as if he were just a funnel for pouring the soup and not a human being. He didn't even have the strength to close his mouth and embrace the death that seemed to have become a greater compulsion than his desire for revenge against the braided witch.

Sometimes, Tarquínio was taken to the nursing home's main hall, where the other residents watched television. There he would remain,

350

prostrate, oblivious to his fellow prisoners of fate. A keen observer might have detected a faint sign of life, a glimmer of despair in his eyes, when during the election broadcast for the next presidential election, the TV screen was filled with the eyes of a familiar face, while a narrator intoned what was written below in a resounding voice, recycling a time-tested slogan:

"In these eyes, you can trust!"

All winds were favorable for Maria Amélia's campaign. A vast coalition was formed with the major parties—larger than the one from the golden days of the Workers' Party (PT)—leaving in opposition, apart from a few smaller groups, the evangelical front, now united under the 'Divine Alliance,' with an end-of-days rhetoric. Their candidate was none other than Bishop Tamarinho Junqueira, stripped of the main source of information about his opponent. He felt powerless, positioned as the underdog in a race where there was no match for the favorite. Even a large portion of his voters, radicalized in the evangelical centers, couldn't resist the allure of the slender woman dressed elegantly in red, with posters scattered everywhere, imprinting on everyone the eyes in which you should trust.

At the height of the campaign, Maria Amélia was urgently summoned to visit her most loyal supporter, Professor Fábio da Mata. He had caught pneumonia, and antibiotics were no longer effective in his body worn down by that incurable ailment: old age. Nonetheless, as if divulging a secret, Maria Amélia spoke to him about a project she planned to undertake, parallel to her electoral campaign. Despite his difficulty hearing and an even greater challenge in speaking, the professor managed to utter, while casting a gaze at her that resembled more a plea:

"Don't do that! The time hasn't come yet."

It might have been the first time the professor had ever disagreed with Maria Amélia. Her response was a smile—reassuring, one might say—and a gentle caress on the dying man's hands. He closed his eyes, perhaps convinced that she had granted him permission to pass away. He died that afternoon.

351

No victory so resounding has ever been recorded in Brazilian history. Maria Amélia was elected with more than 88% of the vote, approaching a level of unanimity that is perilous in politics. There were no grandiose promises, declarations of new directions, or drums heralding a new era. Even Maria Amélia's progressive ideas about governance never made it into the campaign. The argument was both simple and compelling: thousands upon thousands of posters featuring two unyielding gray eyes, each driving home the message: "In these eyes, you can trust."

56

We haven't yet delved into Maria Amélia's other project, the one she disclosed only to Dr. Fábio da Mata on the day of his death. This project unfolded alongside her presidential campaign: Maria Amélia had decided to have a child. More specifically, she wanted a daughter, even though no known method can guarantee this outcome with absolute certainty. There are old wives' tales, popular beliefs, and unverified theories about the timing of intercourse—whether it should be close to or far from the ovulation period—based on the notion that "male" sperm are faster but less resilient than "female" sperm. According to these theories, far from the time of ovulation, the "Speedy Gonzales" sperm cells perish in an acidic environment, unable to endure the wait. Meanwhile, the more patient and enduring female sperm slowly make their way to the egg, ready for fertilization. Some even claim that if the woman climaxes first, the child is more likely to be male; the female orgasm allegedly reduces vaginal acidity, thus creating a more hospitable environment for faster male sperm. Maria Amélia, however, was unconcerned with all of these theories and myths. She wanted a daughter and was certain she would have one—a conviction that Professor Fábio da Mata might have been able to explain, had he not been deceased.

Shortly after launching her electoral campaign, Maria Amélia began her search for the father of the daughter she planned to have. She had considered a colleague from Congress but quickly dismissed the idea. What about Steven? No, she had contemplated the option, even though he had fled to the United States in a state of utter panic. She knew that a mere snap of her fingers, a phone call, or an email would bring him rushing back to her. However, she didn't want anyone from her inner circle or immediate surroundings. A stranger seemed the best choice, as long as he was healthy, strong, and obedient without being intellectually lacking. Maybe a professional prostitute? Or simply someone strapped for cash who'd be more than happy to mix business with pleasure, sharing a bed with a woman who was, even if it's a stretch, the dream of an entire nation. Where could she find such a man?

On the Internet—where else? Maria Amélia, confiding in no one but her old friend about to kick the bucket, logged onto a dating website called "Eager to Be a Mother," and posted:

"Attractive, seductive woman seeks strong, healthy man for a one-time sexual encounter. Recent medical certificate required. Location and terms to be negotiated."

"Terms to be negotiated" was her way of indicating she was willing to pay, and handsomely, if needed. Her mistake. She soon found out that wasn't necessary. Proposals flooded in. After combing through a plethora of profiles and photographs, she settled on a thirty-five-year-old man from São Paulo. He was tan-skinned, slender, and stood at six-feet, one-inch. What set his response apart from the rest was its succinctness: "I'm in. When and where?"

Even in the throes of an electoral campaign, Maria Amélia found no difficulty carving out time to execute her plan discreetly. One detail required meticulous attention: she needed to avoid recognition. This applied not just to the tall São Paulo native but also to everyone else involved—doormen, reception staff, housekeepers, and guests. It was clear that the woman with the trustworthy eyes, whose face was plastered across Brazil, couldn't simply go incognito in any local hotel or motel. She considered flying the prospective father to Paris or New York, where anonymity could be easier to maintain. However, her absence would raise eyebrows, and the man from São Paulo might grow suspicious of the mysterious wealthy woman. Instead, she chose a simpler, more straightforward approach. She suggested he check into a less-than-reputable hotel in Glória and wait for her there. And so he did. Maria Amélia purchased a nondescript dress from C&A, caked her face in blush, wore black contact lenses, donned a wig of the same shade, and put on plain shoes. After greasing the palms of the doorman and the manager with a substantial sum—which was a drop in the bucket for her—she entered the room where the São Paulo man lay in bed, clad only in his underwear. She undressed, unveiling a body that exceeded even the most optimistic expectations of her hired lover, and said:

"Take off those briefs."

In just over five minutes, the man from São Paulo reached his climax. Eager for more, and noting that Maria Amélia was even somewhat enjoying herself, he continued the wild humping until achieving a second orgasm.

"Easy there, stud. That's enough!"

Even though she did her best to disguise it, her voice carried its usual authoritative tone.

"Just a bit more, please."

"You've had your two rounds, pal. That's it, the deal's done."

"Give me your number. We need to do this again. You're way too hot."

"Thank you very much, but it's over."

He gripped her arm tightly.

"Stay!"

"Let me go!"

Outmatched by her partner's physical strength, Maria Amélia decided to take a calculated risk, one she had anticipated. With her free arm, she removed her contact lenses, locked eyes with the man from São Paulo, and repeated slowly:

"Let me go."

A chill running down his spine, he released her. Maria Amélia sprang up, dressed quickly, and stormed out, slamming the room's door behind her. She then walked briskly to Cinelândia and caught a taxi to Barra Shopping, where she had one of her cars parked.

The taxi driver later told his colleagues:

"Shit man, I got a long fare from Cinelândia to Barra. Paid for by a really ragged and greased-up hoochie. The girl must've hustled some sucker."

The sucker lay in bed for about five more minutes, uncertain how to process what had just happened before Maria Amélia had slammed the door and strode purposefully toward Cinelândia. Then he noticed the two contact lenses on the bedsheet. Worms began to churn in his mind, leading him to suspect that he had just been with someone of great importance, someone who had taken great pains to disguise herself. Maria Amélia's piercing gaze had lasted only one-point-seven seconds (don't ask me how I know that), but the tall man from São Paulo felt a shiver when he connected those eyes with the ones he'd seen on billboards across Brazil, on TV, and replicated by the thousands on Facebook and other digital platforms.

"No, it can't be!"

The tall man from São Paulo spoke aloud to the empty room, showing an astonishment that even he could see reflected in the mirror.

In the Lagoa mansion, under the shower, Maria Amélia remembered the lenses. However, delighted by the warm water cascading over her slender body, she didn't give the incident much thought. "It was a minor oversight," she conceded. "But it's probably nothing." With a sense of relief, she thought, "So far, fate has always been on my side."

The São Paulo man only flew when absolutely necessary, when the distance was at least 600 miles and there was an urgent reason. As such, he took an Expresso Brasileiro sleeper bus back to São Paulo, catching the last departure at eleven fifty-nine p.m. He'd arrive early at the Tietê Terminal, grab a cappuccino, and have a couple of Brazilian cheese breads before making any decisions about the issue tormenting him.

It was impossible; he couldn't get a wink of sleep during the trip. Those two eyes that had shot through him for just a brief moment wouldn't leave his thoughts. That fleeting instant had been enough to numb his arms and set free the most incredible body he had ever touched in his entire life. He felt a chill remembering the moment of their first climax, when he had firmly gripped his lover's hair and realized that something hard and sinuous lay beneath.

Braids.

"No, it couldn't be."

He had been betrayed by his subconscious once again. He said it out loud while having an espresso at the Jardim Itatiaia bus stop. He felt embarrassed facing so many inquisitive glances. He shrugged and explained:

"Sorry, I was thinking out loud."

The thought didn't leave his mind until he disembarked at Tietê Terminal at six-thirty on a rainy, cold morning. As planned, he had a cappuccino and ate two cheese breads before taking the subway to Vila Mariana, where he lived. When he was just three blocks from his home, he decided to share his concerns with his best friend and colleague—a person he considered level-headed and who prided himself on never getting into trouble.

He didn't have time to share his concerns.

He was hit by a bus on Domingos de Morais Street. He arrived alive at the hospital and died while being taken to the operating room. His expression was that of someone who had something to say but couldn't.

It's not entirely clear-cut that Maria Amélia had any interference in the event. She didn't plan it, nor did she even focus on the matter, preoccupied only with two things: the election taking place in a few days and an expected pregnancy resulting from her tryst with the man from São Paulo at the Gloria Hotel, whose name she didn't even bother to remember. Furthermore, he was just that day's victim among the more than ten million people who move around São Paulo. In fact, statistics say that at best, one person is run over and killed in the city every day. This doesn't even account for the impoverished outskirts, which are often overlooked.

57

The Square of the Three Powers was packed, far more so than during Lula's first inauguration, with a sea of people filling the Planalto Central and spilling onto the Eixo Monumental. Only two lanes remained open—one on each side—for the passage of official cars and special guests. Maria Amélia, elegant in a red dress and surrounded by heads of state from every corner of the globe, relished the role she loved most: being at the center of attention, admired, applauded, or, at the very least, feared by those who disagreed with her. The attendance of the heads of state of the United States, China, France, and Germany aptly demonstrated Maria Amélia's international prestige. Amidst all these people bathed in the media spotlight was a bespectacled woman who couldn't hide the tension evident in her gaze. Maria da Anunciação had received a handwritten, special invitation from Maria Amélia that presented her with an irrefutable proposition:

> Doctor Anunciação,
> You are summoned to my inauguration. I will not accept a refusal from my Minister of Health.
> With affection,
> Maria Amélia"

"With affection" carried the weight of a stab. The psychiatrist felt a chill inside. More than any sense of honor she might have felt was the certainty that she would now be watched by the "braided witch" around the clock. (She tried to shake off the term, emptying her mind, but it wasn't possible.)

Her subconscious refused to call Maria Amélia anything other than the "braided witch," unable to rationalize the sting of defeat that sought to blur all negative perceptions of the victor.

Minister of Health, in the inner circle. Cornered, under absolute control.

Maria da Anunciação felt her assessment reinforced when she spotted the American, Steven Adams, among the guests. As she approached him, she froze; the lady of the hour momentarily shifted her attention from the cheering crowd to give them a piercing look. Despite this, they spoke:

"I'm surprised to see you here. How is the illustrious colleague doing?"

"Good morning, esteemed psychiatrist. Or should I say, Minister of Health?"

"Ah, he already knows!" she thought.

"Minister?"

"Well, doctor, you're speaking to your immediate advisor, after all. An advisor you can't refuse, let's say, by higher decree."

Both laughed awkwardly, acutely aware that they were trapped in the same cage.

Far from the inauguration, in that place known as "the Marvelous city," two incapacitated individuals were compelled to watch the celebration on television. As for the first individual, readers surely already know who he is. The nurse moved him from his room, where he sat gazing into the mirror, as always, to the TV set in the nursing home's living room. This room was filled with residents who were mesmerized by the young woman with braids, who at just thirty-six was ascending to the highest office in the Republic. It's unclear whether the murmurs of the elderly and some mentally challenged individuals registered with Tarquínio—or if his neurons, damaged by a stroke, could even comprehend the significance of all the commotion. Namely, the total triumph of his mortal enemy. He sat there, impassive, until the festivities ended, and the nurse took him back to his torture room to face the unyielding mirror.

The other incapacitated individual also needs no introduction. After the death of her two daughters, abandoned by her husband—with whom

358

she'd lived nearly three decades without any affection, merely for convenience's sake—the closest friend of Maria Amélia's adoptive mother was struck by rapid-onset sclerosis. Perhaps, it was a choice her own mind made, a way to free herself from the 24/7 torment of her vengeful desires. Even in sleep, she was plagued by dreams; in one recurring vision, she strangled the witch with her own braids. As Maria Amélia's triumph played out in grandeur on the television, Cleide's head slumped to the side, startling the nurse. Bending down to see what had happened, the nurse noticed, for the first time since she started caring for the wealthy woman in the Ipanema penthouse, tears streaming from her eyes. She mused aloud:

"Poor thing. She's moved by the inauguration."

And she too shed tears, touched, not realizing, not even remotely, that the bedridden woman's tears were born of pure hatred.

At the time of the celebratory champagne, after the protocol marathon—the receipt of the presidential sash, the speech to the throngs on the Esplanade, the official ceremony at Congress—Maria Amélia felt a slight nausea. Instinctively, she placed her hand on her stomach. She smiled and thought, almost aloud: "I'm pregnant."

58

"And she is mine alone, belonging to no one else," she completed her thought, mingled with the adrenaline flooding her entire being. Amidst the party that was solely hers, she even entertained a mental exercise—imagining a line of deputies, senators, and wealthy individuals, even married ones, stretching around blocks, as if she were Cinderella waiting for her prince to bring her the lost glass slipper and offer to father her child. Nonsense. The calculated risk of meeting some anonymous man from São Paulo continued to be the best decision, she pondered. "It will be a girl, mine alone, my extension, with no father to butt in."

At her first cabinet meeting, Maria da Anunciação noticed she wasn't the only one feeling intimidated. Seated at the oval table, Maria Amélia assumed the role of a King Arthur, fully aware that her peers paled in comparison on all fronts. When a proposal didn't suit her, a downward point of her right thumb was all it took to silence the room. A despotic queen in her own right, though she couldn't bear being labeled as such, sensing a tinge of irony in such a characterization. She thought of her predecessor, who had insisted on being called '*presidenta*,' with little regard for the objections of language purists. That first female president of Brazil had been openly contradicted by all major newspapers, magazines, and TV stations, and miserably betrayed by her vice president. Given the leeway granted by grammarians, the choice was hers and hers alone: Presidenta Maria Amélia Paranhos Feitosa. The media bent to her will, as did her ministers seated around her, notepads before them like students under the stern eye of a teacher who would tolerate no dissent. Write it down and execute!

Maria da Anunciação opted for the tactic of speaking as little as necessary, fully aware that she wasn't there to be the minister of anything. She only spoke when, mortified by the sardonic remarks of the braided presidenta, she was forced to open her mouth:

"I see our Minister of Health is very quiet. What's on the agenda, Dr. Anunciação?"

And so, she repeated, for the other ministers, the plans crafted by Presidenta Maria Amélia herself and relayed to her by advisor Steven Adams. Advisor to the minister and lover to the president—when she felt the need to satisfy her feminine hormones in the sweltering 100-degree-heat-in-the-shade. Their rendezvous took place at Granja do Torto, where the American had a wing all to himself, equipped with his paranormal measuring devices. That's where they met, attracting attention only from the president's two loyal canine guards, who couldn't speak or give interviews, of course, but who would, if they could, rip the American to shreds in a fit of jealousy.

When sexually satiated, Maria Amélia would often mock her lover:

"Ah, Steven, you and your obsession with measuring people's power! Science doesn't accept it, calls it utter nonsense, and those who have the power scoff because they know they're untouchable amid the endless probabilities to which their games are subject."

"I know very well that I have less prestige with the almighty president than those two dogs."

The president's laughter could even be heard by the uniformed guards around the estate:

"What's this, Steven, jealous of my guard dogs? You had the privilege of being on top of the president, something the entire Congress wishes for."

In moments of extreme tension, the American would always revert to English. And he would tremble, the shaking of someone with no other option but to submit. When he returned to the United States, after the episode involving Dente Grande's death, he had vowed never to return to Brazil and even tore up all the notes he had taken during his research at the Lagoa mansion. But he couldn't resist the appeal—or rather, the summons—of the newly-elected president of Brazil. It came over the phone:

"You must have heard from the news. I've been elected. And I'm summoning you to be one of my advisors. I won't accept a refusal. I expect you at the swearing-in."

Simple, blunt. He complied, even more loyal than her pair of Fila guard dogs, fully aware that he had been, and would always be, a pawn in the hands of the braided president.

Weeks after the inauguration, what had once been a conviction became a certainty. The ultrasound confirmed it: it was a girl.

"I knew it," she said to the doctor who delivered the news, emotion shining in her eyes.

Four months into her pregnancy, the subtle changes in her physique barely scratched the surface of her inherent elegance. In fact, the tiny bump that was starting to show only seemed to add to her charm. She didn't anticipate suffering from any of the typical pregnancy symptoms—

no nausea, no bizarre cravings like wanting to eat jabuticaba mixed with shredded chicken (imagine such a concoction!). Nor did she expect to ever abruptly halt a cabinet meeting, declaring that a minister was going off-topic and ruining the atmosphere. More often than not, the target was the Health Minister.

"Dr. Anunciação, do not overstep; now is not the time to bring up this matter! Please wait your turn and do not disturb the proceedings!"

The poor woman would only speak in hushed tones, making a Herculean effort to suppress her old vanity as a people-expert. The incident in question occurred when the finance minister was discussing the budget, and Maria da Anunciação interrupted him:

"But we can't make any more cuts in Health. It's the most criticized sector of the government."

Her apology counted for nothing. Maria Amélia slammed her hand on the table and ended the meeting.

"The debate will continue tomorrow!"

She abruptly stood up and retreated to her office, where she rested for about forty minutes. Very unusual—it wasn't like her to sleep during the day, aware as she was that life is short and needs to be lived to the fullest, eyes wide open. To her, sleep was death paid in installments, unless, of course, you were dreaming, where you could travel to other worlds, other realities. She was awakened by her loyal butler, whom she had insisted on bringing from her Lagoa mansion.

"Presidenta!"

"Don't call me 'Presidenta.' To you, I'm Maria Amélia."

"There's a truckload of jabuticaba at the palace entrance. It was sent by the mayor of Sabará."

"Ah, damn it, it was that shameless rag."

The shameless rag had come out two days ago with a screaming headline.

"The Presidenta Craves Jaboticabas"

A woman with cravings is a pregnant woman, and she herself hadn't told anyone. It must have been the doctor or her assistant; they were the ones present during the exam. One can never really know where rumors begin. Even someone with all the power—both earthly and supernatural—can't escape the prying eyes, let alone the swarm of sycophants. And so, there it was, at the entrance to the Alvorada Palace, a truck loaded with big, juicy, meticulously selected black jabuticabas. Maria Amélia said to the butler:

"Fine, go ahead. Pick out a basket and bring it. Summon my secretary."

To the secretary, she said to send the truck back to the mayor, with the following note:

Thank you for the jabuticabas.
My craving will be satisfied with one basket. I suggest you distribute the rest to the pregnant women of the municipality.

Maria Amélia Paranhos
President of the Republic.

If she couldn't hide it, the best course of action was to proclaim it outright. And she did so in a statement she drafted and read herself on national television, which was subsequently published in the newspapers the following day:

My fellow Brazilians,

It is with joy and emotion that I announce to all of you that I am pregnant. It will be a girl. On this matter, I ask that you grant me the right to privacy that we all deserve, and which is a part of this government's policy.

Maria Amélia Paranhos
President of the Republic.

The news made headlines around the world. The *New York Times* even emphasized the sudden and remarkable shift in Brazilian customs in an editorial:

Brazil Under a Spell

Brazil's President Maria Amélia Paranhos, 37, single, announced in an official statement that she is pregnant, without naming the child's father. It is incredible that this could happen in a country with the largest number of Catholics and evangelical sects, most of whom are more conservative than the Vatican on matters of social customs, and in a society where the family, based on monogamous marriage, is the cornerstone.
She broke the news with incredible brevity, proclaiming her right to privacy despite the high-profile nature of her position. The National Conference of Bishops, usually conservative on such matters, has not commented on the issue. Apart from some isolated voices in evangelical churches—usually so vocal—there has been none of the expected chorus of criticism. On social media, the news has spread—as one Facebook post put it—'like soybeans across the plains of Mato Grosso.' The state of Mato Grosso is Brazil's soybean heartland.
What accounts for the President's remarkable protection? A source, demanding absolute anonymity, speculated:
"Brazil has been put under a spell."

Steven Adams offered to be the father of the child during a night of intimacy at the Granja do Torto.
"Come on, Steven, don't start. What kind of indecent proposal is this? Imagine Bishop Tamarinho Junqueira shouting in the Senate: 'The child's father is a foreigner.' No, sir, thank you. It's going to stay like this. Fatherless. Only mine. And it's not a child, it's a girl, my girl, my own girl."
From the original group of Lagoa's little parliament, *Nosso Partido*'s birthplace, at least three ventured to ask for the president's hand in marriage. Her response was the same for all:
"Don't be ridiculous!"

59

Back when he was still an active journalist, Tarquínio Esperidião wrote an article for a well-known alternative newspaper of the last century, using the pseudonym "The Demolisher." The title: "New Parents Syndrome." In the article, employing a mocking tone, he attacked:

> It's horrendous having to endure new parents. Unless, of course, you are a grandparent or a close relative, since the disease, or syndrome, is contagious, and the existing vaccine has many side effects. One of them induces a complete disbelief in the human race and its ephemeral passage on this tiny planet. Symptoms of the illness already start during pregnancy. I'm not aware of a more pathetic scene than a pregnant woman stroking her belly with that distant look, while being admired by the husband, who, if he were ice cream, would melt in five minutes. Once the offspring is born, the couple, along with the grandparents and other relatives affected by the syndrome, become filled with the conviction that their little one is unique, exceptional, capable of solving all of humanity's problems when they grow up. And is the most beautiful of all. How cute! The whole thing must be rooted in the species' survival instinct. But it is a drag.

Maria Amélia didn't have the baby's father to join her in the tender ritual of rubbing almond oil on her belly, a gesture she perhaps unconsciously adopted from Adelaide when she had been pregnant with her great-aunt, from whom Maria Amélia had inherited not just her name but a few other peculiarities as well. A near letter-for-letter imitation. Preferably at Granja do Torto, where she felt most at ease, Maria Amélia would lock the door, put on some soft music, and begin the massage. Inside her, the girl (she didn't like the word "fetus," much less the ambiguous term "baby") would move slowly, in tune with her mother's gentle hand movements. This could go on for hours, some of the most productive, when the best ideas formed in the president's mind. It could even be said that a symbiosis was forming between mother and daughter, with the latter literally dictating the best moves the president should make on the complex chessboard of politics.

Don't assume that Maria Amélia's father's sardonic theory could explain the president's sensation. Something more was at play. In fact, a code had been established between the two of them. If a minister

365

presented a proposal laden with political risk, the fetus would respond with two forceful kicks; if the proposals were simply ineffective or harmless, the kicks would be softer. For a good proposal, Maria Amélia felt a gentle— let's say affectionate—nudge from her forming daughter's head. Some of the more perceptive ministers, including Maria da Anunciação, could sense the strange vibration in the room during meetings at the Alvorada, almost as if there was an extra minister present. Unperturbed, Maria Amélia would slide her hand under her skirt and stroke her belly gratefully, unconcerned about what her ministers and other subordinates might think. Maria da Anunciação decided it was best to hold her tongue and become merely an observing minister. However, faced with the Health Minister's silence, Maria Amélia felt three slow pushes, spaced out as if someone was operating a car clutch. The message was immediately understood—a cue for the president to nudge the minister.

"But what's with the silence, Dr. Anunciação? We've been in this meeting for nearly two hours, discussing exactly the distribution of funds for the ministries, and we haven't heard a word from you. Are the finances of the health department really that good? Nothing to say?"

The fetus seemed to perform a little pirouette, giving the impression of amusement.

Maria Amélia smiled and said softly, not caring whether the ministers heard her or not:

"You little devil, once you're born, no one will be able to handle you. Not even me!"

The little devil was only sixteen weeks, but already acting as if she were past twenty. She responded with two light taps, as if to say, without showing much reverence to her presidential mother:

"You're absolutely right."

In the following weeks, as she saw her belly and breasts grow, Maria Amélia was overtaken by an almost uncontrollable desire. The self-massage sessions with almond oil, though clearly extremely satisfying to the fetus, were no longer enough for her, even when pleasuring herself with a more and more engorged vagina. During one of these sessions at

Granja do Torto, she felt an overwhelming urge to call Steven—an idea that seemed to excite the little devil, who hadn't even yet earned the right to breathe on her own. The gentle rubbing within the womb, as soft as a lover's caress, made it clear that the idea was more than welcome. The president didn't even bother to wipe her almond-oil-smeared hands. She grabbed the phone and dialed:

"Steven, come to Granja immediately. It's urgent. Drop whatever you're doing."

He was, as it happened, discussing a new psychiatric care system with Maria da Anunciação.

"Sorry, Minister, I've been urgently summoned."

"Then go, quickly!"

Her response, in the way she spoke, the tone, the facial expression, conveyed the following cascade of emotions: resentment, envy, suppressed hatred, a yearning for unattainable revenge, and even a hint of excitement—unable to contain the imagination of being in the president's place, under the advisor or on top, or sideways, upside down, in any possible way. She couldn't avoid the trembling of her lips as she tried to suppress the word that darted through her neurons, emerging in a suppressed scream.

"Whore!"

Steven knocked softly on the door. Maria Amélia said:

"Come in. And lock it behind you."

The president was lying nude on a red sheet, her legs slightly apart. She gleamed in the light reflected off the oil that covered her entire body.

Steven undressed, tossing his clothes to the side, and proceeded to satisfy the desires of both.

Maria Amélia's pregnancy did not disrupt the government routine in any way. Meetings were held every day—sometimes even on Saturdays or Sundays—and often included the entire ministry. Like a self-proclaimed King Arthur, she insisted that everyone be equal before her. But they were all just puppets or, in some cases, tormented souls, like Maria da Anunciação. However, it was precisely the Minister of Health who, in an

367

unguarded moment, spoke when she should have remained silent. Now in the thirty-ninth week of pregnancy, the little devil twisted and kicked despite the limited space, seemingly dictating the words that then erupted from her mother:

"Shut up, Maria da Anunciação!"

She was no longer a minister, no longer a doctor, even if those titles had once been uttered with pure irreverence.

The unfortunate minister had merely offered a suggestion, choosing her words carefully so as not to seem inappropriate:

"Given your advanced state of pregnancy, for your own well-being and that of the baby girl soon to be born, wouldn't it be better for the president to take a leave of absence?"

After the "Shut up," Maria Amélia continued her speech, now directed at the entire ministry:

"Listen up! I will not be taking a leave of absence. Not today, not tomorrow, and not even on the day of birth. What's more, I've already hired three trusted nannies. I'll pay them out of my own pocket, so no one can make sideways insinuations. My little girl will be right here with me during meetings and even at official events."

The ministers swallowed hard. With her head lowered, Maria da Anunciação did everything she could to dispel the thought that the president's outburst was different this time; it lacked the humor of previous occasions, she seemed out of control, the words didn't feel like her own. If she were a witch, she might be losing her powers.

60

The nurse burst into Tarquínio's room, elated, to find him, as always, stationed in front of the mirror.

"Come, come, Mr. Tarquínio. The big day has arrived."

Tarquínio was then wheeled into the living room, already teeming with people gathered around the television. The atmosphere was like that of a

World Cup victory. Every channel was broadcasting the same monotonous scene: the Granja do Torto compound swarmed with news cars, frenzied journalists clutching their recorders, helicopters capturing aerial footage. The president was in the throes of labor. A glimmer seemed to spark a minor reaction in Tarquínio's brain, and he stammered tremulously:

"Let them die!"

Only the nurse noticed, but she didn't grasp what he had said. She squeezed his hand, convinced that he was joining the rest of the nation in celebrating the birth of Brazil's little princess—his granddaughter.

Tarquínio tried to articulate the word "Idiot!" but only a guttural noise escaped that could mean anything. The nurse took it to mean "wonderful!" and squeezed his hand even tighter, leaving him powerless to correct her.

Maria Amélia had decided to give birth at the Granja do Torto. Not once in her life had she sought treatment at a hospital, not even for preventive exams. The birth of her daughter had to be natural, in an environment free from the smell of disinfectants. Instead of a doctor, she wanted a midwife. Some ministers went to talk to Maria da Anunciação, hoping she could convince the president to be assisted by a medical team. The Minister of Health responded tersely:

"Me, convince her? You go do it!"

The labor was brief. At ten-fifteen in the morning, a girl was born, weighing eight-point-four pounds and measuring nineteen-point-five inches—perfect and radiant. After the midwife severed the umbilical cord, Maria Amélia announced that she wanted to hold a press conference immediately. She rose, resolute, and to the astonishment of the midwife and her assistants, cradled her daughter in her arms and strode fearlessly into the hall where a battalion of journalists awaited. Before sitting down, she held her daughter aloft, the infant seemingly delighting in the barrage of camera flashes that competed with the brilliance of her gray eyes—eyes even brighter than her mother's.

"Here is my daughter. My continuation. She will bear my name: Maria Amélia."

A reporter asked when she would resume her presidential duties.

"Well, tomorrow. Do I look sick to you?"

Tarquínio had an unexpected reaction. He managed to lift his arms and cover his eyes, all while being overtaken by a sudden urge to vomit. The nurse, stunned, began to shout:

"A miracle, a miracle! Mr. Tarquínio has managed to move. It's a miracle!"

At that moment, Tarquínio's desire was to strangle the nurse with the same fervor he had for throttling the president and the bright-eyed little witch in her arms.

The president did not appear at the Alvorada Palace the following day. An official statement was released, noting that Maria Amélia would be taking her four-month maternity leave, during which the vice president would assume her duties.

No one questioned her initial decision to continue working. Her revised stance was communicated to the assembled ministers at the Granja do Torto:

"I was impulsive yesterday when I said I would resume my duties immediately. I have decided to devote the upcoming months entirely to my daughter. Don't involve me in any political entanglements! I will be unavailable."

And she didn't even bother to draft an explanatory note, delegating the official communication to the vice-president.

The president's change of attitude took place during the first breastfeeding. For the first time, she felt something she had never experienced before: the obligation to obey an order dictated by another person, and that person was the little girl who was suckling her milk while locking eyes with her.

"Little devil!"

Indeed, *little devil*. And from the eyes of the little devil came a command that, put into words, was this:

"You won't be resuming the presidency tomorrow. I want you with me twenty-four hours a day."

"Full-Time Mom
President Proves to Be an Exemplary Progenitor"

On the front page of a Brasília newspaper, there wasn't a hint of shame in using the term most shunned by serious journalism, "progenitor." And the tabloid was followed by a flurry of reports in other media outlets of a similar caliber. All of Brazil seemed to have caught the new parent syndrome, to use the term from the old article by Tarquínio Esperidião, the grandfather.

The president indeed gave reasons for all this fuss, taking on the role of a supermom to the delight of the nannies, who found themselves mostly twiddling their thumbs. She bathed her, changed her diapers when it was necessary, and of course, did what was most important: she breastfed her daughter with mathematical regularity, every three hours. The little girl's gifts manifested themselves in the smallest details. By three months, diapers were practically unnecessary. She would stretch her chin up and emit, "Ahm, ahm, ahm," precisely three times when she needed to urinate; four times for a bowel movement.

Nearly at the end of her four months of life, just days before the end of the maternity leave, the little girl was capable of feats usually only documented in children older than eight months, such as combining syllables to form words. Yes, the new Maria Amélia was speaking at four months, even forming phrases—two in particular, as if she were the mother directing a ministerial meeting:

"Don't want!"

Or:

"Want now!"

A French magazine specializing in child development featured a lengthy article under the title:

"The Gifts of the Brazilian President's Daughter"

The little rascal's fame was quickly becoming international.

For months, the nannies and other staff at Granja do Torto had been noticing a change in Maria Amélia's habits and behavior. She didn't seem as sure of herself as she had always been. Sometimes she complained of tiredness, though she never relinquished her caregiving duties. The most notable change, however, was the diminishing sparkle in her eyes. Gradually, their previously vibrant gray hue was becoming dull, resembling the lifeless gaze of a dead fish. She did not resume her role as president at the end of her maternity leave.

The reaction was so intense and spontaneous that Tarquínio Esperidião managed to leap out of his wheelchair. To the tune of the funeral music accompanying the somber announcement from the news anchor, he shouted:

"Hoorah, the witch is dead!"

Nobody in the room even noticed Tarquínio's leap and shout; they were all too choked up, caught in the swell of emotion sweeping across the entire country. Public squares filled as though it were the end of the world, with mourners numbering in the millions.

Back in his wheelchair, Tarquínio felt the last vestige of vitality that had momentarily reactivated his mobility and unlocked his vocal cords fade away. What he heard next only confirmed that the nightmare would continue. The TV host, following the somber announcement from her colleague, said that the president left her daughter to all of us, depicted in a close-up with her enormous gray eyes shining like two headlights. Overwhelmed with emotion, the journalist proclaimed:

"Rest in peace, Presidenta. Your daughter has been adopted by the entire country. She is Brazil's little girl!"

Maria da Anunciação followed the medical team, who were unable to determine the cause of death. The only anomaly was the loss of the sparkle in her eyes.

The psychiatrist felt the urge to smile, to let out her inner satisfaction. But she restrained herself. The little girl was nearby, watching ...

About the Author

TARCISIO LAGE was born in Abaeté, in the interior of the Brazilian state of Minas Gerais in 1941.

As a journalist, he went through the newsrooms of the main newspapers in Brazil and went into exile in Chile in 1970, from where he moved to London and worked for almost four years at the Brazilian service of the BBC. He then moved to Bern, working for six years at Swiss International Radio. He ended his career in journalism as the head of the Brazilian Section of Radio Nederland, in Hilversum.

In addition to *The Weaves of Power*, Tarcisio Lage is the author of three other novels: *Os Muros de Jerusalém*, *Eu, Cidade*, and *Uma Bruxa na Janela*. He has also written children's books and a collection of stories, *O livro negro de Lili*.

Tarcisio Lage lives in the Netherlands.

Made in the USA
Middletown, DE
22 June 2024

55840667R00208